475

Dodger
of the
Revolution

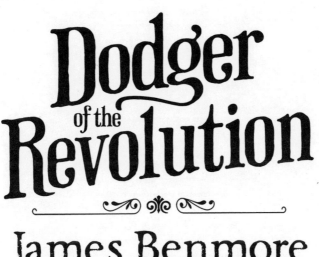

Dodger of the Revolution

James Benmore

Based on a character created by Charles Dickens

HERON
BOOKS

First published in Great Britain in 2016 by Heron Books
an imprint of

Quercus Editions Ltd
Carmelite House
50 Victoria Embankment
London EC4Y 0DZ

An Hachette UK company

A CIP catalogue record for this book is available
from the British Library

HB ISBN 978 0 85705 482 1
TPB ISBN 978 1 78429 288 1
EBOOK ISBN 978 1 78429 287 4

For my grandchildren,
Jessica, Chloe, Cecile, Julian
And the other one who is still on his way

'*Work, comrades all, work! Work, Jacques One, Jacques Two, Jacques One Thousand, Jacques Two Thousand, Jacques Five-and-Twenty Thousand; in the name of all the Angels or the Devil . . . work!*'

Monsieur DeFarge to his fellow revolutionaries
as they storm the Bastille in *A Tale of Two Cities*

Chapter 1

Confessions of a London Opium Smoker

*A short time on from the thrilling events of the last volume, the
reader now finds me at my leisure in what some might call
'The Best of Times'*

Picture me there if you can, laid out good and comfortable on
one of Li Wu's thickest and furriest blankets, shoes off, shirt
buttons undone and sharing a recreational pipe with three
other working magpies. I was just about readying to shut my
tired eyes and drift off into a sweet poppy-fuelled reverie,
when who should appear in that underground den to disturb
my bliss but the pale and pinched personage of Oliver Twist
or Oliver Brownlow or whatever else he was now choosing
to call himself.

And, just as on that famous occasion when we had first
met, I had spotted him before he had me. The smoke inside
that puff-palace was thick, so I had to blink hard and lift
myself up from my prone position before I could be sure
that it was indeed my youthful acquaintance who had just
walked through the far door and was taking off his shoes at
the proprietor's request. I leaned forward and pulled back the
purple silk hanging what screened my room from the other

smoking chambers just an inch to see if I was mistaken, as Oliver's presence in such an establishment made no sense to me. He was, after all, a notorious flat so what he might be doing by himself in a low place such as Wu's of Limehouse was a mystery and one I was still lucid enough to be intrigued by.

Our last encounter had been months ago, when he had paid a surprise visit to the crib I shared with my fancy woman, Lily Lennox, and I had not expected to ever see him again. But there he was, talking business with the youngest Wu boy and it looked as though his appearance had altered much in that short time. He was wearing an expensive-looking suit and a matching hat what he had removed upon entering. My covetous eye admired the suit's style, tailoring and colours very much. It was too bold for Oliver though, what with his stiff deportment and provincial ways, and would have hung far better on some flash metropolitan, like myself. Also, a fair and tidy growth had now appeared just between his nose and upper lip what I would guess he had cultivated so as to cut a more mature figure. If so, the moustache was a failure. He looked as boyish and as unworldly as ever. No matter how hard he tried to fight it, the former workhouse boy still retained his talent for venturing through the slums of my city like he was a Royal prince on an expedition into deepest Africa.

On the occasion of our first meeting we had both been young kinchins and I had marked him sitting on a stone step of a suburban street in Barnet. He was shivering, homeless and as vulnerable to the world as a baby sparrow from a dropped nest might be. But, even in that desperate hour, he still managed to affect the air of one what considered his rough environment to be all a bit beneath him. As I watched him survey those lantern-lit rooms, through which the Wu's led all their most prosperous visitors, I noted that his manner had grown no less condescending with time. I could even tell when the first true breath of poppy vapours entered Oliver's lungs, as he seemed jolted by its heady effect. He removed a snow-white fogle from out of his outer breast pocket and into that he allowed himself a discreet cough. This proved – as if proof was ever needed – that until now Oliver had been a stranger to The Black Drop, and so further forced the question of what business he might have down here.

Wu's was an underworld den in more ways than one. We was close to the docks and below the line of water, so all ventilation went upwards. The opium fumes therefore advertised them-selves upon the nostrils of those walking on the streets above. But only those with connections would know upon which door they should be knocking or indeed what the latest password might be, so it was not the sort of place a cove just happens to stumble into when passing. But, for all his flatness, Oliver was a newspaperman and I knew from our recent encounter that he was a bloody good one, so perhaps he was here on some sort of investigation. I continued peering at him around a brick column, as he moved from one silk-screened smoking chamber to another, inspecting each and every drugged inhabitant he found within them. The place had several of these coloured and silky partitions with oriental lettering upon them what separated the different groups of puffers from each other, and

I saw that it would not be long until he and his new moustache worked their way around to mine.

I felt a surprising panic at the thought that I was about to be discovered here, accompanied by a rare and unusual sense of shame. I scurried back to the mattress upon which my pipe still lay and contemplated hiding myself under the blanket until he passed me by. My three fellow puffers what I had been sharing the oil lamp with was all well adrift already so it would have been a simple deception to pass myself off as another anonymous dreamer. But I pulled up short before doing this and gave myself a swift talking to. Why should I hide from Oliver Twist in such a cowardly manner? I asked to myself as I saw his unmistakable silhouette moving closer on the wall. No doubt he would have more reason to be ashamed at being found in an opium den then I ever would. So, instead of hiding from him, I sat down upon the mattress bench in a brazen manner, leaned closer to the lamp and continued smoking like the carefree sophisticate that I was.

'Bust me,' I pretended to splutter when he at last reached my smoking chamber and pulled back the purple hanging. 'Is that young Oliver I see before me, grown all tall and dressed up smart?' I squinted at him and his face registered some surprise upon seeing me. 'Why, I do believe it is! And they told me that this was an exclusive gentleman's club. It seems like they'll let in any dubious character.' I held out my pipe to him as he waved some smoke away from his face, dipped his head under the low hanging and stepped in. 'Care to partake?'

The silk behind him parted like a curtain and the youngest

Wu entered the chamber as Oliver blinked at me through the smoke. I addressed the Chinese boy beside him, who could not have been much older than twelve.

'Now then Youngest Wu, I wish to raise a matter most delicate,' I said to him after breathing out more smoke. 'It is about Mr Brownlow here. He ain't all that he says he is.' The boy looked unimpressed with this intelligence and I supposed that, like his older relatives, he could not speak much English. 'Yeah, you heard. It is my reluctant duty to inform you that he is was born under a different name and is −' I pretended to whisper this next bit − '*of rather low birth.*' Then I nodded at the Chinese boy and winked. 'So get the money off him up front, there's a good lad.'

I placed the pipe back into my mouth and grinned at the unsmiling Oliver, who had never been much on taking a joke. Youngest Wu tapped Oliver's coat sleeve and pointed at me.

'That there's him, innit?' he asked, surprising me with a cockney accent thicker than my own. 'Now where's that shiner you spoke of?'

Oliver reached into his coat pocket and produced a bright guinea. It was only then that I realised that he had come here looking for me and I felt my whole mood drop at the revelation.

'Thanking you kindly,' the Youngest Wu bowed to us both once the coin was in his fist. 'Have a happy smoke, gents.' Then the boy disappeared from the smoking room in a literal puff of it. Oliver's eyes had still not left me and he cleared his throat before coming closer.

'No thank you, Jack,' he said at last when I again offered him the pipe. He was brushing some small insects from off of the cushion of the rickety chair what stood across from my bench with his gloved hands. It was as if he was waiting for me to offer him the seat before taking it. He also seemed to be a bit perturbed by some of the rats what was scurrying around the outskirts of the far walls, but if he planned to remain down here with me he would have to overcome such genteel sensibilities.

'Suit yourself, Oliver,' I said and placed the pipe down by my feet, 'but you might like it if you only gave it a chance.'

'No doubt I would,' Oliver said as he at last decided to stop faffing and just sit himself down. 'Which is why I shan't be having any.'

As he positioned himself across from me with his hat in his lap and his thin vicar's smile, I was overcome with a dreadful sagging sensation. I could feel the sweet bliss of the poppy, what I had paid a pretty penny for, just dissipate in his saintly presence.

'Have you ever, I wonder, read Thomas De Quincey's book on the subject of opium?' he asked.

'I've read all manner of books,' I replied. 'More than you have, I'd wager.'

'De Quincey describes the substance as highly addictive,' he said. 'I'm also told that it brings on drowsiness.'

'Yeah well, so does most of the stuff you write in *The Morning Chronicle*,' I replied. He pretended to laugh but it was clear he had not come here to banter and my innards grew tight just looking at him. I will admit that of late I had grown fonder of Oliver, as he had provided me with invaluable assistance at the start of the year during my unjust incarceration in Newgate Prison. I may well have been hung, were it not for his aid and so I did not wish to appear ungrateful. But that Oliver – the loyal, heroic Oliver, who had acted with no thought of reward – was not the Oliver what was visiting me now. This here was disapproving, judgemental Oliver and I knew that his fingers was itching to wag already. Here was the Oliver I have hated ever since he told the authorities what my dear old Fagin was all about and destroyed my happy childhood. The opium was working on me hard, altering my disposition and turning me against him.

'Hark this, Workhouse,' I let more smoke blow out of my nose and dropped the smile. 'Whatever business you think you have with me, you don't. I don't take kind to people paying others for information about my whereabouts and I don't wish to be disturbed when in the company of these . . .' I waved my hands over the trio of slumbering magpies dotted about the room in their druggy stupors, who was now exhibiting all the charm of rotting cadavers and thought about how to describe their relationship to me. I had only met two of them a week ago. '. . . Close friends,' I settled on.

Oliver did not even glance in their direction.

'If you have one friend in this entire place, Jack Dawkins,' he said, 'then it's me, whether you like it or not. And while I may not consider you to be the best friend that I've ever had – far from it in fact – you are still undoubtedly my oldest. So I am here to help you. Again.'

'Why, that's very obliging of you,' I said after coughing in indignation. 'But help me with what, eh? I ain't in a condemned cell no more, thanking you kindly. As you can see, I'm free as a bird and doing the genteel at long last.'

'There is more than one way to be imprisoned,' was his flat and aggravating reply.

'You're very fond of your own goodness, ain't you, Oliver?' I said and shook my head in wonder at his nerve. 'Very proud of that halo what balances above your head. You want to take care that nobody knocks it off you.' Oliver ignored my aggression. Instead he reached down and picked up my opium pipe by its stem to inspect it. I guessed that he had never seen one outside of an illustration before and I suspected that he was curious to see how it worked, in spite of his disapproval.

'Jack,' he sighed as he peered in close at the pipe's stained bamboo and at its ceramic pipe bowl, 'I've read many important texts about this,' he continued before placing it back where it was, 'and you'll soon be dependent upon this drug, if you aren't already.' I could not help but chuckle at him and his misplaced melodrama.

'Prison libraries have a lot of books about puffing,' I told him, 'including the one you mentioned earlier and I've read the lot of them. But there are some things about which you cannot learn in no book. I've been smoking pipes with all sorts of exotic ingredients in them since I was ten, or thereabouts. And this stuff has no more effect over me than a strong cup of tea.'

'Your eyes are like pinpricks,' he returned. 'And see how sweaty your rug and pillow are.'

'They was like that when I got here,' I assured him. 'And the pin eyes would be on account of the lack of light, I shouldn't wonder. Now, if it's a proper opium fiend you're after,' I reached down to pick up the pipe again preparing to smoke some more, 'then have a word with old Eddie there. I doubt he's left this den in years.'

Eddie Inderwick was, once upon a time, Fagin's sharpest student and favourite magpie. But that was before I came along – nowadays he was just a faint shadow of a thief. When I had first returned from my five-year incarceration in Australia, I made it my business to seek Eddie out and discovered him here in this very smoking chamber, muttering to himself, wasting away in old clothes and entertaining mad fantasies. It had been a sad sight and he was still at it now, rolling about in restless slumber on the opposite bench, gibbering about some murders he had witnessed and wrongs what had been done to him. I poked him with the end-piece of my pipe so he would quiet himself.

'He's often much better company than this,' I told Oliver as I moved the pipe back to the oil lamp. 'You've caught him on a bad day.'

But before I could suck in some more of those lovely fumes, the pipe was smacked out of my hands by Oliver, so fast that at first I thought that I had dropped it. I was stunned, not just at the action but by the realisation that his hands had been quicker than my own for once. I cried out at the injustice of the dirty snatch but Oliver leaned closer to me and spoke firm.

'I have been sent here to talk some sense into you, Dodger. To convince you that you are letting this poisonous habit destroy you. Do you want to know who sent me?'

'It ain't the Lord Our Saviour, is it?' I winced, rubbing my itchy eye with one finger. 'Cos I'm never in the mood for none of that.'

'It was Lily,' he replied. I felt myself sober up a little by the very mention of her name.

'My Lily?' I asked. 'She's the one what told you that this was where I might be found?'

'She's the one that told me this was where you can *always* be found.'

I was unsure of how to feel about this information. On the one hand, I recalled the shine that my fancy woman had taken to Oliver on their previous meetings and so was unsettled to hear that they had been having further communication without me around to keep a close eye upon developments. But, on the other, I had thought that Lily was lost to me anyway and so to learn that she had been expressing concern about my well being to other parties was an encouragement that I could still win her back.

'Lily paid a visit to the *Chronicle* office yesterday and asked for my help in the matter. She said that you were so shaken by your experiences in the condemned cell that it has caused you to turn to opium and, now that I have seen you, I cannot help but agree with her. You have altered in an alarming way.'

'I ain't altered one ounce,' I snapped back, 'and I take offence at the suggestion. All the danger of the past year wasn't nothing, I don't care what she's been saying. I've just had a bad run of things, that's all. I'll be right again.'

'Are you aware that your hands are shaking as we speak?' he asked in a flat voice.

I crossed my arms quick as he said this, to tuck them away from his sight. But it mattered little, as what he had observed was true. Ever since we had been speaking of Lily the shakes had overcome me again. This was why I needed another drag on my pipe so as to steady them.

For some moments we both sat in silence and I stared at the lights what shone from the opium lamp. I tried to resist picking up the bamboo pipe at my feet while Oliver was watching me, but I wanted to do nothing more. At length, and once I had regained mastery of my hands again, I breathed out and decided to speak a little of what had been preoccupying me of late.

'Did I ever tell you,' I began in a more conversational tone, 'of how I came to be called The Artful Dodger?' Oliver shook his head and looked interested, which was just as well as I was going to tell him regardless. 'It's a moniker what has always suited me, true, but did you know that it was Fagin who first coined the name? One of the proudest moments of my life that was.'

I had pulled one of Li Wu's round tasselled cushions up behind me so I could sit more comfortable against the damp brickwork. I always found talk of my time with Fagin to be cheering, although I appreciated that Oliver did not look back on him with as much affection as I did.

'This was in the days after I had first come to live in his crib after running away from my mother,' I recalled. 'I was still just a kinchin mind, just one of the new bunch of boys what had moved in to his warm Saffron Hill home during the cold winter months of '36. We was all of us jostling for attention from the old devil, who was known to be more generous with the mouthy swaggerers than he ever was with shy boys, but it had been hard even for me to shine at first. There was bigger lads, such as Georgie Bluchers and Jem White, what could beat me at fighting if they wished to, so nobody had me pencilled down as much back then. But that all changed after the old man took us out on our first big finding lesson.'

'You may recall,' I continued, 'during the short time in which you too enjoyed his hospitality, that it was not common for Fagin to risk the grab himself. He preferred to instruct us in his craft from the safety of his kitchen and judge us by our winnings whenever we returned home. But in those early days, and on the rarest of occasions, he would lead us fledgling blackbirds onto the streets himself in order to teach us some tricks. He would wash and cut his greasy hair just for the occasion and put on his one smart suit. And, while I cannot pretend that the man would ever be mistaken for Beau Brummell, you might be surprised at how respectable he could appear when he made the effort. Now, this particular outing was a proper treat as it fell on Christmas Eve and we was all headed to the Lowther Arcade. You know the place? On the Strand?'

'I know it well,' Oliver smiled at the mention. 'That long arcade with all the fine toy shops and those wonderful glass ceilings. My adopted father took me there on our first Christmas together to buy me some toy soldiers.'

'Well, that's just what my adopted father was doing!' I beamed upon learning of this shared experience of ours. 'Only I doubt that your Mr Brownlow expected you to pinch the soldiers for yourself. Fagin, though, was keen to use the festive season as a spur to make ready shoplifters of us all. He knew that the skills we would learn collecting our own Christmas gifts would stand us in good stead for our future careers. We had been over the theory many times, now we was to put it into practice. In pairs of two we was each expected to enter at the south end of the bustling arcade and work our way northwards through the long passage of shops, to see which pair could impress him the most with our findings. The prize, as ever, would be gin.'

'What an appalling way to motivate children,' Oliver remarked.

'Georgie and Jem went in first,' I continued, ignoring him, 'and they bungled it. Like most beginners, they made the mistake of trying to lift what they wanted for themselves rather than what would be good for the dash and they was almost grabbed trying to make off with some model trains what they had to drop in order to escape. Other boys had more success pilfering smaller toys, but these did not add up to much and that was all Fagin ever cared for. But I knew without being told that the real value of all the Christmas window displays was not in the toys themselves but in the distractions that they offered. I convinced Charley Bates – who you'll remember from that day when the three of us all went out on a spree – that we should not waste time even entering the shops. Instead, we loitered around the window-shoppers who was gawping at the many Christmas trees and concentrated on emptying the coat pockets and gowns of the ladies and gentlemen there. We kept moving as we did, so by the time we emerged at the north end of the arcade, our clothes was stuffed with wallets, purses, watches and jewellery. Fagin, who had been watching us close as he sauntered by himself, saw my natural talent for the first time and was good and impressed.'

From the other side of the smoking chamber, Eddie Inderwick was groaning at us. It seemed as though he was trying to turn onto his side so he could tell us to keep our chatter down, but his words came out as one long wheeze.

'Ignore him,' I said to Oliver, who looked concerned. 'He'll drift off again soon. So anyway, that night in Saffron Hill, after we had all grown bored of those ill-gotten toys and discarded most of them, we lined up in Fagin's kitchen to eat this Christmas pudding what he had been preparing all week. He lifted the lid from off his large steel pot to release the steam and we could smell the fruits and brandy within. But before he began filling our bowls he made an announcement:

"Hush my dears, hush," he placed a finger to his lips. "Before I start dishing out this tasty and well-earned pud, I wish to say a few words. And that is to tell you how very glad I am that you've all come to brighten up my humble abode!" Cheers and stamping from the new boys in the line and some banging of pots from the older ones already sat at the long table. "You've made a lonely old man very happy," he said with a flourish, although it was doubtful that he had ever spent a lonely day in his life. "It makes me feel thirty years younger, it does, to be enjoying such youthful company!" Charley shouted out that he must be feeling around ninety then to which Fagin feigned offence, grabbed a nearby wet flannel and threw it straight at his face. Merriment from all around as it slapped and covered its target but Fagin, once he had finished chuckling himself, held the still clean ladle in the air as if halting an orchestra. "My dears, each and every one of you," he continued once we had quietened down, "has what it takes to be the prince of this city if you wish it! I cannot remember the last time this creaking old house had such a crop. Nevertheless," his face turned more serious and he pointed the ladle at us again, "there is a question what needs answering before we feast. And this is the small matter of which one of *you*," he moved the ladle along the line of newcomers as if expecting it to stop at one of us of its own accord, "will be declared *top sawyer*!"

This stilled us. We waited to be told who the finest thief in our company was and therefore who would be our leader. We knew that whatever name Fagin said now would go unchallenged, as we was then too young to pick one for ourselves.

"Every crew needs a captain, does it not?" Fagin continued, confident in our full attention. "And every pantomime needs a principal boy." The ladle was still travelling along the line of boys waiting to anoint the chosen one. "And I know the name of your top sawyer before you do! His name is . . . The Artful Dodger!"

Disappointment rose up from all around. None of us had heard of him.

"Sounds like a lavender boy," cried Jem White in his insolent way, "and he belongs in a molly house, not here." There was much laughter at this, but this time Fagin did not join in with it. Jem knew he had no chance of being our top sawyer after his poor showing at the arcade, so he was already out of sorts with whoever this Artful Dodger person might turn out to be.

"I know what you mean, Jemima dear, I know what you mean," grinned Fagin, coining another nickname what Jem was stuck with for some time. "He sounds like a bit of a sharp one, don't he? A bit of a character." He then began banging the steaming pot with his ladle. "Who is this mysterious Dodger then, eh, and what is so artful about him?" He spoke as if daring the boy to show himself.

But before any young chancer could try and claim the title as his own, Fagin plunged the ladle into the pot. "Why don't we ask this Christmas pudding here, eh?" he said with a wink. "A pudding always knows the truth, I find!"

Fagin then snatched the first bowl from out of Georgie's hands and began filling it with his pudding. There was knowing smiles from the older thieves, who would have doubtless seen this show before when their own top sawyer was announced.

"There's a gold shiner hidden somewhere amid all these plums and prunes, which is worth more than all your day's swipes put together." The full bowl was handed back to Georgie and then Fagin took the next one from Mick Skittles. "And this here coin is of the magic sort and it knows what bowl it is meant to be found in." Once Mick's bowl was full, Fagin took Mouse Flynn's and continued like this until all the boys ahead of me in the line had been served. "And in whichever bowl we find it," he continued as he grabbed at my own and filled it with a bit more care than he had the others, "well, that would be the bowl what belongs to the Artful Dodger, I should think."

He winked at me as he handed me back the bowl and I knew then that I would be tasting metal in my mouth, before I had even taken a bite. I felt like I was being christened.'

Oliver sat there on that rickety chair and I could see that he was not sure of what to make of this rum naming ceremony. I imagined that a serious scribbler such as him might find my fond childhood memories to be a bit on the sentimental side. When he next spoke it was with some hesitation.

'Don't take offence, Jack,' he said after coughing into his fogle again, 'but it sounds to me like any one of you could have been named the Artful Dodger.' The smoke made me blink hard and I asked him what he meant by that. 'I mean that it was all just a bit of Christmas tomfoolery,' he explained. 'That you were merely a random winner, perhaps even an accidental one. How could Fagin have guaranteed that the coin would end up in your bowl?'

I was most taken aback by this stupidity and gave a loud snort to let him feel my contempt. 'You lived at Fagin's house, Oliver,' I said back. 'Did you ever see him perform a conjuring trick what ended up in any other way than how he wanted it to? If he asked you to pick a card then you would always pick the one predicted. There wasn't anything accidental about the Jew so it stands to reason that I was meant to be the Artful Dodger, eh? All the other boys took it to be so.'

'But haven't you ever wondered,' Oliver pressed on in his vexatious manner, 'whether Fagin didn't really care who the

Artful Dodger was? He just knew that there had to be a top sawyer among you, a leader, and that if the business wasn't settled then there would be fighting. So he made a game of announcing the nickname. Perhaps that was the real illusion.' As he spoke, I could feel myself grow hotter at the blasphemy of it. 'And as for the wink?' he persisted. 'In my memory Fagin was forever winking at anyone over anything. It signifies nothing.'

I would have leapt up and given him a proper hiding for his treason had I not been rendered so lazy from the opium. Instead, I just jabbed my finger in his general direction.

'I'm the Artful Dodger, Oliver, and you bloody well know it. You saw me in my prime, there was no faster thief. Fagin knew it, Charley Bates knew it, they all knew it. The very idea that such a name could have belonged to anyone else, that it could have suited anyone save me, is a travesty what I'll not entertain.' The three other occupants in this smoking chamber was all stirring now. I even heard Chinese voices from behind the silk curtains telling me to shush, but I was too hot to heed them. 'Back then,' I kept growling, 'I earned the name on every finding spree. Back then I was the Artful Dodger of every minute of every day.'

'Back then?' said Oliver in a voice much calmer than my own. 'Not now?'

I slumped back down onto the pillow and felt the fire what had just risen inside me burn out just as fast. I looked over to where a small jug of greenish water and some pewter cups was resting on a table. I did not want to ask Oliver to fetch a drink for me – I would not let him treat me like an invalid – and so

I forced myself up from the bench again and poured myself a drop of this dubious liquid. I asked Oliver if he would like some but was unsurprised by his refusal, considering how unwise it was to drink water what you could smell from a distance. But I just needed to wet my throat with it so I spat it back into the cup once this was done. Then I returned to the bed, closed my eyes in exhaustion and thought on all the wrongs of the past few weeks.

'No,' I said at last. I felt relieved at speaking the hard truth of it, the truth of which no doubt the rest of the criminal underworld was already well aware. 'Nowadays, it is starting to seem that I ain't that artful at all.'

Chapter 2

Kingdom of Monkeys

*Recounting the shameful circumstances surrounding
a recent family outing*

'If you really want to hear about it, Oliver, then the first thing you'll no doubt want to know about of is all these noose nightmares what I've been having ever since Newgate. I'd also tell you about all the sweating and the shakes they've brought on and about how I've been doubling up on opium by way of a treatment, but I don't much feel like going into it, if you want to know the truth. However, if you've spoken to Lily, then I suppose she must have told you about what occurred at the zoo, and if so, then I ought to set you straight on that. There are always two sides to every story and this here is mine.

As it was a hot June day, myself, Lily and little baby Robin had all spent the morning picnicking in a small cemetery not far from our crib. I would imagine that someone of your class might look askance upon us poor people choosing to holiday among the tombstones on a summery day, but when you live in the slums there is often no greener, fresher or more pleasant destination within walking distance. And, on top of that, this particular cemetery was the final resting spot of my poor fallen friend Mouse Flynn and his wife Agnes, who had died in childbirth. This departed pair was the true parents of that little item of mortality Robin, who, as you will recall from your visit to our happy home, Lily and myself was raising as our own. So it felt only right that we should take him to visit his family whenever possible. While we was there playing with our adopted son and speaking to the dead Flynns I decided to again raise with Lily a matter most sensitive. See, although our lives had been beset with many shocks and sadnesses over the past few months, there was one thing what gave me joy whenever I dwelt upon it. I had so taken to fatherhood ever since that little boy had come to live with us in our crib, that I had begun to dream of a future where I would be not just a surrogate father to him, but also the natural father to many others. I would soon sire a whole litter of kinchins and educate them all – boys and girls – in the crooked ways of this world. And then – once they was old enough – these junior Dodgers could all provide for me and their mother in our dotage, so there would be a return on the investment. But whenever I mentioned this sentimental ambition to the light of my life, she did not seem as enthused.

"The world's got more than enough people in it, Jack," she told me blunt as she changed Robin's soiled swaddling clothes, "it don't need no others."

"But you make for a good mother," I flattered her, as she finished cleaning his bottom and tossing the soiled napkin into a bush, "and any child would want me for a father, so nature must take its course, eh?"

"Hmm," she replied as she pinned his new napkin into place, but it was obvious that she needed further persuasion. During her whoring days Lily had been taught to take precautions against falling into such a condition and it seemed that she never stopped taking them. Don't ask me what these precautions was, but they had been successful, much to my chagrin. Before I could argue the case for reproduction further, she changed the subject to that of my unseasonal attire.

"Take your coat off, my love," she said as she gave Robin back a little stuffed mouse what he did not like to be without and lifted him back into his baby carriage. "You must be sweltering in this heat."

"I don't like to," I answered. "On account of my scars."

I had told Lily often enough that I hated the sun as it reminded me of my time in Australia and that, even through a thin shirt, the stinging rays could aggravate the many whip marks what streaked across my back. But this was only sometimes true, as the real reason I wore a winter coat in summer was down to the chills what would come upon me if I went without tasting opium for too long, chills I was already feeling despite the church clock above us not having yet struck twelve. I had promised Lily that I would spend the afternoon with her and Robin in Regent's zoo, as she wished to see the new bear. But I could think of other things I would rather be doing, so I tried to tell her that I had business matters elsewhere and that she should take Robin by herself while I went off to be the family provider. This, it seemed, was ill-judged.

"You ain't picked a pocket or robbed a crib in weeks, Jack," she chided me as we wheeled the wicker carriage containing the baby and the picnic basket out of the cemetery. "Which is why there ain't no money coming in other than that what I steal. You've got the Limehouse itch again, don't go pretending otherwise, I can see it on you. Well, there'll be no puffing today. These tickets what I found in that lady's purse are dated for this afternoon, so we're all going to the zoo whether you care to or not. Now, trot over to that there thoroughfare and hail us a cab big enough for this," she tapped the carriage. "I want to see Black Boris."

The journey towards Regent's Park proved to be an unpleasant one. As the hackney cab trundled along gravelly roads, I found myself rocking forward in an uneasy manner what had little to do with the motion of the vehicle. I could feel the sickness coming on again and Lily handed me a fogle so I could dab the sweat from off my brow. Now that I had agreed to remain at her side for the rest of the day, she had become more sympathetic towards me and said that she was only making me spend time away from the poppy for my own benefit. She again entreated me to remove my coat, but I remained reluctant. I thanked her for her concern as I gripped tight onto the wooden seat to hold myself in place.

Once we was through the southern gates of the zoo I did begin to feel a little better and, as we pushed the baby carriage up the shrub-lined promenade towards the bear pit, Lily at last managed to convince me to remove my coat and enjoy the weather more. Her attitude had softened towards me by then and our chat became more cordial as we neared Boris the mighty black Russian, about whom there had been much talk about town. The new bear was proving to be a popular attraction and there was at least three dozen spectators gathered around the square iron barriers what surrounded his pit and they was all very distracted by the ursine celebrity. Boris had obliged his adoring audience by climbing a stout wooden pole in the centre of his pit, so as to display himself proud and high but was still at a safe distance. Many of the gentlemen watching him was holding out buns on the end of long sticks, attempting to feed him, to the delight of all.

"Fancy doing likewise?" I asked Lily and nodded towards the stall where they sold the buns and implements. She shook her head and lowered her voice.

She halted the wicker carriage before we became part of the crowd ourselves. "I'd rather watch you work your mischief." Lily smiled her wickedest smile. "See how distracted they all are," she indicated the congregation. "Dipping conditions are perfect, don't you reckon? You can circle that pit easy and once you're done, you can hide your findings underneath Robin's crib here."

In all truth, I could feel my left hand start to twitch at the very suggestion. Perhaps it was just the heat, but a discernible sensation of dizziness came over me at the thought of picking any pockets without having prepared myself for the task first.

"Yeah, I don't know about all that, Lil," I whispered back. "Any experienced thief will tell you that it ain't clever to work in an enclosed space such as this here zoo on account of there being no handy cuts to escape down. And I wouldn't want to risk you and the baby getting into no bother."

"Oh, but when have such things ever troubled you in the past?" She laughed, and I understood now that she had brought me here to be tested. "We'll be alright. You go brush up against some pockets, why don't you? It always used to give me a buzz to see you do it."

Her clear excitement at the prospect of witnessing me work my art again made her seem so very beautiful that I longed to satisfy her desire and return from the pit with many pilfered love tokens. Doubtless she would have been so attracted by my success that we would have gone straight home afterwards and set about making babies. But my hands was too clammy, I could not even remember my last dip and I knew that I was just not up to it.

"Not today, Lil," I replied and felt limp as I did so. "I ain't much in the mood. Perhaps next time." Her smile vanished and she turned from me. She shoved the baby carriage off away from the bear pit and walked off deeper into the zoo. I trotted after her.

You're a married man, Oliver, so you know well what they can be like. Lily remained in a huff for a good ten minutes as we negotiated the aviary walk, where bright-coloured caged birds screeched and squawked at me as if they was all expressing Lily's irritation on her behalf. At last, we came to a tree-lined avenue where a hut had been built in which ladies could go to relieve themselves and Lily broke her silence to tell me that she needed to pay it a visit. She told me to watch over the baby until she got back and so I wheeled the carriage over to a sheltered bench, and with one hand on the side so it would not roll away, I let my eyes rest for a spell. Robin was happy enough squeezing his toy mouse and it felt good to allow myself a little doze in Lily's absence.

"Watch out, constables, it's the Artful Dodger!" yelled a high-pitched voice not far from my earhole, causing me to start up from my nap in fright. "Arrest him quick afore he pinches one of the efelants!"

Young laughter rippled all around as I woke to find myself surrounded by the boys from the Low Arches, a rascally gang of six. From the little noise they had made in their approach they may well have dropped down from the trees above like chimpanzees. They was all dressed up flash and colourful, as I used to do at their age, in clothes what was far too big for them, and they seemed to have found sneaking up upon my sleeping self to have been a most amusing jape.

"Sorry for the disturbance, Mister Dawkins," grinned the closest boy on the bench beside me, as the others continued giggling at my momentary confusion. "But we'd like to make an introduction if you don't much mind?"

I was a bit embarrassed to have been caught unawares by these youthful admirers of mine. The Low Arches boys was a band of keen and industrious urchins who was local to Seven Dials and their leader, the imp what had just woken me up in so rude a fashion, was a boy of about thirteen called Joe Muckraw. I was familiar with Joe and his little collective as I had become something of a Fagin figure to them in recent months. They all grew up knowing the Artful Dodger by reputation and so they're forever buzzing around my haunts in the hope of ingratiating themselves. Now I'm more than happy to encourage them in the ignoble art although, unlike the old Jew, I would never let any of the thieving buggers inside my own crib if I could help it. But they've often been known to knock on my door to ask me to inspect whatever findings they may have acquired during the day, or to ask me to play the fence if I think there is a profit in it, which there often is.

"I don't need eyes open to know when you're about, Muckraw," I smiled back at him. "You have a very distinctive odour."

This got him back where it hurt and his ratty little face crumpled as his pals directed their laughter away from me and towards him. I knew Joe to be very sensitive about his cleanliness, as he had been born a mudlark boy, meaning that his late parents had both been river dredgers. The first time I met him he had more dirt up his nose, behind his ears and under his fingernails than a person exhumed, but that was over a year ago. Nowadays he had declared himself to be the top sawyer of this little gang and so he was making more of an effort to wash himself.

'Perhaps you ain't heard,' he informed me as he jumped down from the bench, placed his thumbs into his waistcoat pockets and puffed out his chest. 'Nobody calls me Joe Muckraw no more. I'm The Slippery Soap these days,' he nodded at his gang with misplaced grandeur, 'because I always get away clean!'

'Come up with that yourself, did you?'

'Yep,' replied the self-anointed upstart. 'Like it?'

I stretched my back before answering. Reclining on that

bench had antagonised my scars again and put me even further
out of humour.

"I ain't certain that I do, Joe," I answered and I saw the puff
go out of him. "But it's clear to all that you can imagine no
more elusive object than soap, so what can we expect?"

His boys sniggered again to his obvious displeasure. Perhaps
this was a bit cruel, but Joe Muckraw had made the mistake of
trying to humiliate me and so it stood to reason that he should
be paid in kind.

"Soap is famous for being hard to keep hold of," I continued.
"It is not steady, but all over the place. It is a liability, Joe, and
you would be ill-advised to name yourself after a famous liability." Before he could respond to that, I turned to the others
and noticed that there was one boy standing among the group
who I had never seen before. He was a couple of years younger
than the rest. "This who you want to introduce me to, is it?"

"Pleased to meet you, Mr Dawkins sir," said the new boy.

"What's your name, son?"

"Nick, sir."

"That all?" I asked. "Not named yourself after a household
toiletry like Joe here?"

"Nah," he shrugged. "I'm happy with Nick."

"Good for you, Nick," I nodded in a languid way. "And
besides, the great thieves never come up with their own identities," I cast a disapproving glance towards Joe the Soap as I
said this, "but instead we have our criminal names given to
us by older, respected crooks. And we in turn are expected to
bestow suitable monikers on any gifted, younger thieves what

we might notice showing promise. In this way reputations are given as well as earned and in my view, we should look with derision upon any flash youth what might try to buck this time-honoured tradition."

"You must be very honoured 'bout meeting Mister Dawkins here, eh Nick?" interrupted Joe, pretending to be unconcerned by my criticisms. "After all, this is the man they used to call Lummy Jack, Fagin's Favourite, the Artful Dodger. People considered him to be the patron saint of all thieves, once upon a long time ago. He used to be top sawyer of the Diallers, you know. A high distinction back in his day."

It was my turn to drop the grin, as I turned my attention back to the cheeky sod.

"I still am top sawyer in Seven Dials, Muckraw," I spoke low and with deliberate threat. "And it ain't advisable to go pretending otherwise, even in fun."

"That ain't what we hear," piped up Venetian Vince, a swarthy youngster who, despite his nickname, was born in Maidstone. "We hear Tom Skinner runs things there now, and that you ain't done much of anything since you was released from gaol."

"Tom acts as my Prime Minister," I explained. "But I remain the monarch. And monarchs, as we all know, don't do nothing if they don't wish to."

Vince smirked at me. Joe smirked too. I noticed that they was all smirking, save for newcomer Nick.

"So you're just as sharp as you ever was, eh Dodge?" asked Joe as he took a couple of steps backwards. "Still top sawyer?" The other boys had been edging backwards too and it was becoming apparent they was up to something tricky. "Then how come, Jack the Puffer," he sneered with undisguised delight, "you ain't even noticed what we've stolen from you yet?"

Even then, I am ashamed to record, it took me a full second to fall upon what he was referring to. But, as soon as I did, something inside just dropped and I cried out in alarm. The wicker carriage had vanished.

I jumped up from my bench in horror. "What have you little bastards done with my son?"

But already the Low Arches boys was scarpering off in different directions, all of them cackling at me like demons. The only one still within reaching distance was new boy Nick and I grabbed hold of his arm as he tried to escape. I yanked him back so hard that I could have pulled his limb off if he'd resisted more. I shouted into his terrified face.

"Give him back now," I warned him, "or you're going in the bear pit!"

This Nick struggled to get away and spluttered something about not knowing where he was. "Some other boys wheeled him off while you was dozing, Mr Dawkins, sir," he answered fast as I twisted his arm. "They're only having a laugh. It weren't my idea or doing."

Joe Soap yelled at me from the far end of the lane. "They've taken him to the reptile house," he grinned. "You best hurry Dodger, afore the snakes swallow him."

I released the boy and raced off towards this part of the zoo, sheer panic spurring me on to run faster than I ever had before.

I shoved my way past any strolling couples what obstructed my path and shouted my adopted son's name at the top of my voice. My heart pounded at the very thought that I might lose him for good and I became even more terrified thinking on how Lily would react. My distress was made worse by not really knowing the whereabouts of the reptile house, and instead I came to the elephant paddock at the north garden. Spectators was lined up to gaze through the bars of the enclosure at the long-trunked beasts bathing themselves in their pond.

"Which way's the reptile house?" I demanded of the congregation but, being all of the genteel middle-class, they pretended to ignore the frantic cockney in their midst. So I instead directed my question towards the three white-robed black men in the paddock who was helping to scrub the elephants. These African attendants did not appear to speak much English, so I moved my arm like a snake and hissed. They nodded and pointed me in the right direction.

Soon I came to where the reptiles was kept. This corner of the zoo was far less populated than the rest. To my great relief, there the abandoned baby carriage stood under the shade of the wooden pavilion. I approached it, ready to gather up the precious boy safe into my arms. But when I peered into the carriage I instead screamed out in fright. The carriage's only occupant was a green snake slithering itself into a tight coil.

I staggered backwards and almost fell down from the shock of it. Then I heard the unmistakable sound of my baby boy crying and I spun around to see him in the arms of Joe Muckraw at the top of a grassy mound to the left of the pavilion. Joe was cradling little Robin, flanked by two other boys who must have been the ones what had made off with the carriage in the first place. How they had managed to pinch the snake was bewildering, but I was too hot and angry to enquire and began cursing up at them. Joe looked down at me and jeered.

"We was only larking about, Dodge," he said and rocked my baby son to try to settle him. "Take a joke."

I was just about to march up that little grass hill and snatch Robin back when something even more fearsome reared into view behind them. Lily Lennox in her green summer dress, looking like she was poised for a kill, uttered something to the trio of baby-nappers what I could not hear from that distance, but seemed to strike terror into them. With one swift action she grabbed the child out of Joe's arms and gathered him safe into her own. The other two Arches boys fled in opposite directions, but it turned out that the Slippery Soap was not going to get away so clean after all. Instead Lily kicked him hard in his stomach. Joe doubled up and tumbled down the small hill towards me.

I turned back to the baby carriage, reached inside to grab the snake and, before it had a chance to strike me, flung it back towards the pavilion for someone else to worry about. Then I wheeled the carriage up to where Lily was, congratulating her on her successful recovery of our baby and planning on stamping on Soap's fallen body myself as soon as I got the chance. But once the baby had been placed back inside the wicker carriage, Lily began pushing our child away from me.

I followed after, making all manner of feeble excuses and apologies, and then she spun around.

"Stay away from us, Jack!" she seethed with more hostility than I had ever before known from her. "You ain't a suitable father for this, or any other child. You're a wastrel and nothing more and the quicker I can get him away from you, the better!"

"Don't be like that, Lil," I protested, "it weren't my fault. It was all the doing of these here kinch–"

"You don't provide for us no more, you can't protect him," she continued loud enough for the whole of Regent's Park to hear. "What possible use are you to either of us?"

As I was struggling to find a reply to this, she moved in closer and spoke with what sounded like genuine sorrow in her voice.

"What happened to the man I fell for, eh, Jack?" she whispered. "Did Newgate take him after all? Cos I ain't seen him in a while."

I was at a loss as to how to respond to this and muttered something in my defence as she turned and pushed the carriage away towards the exit. She left me standing there dumbfounded, as she spoke her cruellest cut yet.

"You're the last man I'd ever have a child with," was what I thought I heard her say.'

Chapter 3

A Disappointed Drudge

*My conversation with Oliver continues and
a cruel deception is revealed*

Oliver had not uttered a word while I had been relating my sorrowful tale to him and it was instead Eddie Inderwick who at last interrupted me. My fellow puffer was, once again, seized by one of his nasty coughing fits and he gripped his stomach as he curled up and hacked it all out. Then he rolled over on his stained mattress to face my side of the smoking chamber. He scowled at me as if he considered his pain to be somehow my doing and told me to shut my yapping, before pulling a ragged blanket over himself, returning to sleep. Oliver looked upon him as though he was some colicky baby what we must be careful not to disturb.

'Don't be deceived,' I said as Li Wu entered through the silk curtains with a clean jug of water and poured me out a fresh cup. 'Eddie can be quite the conversationalist when the mood takes him. Even if it is only to himself.'

The Chinaman filled up the rest of the pewter cups what was lying beside each of his paying customers. As he did so he placed a finger over his lips and told me to shush. I apologised to him and he scuttled off without even acknowledging my visitor.

'There are times,' I remarked to Oliver once Li Wu had left the chamber, 'when I wonder if that Chinaman thinks he's running the British Library or something.'

Oliver seemed unoffended at having been ignored by the proprietor of this opium den and waited for me to finish wetting my throat. Then he leaned in further and asked me if I thought that it truly was over between Lily and myself.

'When I got back to our crib early on the following morning,' I said once my cup was drained, 'I found that she had gone. Not only that, but she had removed most of her things and all of Robin's.'

'That was terribly fast,' observed Oliver. 'Where were you while this was happening?'

I picked up my opium pipe and inspected it from a number of angles.

'I had spent the night here,' I admitted and avoided meeting eyes with him. 'Smoking my cares away.'

'I see,' he sighed.

'She left me a note to say that she was taking him by coach and horses to live with her childless sister and her husband, the poor little mite. They're up in Rochester in Kent and are a right pair of flats by all accounts. The husband's a schoolmaster, she's a seamstress and neither sound like much fun. Robin won't grow to be happy and bright under their roof, I don't care what Lily says.'

I took another hard puff of that pipe and shut my eyes. I had a deep desire to just ignore Oliver and lie back down onto my mattress, but it seemed like he was not going to allow it.

'She still cares for you, Jack,' he told me. 'She told me so herself.'

'Yeah?' I murmured with my eyes still closed. 'She's got a rum way of showing it.'

'I must say though, I agree with her,' he added. 'The child is better off away from your bad influence.'

My eyes snapped open again and I sat up straighter, ready for a confrontation. 'That ain't for her to decide though, is it!' I barked at him. 'The boy was mine, unnerstand? Not by blood, I grant you, but all other rights. His true father, Mouse Flynn, was a Saffron Hill boy and he was like a brother to me. This made Robin my responsibility and, therefore, my boy to raise. She *stole* him from me, hear?' I stressed the word as if stealing was the worst crime a person could commit.

I realised then that I was shouting and I received some complaints about the noise from some disturbed sailors in a neighbouring smoking chamber and some of the older sons of Wu.

'I'm sorry if my words offended, Jack,' Oliver said although he did not look very sorry. 'But let me ask you this. Would you tolerate a thief who stole not just your baby from you, but Lily as well? Who stole all of your earnings and your gang of Diallers too? Who took your talent for thievery and the standing that, until very recently, you enjoyed among the criminal community? Because that,' he pointed at the now almost extinguished opium lamp, 'is precisely what you are allowing the poppy to steal from you unchallenged.'

The light was starting to die inside that little chamber. I

looked down to the bamboo pipe what I cradled in my hands and knew that there was no longer any use in refuting these truths. The opium had rendered me low and I was overcome with remorse at the deplorable state I had let myself fall into. I could not meet Oliver's eye when I spoke next and I must have sounded like a whimpering adolescent.

'Why do you care?' I sniffed, vexed with him for being right. 'It ain't like you want me to get better so I can go back on the thieve, is it? It should please you to find me so reduced. It proves that your philosophy was the right one.'

Oliver got up from his chair and sat down upon the mattress next to me. When he spoke next it was with a kindness in his voice that I was not ready for and I could feel myself becoming most emotional.

'You may not find this easy to believe, Jack,' he said as he offered me a handkerchief on which to dry my eyes, 'but, when we met as children, I admired you very much.' I waved the fogle away, but let him go on speaking. 'I was very frightened of London when I first arrived here, it seemed so wild and chaotic, and had you not befriended me I suspect I would have perished. You were so fearless to my provincial eyes, so competent and quick-witted, so full of life. So it pains me to see you like this, Dodger. I would much prefer it if you recovered yourself and those fine qualities you once possessed, regardless of my feelings about your dubious morality.'

'I wish I could,' I confessed at last. 'I would love to cast off the spell of the poppy and just be done with it. But it ain't that easy.'

'Do you know what I think would fix you? Occupation.'

'I've got lots of occupations,' I reminded him. 'I'm busy, busy, busy, me. I'm a pickpocket, a cracksman, a top sawyer to a large criminal gang.'

'You are none of those things anymore,' he corrected me. 'And that is your problem. You need new challenges, Jack. You must find something that will distract your mind from all this,' he tapped the opium lamp with his foot as it snuffed itself out. 'Find an occupation. Go on an excursion. Be the Artful Dodger again.'

I considered this and knew that, in spite of myself, it was sound advice. My life had become stagnant with the success of the Diallers, I had climbed to the top of my profession and thought that there was nowhere higher to climb. I had retired too young and this terrible lethargy had been the unwelcome result.

So I forced myself up from my slumped position and reached over to the small wooden table on top of which the jug of green water was balanced. Oliver watched my movements with interest and his little moustache twitched as if he knew what I was planning to do. I took hold of the jug and emptied the dregs over my head as he smiled in encouragement. Then I gave my face a wash with my hands and got up to pace around the smoking chamber for a spell, taking care to avoid those asleep on the floor.

'That's a good start, Jack,' he said. 'Refresh yourself.'

I was glad now that Oliver had come here to listen to me. I talked all my woes through and I became most grateful to him as I felt myself sharpening up. He had, not for the first time, proven himself to be a good if unlikely friend. And, I thought, if it was true that Lily had searched him out for my benefit, then it showed that, contrary to what she had said on that day in the zoo, she did still care for me. So perhaps I had not lost her after all.

'Everything you've said here is true, Oliver,' I announced as I picked up my coat, what I had earlier dropped without a thought onto the dirty ground, and flapped the creases out of it. 'The poppy has stolen too much from me and it is time to get it all back.' I put on the coat with some flourish and tried to recall where I had left my hat or if indeed I had even come in here with one. I spotted a crumpled black topper what might belong to me wedged underneath the bench on which I had been lying. 'I'm going to remind everyone who the Artful Dodger is and why I'm him. Then, I'm taking charge of my gang again.' I held the hat by its rim and punched it back into shape. 'But, most of all, I'm getting my lady back. Lily and myself will be as one again in no time,' I assured him as I slapped myself in the face in an effort to further throw off the effects of the drug.

At this, Oliver, who had been nodding in approval at most of my words, altered his manner.

'I'm not so sure about that last thing, Jack,' he said after another little cough and in a graver tone than before. 'It sounds as if Lily has made her decision and perhaps you ought not to pester her further.'

'It's Lily I want,' I said as I set my hat at the particular angle that I liked upon my head, 'and no one else will do.'

'That is a pity,' he said with a small shake of the head. 'As down that road only disappointment lies.'

In my fidgety pacing I had reached the far end of the smoking chamber and in between us lay two of the slumbering puffers. I pulled up short when Oliver said that and asked him what he meant by it. He stood up. In his unbefitting tweed suit and with both of his hands holding onto his hat he looked most unlike that small orphan boy I once knew.

'I'm afraid Lillian doesn't love you anymore, Dodger,' he announced, like he was some doctor about to deliver fatal news. 'Not in that way. She loves someone else. She asked me to tell you.'

My eye's was stinging again from the fug that remained all around and this caused me to blink in agitation. He raised his left hand up to his face so he could scratch his moustache in a gesture of nervousness.

'The sordid truth,' he continued in his unsteady way, 'is that she and I have become intimate. There, it is said.'

I shifted from foot to foot and eyed him.

'This is what I really came for,' he raised his chin as he spoke. 'So that I could tell you how things are, man to man. I have taken her for my mistress.' It was as though he had struck me, strong and sudden, with a hidden whip. I opened my mouth in amazement, but no sound followed.

'You're lying,' I stammered at last.

'I'm afraid not,' he shrugged. 'I know this must be upsetting for you, but I hope things can remain cordial between us.'

I have never been so overcome with the hot urge to kill

someone as I was then. I shook my head and told him why he was mistaken.

'Why would Lily,' I sneered at him, 'choose a flat like you over a flash cove like me?'

'Because I am a gentleman,' he replied without missing a beat. 'And you are of the gutter.'

Then he smirked at me.

I charged at him, leaping over the first sleeping puffer with the full intention of strangling Oliver where he stood. But I was still disorientated from the opium and before I could get to him I tripped over the body of Eddie Inderwick, what sent me crashing downwards. I stumbled to get up but I was then tangled up in the purple silk hanging what I managed to pull away from its hooks as I fell again to the floor. From around the den I could hear people cursing me in Chinese as well as in English as I tried to unwrap myself from the silk. I could hear Eddie Inderwick swearing at me from the floor.

'I'm going to rip your treacherous tongue out, Twist!' I raged as I struggled to stand without tripping over the fallen hanging. I was all turned around and I had to search for where he was hiding himself before lashing out again. But, before I could find him, I was seized by three older members of the family Wu.

'Out!' ordered Li Wu as he and his two older sons grabbed me before I could do more damage. 'No more smoke for you!' My limbs had been thrashing around in an attempt to hit Oliver wherever he was hiding within the heavy fog, but now these Chinamen had me restrained. Oliver appeared to have dashed off somewhere, but Eddie was sitting up and scowling at me.

'You've had more than enough sweet smoke, Dodge,' Eddie advised me rubbing his hurt head. 'Do as the Orientals say and go home now, if you still have one.'

'Not till I've settled Twist!' I shouted and kept casting my eyes about for my false friend. 'Where'd he go?'

'Where did who go?' asked Eddie.

'The cove I've been talking to all night,' I exclaimed. 'Who else? The one what was sat in that there chair.'

Eddie looked towards the chair and then back to me. His expression was confused.

'You know who I mean!' I turned to Li Wu. 'The man who your son led in here. Twist paid him a shilling to dig me out.' The old Chinaman asked me which son I meant, indicating the two men what was both holding me by an arm each as I tried to wriggle myself free. 'Not these,' I said. 'The little boy what works here. The kinchin with the cockney accent.'

Li Wu looked offended at the very suggestion. 'I allow no child here,' he told me with a raise of the chin and an accusing eye. 'Too many dangerous characters!'

Eddie then spoke me in a sympathetic voice. 'There ain't been nobody else down here save for us puffers, Dodge.' He got up on his knees and crawled over to the chair what I now noticed had Eddie's flat cap resting on the seat. Even then I was still confused. Had Oliver been sitting on it all this time? 'You've been talking to a chair for the past hour,' Eddie explained. 'I tried to tell you to shush, but you just got louder. Don't feel embarrassed, we've all done it.'

I stopped wriggling then and the Chinamen loosened their grip on me as the mist around began to part. Once the hat was on his head Eddie walked over to the oil lamp and tapped it with his unbooted foot. It was empty.

'Unless you've some shillings left for a fill-up,' he remarked and bent down for his shoes. 'It's time for us both to head home.'

Still, I stood there dumbfounded. I took one last look around that hazy opium den for any sign of Oliver Twist, before accepting the truth that he had never been here at all. I blinked my watery eyes again, shook my head and felt a proper disgrace.

'I've hallucinated before,' I coughed and addressed the Wus, who was busy repairing the damage to the curtains. 'But never so deep.' There was a palpable relief at realising that what I had just heard about Lily was only a dream, but this was minor when compared to the humiliation of the scene. 'Sorry about the fuss,' I offered.

'*Out!*' Li Wu reiterated, pointing towards the staircase what would lead me back up to Narrow Street.

We who smoke often lose track of time, but I had not expected blazing midday sunshine to greet me as I stepped out onto the dusty street. I raised my hand up to protect my eyes from the blinding rays and could tell that it must be early on a Monday morning without needing to consult a watch. The road was thick with carriages transporting bags of exotic spices and expensive silks away from the docks and onto the Limehouse

Causeway. I was also surprised that I had not heard all of this down below, as the cries of busy tradesmen as well as the sounds of galloping hooves echoed from all around. I bade farewell to Eddie, who limped off to find a bench to sleep on, and then I headed towards the river. I was not ready to return home yet. I had more thinking to do.

Down by the riverside I found a spot overlooking some barges what was being built down on the muddy banks and I removed my blue coat. It had been a good coat when I had first stolen it from a restaurant cloakroom two years before, but now it was covered in dirt and coming apart at the stitching. Keeping something so worn just made me look like a vagrant, so I considered hurling the rotten garment into the drink.

Occupation. That was the message Oliver had come to deliver, even if he was an Oliver of my own dreaming. I leant on the wooden fence for some time and I raised my hatted head up to the clear sky to let the sun colour my face and help rid me of that drug-fiend pallor I had acquired of late.

New challenges.

Although the day was hot and my eyes was shut I could feel a cool breeze coming up the river and hear the barge-builders toil over their vessels, hammering nails into wood and cursing one another in good fellowship. And I knew that I could not tolerate my own wretchedness any longer.

What would Fagin say – he who had named me and anointed me top sawyer – if he could see me now? A man whose hands trembled when he even thought about picking a pocket, who let lethargy rule him and children laugh at him. He'd be disgusted by me and now so was I.

Find an occupation, he would be sure to agree. *Go on an excursion.* And, most important of all – *Be the Artful Dodger again.*

Chapter 4

London Smells

In which I go in search of new and exciting employment opportunities

London in the summer is made up of a variety of overpowering smells, as there is not enough rain to wash them away. Coal is a dominant one, along with beer, sweat, grease, tobacco, and, of course, excrement – both human and animal. And each vicinity emits its own discernible fragrance. Bethnal Green sewage, by way of for instance, is of an even fouler sort than most other places and the only people who think otherwise have never left Bethnal Green. The sewers of Kensington smell like a veritable flower garden, but only by comparison. Billingsgate smells of rotten fish, Smithfield of rotten meat and Covent Garden of rotten veg. There is also a notable difference between the quality of perfume a woman might wear to a society pleasure garden to that what she might put on while standing outside a brothel. If I am honest, I have always preferred the latter.

There are certain streets down which I could walk with my eyes shut and just let the familiar smells guide me. Field Lane is one such path as it leads me straight past Fagin's old home, where I can always detect bacon and sausages in the air even if he is no longer the one frying them. Saffron Hill has not smelt of saffron in centuries and nowadays the principal fragrance is gin, which I find to be just as enchanting. However, of late it is also overrun with roving dogs, who leave their own evil stink upon every corner and are known to growl at strangers. This does not include me, of course, and, as late afternoon turned to evening, I marched past them unhindered, following the strong smoky trail towards the Three Cripples public house.

Tobacco pervades the Cripples as much as opium does Wu's of Limehouse. Even the wallpaper inside matches the unhealthy colour of an old smoker's last tooth. As I pushed open the two heavy doors of the pub, I inhaled hard and enjoyed the strong puff before entering further, in a confident fashion. This rookery was where I had grown up, it was my home turf and I wanted all the Cripples regulars to be impressed by the very sight of me.

'No, ladies and gents, your eyes ain't playing tricks on you,' I announced to the room as I occupied a central spot where I could be viewed by all, 'Saffron Hill's most famous son has indeed returned. But please don't make a fuss about it, I don't want no special treatment.'

The many rough-faced denizens of that pub stared at me from their various tables and nooks. I recognised few of them and it seems they did not recognise me either. So I shrugged that off and strolled straight through the bar, taking care to display the sort of swagger what would have people asking questions about me. There I laid a warm hand of greeting upon the small and crooked frame of Old Lively. He was sat without company, nursing his usual pint of half-and-half and, once we had said our hellos, I rapped upon the bar with my other hand to draw the attention of the sullen girl serving.

'A bottle of White Fire to share between myself and my favourite uncle here, please Ruthie,' I smiled at her.

As soon as I spoke I sensed some female figures approaching us from a dark corner of the saloon, no doubt drawn to me by the likely promise of a free drink. The old hunchback was so pleased by my generosity that he near straightened himself out and he began telling me what a good boy I was. Old Lively was not my real uncle but he had been one of Fagin's closest business associates back in the good days and so my affection for him ran deep. He was a local trader who had prospered from selling high-quality stolen goods he purchased from Fagin, so the two of us had often been known to spend many a nostalgic hour in this here pub, lamenting the loss of the crafty old Jew. I was very much looking forward to enjoying such a session with him now as, although I was sworn off the poppy, this did not mean that I could have no gin. However, I was about to be corrected on that score.

'We ain't serving you, Dodger,' sniffed Ruthie. She crossed her arms and lifted her chin in a confrontational manner. 'It's been ruled.'

'Ruled?' I was most taken aback. 'Who by?'

'By the family,' she informed me. 'All seven daughters.'

'But not by your old man?'

'It's on account of our old man,' hissed the flint-eyed girl, 'that we made the rule. We're all sick of you taking advantage of his sentimental nature.'

'Where is he?' I demanded. 'I wish to speak to the patriarch himself. Don't fret, Lively,' I assured my disappointed companion. 'Barney'll set us right, he always does.'

'Not this time,' Ruthie persisted. 'Your bill's too high, has been for years. You've been coming in here and putting it on account and he's been indulging you. But until you pay what you already owe – which is a small fortune, I needn't remind you – then your patronage ain't welcome.'

'Good for you, girl,' cheered a familiar female voice from behind me. 'Jack always wants my favours for nothing 'n all.' I turned to see who it was and found myself confronted by a red-faced, heavy-carriaged harlot of my acquaintance, who winked back all mischievous. 'But I'm five shillings,' Greta said as she approached with two other whores flanking her, 'same as ever I was.'

'And you're worth every one of them, Greta,' I complimented her. 'But I mean to stay true to my Lily, in spite of what you may have heard.'

I had got myself entangled with this large lovely some years before, but had regretted it even then as she had been the friend of my first love, Ruby Solomon. But her manner was playful enough and her two companions, Pickled Liz and Ebony Bet, smirked at her cheek.

'P'raps though,' I ventured, 'seeing how I've been more than generous to you ladies over the years, you might now want to stump for some gin to share?' I indicated the bar.

Greta laughed in a long and throaty way at so outrageous a suggestion and I felt a strong bitterness at this. Before my incarceration I had come to this establishment often and had been happy to share my wealth with her and many others, so it burned now to see how little credit my former largesse had given me.

'Some Low Arches boys was in here earlier,' Greta snorted. 'Told us what happened at the zoo. We all roared, as you can well imagine. Even Lively.'

I glanced towards my elderly friend, who looked away and lifted his pewter pot as if to drink from it, but I got the distinct impression that he was trying to stifle a smile. I was about to take the assembled drinkers to task for their disloyalty, when Barney appeared at the far end of the long bar, his manner all of a flap. But his fat, wrinkled face lit up when he saw me.

'Dodger, you rascal!' he cried in what seemed like genuine delight and he came scurrying across, squeezing his hefty self past another of his busy daughters to rear up beside Ruthie. 'It's been too long, my boy. Too long. Has Ruthie offered you a drink yet?'

'She was just about to, Barney,' I beamed.

'No she wasn't, Barney,' his sixteen-year-old daughter refuted. 'We've been over this Pa, he never pays his bill and he offers drinks to half the pub 'n all. He takes you for a fool!'

'Come now Ruthie, its only the Artful!' Barney waved her concerns away and reached for a bottle of White Fire from behind him. 'Fagin's boy, remember? Oh, you don't remember

Fagin, you was too young when he passed.' He unscrewed the bottle with one hand and picked up two small glasses with the other. 'But he was a marvellous cove, weren't he, Dodge!'

'I don't want to hear about some dead fence again, Pa,' complained the girl, watching in dismay as her father poured me a drink. 'You treat this'n here better than you do your own daughters! But he ain't your son!'

Barney gave her a look what communicated that he sympathised with her frustrations, but he was powerless to do anything about it. Then he patted her on the head, which did little to cool her temper, and told her to mind the bar while he took me off for a discreet conversation elsewhere, just the two of us. He budged Greta and company out of the way as he did so.

'Ta for the medicine, Barney,' I said once we was behind the wooden partition what separated this corner of the pub from the main bar and I had taken my first swig of the gin. 'I've been a bit short of late, so I was counting upon your kindness.'

Barney gave me a gummy grin once we had sat down and chinked glasses. He and Fagin had been as thick as brothers when I was a kinchin and I had never received nothing but care, generosity and affection from this quarter, both before and after my years away.

'We don't see enough of you around here, Jack,' he said after sinking his own. 'I was starting to worry we had lost you to the white smoke for good.'

I recalled then that my last conversation with Barney had not been a happy one. I had asked him to lend me some money as I was already finding it too hard to steal my own, and he had refused. He had expressed concern about how much time I was spending among the opium clouds and had told me that he would not pay for any more. I had responded by telling him he could stick his piss-tasting gin and that I would never darken his rotten pub again. As this forgotten memory re-emerged, I placed my hands over my temples in shame and apologised for it.

'It's forgotten,' he said, waving it off. 'All your friends know that you ain't been yourself since that Newgate unpleasantness.'

'No, I ain't been,' I admitted, deciding against denial. 'But that's going to change from now on, Barn. I mean to get back to who I was.'

'Glad to hear it!' He poured himself a refill and went to top up my own glass.

'I need to sort out my finances first, though,' I told him. 'Which is what I wanted to see you about.' At that he stopped pouring and his body slumped.

'We've been over this, Jack,' he winced. 'I don't mind sharing what's mine, but I won't lend coin. It ain't doing you no good.'

'I ain't asking for loans,' I said and shuffled forward so we could not be overheard. 'I'm on about a job.'

Before I had gotten involved with Weeping Billy Slade, a business what had resulted in my arrest for a murder I had not committed, I had been making a decent living as a burglar for hire. I had enjoyed a reputation for being the most skilled cracksman in the London underworld, employed by wealthy clients who did not have the steel to perform their own cracks.

Many of these affluent customers had come to me through Barney, who ran a good line in introducing middle-class villains to criminal-class tradesmen, to the benefit of all.

'I ran into Herbie Sharp earlier today,' I told him, referring to one of the Diallers who lived near my crib, 'he reckons you've told Tom Skinner about some foreigners what are in the market for a thief. And that the money involved is considerable. This true?'

'Herb's got too much mouth,' Barney responded, wiping the drink from his own with his shirtsleeve. 'But yeah, there's been some interest. What of it?'

'Why didn't you come to me?'

Barney sighed.

'Tom runs the Diallers now, Jack. You ain't as reliable as you was once. And besides, you can never be found.'

'But this is just what I need,' I insisted, prodding the table with my finger. 'A big job, to put me in cash and restore my reputation. Who are they?'

'A French man and his French wife,' Barney said. 'Mulattoes both. But their coins are British and they don't mind spending them. They come in here one night, hooded like a couple of killers would be, claiming that they've heard it said that this is the place to come for a burglar.'

'What's the job? Why is the money so high?'

'It involves travelling to Paris,' he replied. 'That's where the crack is. Aside from that, they was very secretive.' He tapped his nose then, as Fagin used to do.

'Has Tom taken it already?'

'Too busy,' Barney shook his head. 'Doing your job, I should think. I'm to set up a meeting between the French and the assigned cracksman once Tom's decided who the lucky Dialler is.'

'I'm the lucky Dialler!' I declared. 'Set up a meeting with me.'

'I don't know about all that, Dodge. Tom says–'

'Tom won't mind,' I assured him. 'Send a message to the French, telling them that the underworld's finest burglar has taken an interest in their business and that I can meet them here to discuss details at their earliest convenience. And talk me up a bit, eh? Let them know what quality of thief they'll be getting.'

Barney huffed about this for some more moments, but I knew he'd agree if I kept on and, sure enough, he soon relented.

'Alright, I'll see to it,' he nodded. 'Come by here at three tomorrow. But don't be late, don't be drunk and don't be foggy-headed neither. It's a good job, Dodge, a fine opportunity for any thief and I'd hate to see it go wasting.'

'Cross my heart, it won't,' I grinned and knocked back my gin. 'This is a new start for me, old uncle, and I mean to take it serious. Now how about another drop, eh?'

Instead, Barney put the stopper back in the bottle and began to get up again.

'Lets see how you do tomorrow,' he said in a firmer tone. 'And, if you do get the job, then perhaps you can see your way to paying that bill off, eh Jack?'

Then, after a brief farewell, he returned to the bar to talk business with his daughters.

Most of the time, as I strut about these slum streets to which I am to the manor born, I feel cocksure and proud to have been raised among the lowliest and most destitute of the city. When you are of a class what is expected to starve before your childhood is out, you should wear your continued survival with honour, as a refutation to those above who would, without a thought, stamp you out like vermin. But on that particular summer's evening, as I passed by dilapidated tenements, nag carcasses and dead-eyed vagrant congregations on my way home to my crib, a crib what until last week I had shared with beloved Lily and our adopted son, I was struck by a rare jolt of discomfort about it all. I still did not know to where Lily had fled after depositing Robin with her God-fearing relatives, but could she have ended up anywhere worse than these here rookeries? Now that she had abandoned me here, in this wild and barely charted land with its violent men, brutalised women and ragged and shoeless kinchins, I saw its injustices anew and grew weary of them. Perhaps a trip to fashionable Paris would be just the thing to help me cast off the London stench.

With these despondent thoughts, I turned into Five Fingers Court and saw the riotous and bloody scene what I had been able to hear all the way up Crooked Arm Way. In the corner of the yard was an upturned costermonger's cart with shattered wheels what had been abandoned there some weeks before. In the middle of the road was two brawny coves circling each other, both with their shirts off, delivering sharp bare-fisted punches into the other's face as a cheering crowd looked on from every surrounding window. One of these street pugilists, known only to me as the Larkey Boy, was by far the crowd's favourite and he had already cut open Pugg Junior's face with his bungs, taps and fibs. It was Pugg's blood what was decorating the straw-strewn paving below and his battered body what crashed backwards onto the cart, much to the joy of the onlookers. The smell here was of blood and sweat and I stuck close to the walls as I crossed over to my doorway, rather than join in with the crowd. By the time I was upstairs and in my crib the fight was over, wagers was being disputed and Pugg Junior's battered self was being removed from the scene, on an old stretcher, no doubt to be nursed into recovery who knows where. Night had not yet fallen, but I drew my curtain and felt nothing but uncharacteristic contempt for my own neighbourhood.

I had spent the last couple of hours in the apartment of one of Greta's friends in the hope that this would help me to forget about Lily. But if anything the experience had just made me feel even more alone and out of pocket. But before I had left the Cripples, Barney had donated a bag of vittles for me, food what I suspected might have been intended for himself before I had happened to mention that my bachelor cupboard was bare. I now placed this bag onto the wooden table and took out the dusted hambone and four-penny bran loaf and began to search for that bottle of claret what I had stored around here somewhere. I was disappointed to discover the bottle was empty, as I did not recall finishing it the last time I was here. So I ate my dinner dry and in glum silence, thinking on all my troubles.

Afterwards, I went through to the larger room what contained, among other things, the brass bed, what until last week had been home for two. Also here was Robin's cot and a round tin bucket, sat in the corner with its white line of salt circling the inside top. In this bucket there was a pile of washed cloth nappies and large pins. Even the sight of that managed to sadden me. All around the room there was various evidences of a baby what had lived here, such as the swaddling clothes he had since outgrown, expensive creams I had stolen for him, countless soft toys and his favourite spinning top. I was too tired to clear any of these away and so I instead crossed over to the foot of the bedstead and pulled the right-hand brass knob, which came off with a squeak.

Down in the hole of the bedpost rested a small circular tin what was the size of a pepper pot. I clawed it out with my fingers and removed the lid to see how much brown substance it contained. It was almost full. I had several other opium tins secreted around the place, as Lily had never liked me to keep it anywhere that little Robin might discover it. On the journey home from Saffron Hill, I had promised myself that I would locate all these hidden stashes, gather them up and dispose of them. But now I felt the weight of the full tin in my hand, I reconsidered this action and instead contemplated smoking what I still had left and then calling it quits. That would be just the thing to relieve me of all the pains I had suffered through that day and so I lifted it up to my nose and had a little sniff.

'I wouldn't do that if I was you, Mr Dawkins sir,' said a voice from behind me and my whole self jolted at the shock of it. 'You'll need to be at your best tomorrow, sir, for the French.'

In one instant I dropped the tin, grabbed a long skittle bat what rested on a nearby chest and spun around to face the interloper. There, leaning against the doorway I had just walked through, was a lad of about thirteen, all cocksure, a hand in one pocket and a toothpick in the other, what he had raised to his mouth.

'Apologies, sir, I did not mean to surprise you. Well,' he shrugged, 'I s'pose I must have done, otherwise I'd a knocked. What's the use in denying it?'

'Where'd you come from?' I demanded. 'And who are you?'

'Nick, sir,' he replied and stopped picking at his teeth. 'Remember? From the zoo? Joe Muckraw made the introduction.'

'Yeah, I remember you,' I growled, still not lowering the bat. 'No Nickname Nick.'

'I've come to apologise, Mr Dawkins sir, for my disgraceful behaviour at the zoo. It was not my idea to steal your son from you, sir, that was Soap's, as you can no doubt imagine. I could have warned you of it, yes, only I did not wish to peach upon my fellows. You can understand the dilemma, Mr Dawkins, I'm sure. But I wanted you to know I did not approve of the jape and that I have the upmost respect for a thief of your standing.'

'Respect, you reckon?' I scoffed. 'Then how come you sneak

into my flat like this, eh? There ain't nothing respectful about appearing out of nowhere, Nick, as if from a puff of – oh bust me!' I lowered the bat in sudden disappointment. 'I know what this is.' I moved over to the side of the bed, sat on the end of it and sighed. 'You're another fucking hallucination, aren't you?'

Nick looked offended. 'A hallucination, sir?' he said stepping further into the room. 'I should hope not.' Then he produced something from out of his jacket pocket and tossed it towards me. 'Nice catch,' he said as I grabbed it with one hand. It was that stuffed mouse what Robin had liked to play with. His favourite toy. 'It fell out of your son's baby carriage, sir and I had a mind to return it to you. Could a hallucination do that, I wonder?'

I squeezed the soft mouse and felt another ripple of sadness run through me. It was unlikely that I would get to return it to Robin any time soon and before long he would have grown too old for it.

'He ain't my son,' I murmured as I brushed at its now grubby grey felt. 'His true father was called Mouse, which was why we gave him this.'

I looked up at No Nickname Nick again. The boy was now kneeling down at the end of the bed, picking up the brown opium what had spilled out of the tin and putting it back. It was unlikely that even the most potent poppy dream could do that.

'So what's your game then?' I asked him once he had the lid back on. 'How do you know about the meeting tomorrow with the French? And what have my recreational preferences got to do with you, anyway?'

'Begging your pardon, Mr Dawkins sir,' he said, 'I know that breaking into your home was never likely to endear me to you, but I wished to demonstrate how skilled I am at both the burglary and at the spying.'

'Well, I'll give you that,' I admitted. 'I didn't hear you come in.'

'That's because I was here before you entered, sir, please don't be angry.'

'Here already?' I cried in outrage. 'Watching me eat and piss in the pot?'

'I was here for a good ten minutes before you was, Mr Dawkins, I came in through the window while your neighbours was distracted by the fighting. I watched you cross the courtyard as I drained the last of the claret, sir, another thing I ought to say sorry for.'

'You're a little sod!' I said and stood up again. I was contemplating giving him a good smack, which would, of course, prove his existence one way or another. 'And you're going to be leaving through the same window,' I said instead.

'Now if you could just hold yourself for a moment or two, Mr Dawkins,' he said, taking one step back. 'And grant me an audience. It concerns those French mulattoes you're meeting tomorrow.'

'How do you even know about them? Such things should be kept secret.'

'Herbie Sharp told me about them,' the boy explained, which made sense. Herb really did have too much mouth. 'He said the money would be considerable and I liked the sound of the job for myself, y'see, on account of my particular skills. Skills what make me the perfect crim for a Parisian crack. So I scudded straight to the Three Cripples to apply for the position, only to be told that, just moments before, you had left with some harlot having already arranged a meeting for tomorrow. Well, I knew that I could not compete with a thief of your reputation, Mr Dawkins sir, and nor would I try. But I did want to offer my services.'

'What do you mean, "particular skills"?'

'I am French,' he replied.

'You don't sound it.'

'I'm a Londoner by upbringing but my parents was French, sir, and my mother taught me the tongue. Allow me to demonstrate.'

Then he began jabbering away in what sounded like good French, but I was not one to judge. When he finished he smiled and told me that he had just counted to twenty. 'I can carry on to a hundred, sir,' he added. 'If you'd like me to.'

'Can you converse in it?'

The boy seemed less confident about this.

'My mother taught me helpful words and phrases,' he admitted. 'Such as hello, good morning, good evening, thank you and I love you. But she died before she could impart much more.'

'And your father?'

'My full name is Nicolas Rigaud. My father was a famous French criminal, although I do not claim to have ever met him. But I am told he was a very successful man before a house fell upon him, sir. A blackmailer by trade.'

For all my annoyance at his intrusion, I had to admit that I was becoming curious about this here Nick. He had a thick cockney accent like all the other Low Arches boys, but his manner and vocabulary was more genteel. He might have looked like a typical rookery boy but he acted more like a middle-aged valet and I was starting to enjoy being called sir all the time. It seemed that his French mother had done a decent job on him before she snuffed it.

'This is all well and good, young Master Rigaud,' I said, and walked out of the bedroom and back into the kitchen. 'But I don't need no help. I'm the Artful Dodger and can manage any task, regardless of the language.'

'You'll need an accomplice, Mr Dawkins sir,' he said, following me out of the room, 'all cracksmen do. To crow, or distract, or to climb through holes what you are too big for. You've seen how useful I can be in that regard. And I could use the apprenticeship, as well as the patronage.'

I had crossed over to the front door and was just about ready to show him it when I turned to ask him what he meant by patronage.

'Its like you said at the zoo,' he said, occupying the centre of the room. 'Reputations can be given as well as earned. If people was to hear that I had helped the Artful Dodger himself perform a high-earning and adventurous crack, then that would set me up as a top sawyer among my own little gang. I could, perhaps, even supplant the Slippery Soap and advance myself in this world.' Then he stepped forward and spoke in a whisper. 'And I can help your reputation too,' he said.

'What d'you mean by that?'

'I'm saying, Mr Dawkins,' his smile became awkward, 'that if we was as successful a pairing as I think we would be, what with your years of experience and my burgeoning talent, then that might restore your name to its former glory too, eh? Because, I don't know if you're aware of this, sir, but your legend has become a little tarnished of late. Some scurrilous rumours have circulated concerning trembling hands and suchlike. But if we was in it together then I could take care of that side of things, at your direction, of course.'

I removed my hand from the door and glared at him hard. I felt like taking him to task for his impertinence, but despite my hurt pride, I knew he was right. It would be advantageous to take an assistant with me if I was to complete the robbery this French couple had in mind and I could think of nobody more appropriate than this ambitious young shaver. He was a boy, which meant that I would be in charge of things, and talented, which meant that I could get him doing all the work.

'Good at pickpocketing, are you?'

'Very,' he nodded. 'But that don't mean I couldn't benefit from instruction.'

'I'll tell you what,' I relented at last. 'Come to the meeting with me tomorrow if you care to. And if you don't make a nuisance of yourself, I'll consider taking you on as an apprentice.'

The boy grinned wide and said something what sounded like '*mercy bercoo*'.

'It means thanking you kindly, Mr Dawkins sir,' he explained.

'The pleasure is all mine, Nicolas,' I nodded. 'Call me Dodger.'

'Dodger it is!' he beamed.

'Now bugger off home if you have one,' I said and reached for the door again. 'I need an early night.'

Chapter 5

Meeting with Monsieur L

*Wherein I learn that I am not the only one wishing
to remind the world of who I am*

'Madame, Monsieur!' Barney's rasping voice declared as I heard him shuffle his Gallic guests through into his little taproom round the back of his bar. 'The Three Cripples welcomes you and your good lady wife back! I've reserved this room special so you can have some privacy when the tradesman arrives.'

Small slits of light shone in from the taproom and I levelled my eyes with them so I could try to survey the couple unseen.

'We're lovers of the French nation here,' Barney was saying as his great bulk hove into view. He drew a chair back from a round table and offered it to the lady. 'And we promise not to bring up Waterloo,' he chuckled, 'if you're prepared to keep it buttoned about the Hundred Years War.' Barney knew from their previous visit that they was teetotallers, a disappointment to him, as he was hoping to shift some of that beer he over-charges on. So instead his family had laid out their least-stained white cloth over the table and produced their finest stolen china set for afternoon tea. Through the peepholes I had a good view of the table, the teapot and the iced cake standing in the centre but, from this angle, I still could not see the faces of who I was about to introduce myself to. Just minutes before I had watched the pair of them approaching the pub down Field Lane, but they had both been wearing these long, black, unseasonable travelling cloaks, and, until now, I had not heard their voices either. The man spoke first.

'She is not my wife,' he said, still not yet visible as he was in the corner of the room where the pegs for the coats was. 'I am her brother.'

'Begging your pardon, Monsieur L,' Barney responded. 'Now you mention it I do see a family resemble—'

'Why is the tradesman not here yet?' the Frenchman interrupted. His accent was haughty and they was taking an age to remove those cloaks. I began to wonder if they was ever going to come into my line of sight.

'Rest assured, Mr Dawkins will arrive in a—'

Barney was again interrupted, but this time the brother was addressing his sister in their mother tongue. He sounded vexed but, as he prattled, she at last came into view. I watched her from behind as she moved over to the table and inspected the cake. She was tall and wearing a blue dress with black lacing, elegant but not so much that it would look ill-suited to this dirty vicinity. Then she moved around the table and took a seat, affording me a perfect view of her, and poured herself a cup of tea. She was one of the most striking women I had ever seen. Her skin was brown and very beautiful and if I had beheld her in a portrait I would have assumed that the artist had flattered her, as nobody in the real world could have so flawless a face. I reckoned her to be older than myself, perhaps by about ten years, but those who have an easy time of it age better than those of us who have it rough. So she must have had a very sheltered life, I guessed, to appear so untouched by it.

She looked a lot more composed, however, than her brother sounded. He continued talking to her from the side of the room what was concealed from me, and his tone was nervous and full of contempt. It sounded like he was trying to convince her to leave, but she was well planted by then and lifted her teacup to her lips before muttering something to him what seemed to shut him up.

He at last joined her at the table and I saw that he was an upright man of good deportment and wore a discernible expression of distaste for his low surroundings. I was surprised that Barney had not gleaned that they was related, as they was almost identical apart from their sex. The suit he wore was from a fine tailor, but it was not new and my pickpocket's eye had noticed no studs or trinkets adorning either of them what would make it worth the thieve. They looked like people for whom money had run out, and I became even more curious as to what their business here might be. On their initial visit to the Cripples they had given Barney scant details about themselves save for a drop box in Clerkenwell where he would be able to message them. The man had provided no other name for himself than Monsieur L.

'I'll just go and see if the tradesman has arrived yet,' said Barney once he had finished faffing around them. I caught a quick and impatient glance directed from him towards my peephole. I had requested the use of this secret partition what I knew separated his taproom from the rest of the pub so I could spy on them first, as Fagin used to do whenever he conducted business here. The air was dusty in that cramped space and there was dormice at my feet so, once I had satisfied myself that I had seen enough to give me some advantage over them, I stepped backwards, all silent, out of the low partition and crawled my thin frame out into his storeroom.

'They cut the cake yet?' whispered No Nickname Nick as he replaced the secret door after me. 'Cos I fancy a taste of that myself.'

'You won't be meeting them just yet,' I told him once I had stood up again in that small, musty little room what was full of unmarked barrels, caskets and mysterious bags. 'Your young age could put them off,' I added, noting his dejection. 'Wait until they get to trust me, then I'll insist upon bringing an assistant.'

'Alright then,' he shrugged. 'But leave me a slice, eh, Dodger? It's mine, don't forget.'

Nick had arrived early for this meeting, his face pink from running, and had brought with him a blue-ribboned cake-box what he had acquired from a bakery in Holborn that morning. 'I've no inkling as to what's inside,' he had panted while Ruthie unwrapped it, 'nor can I take it back, as they don't give receipts to shoplifters.' It turned out that the cake within was a glorious buttercream creation, but it had the words Happy Birthday written across it in light-blue letters, which we had needed to pick off before taking it in.

Barney joined us in the storeroom then and spoke in his lowest hush yet. 'Come now, Dodger,' he said. 'Johnny Crapaud in there won't linger forever. Time for you to get back to work.'

I nodded, clenched and unclenched my fists to make certain they held steady and patted my jacket pocket to check that the brown envelope was still there. Then I stepped out into the crooked pub corridor, winking at Nick as he wished me good luck, and entered the taproom.

'You must be Monsieur L,' I said as I shut the door behind me so that there was only the French siblings and myself in there. 'Pleasure to meet you. My name is Jack Dawkins, known to many as the Artful Dodger, and I gather that you're interested in securing my services.'

I could see the man hesitating about whether he should get up as I approached, perhaps wondering what the etiquette was for greeting a robber. I sensed fear from him and knew then that he had not spent much time amongst underworld people. When he did decide to rise from his seat and extend an arm, he managed to spill some tea over the tablecloth, what seemed to cause him much embarrassment. He began mopping it up with a napkin and cursing to himself in French.

'This is my brother, Jerome Lamoreaux,' said the sister, who had not moved. 'And I am Celeste. It is a pleasure to meet you also.'

'I can't help but mark,' I said as I took the only other seat at the table, 'that you ain't yet touched the cake.' I picked up the silver knife and reached for her plate. 'Shall I be mother?'

Once I had served us all with a slice each I sat down, picked up a little fork and took a bite of mine as they watched me in silence. I made a big noise to communicate how delicious the cake was and encouraged them both to try theirs.

'Marie Antoinette would have had us believe that you lot are obsessed with cakes,' I observed. 'It ain't poisoned, if that's what's worrying you.'

Celeste picked up her fork then and gave her brother a look what appeared to be an instruction for him to do the same.

'Excuse our stiffness,' she said after having taken a taste. 'My brother and I are unused to dealing with criminals. *Pardon monsieur*, does that word offend you? Criminal, I mean.'

'Just a word, innit,' I answered, with half my mouth full.

'Good,' she answered. 'We are looking for someone who will be honest with us about their dishonesty.'

'We want a thief,' said Jerome, quick and blunt as if he'd been holding the sentence in for some time and could contain it no longer. 'But a capable one, not some oafish delinquent. It is for a sensitive task so discretion, skill and intelligence are required.'

'Well, you've come to the right man,' I told them and poured myself some tea. 'Because I've got all of those qualities and more besides.' I gave Celeste a cheeky little wink.

'We were told that this public house was the place to come for such connections,' she nodded in a business-like way, 'and your Hebrew friend promises us that you are just the man for us. You have experience in stealing to order?'

'Mademoiselle, you will not find a more professional thief in all of London than the Artful Dodger,' I boasted. 'Now

I won't speak of particular jobs, on account of that discretion you value so much, but my experience in the trade is unmatchable. I've cracked plenty of great houses on demand for wealthy gentlemen. I've stolen priceless necklaces from occupied rooms, located missing jewels for eccentric lords. In this city I've picked more pockets than your city even has pockets. I've been to Australia and back and I've even escaped from Newgate prison. That was at the end of last year, you can check the records if you don't believe me. It was reported in all the newspapers.'

'Australia? Newgate?' sniffed Jerome with a wary look at his sister. 'You sound like you're no stranger to arrest.'

'And yet, I stand before you now as a free man,' I smiled back at him. 'Or would you rather hire someone who ain't learnt no lessons yet? More to the purpose, Jerome, is that I do not perform my hard-earned skills for gratis. I've heard tell that the money you're offering is generous and should like to know more. What assurances do I have that you're good for it?'

'If you were familiar with the name Lamoreaux, Monsieur,' remarked Jerome with scorn, 'then you would be embarrassed by such a question.'

'But I ain't familiar with it,' I replied, licking the cream from off my fork. 'So I would appreciate payment up front.'

Jerome turned to Celeste and again spoke in agitated French. They exchanged dialogue for a few seconds and then he got to his feet, walked over to the hat-stand and began gathering their cloaks.

'You off?' I asked, leaning back on my chair.

'*Excusez-moi,*' he said, readying himself to leave and indicating for Celeste to do likewise. 'We made a mistake in coming here. Please accept our apologies, Monsieur, and forget this conversation happened.'

'Please yourself,' I shrugged and stood as if ready to wish him farewell. 'No harm done. I wish you good luck in all your future endeavours, Monsieur Cupidon. Although I hope you ain't fixing on going too far, as you'll have trouble getting back to France, I reckon.'

It took a few moments for the surprise to register on Jerome's face, but when it did he looked as though I had just shot him through the heart. I kept my eyes on him as he turned his head towards Celeste and then back to me, his eyes widening in alarm.

'Why do you use that name?' he hissed. 'Where have you heard it?'

'It's yours, innit?' I said. 'Jerome Cupidon. And not Lamoreaux, as she said.'

'MY NAME *IS* LAMOREAUX!' he shouted with a sudden, babyish outburst of defiance what shocked even me. 'And I refute the other. How did you hear it? Who told you of me?' Celeste then spoke to him in stern French, but Jerome was becoming too emotional to heed her. 'Are you in league with our enemies?' he demanded.

'That cloak you came here in conceals you well,' I said, in a calm voice, although I was most taken aback at how much my mentioning his true identity had upset him. 'But not near enough.'

'You recognised us?' asked Celeste, with more curiosity than outrage. 'This surprises me. We are not known in this district.'

'That weren't my meaning about the cloaks,' I explained and reached into my jacket pocket for the brown envelope so I could relieve Jerome from his obvious distress. 'I mean to say they don't conceal your pockets well enough. And you ain't leaving these isles without these here travelling documents, Mr Cupidon, so you best take them back.'

Jerome cried out again and snatched the envelope from me. His sister, however, seemed to find it quite droll.

'You picked his pocket!' she laughed. 'I told him he was keeping them unguarded.'

'How is this possible?' Jerome raged as he rifled through the papers within, ensuring that it was all there, including the passport what had told me his true name.

'I scraped past you at the top of Field Lane,' I said and took a seat again. 'In this hot weather those outfits make you more conspicuous and they restrict your vision so it weren't hard. Don't feel sore about it, Mr Cupidon, greater men than you have had their pockets lightened by me.'

'I did not notice you anywhere,' Celeste remarked with an air of suspicion. 'And I am very vigilant about thieves.'

'Which is why I charge premium rates, Miss . . . Lamoreaux or Cupidon? I didn't pinch your passport. What would you like to be called?'

'I told you,' she smiled. 'Celeste.' Then she turned back to Jerome, who was still huffing and pacing around and told him to sit with us again. 'It seems as though he is the very man for the job, this Dodger.'

I liked the way she pronounced my nickname, without the second d and making a light growl out of the 'ger'. I could not help but wonder if, like many genteel ladies before her, she found herself attracted to my urchin charms. Jerome, meanwhile, did rejoin us but with a show of reluctance. His eyes was a little watery and his chin trembled as he spoke.

'I suppose I should explain the confusion, as our surname is pertinent to our business,' he sighed, taking another stab at the cake. 'Lamoreaux is our family name. By right if not by law. We are aristocrats.'

'Is that right?' I asked, lifting my teacup to my mouth and sipping. 'Then how come you've got so much black in you?'

Both siblings desisted in their mastication then and exchanged astonished expressions. Perhaps they thought that I had not noticed that they was mulattoes, or maybe they had hoped that I would be too polite to mention it. Either way, they was wrong and Jerome, in particular, looked horrified by the question. He lay down his fork.

'There was such a thing as the French Revolution, sir,' he spoke with a strong tone of rebuke, 'or perhaps you've never heard of it. 1792! Our grandfather's head was guillotined off and dropped into a basket with countless others. But revolutions do not alter our heritage. We are the only descendants of the Marquis de Lamoreaux.'

'Good for you,' I said, laying the teacup down again. 'But

that still don't explain your dusky hue. Or, what is more important, why you need to hire a cove like me?'

Celeste laid a hand upon her brother's arm as he glared at me in indignation, answering for him.

'Our grandmother was called Cessette Cupidon,' she explained and seemed a lot less sensitive about her race than he was. 'And our grandfather first met her about ten years before the revolution. He was in Saint-Domingue, a French sugar colony on Hispaniola Island where he owned some plantations. She was a slave and bore him one son, our father.'

'So you're illegitimate,' I nodded. 'Or at least your father was. No need to look so embarrassed about it, Jerome, I don't care one way or another. I can't even count on one hand the amount of people I know who was born in wedlock, including myself.'

'We are legitimate,' Celeste corrected me. 'We just can't prove it.'

'Our grandparents did marry!' Jerome tapped the table with his middle finger. 'But in secret. In those pre-revolutionary days he could do little else to avoid the scandal of freeing a slave and taking her for a wife. He hoped to reveal the nuptials and legitimise our father in a later, more enlightened age. And of course, such an age did come but he, among others, had to meet with Dr Guillotine for it to happen.'

'The Lamoreaux estate is vast,' Celeste continued. 'A palace almost, and, because we have no proof that we are the rightful heirs, it is currently in the possession of another branch of the family. But its true value is in the glorious artwork that covers every wall. It is in the glittering chandeliers that hang from the ceiling. It is in the furniture, most of which dates back to before the time of the Sun King. It is in the wall-length mirrors – those that were not shattered by the revolutionaries – it is in the trunks of jewels, a veritable pirate's horde. It is in the orchestra of priceless instruments contained in the music room. It is in the gold and silver,' she sighed, 'the like of which you can only dream of.'

'A single hairbrush from a boudoir in our family's home,' Jerome added with malicious pride, 'is worth more than any of the stolen items that you will have cluttered your tiny hovel with.' Celeste scolded him for his manners, but he ignored her and besides, I paid his insults no mind. My pilfering heart was beating too fast at the descriptions of all these wondrous treasures.

'As much as I would relish the challenge to crack such a place,' I said, knowing that if I had a tail it would be wagging hard, 'I don't see how I am supposed to steal the entire palace. If you could just give me a list of which particular items from it you require, the ten or twelve main prizes, then perhaps I can concentrate on those for now.'

The siblings exchanged amused glances.

'We don't expect you to burgle the estate!' Jerome said with unsuppressed mockery. 'We mean for it to be our home.'

'Then what am I for?' I asked, disappointed. I felt like I had had something shiny dangled in front of me and then snatched away. 'I'm a robber. That's why you're employing me, ain't it?'

'The marriage certificate,' Celeste said in a quieter voice. 'If we could get it back then it could be presented to a court and the estate would be ours. But unfortunately, it is in the clutches of a man who despises us and cannot be reasoned with. And nor would we wish to even if we could. His name is Hugo DeFarge and he . . . '

Her expression had become most pained as she mentioned this DeFarge person. She flicked her eyes towards her brother, as though appealing for him to tell me the rest.

'He is a dangerous man, sir.' Jerome said. 'An evil brute.' Then he reached over to touch her hand. 'He killed our father.'

'Sorry to hear that,' I said as Celeste lowered her head and stared at her unfinished cake. 'He sounds a right menace. I take it that you want me to go and steal the marriage certificate from this DeFarge, then?'

'That is why the money is high, yes,' Jerome nodded. 'He lives in a wine shop in the Saint-Antoine district of Paris. His family have owned it for centuries and we have it on good authority that the certificate is there.'

'How did he get it?'

'That's not relevant to you, is it, Monsieur?' he snapped. 'All you need to know is that this is a man who hates all descendants of aristocracy, and we Lamoreaux in particular. He lives to torment us. His ancestors were fierce revolutionaries, his grandfather led the storming of the Bastille and his grandmother was a famous and feared *tricoteuse*. She was a bloody terror by all accounts and he has inherited her lust for noble blood. The DeFarge name has become famous among the Parisian proletariat and so Hugo is a celebrity among his class and community. That is why we cannot employ a French thief for the task. They could betray us for him. We require an outsider.'

'I hate to keep banging on about the money,' I said, once I had finished my cake and was contemplating cutting myself a second slice. 'But tell me more about the money. Barney told me the sum and I'm curious to know when I would get it.'

'When the document is produced, of course. My sister and I will travel to Paris with you and, once you have been successful in acquiring it we will take it to our lawyer there who will do the rest.'

'I'm accustomed to receiving a deposit before I accept a job,' I told him. 'A healthy one.'

'Impossible,' he shook his head. 'Our wealth hinges upon us claiming our fortune, so there is no money until then.'

'Well, you'll have to give me something as I ain't leaving London on faith alone. And I shall expect you to pay for my travel, lodgings, 'n all,' I added. 'For both me and my assistant.'

'Assistant?'

'An ambitious youngster who shows great promise in the cracking line,' I raised my voice a measure, as it was more than probable that Nick was hiding behind those painted panelled walls, peeping on us, 'and who can speak your language fluent. That'll come in handy if I'm to locate a document I can't even read.'

Jerome looked disgusted by my demands and was about to respond when Celeste, who had seemed a bit distracted in the last few moments, to the point where I had wondered if she had even stopped listening, intervened.

'Very well,' she agreed with her elbows on the table and her hands crossed as if in prayer. 'But the assistant receives no extra, you pay him from your own earnings. If this is unacceptable, then don't bring him. Actually, don't even come yourself, we can easily find someone else.'

'Doubtful,' I responded. 'But it don't matter cos I accept the job and am keen to start. Shall we shake on it?'

I then raised myself out of my chair to offer them my hand, but they was both hesitant to take it. Instead, they began discussing the matter between themselves as I just stood there like a fool with my hand outstretched. I glanced over to where the peepholes was and hoped that Nick could translate this for me later. At length, Jerome turned to me and stood up also.

'We have our thief then,' he said as we shook. 'And our business is set in motion. We wish to leave for France immediately, Monsieur Dodger. Tomorrow at noon would be best.'

'That's very well with me, Jerome,' I said with a grin, 'very well indeed.'

I was finding myself experiencing a proper lift at the thought that I was about to set off on such an exciting excursion. I felt no fear at all about running afoul of this Hugo DeFarge character as, while he was no doubt fearsome in the eyes of these tender aristocrats, I was well used to encountering such villains and was sure to get the better of him. And, what was best of all, I could feel the old buzz coming back, not just at the thought of the payment I would receive for this job, but for the job itself. It had been a while since I had cared so much about a crack, since before the opium had gotten ahold of me. I had known a few drug fiends in my time what had conquered their habits by occupying themselves with newer, fresher excitements, so I hoped that this enthusiasm was a sign that I was already on the mend.

'I have just one more question before we discuss details,' I told them before I sat down again. 'Are you planning on eating your cake, Jerome? Cos I hate to see good confectionery go to waste.'

And so it was agreed that my assistant and myself should meet these Lamoreaux heirs tomorrow at midday. They was staying at the Golden Cross Hotel near Trafalgar Square and, once a suitable deposit was produced, from there we would ride a carriage to Dover. Once these arrangements was made Jerome insisted that he and his sister leave this rotten vicinity forthwith, and so we bade each other farewell for now. Although I flattered myself that had he not been so insistent, Celeste might have remained conversing to her new burglar friend a while longer, as I had an inkling she had taking a fancy to me.

Once they had gone Barney scuttled into the taproom to ask me how it all went, with Ruthie followed in after to seize possession of the cake. But before she could remove it for her and the other daughters, I reminded her of where it had come from and cut off a slice for the boy behind the peephole.

'Come in and join us, Nicky,' I said to him and raised the

slice up on a plate for him to see. 'We've something to celebrate, you and me.'

When Nick did walk through the taproom door, after having been pushed out of the way first by Ruthie in her hurry to escape with the last of his cake, his manner was more subdued than I had expected. I thanked Barney again for arranging the meet and he patted me on the shoulder and told me that he had never doubted that it would go well. Then young Nick and myself was left alone to discuss travel plans as he sipped at whatever cold tea was left.

'You're upset,' I remarked, noting that he had said about three words since coming in there, a contrast to his earlier verbosity. 'But Nick, I had to tell them that it was me what pinched those passport papers off him. I needed to impress and I don't know if they'd have gone for it otherwise.'

Nick replied with a small nod and assured me that he wasn't fussed either way.

'You've got a lot of talent for your age, Nick,' I complimented him, and it was not just gammon. 'You cracked my crib, lifted that cake, pinched that passport. You remind me of me.'

'*Merci beaucoup*,' he said as he slurped the last of the tea from Jerome's cup.

'We're going to make a good team, I reckon.'

'Yep,' he said, after he had lifted up the saucer and tipped the spillage into his mouth. 'The thief,' he placed the china down again and gave a small smile, 'and his assistant.'

It was hard to tell which of us he thought was which.

Chapter 6

The Golden Cross

*My French excursion begins! And I learn a number of
interesting things about my travelling companions*

My Beloved Lily,

I have not been sleeping well these past few weeks and the
fault, my petal, is all yourn.

Ever since you fled our crib I have been suffering torments
the like of which I have never known before and what
can only be remedied by you coming back to my loving
arms and sharpish. Here is some news what might help to
provoke your return — <u>I am soon to be rich.</u>

I know, my gentle feather, that you may have heard me
make similar boasts over the years, boasts what have all
resulted in naught. But this time my prosperity is assured.
I have been engaged by some affluent French persons and
they have promised me a fortune to perform a task what
will be child's play for someone of my talents.

The job in hand involves me journeying to glamorous
PAREE, a city what is famed for the beauty and accessibility
of its womenfolk. However, I resolve to remain true to you,

so do not worry yourself on that score. I would hate for jealousy to get the better of you now, my too-absent flower.

Anyhow, I may be abroad for a week or two as there is at least three days travel either way, but when I return I hope to be a different man in more ways than one. You may be interested to learn that I have not breathed in so much as a whiff of the poppy smoke in over a week. I hardly ever think about it anymore. So that's all good and done with, I can promise you!

Perhaps you will have forgiven me my trespasses by the time of my return. If so, you are still welcome to join me in my new genteel lifestyle.

If not, my honey bee, then <u>it's your loss!</u>

Hope this finds you well,
Your patient-but-not-too-patient lover,

Jack Dawkins Esq

<u>Postscript.</u> I'm still vexed with you for running off with my adopted son, but can learn to forgive in time. Forgiveness is a virtue, I say.

'Perfect,' I said to myself, after I had lain my pen down on its blotter and blew upon both sides of the sheet so the ink would dry. 'If that don't soften her heart, nothing will.'

Then I placed it within an envelope with *For Lily Lennox* written upon the front and put that inside my jacket pocket alongside a stolen passport and an unsigned bank note. I left my crib, dragging my sea-green travelling trunk behind me as I hailed a cabriolet from Monmouth St to Saffron Hill, where I met with young Nick. I then took the time to dive into the Three Cripples to deliver the letter to Barney, instructing him to give the missive to anyone who came in claiming to know where Lily had got to, or to the lady herself, should she pass by. Then, after saying a hearty farewell to him and his uninterested daughters, Nick and I set off for the hotel where we was to rendezvous with these French siblings. While I was doing all of that I thought of one thing only.

Opium.

It seemed that my optimism on the day before was misplaced and that the Drop was not done with me yet. In all truth, so shaky was I that morning, that it had been a struggle to make my handwriting in any way legible and I had spoiled parts of my love letter with a number of unsightly inkblots. I had been fighting tiredness all day, as fiends do not sleep so well when we go without, and now I was sweating hard as we neared the hotel where Jerome and Celeste was waiting for us. I was patting my brow with a fogle so much that young Nick remarked upon it.

'Too hot for that jacket, Dodge,' he advised as our cab neared the end of the Strand. He had his own folded on his lap. 'You'll enjoy the weather more with it off.'

'P'raps, but I do not wish to appear slovenly in front of the clientele,' I said, feeling sweat patches form underneath my shirt. 'It'd be unprofessional.'

The chills stabbed at me again as we reared up outside the

Golden Cross Hotel and I resisted the urge to button up even tighter before dismounting. I was already starting to feel better now that the horses was stood still, but I had to wait a few moments before I was steady enough to step out of the cab and into the bright sunshine of that noisy street. The coachman regarded me with some suspicion as I reached up and paid him his fare with the last of my coins. I guessed that my appearance must have worsened during the journey. My left hand twitched as I took the coachman's change and I worried that the Lamoreaux might be so disgusted by the sight of me that the job would be cancelled. However, I need not have concerned myself with that, as Celeste was ready to call the whole business off over another matter.

'Your assistant is a child?' she exclaimed as she and Jerome came out of the hotel doors to meet us. 'Unacceptable.'

'Don't let his youthful looks fool you, Celeste,' I assured her after I introduced the siblings to my new accomplice. 'Nicolas Rigaud here is as skilled a tradesman as any I have met. Your affairs are in safe hands.'

'I don't care for that!' she scolded me. 'It is the morality of the thing. How old is he? Ten?'

Nick replied to her in French with a deep bow, despite not being the one addressed. It sounded like he was telling her his age and when she expressed disbelief, he told her another one.

'He's thirteen,' I insisted. 'At that age I was up to all sorts of perilous activities. I was packed off to an Australian prison around then. Taking him to Paris will be more of a holiday than a hardship.'

'Tell them, Jerome,' she beseeched her brother. 'Tell them that we cannot ask so young a boy to endanger himself for us, can we?'

Jerome seemed much less offended by Nick's age than her, but he stooped a fraction to address the boy in his own language. Nick replied with some sentences what sounded alright to my English ears, but what made the Frenchman wince.

'His vocabulary is limited,' Jerome announced after some further exchange between them. 'His accent grates and his grammar in French is even worse than yours is in English. My sister is right. Unacceptable.'

We was having this conversation on a busy part of the road, not far from the square and so I encouraged the four of us to step away from the rush of pedestrians and up a quieter narrow road so we could speak of our criminal plottings with greater freedom. Once we was far enough away from any passing eavesdroppers, I explained to them why I would not be going on this expedition without him.

'I've already thought of a plan as to how I'm going to pinch back your granddad's wedding certificate from out of this shop and I need him for it. Boys are invaluable to the burglary trade and most of us start out much younger than him. And he speaks better French than I do, so don't fret on it.'

'But I do fret on it!' she snapped back. 'He just told my brother that he was an orphan, but what would his mother say if she was alive? I forbid this.'

'My mother, mademoiselle, would admire my industrious-ness,' Nick told her with some pride in his voice. 'She could never bear laziness and one of the things she said to me on her deathbed was that I should apprentice myself to Mr Dawkins here, who she admired very much. You won't let me get in no danger, will you Jack?'

'Course not!' I said and ruffled his mop of dirty ginger hair. 'He's like a son to me, this one, or rather a younger brother. I'd risk my own life before I ever would his.'

'So would I!' Nick said and we both chuckled at it.

Celeste still seemed unhappy, but Jerome was already moving the conversation on to other matters.

'I have booked a carriage which will get us to Dover before nightfall, and an inn there for the night. We cross the channel at daybreak. Until then, perhaps we should proceed into that coffee-house,' he pointed his cane towards the nearby establishment, 'and we can discuss your deposit.'

Once the four of us was all huddled around a table by the window and had all ordered ourselves some lunch, Jerome began unbuttoning his shirt.

'As I told you yesterday,' Jerome said once he was naked to the navel, 'until our fortune is recovered my sister and I are in straightened financial circumstances. And if we are to pay for all travel expenses then there is no money for a deposit.' Celeste looked horrified at what he was about to do, but he reassured her in French and then lifted the small gold chain, what he had been wearing around his neck, over his head to hand to me. 'This colonial crucifix,' he said in a solemn voice, as he dangled it from the chain close to the light of the window, so I could see how valuable it was, 'belonged to my late father. It was given to him by his Caribbean mother and it hung around his neck until the day of his death. I received it soon afterwards and it is among my most treasured possessions.'

'Sentimental value won't pay my bills, Jerome,' I told him as I took it into my own hands for closer study. 'But, I admit, this does look like real gold.' It was a Catholic cross with the body of Jesus on it, but it was nothing like the more ordinary ones I had come across in my many years as a London thief. It had distinctive markings upon it what marked it out as foreign and it glinted under sunlight. I showed it to Nick and asked him if he thought it was an adequate down payment.

'If I picked that from a pocket,' he said at last, 'I'd be well happy.'

'Me 'n all, but it ain't enough for the two of us,' I decided. 'What else you got?'

Both the siblings looked pained to have their family heirloom valued in such a mercantile fashion, but Celeste went on to tell me that they had similar portable goods in their Parisian apartment, which we would receive upon arrival. 'Jewels and other valuables,' she said and cast a guilty look towards Nick. 'Enough for the two of you.'

'Very well,' I nodded and began unbuttoning my own shirt as Jerome buttoned up his. 'We accept the terms.'

And, as I hung her grandmother's crucifix around my own neck, she muttered something to herself in French. I asked Nick to translate it for me.

'She said that it's a small price to pay,' Nick smiled, pleased with the chance to show Jerome that he had underestimated his linguistic skills, 'to get back what was stolen from her.'

'See,' I said to them once my shirt was buttoned up again. 'He's worth every penny.'

The ride down to Dover was slow, bumpy and tiresome and I suffered for it all the way. Our luggage was strapped to the top of the Dover Mail carriage what Jerome had booked for us and I could only think about what was up there, hidden at the bottom of my travelling trunk, wrapped up safe within a pair of my cleanest undergarments. A glass vial what was intended for medicinal liquids but what was now packed tight with opium from three of my separate stashes. I had done a decent job of not touching any of that substance since my alarming Oliver Twist vision, but still I had wanted to keep it handy in case of an emergency. I hoped not to smoke any while on this job, but I had not been able to divorce myself from its proximity just yet.

The French siblings seemed as morose as I was on the journey down and it was clear that all three of us adults wanted to be left alone with our thoughts. However, we was unable to do this on account of young Nick. He spent the first hour of the journey bombarding the siblings with many personal questions, both in their language and ours, most of which they either evaded or refused to answer.

'How you two fixing to divide up the estate once you have it then?' he queried at one point. 'Half and half?'

'It is a condition of the Lamoreaux will that only the male

line may inherit,' Celeste informed him, and if she felt bitter about that, then she hid it well.

'Don't that bother you?' Nick persisted. 'It'd bother me if I was you.'

'My sister and I are as one,' Jerome answered for her, taking her hand. 'Celeste will of course benefit greatly from my boon.'

'Not when you get yourself a wife, I'd warrant!' Nick laughed. 'The moment you get married, you'll be forced to put her first and Celeste here'll get the shove.'

'I do not intend to take a wife,' Jerome sniffed.

'Why not?' Nick kept on. 'You a lavender boy?'

Jerome turned to me. 'Will the child be this irritating all the way to Paris? And, if so, can you entertain him? My sister and I have our minds on other things.'

I decided that Jerome was right, keeping Nick occupied on this long journey was a duty what fell to me. I therefore spent the rest of our trip down to the English Channel playing 'What My Little Eye Spies' with him and this went some way towards distracting me from my poppy craving. As we played, both the siblings stiffened and withdrew into themselves even further. It seemed to me very likely that my young assistant had managed to strike a nerve with the both of them.

We spent that night in the sort of quaint little hostelry they go in for in the English countryside – all Toby jugs, upside-down horseshoes and patriotic prints depicting Nelson's naval victories upon the walls. We had arrived late and was booked to leave Britain at first light, so we had left all of our luggage downstairs in the reception room from where they would be loaded onto the vessel by porters tomorrow morning. This meant that I would be separated from my opium for one more night and perhaps, I reasoned, that was a good thing. The siblings was to share a chamber together and, from what I gathered, it was the largest suite in the inn. Nick and I was to sleep in a room more suitable for servants. This rankled, but, as I was not paying, I could say little about it.

Nick went to sleep as soon as his head touched his pillow, but slumber did not descend upon me so easy. It was a hot, airless night and I was so desperate to forget about the opium downstairs in my trunk that I contemplated going for a late-night prowl along Dover's Marine Parade. There I would doubtless chance upon some sailor-ready harlot with whom I could while away the rest of the night. But I resisted this impulse, as I was resolved to stay faithful to Lily from here on, even though I had no reason to think that she might be doing likewise for me. And, besides, I did not have enough coins for that.

So instead I got out of my uncomfortable bed, crept out of the chamber wearing my nightclothes and found myself tiptoeing down to the saloon bar below in the hope of finding someone who would serve me some spirits to make me drowsy or, better yet, stealing a bottle for myself. But when I reached the foot of the staircase I found that I was not the only guest who was suffering from sleeplessness. Celeste was sat alone at a table in the bar of the hostelry, with a window open just a couple of inches, breathing in the night air.

'The rightful heir to the Lamoreaux estate is a loud snorer,' she said by way of explanation as she saw me approach. 'You may join me if you wish.' She was wearing a respectable night robe and had a glass of red wine on the table in front of her. 'The landlady poured me this before retiring to bed herself,' she said and pushed it my way as I took the seat opposite hers. 'But, wherever it is from, it is not French.'

'I thought you was teetotal, anyway,' I said as I took the glass and had a long, greedy swig. I was glad that she was facing outwards at the dark coast what was just about visible from that window, as I suspected that my hasty consumption of the drink might have seemed to be more from need than pleasure.

'Jerome is teetotal,' she clarified. 'He has no vices to speak of. And I behave myself when I am with him.'

'And what about when you ain't with him?' I asked, with unconcealed interest. 'You behave yourself then?'

'No,' she replied, in a sad, faraway voice. 'Not always.'

A silence passed over us then as she continued looking away from me in an arch manner. It was as if she thought I was an artist and she was posing for a portrait. I continued sipping at the wine as she breathed in more of Dover's salty air.

'There are many things that he cannot forgive,' she sighed at last. 'There is such an anger in him. But he and I have . . . made an agreement.'

'About the estate?' I asked. 'He'll share the wealth with you provided you play the good sister? Is that the thing?'

'Oh, I do not care for the wealth!' she answered and, for a second, I almost believed her. 'At least not as much as Jerome does. He burns at the injustice of the inheritance not being ours. In particular, he despises our great-uncle Lucien, who has possessed the Lamoreaux estate for all these decades and plans to leave it to his own heirs. But I care less about that and want to claim the estate for different reasons.'

'And what reasons are they?'

'Not your concern, Dodger,' she said then, turning her head to face me with a polite smile. '*Excusez-moi, monsieur*, I don't know why I share so much with you. I must be in a melancholy mind. Time for bed, I think.'

'Yours or mine?'

'I am not that badly behaved,' she answered, to my great disappointment. There was no escaping the fact that here was a very beautiful woman and a night-time tumble with her would be just the thing to clear my head of Lily's abandonment. As I had sat there listening to her talk in that attractive accent of hers, I found myself becoming so aroused that I had struggled to pay attention to any of it.

'I shall try again tomorrow, then.' I smiled back and drained the last of her wine as she shut the window. 'That tasted alright to me,' I observed once the glass was empty. 'You must have a less sophisticated palate.'

'Before I go,' she said, leaning over to touch my arm. 'There is something I should like to say without Jerome overhearing.'

I leaned in closer also, wondering if this might be going where I hoped. Perhaps a cheeky little kiss before bedtime was on the cards after all.

'He is terrified of Paris,' she said then. 'You will notice this as we get closer to the capital. He has a dread of it.'

'But he's from there, ain't he?'

'No, not really,' she shrugged. 'I was educated in the Sorbonne but Jerome left the city when he was young. He has spent most of his adult life in other European capitals, such as your London.'

'Is it cos Paris is where your father was murdered?' I asked. 'By this Hugo DeFarge?'

She nodded. 'DeFarge is the source of much of his anxiety, yes, but not all. He fears our great-uncle Lucien also.'

'The old man?' I spoke with some incredulity. 'Your grand-father's brother? But he must be about a hundred years old by now, if he's had the estate since the revolution.'

'No, but he is very elderly. Moreover, he has three grown sons who are all high-ranking officers in the National Guard. So Jerome is under the impression that these men will set out to kill him if they discover that he has returned to French soil.'

'Is he right? Will they?'

'Kill a man whose very existence threatens their vast inher-itance?' she answered, before leaving me there alone in that bar. 'Of course. Wouldn't you?'

Chapter 7

A Petty Demand

*Whereupon crossing the English Channel turns out
to be a greater trial than I had anticipated*

The Dover-to-Calais steamer what we had booked passage
aboard on that bright June morning was called the *Lucie Manette*.
Once all the baggage was piled up between the two paddle
wheels and the mail was loaded, we passengers shuffled our
careful-footed way along the pier-plank and crowded ourselves
onto the small deck. There must have been about three dozen
travellers, including myself, Nick and the cloaked siblings, and
I wondered why those two was still dressed as if for winter and
why so many of the others was clutching umbrellas. It was not
until the captain's bell had been rung to cast us away, the funnels
was roaring and the two piston-rods was pumping hard that I
understood the need for such protection. The unsheltered deck
was soon bombarded with sea-spray once the steamer was in
motion, and it was an effort to stand steady. Nick fell victim
to the biggest splash, as he had stood too close to the pistons.
He did not seem much amused as the three of us all laughed
at his drenching.

Jerome, who had already warned us all of his poor sea-legs,

had positioned himself up beside the tiller where he could keep his eyes fixed upon the horizon ahead, while Nick went off to sulk and find somewhere dry to sit. Celeste and myself was huddled towards the back of the vessel, squashed between a group of big-bearded European men and their fur-coated wives. To their eyes she and I may have appeared like a happy couple, perhaps setting off for a romantic honeymoon together, and it seemed as though Celeste wished to encourage this misperception. She took my hand and pressed herself close against me in an intimate fashion, to complete the picture of marital bliss. She moved her lips towards my ear as if she meant to bestow upon it a light kiss.

'It was the boy, wasn't it, Dodger?' she whispered. 'Who picked Jerome's pocket.' I was a little startled by this unexpected question and it took me a moment to fall upon what she was referring to. 'I recognise him now. He was loitering about when we approached that public house where we met and he bumped into my brother. So it was he who stole the passports, and not yourself.'

'P'raps,' I conceded. 'What difference does it make?'

Celeste shrugged by way of response as the steamer continued moving away from England, clouds of smoke billowing from its funnel. Then, after a short time, she spoke again.

'*J'ai une petite demande*,' she said, with a smile. 'It is French for "I have a small request".'

'Oh, do you now?'

'*Oui*. I wish for you to perform me a service.'

'Well, what is French for "I ain't your bloody servant?"'

'It matters not, because you are,' she replied and squeezed my arm. 'What else would you call someone of your class who is employed to work for someone of mine?'

I could think of no immediate retort for this cruel though inarguable observation, but it had annoyed me. I had always hated the servant class, those who are so proud of their honest day's work and their crawling obedience to genteel masters and so I did not care to be identified as one of their kind.

'What I want,' Celeste continued, 'is for you to pick a pocket.'

Another splash of salty cold spray from the channel wetted my unprotected head. 'What for?' I asked, with no small measure of belligerence. Lily had asked me the exact same question in Regent's zoo and I was just as disinclined now as I was then. 'Jerome has a wallet with enough cash for the journey, from what I can see. We don't need to risk the dip.'

'We will need French currency soon,' Celeste said, regarding me with a suspicious eye. 'Your professed talents will need to secure that for us. I will not ask the child to steal for me.'

I wiped the seawater off my face and shook my head. 'Any good dipper will tell you that this ain't the place for it, Celeste. We're in an enclosed space and you always need a tidy exit. What am I meant to do if I get caught with my hand in the honey jar, eh? Jump overboard? No, forget it.'

'I desire a demonstration here, not a real theft,' she whispered. 'Jerome, as you observe, has a wallet stuffed full of English notes. Bring me that. If you are seen stealing it by those around him, you can simply reveal that you and he are travelling companions and that it was all a fun game. Jerome and myself will defend you.'

Another gentle rock from the boat allowed her to press her lips even closer to my ear.

'Work your way around the port side of the boat towards the tiller, steal Jerome's wallet and then circle along the starboard side, where I shall be gazing out to sea. Then, I want you to do one more thing. I have an object in my outer cloak pocket – something that will be of particular interest to you. See if you can take it off me without my feeling it. If your reputation is deserved, this should be simple.'

'I'd rather stay here with you, if it's all the same,' I answered, firm.

At this Celeste's manner altered. When she spoke next, although it would have been imperceptible to the passengers around us, it was with greater aggression and she poked my chest with her long fingernail.

'My father was an opium fiend,' she said, and her words was cold. 'So I know what I see.'

'And you think *I'm* one?' I replied, in a display of outrage so convincing that I almost believed it myself. 'Why, I've never been so insulted in all of my—'

'You have a fiend's dark eyes,' she interrupted me, 'your hands shake, more often than not. You sweat, even when indoors and in the evening. You mumble to yourself when you think no one is looking. All of these traits remind me of him. His skin smelt as yours does.'

'I haven't been well,' I protested. 'A summer cold, that's all.'

'I remember my father telling me similar lies.'

I was stunned by these cruel observations, and, for a few long moments, I could think of nothing to say. Until then I had been under the honest impression that I had managed to conceal my sickness and so to hear how transparent my condition was came as something of a shock.

'Does Jerome know?' I asked.

'I doubt it,' she replied. 'He is not as old as I and has fewer memories of our father. And what he remembers, he remembers very differently.'

'I haven't puffed in days,' I answered, trying and failing to keep the shame out of my voice. 'And besides, being a fiend has never interfered with my work. I can still perform the dip.'

'Prove it.'

More heavy spray covered the deck of the *Lucie Manette* and even the passengers with umbrellas complained. The weather conditions was tranquil enough, but we was moving at a fair clip so it would not be easy to traverse the slippery wooden deck, let alone execute her request even when well. But, as I felt her hand tighten in mine as if in encouragement, I knew I could not refuse.

'If I say no,' I asked in a last stab at defiance, 'what are the consequences?'

'If you refuse,' she replied, 'or if you try but fail, we will say farewell at Calais. My brother and I will pay for your return ticket and perhaps give you and the boy a little more for your trouble. But we will not require either of your services further.'

'But what if I succeed?' I asked, pulling her up short. 'Cos

I don't do nothing for nothing, Celeste, regardless of your suspicious nature.'

'If you succeed,' she answered, following a few seconds thought, 'then you can keep half the contents of Jerome's wallet and whatever you may find in mine.' Her other hand was covering her pocket so it was hard to see by the bulge what it might contain. 'Also,' she added, with a smile most flirtatious, 'you will be granted a kiss, if you still want one.'

'From you or from Jerome?'

She laughed. 'Whichever you prefer.'

I looked back over my shoulder towards the white cliffs what was getting smaller all the time and I reflected upon what I wanted to achieve from this French excursion. As much as it was for the promise of a financial reward, I had also wanted to prove to myself that I could regain my lost artfulness. And I supposed that now was as good a time as any to give that a try.

'As you wish, milady,' I said as I released my hand from hers. 'I shall take a stroll around the boat and be back before England has even vanished from view. Be a good girl and don't look away from the sea until I'm back. Otherwise it's cheating.'

And with that, I blew her a kiss and began to make my way around the narrow port side of the steamer. The rails of the deck was all lined with passengers staring out to sea. There was some benches what was occupied by grumbling old ladies holding their frilly hats down tight to stop them blowing away. The talk, from what I could overhear, was all in English and I saw Nick facing out to sea and listening to some old gentleman singing a popular Irish ditty beside him. 'Rich and rare was the gems she wore,' the old man crooned in an unhappy voice, as if he thought that concentrating on getting the lyrics right would help him ward off seasickness. The floor was wet as I passed by their backs and I had to take care not to slip. My stomach tightened as I thought about whether or not I would achieve a clean dip and I hoped it was just the churning of the pistons and the turning of the paddles what was causing this unease. But I was also beset by doubts about my abilities and I had a horrid feeling as I approached the tiller what Jerome stood beside, that this experience was going to be even more humiliating than my inaction at the zoo.

But, as I drew closer, I could see from Jerome's slumped rear posture that he too was feeling the harsh effects of a sea voyage and was, therefore, the perfect plant. What with the paddles, pistons and roars from the funnel, not to mention the Irish balladeer, who was getting louder by the verse, it was unlikely he would hear me approaching so long as his eyes remained fixed ahead. I had already observed in which pocket he kept his wallet and I concentrated hard on holding my hands still for the dip. They was obeying me for now, so I checked about to see if anyone was watching me slide towards him and, once confident that the wind was favourable, I struck.

A pocket well and truly picked! I even surprised myself with how fast and how elegant the execution had been, as my left hand had removed the wallet from his pocket and placed it into my own with as much ease and dexterity as it had ever done. I wondered for what possible reason I had ever been worried as I kept on moving, before Jerome had a chance to feel for his loss. I was so glad that I would be returning to Celeste in triumph that I wanted to hoot in delight as I edged my way back to the starboard side where I had left her.

As I returned to the stern of the ship I saw the back of Celeste's distinct black cloak flapping in the gentle breeze. She had now positioned herself in one of the few spots what was away from the other passengers and so, buoyed up by my success with Jerome, I headed straight towards her for the second dip, confident that this would prove even more simple than the last. I spied the small mystery bulge in her cloak pocket as I inched closer, and noted her loose posture what hinted that her mind was elsewhere. Again, I made the old familiar moves and, as before, I emptied the pocket with the greatest of ease. But, unlike before, I was far from delighted about what my left hand found in there.

I had only taken a couple of steps away before I recognised just what my hands had just taken possession of. I had held the cold, glass object many times before, except that now it felt a lot lighter than the last time I had touched it. I stopped dead and turned, expecting to see Celeste there, laughing at me. But she was still staring back towards where England once was and, as I moved back towards her, a sharp, sudden fury seared through my whole body.

'You're a thief,' I hissed at her.

'So are you,' she sighed, still staring out to sea. 'And a very good one, it appears. Congratulations Jack, I did not feel a thing. I was wrong to doubt you.'

'You was wrong,' I shouted, not caring about what unwanted

attention it might draw, 'to go through my trunk! This is my personal affair and not your concern.' I pulled the glass vial out of my pocket and confirmed what my fingers had already told me. Aside from a light dusting of brown residue at the bottom, it was empty of opium.

'This morning, before you awoke, I escorted our luggage down to the ship with the hotel staff,' she explained, as my other hand covered my face in horror at the crime. 'I told them that your green trunk was mine and that I had lost my key. The porters were all very obliging and one of them picked the lock for me. I was just curious to see if my suspicions about your bad habits were true. I was sad when I discovered that they were.'

'Oh, very droll!' I pretended to laugh. 'A very humorous jape indeed. But where is it, Celeste? Where's my poppy?'

'It is in the sea,' she responded.

'IN THE WHAT?'

'I threw it in there around the time that you would have been stealing from my brother.'

'Well, prepare to get scattered yourself!' I declared as I stepped closer and grabbed hold of her by the arm. 'Cos it seems only right that you should follow my hard-earned poppy into the drink.'

'*Excusez-moi, Mademoiselle?*' a voice from behind me interrupted. I turned to see a group of hawk-nosed Frenchmen had gathered and they looked to be most distressed by my uncouth behaviour towards a lady. The closest man asked Celeste something in French, what had the ring of *is this man bothering you?*

about it. Celeste replied with a sentence starting with *non* but the heroic Frenchmen continued to regard me with distaste and so I released my hand from her arm. Somehow she managed to convince them that I was of no danger to her and so, with some stern, warning glances directed my way, they agreed to leave us with our private dispute. But I found myself not caring about them very much, all that concerned me then was how I was going to cope in a foreign land without any opium close to hand. I began breathing in and out in order to calm myself down. As much as anything, I had shocked myself by what a violent reaction I had exhibited when learning of its loss.

'From your hostile response, I take it,' Celeste said once we again had that part of the stern to ourselves, 'that you no longer wish to claim that kiss?'

'Why did you do that, Celeste?' I demanded as I felt my heartbeat return to its regular rhythm. 'I've done nothing to harm you.'

'It was not my intention to be cruel, Dodger,' she explained. 'But we have already given you a cherished heirloom as payment for a job you have yet to carry out. And we have agreed to give you even more once we are in Paris. I just wanted to ensure that you are worth it, and so wished to set you a couple of tests. Tell me,' she asked, 'did you steal Jerome's wallet?'

'Yeah,' I sighed and patted my full coat pocket. 'With ease.'

'Then congratulations,' her smile was sad, 'you passed the test.' Then she turned her head back to the wake of this boat into which she had thrown my precious drug.

Around two hours later, the mighty paddlewheels of the

Lucie Manette at last delivered us to our destination of Calais Harbour. I had spent the rest of that journey portside with my young assistant, as it did not seem wise to remain beside Celeste, in case I was again gripped by the sudden urge to throw the cruel woman overboard. Nick could tell that I was in a foul humour, although I did my best to hide the reason from him, as I suspected that he too would have been disappointed to learn I had been carrying opium with me. Instead, he jabbered away about how excited he was to be back in France, although he only had dim memories of his early years there.

'I've crossed this channel before, you know, perhaps on this very boat,' he told me as our steamer aligned itself along the long, curved and seaweed-strewn pier. 'Only, back then my mother and myself was travelling in the other direction towards England. I would have been about three then, I s'pose,' he sighed. 'I thought I'd forgotten all about it until today. This journey has unlocked a memory.'

I took his hand in mine as we followed the other passengers across the slippery gangplank and onto the pier. We was separate from the Lamoreaux siblings as we disembarked and was all herded along the pier and onto a dry-dirt road what was fenced off with ropes.

'They ain't arresting us, are they, Dodger?' asked Nick in alarm, when he saw the waiting uniformed men with their stiff hats and stern expressions.

'Nah, this is just Customs House,' I explained to him as this rope path led towards a large building with the words *Liberté, Égalité, Fraternité* painted upon it. 'Time to get your papers out.'

The first official we encountered within that house was blocking our pathway into France. As he inspected the passports we presented him with, he peered through his drooping eyes at me in particular, as if he could tell just by looking at me that I was a thrice-convicted criminal who he should not be letting into his precious country. But there was no stamps or signals on our documentation to betray either Nick or myself, as neither of our passports belonged to us anyway. I had purchased them from Herbie Sharp on the afternoon before leaving London as he ran a nice line in stolen passports.

Before we could enter the town of Calais, we was all instructed to wait in a large room where we was soon reunited with Jerome. He told us that French law meant that the authorities had to unload our luggage and that they could inspect them if they so wished. This information, I must confess, provoked in me a begrudging gratitude to Celeste for having erased the chance that I could have been mistaken for an opium smuggler but, when she too joined us in the Customs House, I took care not to show it. Jerome sensed this new hostility between his sister and myself in an instant and demanded to be told what the matter was.

'Ask yourself this, Jerome,' I replied as I eyed his sister with undisguised disdain, 'how would you like it if someone went sneaking through your things on the sly and took your possessions without asking?'

Celeste looked as though she was already bored of my indignation and turned to her brother.

'When the luggage arrives,' she said, 'we will need to

give the porters a gratuity. See that you have your wallet ready.'

Jerome agreed and began rifling through his pockets for the wallet what Celeste and myself both knew he would not find. She winked at me as he became more panicked in his search, her point made.

Chapter 8

The Road to Ruin

In which I discover that France has been having her own
problems of late, without the likes of me showing up

The driver of the *diligence* stagecoach must have pitied young
Nick for having to endure the company of three such miserable
adults. Our travelling party of four all sat behind him in the
small cabriolet what was fixed to the body of his coach. By
positioning ourselves within the close proximity of this man,
who we had already established spoke not a word of English,
we separated ourselves from the rest of the thirteen-strong
coach behind us. We was keen to sit apart from other travellers
so we could be free to talk of secret matters should we wish
to, although, as the stagecoach's seven horses pulled us out of
the garrison-town of Calais and southwards towards Paris, it
seemed that only one of us was in a conversational mood. I was
not talking to Celeste on account of the lost opium, Jerome
was not talking to me on account of how I stole his wallet,
but he also wasn't talking to Celeste as she was the one what
promised me half of the winnings without consulting him
first – a promise I was insistent they must stick to. For her
part, Celeste was not talking to either Jerome or myself, but

that seemed to be because we was both boring her rigid with our moods.

Nick, however, would not shut up. He was abuzz to be back in the land of his birth and, in between more games of What My Little Eye Spies, he seemed to thrill at almost everything he spied there, no matter how ordinary.

'It looks like England,' he observed, as we trundled through the French countryside on this sweltering June day. 'We'll give it that. But there is a different air, don't you think, Dodge? A different attitude.'

His enthusiasm for foreign travel became infectious, and, after I had spent enough time brooding upon my loss at sea, I began to take an example from him. I found myself enjoying this chance to breathe in the fresh country air and take my first real look at France in all her hazy and foreign glory. He was right of course. Over there they have rain-parched fields of faded green just like we have at the height of summer, the winding country lanes was no straighter or better tended than ours and the hot weather brought out just as many mayflies. But, despite all these similarities, the sense of holiday was invigorating and I began to feel that I was going to make it through the day without taking a puff after all. France was already having a restorative effect upon my disposition and, ignoring Nick's chatter, I let my eyes rest for a spell as the movement of the vehicle rocked me all gentle and I began to feel at peace.

'Merrrrde!'

Our coach driver had roared that word in a throaty, furious

voice, causing me to jolt awake again as the *diligence* drew to a sudden halt. Then he went on shouting more angry words, what could be never be mistaken for anything other than swearing in any language. On opening my eyes I found that we had been travelling along a dusty avenue what was lined with little trees, but our path was now blocked on account of some half-dozen vagrants what was shuffling about ahead of us. Nick sat up straight and stared at them in wonder, as if he thought these here was typical Frenchmen rather than just a bunch of beggars. The coach driver, meanwhile, continued expressing his outrage at them as they just stood there in our way, eyeing our horses as if they was a rival gang. Our driver raised his whip in the air and gave it a mighty crack what shocked his nags into continuing onwards and the vagrants scattered either side of the coach so as not to get trampled under hoof. One of the vagrants, a half-dressed, rangy individual who could have been mistaken for a scarecrow, was on the far side to me but I saw him glaring at the four of us sat on the cabriolet with undisguised hatred. Then he opened his gummy, yellow-toothed mouth to rasp something at us before we passed.

'*Ruin! Ruin!*' it sounded like he was wheezing. '*Rappelay Ruin!*'

Jerome, who was sitting the closest to this undesirable cove as we passed him, kept his eyes fixed straight ahead but the vagrant was not to be ignored.

'*Bor jwa!*' he declared and then launched a sizeable missile of spit, what soared through the air and landed straight onto Jerome's delicate cheek. Nick gasped with what sounded like a mixture of both shock and amusement as it hit. But, if you think that the rightful heir of the Lamoreaux estate was simply going to respond to that with a resigned and weary humour, then you would have been mistaken. Instead, Jerome cried out in horror, his whole body went into a spasm of revulsion at the assault and he would not calm himself until his sister had produced a small, frilly handkerchief from under her cloak and wiped the offending mess clean off. Then Jerome leaned out of the window and issued forth a volley of raw French vocabulary, what I guessed from the delivery was not a diplomatic attempt at class appeasement. There was a fierceness in his voice what would have been most impressive in its bravery, had the horses not been moving at such a trot that it was impossible for the spitter to catch up.

Some female vagrants was also up ahead on the roadside and wore matching expressions of contempt. They too was chanting *bor jwa, bor jwa, bor jwa* and flapping their arms at us in a duck-like fashion. I asked Nick if he knew what that meant.

'*Bourgeois,*' he said and thumbed at Celeste and Jerome, 'is what people like us call people like them.'

As we passed these rough and rude women, Jerome rolled up and tossed them Celeste's frilly and spit-covered fogle as an insult. The women began fighting over it.

'The first thing you must do once our fortune is regained,' Celeste sniffed before we all returned to silence, 'is buy me a new one.'

The rest of the long day of travel was a tiring affair, as we traversed the hilly landscape and passed by many fortified towns, medieval churches, farmhouses and vineyards. Although France remained pleasant to look at, I recall feeling an increasing sense of unease as we continued downwards into the country, an unease what seemed to emanate from the people. Having never been to France before I was unqualified to judge what was or was not unusual behaviour for these provincial sorts, but you did not have to be a seasoned explorer to recognise when the natives was restless. And these natives was so restless they looked to be preparing for battle.

Armed with what looked to me like makeshift weaponry – such as picks, pikes, rakes and other rusty gardening tools – there was droves of determined countrymen and women moving along the main road what led to Paris. More of them seemed to join in with the march the further we travelled, pouring in from every village lane and avenue into the main traffic, until the roads was most crowded. They was not like the vagrants we had encountered earlier – or at least most of them was not – they seemed more like labourers and farm-hands and most ignored our carriage. Many carried sticks with sacking over their shoulders what would have contained food, while others carried bundles of corded firewood. Often, and in a show of good fellowship, singing would break out from a number of the groups and they all sang the same rallying tune, to which everyone seemed to know the words, all the way along the track.

'Oh, I remember this,' Nick declared with great delight on hearing the tune. 'I can't remember who sung it to me though,' he added before trying to hum along to the melody as well.

Even as the day began to darken, we could hear the same song being sung around campfires lit far off in the fields.

We passed a large windmill around what the grass had grown tall from neglect. The wooden vanes was not turning, but each of them had aggressive graffiti painted onto them in bold strokes. All four vanes bore the same violent promise. *Mort au Petit-Bourgeois!*

'What my little eye spies,' I muttered to myself after considering all that I knew about French history and drawing one very unsettling conclusion about what was going on in this land, 'is something beginning with R.'

Before nightfall descended, the *diligence* arrived at a humble coach-house in another fortified town and all the passengers alighted and secured themselves bed and board. Our driver was known to the landlady and no doubt she would reward him for bringing us to that hostelry in particular. She apologised to us in French about something as Jerome, myself and the driver was unloading our luggage from the top of the stagecoach.

'She has a young man who usually provides this service for guests,' Celeste explained as we heaved the trunks through the coach-house and to the last unoccupied bedchamber. 'A porter. But he too has joined the march to Paris.'

'What they all marching over, anyway?' asked Nick. 'I thought that we French had already killed our royalty?'

'Unemployment,' Celeste answered him, as we was all led upstairs to the only chamber they had available what could accommodate all four of us. 'From what I overhear. The people are angry with the government about the National Workshops.'

'What are they?' Nick asked.

'They provide jobs for people all over the country,' Celeste replied, as we entered the chamber with two big double beds and a portable changing screen between them. 'The Second Republic promised not to close them and are now threatening to break that promise.' She said this in a tone what hinted that the subject exhausted her and that she would appreciate him leaving it alone now.

'Who are the Second Republic?' he persisted.

'That is the name of the current government.'

'Why are they breaking their promise?'

'I don't know, child,' she sighed. 'Because of money, I would guess. Would somebody please open that window? It is too hot.'

I agreed and then threw open the large painted wooden blinds to let in some air. The window overlooked the courtyard where some of the other travellers was already sat around tables, enjoying a bottle of wine together before bed and smoking tobacco pipes. I envied them.

'If the porter already has a job,' observed Jerome, who was most aggrieved that a man of his standing should have to suffer the indignity of carrying his own luggage, 'why does he wish to protest unemployment of all things? Sounds more like shirking to me. Or idiocy.'

The landlady was still fussing around us in the bedchamber, but it seemed that she could understand more English than Jerome had expected, as she seemed hurt by this insulting mention of her son. She answered, in her own language, in a sad and bitter way, what sounded like a reprimand to her paying guest. I could not understand her, but she spoke at length and uttered the word *ruin* as everyone else had been doing all day. Jerome's haughty manner altered as the middle-aged woman spoke with a certain pride. I had been watching this exchange over by the window and Nick walked over to me and whispered a translation.

'She's telling him that the porter is her only son,' he said, as I perched myself on the windowsill and tried to breathe in some of that pipe smoke what wafted up from below. 'And now she's saying something about how her other son is *mort*. That means dead.'

Celeste seemed to be apologising to the woman on behalf of her brother and, before the door was shut after her, she was given a generous gratuity by the Lamoreaux.

'Her son was killed in Rouen,' Nick went on, explaining the word what I had been hearing all day as ruin. 'Which is a place, by the sound of things. Killed fighting soldiers, he was. Am I right?' he asked Celeste.

'Right enough,' she nodded. 'The poor woman worries that her second son will be killed too, while trying to avenge his brother.'

'Yes!' Nick cheered, congratulating himself on his ear for the language. 'Told you my French was good.'

I looked at Celeste who was now sat over on a bed, her shoulders slumped, looking even more miserable than her brother, which was some feat. Jerome circled the bed towards her and placed a hand upon her shoulder. He whispered soft French into her ear, too quiet for Nick to overhear, but whatever it was he was saying it seemed to be a comfort to her.

Soon after that, the siblings pulled the portable dressing screen across, separating their side of the room from ours and wished us goodnight. Darkness had not even fallen yet on that long day, but Nick bedded down also, leaving me to continue sitting by the window, watching the last of the sun set over the courtyard. The men below my window was still chatting around their table, another bottle of wine had been opened and their conversation sounded ominous. I noticed a piece of graffiti across the yard. Scrawled in charcoal across the walls of the stable was the words *RAPPELEZ ROUEN!*

An hour later I shut the wooden blinds to deaden the noise from below and block out the bright moonlight. I was feeling empty and went to bed knowing that my dreams would be unkind and that, had my opium not been cast into the English sea, I would have taken some by now without question.

The only thing more vexatious than being woken up first thing in the morning by the sound of a cock crowing, is when the cockerel in question has an annoying French accent. One such offender had positioned himself right outside our chamber window and was making me regret not shutting the glass window, as he cried out his proud rendition of cock-a-doodle-do, a tune what bore similarities to the English version but sounded, to my ears, to have ungainly pretensions of grandeur about it. Not only that, but this unwelcome alarm was also matched by the cacophony of noisy men rallying others into a revolutionary fervour beneath us, as well as that of some honking geese. It was not so easy to tell the difference between those two sounds.

Nick was not in the bed chamber when the rest of us awoke, but I was unconcerned as a lad like him would always show up for breakfast. I did wonder if he too was outside in the courtyard, and so, wearing only my underthings, I crossed over to the window and opened the blinds. Morning sun filled the room and, below me in the yard, a grey-bearded man in his late-sixties carrying a long staff was stood on a barrel, delivering the most impassioned speech I had heard yet among these revolutionary sorts. Several younger men in workmen's blouses crowded beneath to cheer his every statement, as he banged his staff against the barrel, making more mention of Rouen and railing against the *petite-bourgeoisie*. I did not hear Celeste approach from behind until her hand was on my shoulder.

'He doesn't seem to like our kind very much,' she observed. 'He blames the recent troubles here in France upon the complacent gentility. Which, I suppose, is us.'

'Which I suppose is *you*,' I told her. 'He ain't talking about me, is he? I'm of the people.'

'Oh, you think so?' her smile patronised me as though I was a small child who had just declared himself a soldier. 'You see yourself as a revolutionary, do you Dodger?'

'In my fashion, yeah.'

I looked down upon the small band of dusty rebels as they

gathered their various farming tools what they no doubt deluded themselves would serve as sufficient weaponry against military guns. Aside from the old man, they was all my own age or younger and they looked to be a brave enough bunch, patting each other on the back in encouragement for what they was about to do, chanting what I supposed must be patriotic slogans. And I knew that, in spite of what I had just said, I was nothing like them.

'These principled young men down here,' I said as I watched them all troop out of the courtyard of this inn and onto the main road singing that now familiar song, 'are a collection of prize-winning idiots.'

Celeste gave a small laugh as if I had just expressed a thought of her own.

'All that most of them will gain from any revolution,' I continued as I watched the packed yard empty of vehicles save for our *diligence* coach, 'is a shot of lead through the skull, just like the landlady's dead son earned himself. They'd all be better off staying at home, in my view.'

'What noble sentiments,' Celeste smirked. 'You truly are the people's hero.'

'I stage my own revolution against the ruling classes every time I pick a pocket or crack a crib,' I turned on her. 'When you're born into poverty, like I was, stealing from those above you is the last word in defiance. But no sensible London crim would ally themselves with a cause what could kill them, least of all when there's no profit to be made from it.'

'Is that so?' she remarked and indicated over at the stable

doors where I had noticed the graffiti last night. 'Then what is your assistant writing on that barn?'

There, across the other side of the yard, standing with his back to us, was No Nickname Nick and he seemed to be adding his own sentiments to the collection of political slogans about Rouen what was already there.

'Nicolas!' I shouted over to him. 'Come in for some breakfast. We'll be on the road again in no time!'

Nick turned, smiled at us and dropped a lump of black chalk onto the ground. As he darted across the courtyard towards the door of this inn, I read what he had been scrawling on the stable walls in his own rough hand.

Mort a la Seconde Republique! it read.

'It's true what he says,' Celeste remarked before turning away from the window. 'His French really isn't that bad.'

The rest of the journey into Paris was a far more pleasurable experience and perhaps, I could not help but hope, this was because I had not been at the puff in the past few days. I was travelling now in my whitest shirt, with the sleeves rolled up, the top half unbuttoned. I was enjoying the sunshine for the first time this year. The occasional city milestones we passed began to display numbers low enough to start getting excited about, and, as our carriage trundled past another marching mob of revolters who was all singing that one uplifting song, Nick and I could not help but whistle along to it in a merry way.

'The song is called *La Marseillaise,*' Celeste informed us upon inquiry. 'It is very popular in France, especially among those with a revolutionary spirit.' It was notable then that neither she nor her brother joined in with it.

As the day continued, our carriage put some distance between ourselves and the marching protestors and we saw far fewer countrymen as we travelled further south. Around these parts there was the occasional woodsman loping along with an axe over his shoulder, but few other travellers. Nick and myself had started singing our own London songs by then and our raucousness seemed to annoy Jerome in particular. Indeed, the closer we got to the city, the more stiff and agitated he became and I remembered what Celeste had told me about how much he dreaded the place.

'Not far now,' Nick beamed and pointed at the first milestone we had seen for hours. It read PARIS 5 KILOMETRES.

'You seem to be in a happier mood today, Dodger,' Celeste observed, as I was laughing at something droll Nick was saying. 'In which case,' she smiled at me in a knowing way, 'you are very welcome!'

Chapter 9

Servants

Entering Paris on the track of a storm

We had not been in the capital for longer than ten minutes before Jerome started moaning about how anxious the place made him. Our stagecoach had thundered past that magnificent arched monument they call the Arc de Triomphe, but we was not even halfway down the Champs-Élysées before he began making his dark observations.

'Terror everywhere,' he remarked as we all surveyed the broad and elegant promenade. 'Can you not feel it?'

'No, not really,' I answered as I looked at all the luxury shops and fashionable cafes we passed and I admired and coveted the many signs of affluence. 'There ain't even a lot of people about.'

'That's what terrifies me,' Jerome trembled. 'Why is everything so quiet?'

But despite all his moody forebodings, I had to admit I was good and impressed with Paris already, even if half its populace was in hiding. The architecture was awe-inspiring, the fashions was striking and the people who I did see walking about looked rich enough to be worth stealing from. I could

JAMES BENMORE • 122

feel the joy of the dip returning, a joy I once feared I would never feel again, at the sight of such an unsullied patch for me to go finding in. I was keen to get out of this vehicle so that I could start exploring.

The stagecoach at last came to the conclusion of its two-day journey, just before a public square at the end of that long road. In the middle of the square was a giant, ancient-looking stone pillar with ornate statues and fountains gathered about it.

'What is that thing?' Nick asked, once all the passengers and luggage had alighted the coach and the driver had rode away. 'And what are all them etchings marked onto it?'

'That is an Egyptian obelisk and this is the Place de la Concorde,' Celeste explained to him. 'You'll be interested to know, my little Jacobin, that here was where the largest guillotine of the revolution once stood.' Nick's imagination was indeed captured by this historical titbit and he demanded to be told more. 'Our grandfather was executed here,' Celeste continued in a sorrowful way, 'so was King Louis, Marie Antoinette and countless other aristocrats.'

'The filthy rabble of the city all crowded around here in their thousands,' Jerome scowled as he beheld the now bloodless scene of the crime, 'as good men and women were brought to their knees and beheaded. That infamous whore, who our father's killer is still so proud to call a grandmother – the disgusting Madame DeFarge – would have been here among the audience. Knitting and jeering at the fall of her betters, *tricoteuse* that she was.'

Then, and with a surprising smoothness of action what

was almost graceful, Jerome reached back into his throat and launched an impressive spit in the direction of the obelisk. Even Celeste seemed shocked by it.

'Please, brother,' she then said as he wiped the spittle away from his mouth. 'Do not mention Madame DeFarge again. You know how I hate even hearing that accursed name.'

'Well, that was all a while ago,' I said, taken aback by their venomous attitude towards an event what had passed into history decades before either of these Lamoreaux bastards had been born. 'Let us concentrate on the present for now, eh? Are your aunt's lodgings far from here? Only it's getting late and I don't fancy carrying these trunks any greater distance than necessary.'

'Aunt LeFleur's apartment is not far from Les Halles,' Jerome said, as if that was supposed to mean something to me. 'And some servants are there waiting upon our arrival.' He lifted up his travelling cane into the air to hail one of the many cabriolets heading in our direction. 'Perhaps you can pay for this part of the journey out of that money you stole from me, Dodger?' he sniffed. 'I am keen to get myself safely indoors also.'

Neither Celeste nor Jerome had spent much time in Paris over recent years. But they still had local connections what had secured an apartment for us to stay in over the next week or so. Old Aunt LeFleur was on their mother's side and she lived here for most of the year, but liked to leave the city in the summertime and so had allowed her niece and nephew to stay at her house.

'A convenient arrangement,' snarled Jerome after the four

of us had been standing outside a large, rusting iron gate in a Parisian backstreet for what felt like an age, 'or so it would be if only someone would grant us entrance. Where are these wretched servants? *Maria! Gaspard!* These streets are too treacherous for us to remain out here for long.'

Jerome continued rattling upon the ivy-tangled bars with his cane and shouting these names at the windows above and into the courtyard beyond, for such a long time that we all began to accept that the place was deserted. But, just before we was all set to leave, an elderly man with a wooden leg appeared from the length of the courtyard. The slow *tap tap tap* of his artificial foot echoed through the passageway as he approached. He seemed to take forever to reach the gate and his mouth was opening as if he was trying to say something, but nothing could be heard. This, I gathered, was the servant Gaspard. Just before he reached the gate with a large set of keys, a girl appeared from behind a door in the courtyard and stomped over to us in a surly huff. She snatched the keys from out of the hands of the one-legged dodderer and unlocked the gate, as Jerome scolded her about, I suppose, her tardiness and sullen demeanour. She was about nineteen, black-haired and rough-cheeked and she gave a shallow curtsey by way of apology what did not much smack of sincerity. Then she led the four of us and our luggage through the dark passage to the open courtyard, what was full of dying plants in cracked clay pots, and then up a winding iron staircase to a third-floor apartment, as the wheezing old man hobbled behind us at some distance.

The apartment, although large, was dirtier than I had expected

and was in a state of some disrepair. The carpet was stained with
what I would suppose was rainwater, considering the state of
the roof. The furniture was close to dilapidated and it all stank
of too many budgerigars, many of which was dead in their
cages. I had lived in far worse places over the years, and Nick
had little to complain about either, considering that back in
London he lived under railway arches with the other boys in
his gang. But both Jerome and Celeste seemed to be shocked by
the poor conditions of their aunt's home and took their disgust
out upon Maria the servant-girl. This worsened when, upon
his exploration of the other rooms of the crib, it came to light
that Maria had been sleeping in Aunt LeFleur's chamber since
her absence from the city and Jerome, if his outraged reaction
was any clue, was not best pleased about such impertinence.

There was two bedrooms in the main apartment and both
of them was spacious, comfortable chambers – far superior to
those what we four travellers had been sharing on the journey
here. And so I assumed that we would be enjoying a similar
arrangement tonight, with the Lamoreaux siblings occupying
one and myself and Nick sharing the other. But in this assump-
tion I was mistaken.

'The servants' chambers are below,' Jerome informed me
before I could carry my small green trunk into the second most
luxurious room. 'You and the boy will sleep down there, of
course. Gaspard's room has two other beds in it.' The old man
with the wooden leg had only just made it through the apartment door and looked unhappy to hear his name mentioned
in a foreign sentence.

'Let the old boy enjoy his solitude tonight, Jerome,' I said and tried to push past him into the chamber, 'Nick and myself ain't the feudal system sort, so try not to keep mistaking us for servants, eh?'

'My sister will sleep in this room!' he protested as he blocked the doorway. 'And I shall have the other. The underclass have been exploiting our family line for long enough!' He cast a stinking look towards the servant-girl. 'I will not have my aunt's bedroom subjected to criminals, especially English ones!'

'English criminals what are here to help you, or have you forgot? And this here deposit,' I tapped the golden cross what hung beneath my shirt, 'ain't worth the risk alone. So if I find any valuables worth having in that bedroom, I'm taking them by way of further payment.'

'I'll kill you first!'

'*Jerome!*' his sister snapped from behind me. Then she spoke to him in French, her words sounding sharp and strict. He tried to whine back at her in a defiant way but he soon withered under her verbal discipline. 'And as for you Monsieur Dawkins,' she addressed me in a no less severe manner, 'I have jewellery belonging to me here inside a safe. I shall open it later this evening and you can select from it what you feel is adequate payment for both you and your assistant. This will still be a mere fraction of what you shall receive after our estate has been retrieved, however.'

'Glad to hear it,' I said, still staring hard at Jerome as she spoke.

'But until then,' she continued, stepping forward to position herself between the two of us, as if to defend him from me if necessary, 'you and Nicolas *will* sleep with the other servants if my brother wishes it.' Jerome smirked as she said this. 'Let Gaspard take you to his room,' she continued, 'while Maria prepares us a meal. And, after that, we shall discuss the details of your particular service. You can take every diamond in this place, for all I care. For us, the marriage certificate is worth so much more!'

Later, once night had fallen and the small dining room was lit by just one short candle, shoved into a bottle covered with wax, the subject turned at last to the business of cracking this wine shop. Maria had prepared us a low standard of meal and so had suffered another scolding from Jerome as a result but, once this had been digested, she produced some bread and cheese as well as some wine, what only I drunk a glass from. Once this was poured the elderly servant asked if he could retire to his room, although nobody heard him at first, on account of his weak voice. Maria was instructed to wash the crockery before she too could leave us. Nick had been very quiet ever since we had arrived in this place, although he had been helping the servants in the kitchen of his own volition and feeding the remaining birds. But now was the time for us all to plan a course of action for tomorrow and so he was summoned back to the table. And, even though neither of the two servants spoke English, the door was shut firm on that room so we could speak of criminal matters with freedom.

'So, tell me more about this Hugo DeFarge cove,' I whispered the name. 'Anything I might be able to use.'

'We have told you all you need,' Celeste remarked as she poured me another glass and we ignored the rowdy shouting what was coming up from the street below. 'He is the man who killed our father and he has somehow acquired the wedding certificate that proves our legitimacy. He contacted us through family friends to say that he will either sell it to us at a ridiculous price, or sell it to Lucien Lamoreaux, who will no doubt destroy it. We want neither of these things to happen so you must steal it back from his shop in Saint-Antoine.'

'Do you know where in the shop it might be kept?'

'Of course not,' she said, as Jerome began scratching away at a piece of paper with his pencil near to the candlelight. 'That is your problem to solve.'

As soon as he finished with his drawing Jerome spun the paper around and held it to the light so that Nick and myself could view the image. I looked down and saw a sketch of a black-eyed, long-faced and bull-necked rogue staring back at me. Even though I had never seen DeFarge myself, I had a strong suspicion that this was not a flattering likeness. Jerome had drawn one thick eyebrow what covered most of the man's forehead, a drooping nose, large elephant-like ears and two deep scars on his cheeks. Beside me, Celeste peered over at the drawing also.

'You know how I detest the man, brother,' she said after having surveyed his artwork. 'But this picture will mislead the Dodger. DeFarge is not so hideous.'

Jerome ignored her and tapped at the two scars.

'Our brave father gave him these,' he said, with some pride. 'Just before he received his own fatal wound. So, regardless of how accurate my drawing is, you will know him by them.'

'You've met him?' I asked, as I took the drawing from him, folded it up and placed it into my pocket for later consultation. 'When?'

'DeFarge was at our father's funeral,' Jerome said. 'That was the last time either of us saw him. He was not among the mourners. We saw him lurking behind a leafless tree on that cold winter day, as our father's coffin was lowered into a hole in Père Lachaise cemetery. I assume he came to assure himself that the job was completed.'

'How come he wasn't arrested for killing your old man?' Nick asked. 'You can't just loiter around funerals of men you murdered and not expect trouble.'

'Our father . . .' Jerome glanced towards Celeste, whose own eyes was fixed upon the candle flame, 'was a beautiful man in many ways. But he suffered from demons. I believe my sister told you that he was an opium fiend.' I nodded as Nick expressed surprise at the news. 'Well, I'm told that this affliction brought him into contact with the Parisian underworld, which is how he met Hugo DeFarge. DeFarge used our father's weakness terribly and he came to be in his debt. There was a swordfight before long and our sweet father lost.'

'Hugo DeFarge is a man,' Celeste spoke then, in a quiet but bitter tone, 'who is as motivated by hatred for our class as his notorious grandmother also was. So he must have delighted in corrupting our father, cheating him out of his possessions and rendering him low.' As she said that I heard the pain in her voice and felt how raw the subject must be for her.

'But all that matters,' Jerome sniffed, as though he had shared more than enough family secrets with mere tradesmen such as Nick and myself than he had ever meant to, 'is that you avoid him. He is deadly. Do not fall into his clutches. Steal back our document and leave that place as quick as is possible. I give you that picture solely so that you might know who it is you should be avoiding.'

'I've no intention of avoiding him,' I told them and helped myself to some more of their soft blue-veined cheese. 'If anything, I'll be introducing myself to him. I'm going to be getting so close to Hugo DeFarge that I should be able to give him a kiss on that scarred cheek of his.'

The siblings looked perturbed by this declaration and I could see that the delicate art of breaking and entering was lost on them.

'A decent burglar doesn't just bust into a place without having scouted it all out good and thorough beforehand,' I told them but it was for the good of Nick's education also. 'It all requires a bit more finesse than that. First, he familiarises himself with its comings and goings, has a little explore around the building, surveys its strengths and weaknesses. And this here crack is in a wine shop what should make the job very easy. A place of business is always easier to monitor than a private address, as you can just go in as if you're any other customer and get a feel of the place.'

'So your scheme is to just hand over money that you stole from my wallet to that hated enemy?' Jerome exclaimed in disgust. 'While getting drunk with it!'

'Yeah, I intend to get lit up good and proper at your expense.' I grinned and raised my glass at the thought. 'But I shall have my younger brother with me,' I added and nudged Nick. 'To keep me from getting into too much trouble. By this time tomorrow, he and I shall be friends with every cove in that place, including your father's killer. And that, my Gallic friend, is how I intend to learn where the wedding certificate is hidden.'

'You will seem out of place!' Jerome told me. 'Hopelessly so! This revelation may shock and amaze you, Dodger, but not everybody in Paris speaks your language as well as my sister and I, and your assistant understands our language better than he speaks it, so don't place too much faith in him. Not only that, sir, but the English are about as popular here as we French are in your country. You may well receive a blow to the head by some old soldier who wishes to recreate Waterloo, with you cast as Lord Arthur Wellesley. DeFarge's wine shop is a rough and hazardous place.'

'Well, I'm a rough and hazardous individual, so I'll fit in better than you're giving me credit for,' I said after finishing my second glass. 'Cities have their differences, but their slums are all the same. Indeed, I'd wager that the patrons of that wine shop and myself will be firm friends before long, regardless of our uncommon tongue. I'll find your document, Jerome,' I promised him. 'Just give me some time to ingratiate myself first. I need to learn where the valuables are kept. I have a plan what I think might help.'

I then produced something from out of my pocket and showed it to them. They did not understand the relevance of it at first but, once had I explained my thinking to them, I told Nick to fetch a pen and inkwell. Celeste, who had been listening to me with a deep and concentrated look on her face, what was now only half-lit by the candlelight, admitted that the scheme might work and offered to help me with it.

'That is quite clever,' she said once she had lain down the pen and the ink was dried. 'And, furthermore, DeFarge would never suspect someone like you of being in league with people like us. Also, I am told DeFarge himself speaks a little English. He may even approach the two of you.' Jerome whispered something to her in French, but she ignored him and touched my hand as if trying to focus my attention upon her. 'And here is another detail about our Monsieur DeFarge that I think you may find useful. He is a family man.' Again, Jerome said something in French to her but she replied in English. 'It *is* relevant, Jerome,' she said, her eyes like flint as they locked with mine. 'His wife is dead, but there is a son. Younger than him,' she pointed at Nick, 'called Jean-Pierre or Jean-Claude or Jean-Something. Jerome,' she spoke to him, but kept her eyes fixed on mine with this unsettling intent, 'what did she say the child was called again?'

'Jean-Jacques,' he said, in a still tone.

'*Oui*,' she nodded, with a strange and sinister smile. 'The apple of his father's eye, as you English say. So perhaps, if you are unsuccessful in finding the document, then you can steal something else precious of his with which we can trade.'

The room had become much blacker now and I needed to blink hard on account of the close light as I made sense of what she was insinuating. I glanced over at Jerome and then at Nick and saw from their faces that they was as bothered by her wicked suggestion as I was.

'You hired us as thieves, Celeste,' I told her straight. 'Not as kidnappers. I don't care how large the reward, I don't go around hurting or scaring kinchins.' Celeste looked horrified by the accusation.

'I don't mean that you should hurt him!' she exclaimed, looking to her brother for support. 'What a vile thing to think. I'm the last person that would ever suggest such an act, aren't I Jerome? I simply mention this so you know what is dearest to DeFarge and that perhaps, if you lead the child away to somewhere safe – and where could be safer than here? – then we will have something to bargain with. Doesn't that make sense as a plan?' Jerome looked as unconvinced as I was at her reasoning for mentioning the child.

On the other side of the table, he rose from his chair. 'Forgive my sister, Mr Dawkins,' he said as he took another unlit candle and lit it from the one in the bottle. 'But she has had a long few days travelling and must be tired. Of course, the child shall not be bothered in our pursuit of the document. No fortune is worth such a mean and lowering tactic.' Celeste's whole body slumped a little as he came around the table, as if to lead her away. It was as if she had drunk too much and he was stopping her from disgracing herself further, although she had not touched a drop. It was the first time I had seen the younger sibling express any true mastery over his older sister. 'No doubt we could all use some sleep,' he continued then and turned to me. 'The servants will rise early to attend to us and I, for one, will be grateful for a civilising shave after all this travelling. Gaspard could give you a shave as well, Dodger, but if you are trying to pass yourself off as inconspicuous in Saint-Antoine then it would be better if you remained unkempt. Very well. Tomorrow we shall direct you and the boy to the shop and then await your return. And at last,' he added before we all retired to our very different bed chambers, 'we will learn whether or not the Artful Dodger is worth the riches that have already been paid him.'

Gunshots could be heard from somewhere far off in the city that night as Nick and myself bedded down in the tiny servant's chamber. The wheezing old man snored through, but neither myself nor my young friend was ready to go to sleep just yet.

'When they talk amongst themselves,' I asked him, 'what do they say?'

'I can't follow them,' he whispered back. 'It's either too fast, too high-class or in riddles. I follow the servants better. They wasn't told that I could hear French so they talked in a more simple, open way when I was helping them in the kitchen. My mother was a scullery maid and that Maria girl speaks just like she used to. I can't hear a word that old geezer says, though,' he pointed at Gaspard.

'I bet she hates Jerome,' I said. 'I would if I was her.'

'Yeah, but not as much as she hates Celeste,' Nick told me. 'Calls her a *putain* behind her back, which means whore. She covets all her nice dresses and jewels what are kept here in her aunt's apartment. I heard her tell the old man there that the jewellery box what was offered to us to pick our payment from was the least of them. There are lots more jewels and diamonds hidden away in some safe, which the girl reckons she will crack open in a week or two once the fighting is done.'

'Did she now?' I considered this information as some more gunfire was heard, this time a little closer by. Some footsteps came running down the street just outside and someone was chanting something as they passed. Then the city fell silent again.

'Maria told the old man,' Nick continued in an even quieter voice, 'that the Cupidons will regret their hard treatment of her in less than a week. Then, she reckons, they'll be serving on her, while she'll be the one wearing the pretty dresses and diamonds. She reckons that if they refuse their new roles their throats will be cut. Not by her, but by someone, she reckons.'

'Well, lets hope she's wrong about all that,' I said, before leaning over to snuff out the last candle, 'else we'll never get paid.'

Chapter 10

Claret on the Cobbles

Introducing myself to Parisian society

The most glorious collection of home furnishings I had ever before seen, outside of a private property, was behind the first glass window we passed on the Rue Montorgueil the following morning. I was so impressed by the fine display that I made the others stop so we could all admire the set of silk-upholstered suites, the gilded chests, the bronze busts, the marble statuettes, not to mention all these little porcelain clocks what made my own ticker beat faster as I imagined smashing the glass and taking them for mine. Precious china was stacked tight into dressers, elegant dresses was hanging from rails, fancy hats was piled on top of one another. Seeing such opulent stock crammed into a shop of that sort told me everything I needed to know about the prosperity of modern Paris.

It was in tatters.

'In times of affluence,' I observed to both Celeste and young Nick, as we enjoyed a brief pause beneath the trio of golden balls what hung above us, 'a lowly pawnbrokers such as this here would never be stuffed with such treasures. It must be a buyer's market.'

Celeste had no interest in my economic observations and did little to feign any. Instead, she was keen to hurry us along to the Saint-Antoine vicinity, where she could point me in the direction of the DeFarge wine shop and leave us burglars to it. She wanted to return to Jerome, who was refusing to leave the apartment, having become so terrified by the sounds of fighting on the night before.

'Most shops,' I said as she led us through the maze of narrow and winding backstreets, 'are either locked up tight or half empty. I wonder if the banks are too. What day is it today?'

'Friday,' she replied, as we cut through one of many long tiled passages of boarded-up shops. 'Although it does feel like a Sunday, I will admit.'

Most of the populace seemed to be in hiding, which I thought peculiar, considering the sticky weather. The few Parisians we did happen to pass while on our journey was all carrying axes, wood-saws, stone hammers, cutlers' knives or other domestic tools what could be used as weapons if the circumstances demanded it. Walls was covered in aggressive graffiti, often painted, sometimes chalked and the only word I recognised was 'SANG,' which was seen everywhere.

Nick and myself had done our best to dress in as inconspic-uous a way as possible, with hats and light jackets what was appropriate for the weather. It felt unnatural for a peacock such as myself to wear these bland and colourless clothes, but sometimes we must sacrifice fashion for the job at hand. A red neckerchief was the only flair I had allowed myself and this was only because I had seen so many men wearing similar ones the day before. I had been given some French sous before leaving and had already purchased some common labourer's tobacco from one of the few open shops and some boiled sweets for Nick. From just the smallest sniff of the leaf, I could tell that it was going to prove a mild and uninspiring substitute for the opium I really craved, but I had not purchased it for my own enjoyment. Instead, I hoped it would help me blend in. I had enough to offer to others should I need to ingratiate myself with a smoker.

The three of us came to a main thoroughfare, where there was a large crowd. They was in their thousands here, marching through the Rue de Rivoli waving plenty of those three-coloured flags of the nation in the air as they went. Every hat boasted a tricolore cockade and that famous tune, *La Marseillaise*, could be heard on all their lips. From their dress it seemed that a good deal of these marchers was country folk like those we had passed on our journey down here.

'Revolution!' Nick cheered as we reached a massive building what appeared to be some sort of town hall. Here the marchers had all halted to yell abuse and spit. 'Has it started yet? Is this it happening here?'

'Nobody's getting hurt,' I replied as I noticed that the troops guarding the building had their weapons ready, but was not opening fire as they kept the mob at bay. 'But I ain't ever been in no revolution before, so I don't know what I'm looking at.'

'The possible revolutions of other countries are none of your concern, boys,' Celeste reminded us as she came to a sudden halt. 'Retrieving what belongs to me is.' She tightened her hood some more and began giving us directions to the wine shop. 'If I go on with you any further I might be spotted by DeFarge or one of his accomplices,' she explained. 'He would be sure to know me by my likeness to my father.'

'Get going then,' I nodded. 'We could do without being seen with you 'n all.' I turned to Nick. 'Would you be able to find your way back to her crib from here if we get separated?' He thought about it, then nodded. 'Well, let's hope so. If the two of us do get lost then we'll meet you, Celeste, at that big ugly church what we passed at the end of your road at midnight. With a bit of luck we'll have the wedding certificate for you by then.'

And with that, Celeste turned back to where she had come from, leaving my young assistant and myself to meet Hugo DeFarge alone.

A large cask of red wine had smashed on a long cobbled street leading into Saint-Antoine. The dark red stain of it covered most of the narrow passage and it was sticky and foul-smelling enough for it to have happened some days ago. A couple of mongrel dogs and some old vagrant was crouched over the spillage, licking up what remained.

'That's disgusting, eh, Dodger,' Nick remarked as we stepped past the wine-licking vagrant. 'Degrading himself in full view like that. I could not imagine falling so low.'

'Me neither,' I said, and I placed my hand in my trouser

pocket to assure myself that I still had that full purse. I was looking forward to buying some wine and consuming it from a glass, like the civilised person I flattered myself that I still was.

The suburb of Saint-Antoine did not strike my slum-born eyes as all that rotten, considering everything I had been told about DeFarge and his shop, but then the Lamoreaux no doubt had different standards about what might constitute a pleasant urban environment than mine. True, the lanes around here was so narrow that every corner had its plaster scratched off from where wide carts had no doubt failed to make successful turns and such an incident must have made the aforementioned wine cask topple from its vehicle. Meanwhile, the mustard-brown buildings either side of us made up for the lack of space down here, as they was all five floors and a garret. This meant that, in spite of the sun, the vicinity was cast in shadows and was far more populated than many of the other backstreets I had travelled through to get here. It was as if I had lifted a rock in an otherwise tidy garden and discovered where all the insects had been hiding.

All the wooden blinds along the road was thrown open and bullet-holed tricolore flags hung from washing lines between the houses. Big groups of men and women crowded outside every shop and above them full-throated voices hurtled across from all windows. I noticed one hard and heavy cove standing outside his butcher's shop, with blood dripping from the cleaver he gripped, onto the cobbles below. He was whispering with a number of shorter porkmen, as if they was either plotting a murder or discussing one they had just committed. As myself and Nick passed by them they eyed us hard and I then noticed that other locals was doing likewise and that we was the subject of dark discussion from all corners. Beside me, Nick, perhaps feeling nervous from all the hostile glances we was attracting, begun to whistle *La Marseillaise*, with which he had become most taken on our journey down here. But instead of helping us to fit in, it had the opposite effect. People along that street stopped what they was doing and stared at us all the harder.

'Even your whistle has an English accent,' I told him.

The wine shop we wanted was on a tight corner and there was no colourful sign hanging out the front like a British pub would have, nor any name or nothing else what might signify that we had reached our destination. How such a place was expected to attract passing custom was a mystery, as the only thing what marked it out as a den of drink was two upturned barrels stood outside and a trapdoor into the cellar. The front door was open, although it was hard to see within due to a thin red sheet what hung over the doorway from the inside. On the street outside was a small gang of young kinchins playing at soldiers, pretending to shoot at one another with wooden sticks. These excitable lads was younger than Nick by a few years and one of them ran straight into him by accident as we crossed to enter the shop. His playmates all laughed to see him collide with a bigger boy, as if expecting to see some trouble and the lad stepped back from us mumbling something what may have been an apology. But Nick responded by miming a gun of his own and shooting the lad, before winking at him in fun. This got him a laugh from the young gang and the colliding boy feigned a wound and fell down there in the middle of the road. Then his friends all lifted their sticks and shot at Nick as he too play-acted a bloody death. It occurred to me that there was a chance that one of these here boys could be the son of Hugo DeFarge and so I was glad that Nick was already making an effort to befriend them. I continued into the wine shop alone. Sweeping the red silk sheet aside, I entered the unlit bar with a good deal of anticipation. The smell of wine and cork was both powerful and very pleasant. I could already taste the grape, I thought with a smile, just seconds before someone's fist hit me hard on the side of the head, knocking my hat off.

I yowled out in pain and stumbled to the floor, as the door slammed behind me and I heard a lock turn.

'Who done that?' I almost demanded in outrage, as my hands raised up to cradle my bashed forehead and my knees collapsed down onto the sawdusted floorboards. I say 'almost' because I was in such shock over the sneaky assault that I could not yet articulate an enquiry into who the culprit was, or for what earthly reason they might have struck me. From down there all I could see was about half a dozen pairs of thick, trousered legs and a couple of long dress skirts surrounding me. The legs all stood as if they was just itching to kick a man while he was down and I looked upwards to see if any of these bodies had friendlier top halves. Alas, no.

'If any of you ugly lot happen to be the proprietor of this establishment,' I said, as six pistols, two muskets and one lengthy sword blade was pointed right at my throbbing head, 'then I would like to lodge a formal complaint.'

The fierce congregation of French thugs sneered back at me and the closest man growled something. Behind me the knob on the front door rattled and I heard Nick's voice from the other side. 'Dodger!' he called through the small curtained window beside it. 'Let me in. The door's locked.' I could hear those kinchins out there giggling at him as he became more distressed.

'That's my little brother out there,' I told my assailants, as I grabbed onto a nearby chair and begun hoisting myself up. 'Either let him in or let me out, will you? Else you'll answer for it.'

A man to my left pulled the chair I was using out from under me and another man to my right kicked me in the ribs. I fell flat on the floor then, as they took turns to shout aggressive questions at me. By now, the anger and humiliation what I felt at this attack should have been replaced with terror, as it became apparent that I had stumbled into real peril here, but I did not feel any. After all, I had been the top sawyer of a crooked London gang and you don't get respect from the likes of them by pissing yourself whenever a gun is pointed at you. I had lost confidence in my talent of late, but not yet in my steel.

'I came in here for a drink!' I snarled up at them. 'This is a wine shop, innit?' Then I held up an invisible bottle and made a drinking motion with it. Above me, one of the two kickers made as if he was about to deliver another, but I raised an arm and pointed a finger at him. *'Don't!'* I warned him and, to my own surprise, this did hold him steady for now. He was a big, bearded man and he looked at the other kicker for direction. I then noticed two interesting things about this second man.

The first was that he reminded me of Bill Sikes. He had the same brutish demeanour, the same violent eyes and cruelty just emanated from him. And the second thing worth noticing was that he was dressed in priests' clothing.

This brute priest shook his fist in a very deliberate way, what was no doubt meant to communicate that it was him who had punched me upon my entrance. Then he issued some orders. The bearded man grabbed me under the arm, forced me to my feet and then I was pressed hard against a wall so that he could shout questions into my face all the easier. His intimidating Gallic nose was near enough to mine that it blocked out the rest of the room, his hands was shoving into my chest to keep me still and everything he said sounded loaded with threat. The rest was all now squabbling amongst themselves, as if discussing what should be done with me.

Outside the shop, Nick was still calling out through the window but he was attempting to speak in his rough French now. The priest responded with a nod towards one of his armed cronies and it seemed like he had just been given instruction to deal with the child. This pistol-wielding cove edged towards the door and now the terror started to strike.

'Nick! Run!' I shouted through to the window. 'They've got guns. Get away!' A shaft of daylight entered the gloomy shop as the door was opened and the silk curtain pulled back. 'Don't you hurt him!' I raged from my position up against the wall, as the man with the pistol stepped out onto the street. 'He's a boy! I'll kill you if you do!'

They all fell quiet then and the bearded chest-shover squinted at me with suspicion before barking another question. Here though he was speaking to the others and I heard the word *gendarme* in there. Then, from the back corner of the bar, somebody at last spoke my language.

'Nobody's going to hurt your boy, Londoner,' said an Irish accent. 'What sort of people do you think we are?'

This man was shorter and younger than the others, wore cheap round spectacles and a neat, unbuttoned pea-green waistcoat. His spectacles was at a slight angle as he pushed his way through the mob to get to me but there was little else what was humorous about him. Like the rest he carried a firearm, in his case a rusty barker what he at least had the decency to not point at me and kept hanging at his side.

'Well, just what sort of people d'you think you're coming across as?' I answered back as I continued struggling against the grip of the bearded man. 'Gentle bookish types?'

'What business have you in this place?' he asked, in a soft but unfriendly voice, as he drew near. 'Wine, so you say. But why *this* place? We are not a shop that advertises to tourists.'

'I ain't a tourist,' I shot back and nodded over to the racked wine bottles what was covering the back walls. 'But I am a drinker. My younger brother and myself was just passing by. We hoped that you might serve us with some refreshment. We're new to the city and are looking for some cheap lodgings and food. We thought that this might be a good place to ask after it while I wet my throat. But if our coin ain't wanted, then I'm happy to spend it elsewhere. There's no need to be so bounceable about it.'

The Irishman then translated all of that to the hardened congregation – or at least the nub of it – and this caused plenty of ardent conferring. From the way that the others responded to the man in the priest's collar it was clear that many hated him as much as I did, including the women with the weapons who looked, to my trained eye, like working whores. Several of the older men that the priest was busy barking orders at wore cavalry jackets with horizontal gold braiding, only they was far too worn and dirty to have seen service any time this decade. All of these people sported that tricolore cockade about their clothing what identified them as revolutionaries.

The man who had been sent outside to talk to Nick returned and shrugged when spoken to. 'Your boy ran,' the Irishman told me. 'He needn't have. We just want to know who y'are.' Then the bastard with the beard, who had been holding me against both the wall and my will, addressed me in French. It sounded more like a statement than a question and I could only stare back at him. The women laughed, and around the room all weapons was lowered. The priest threw his hands into the air like he had lost an argument.

'They now believe that you speak no French,' said the Irishman with the smallest of half-smiles. 'Because if you did, you'd never look so unoffended by the vile thing Armand here just said about your mother.'

This Armand then grinned at me as the others chuckled and he released me from his grip. I nodded and smiled back, my face a picture of gratitude.

'Hard to be offended by people so foul that a dog wouldn't

fuck 'em,' I said in a sweet tone. The Irishman straightened his spectacles and coughed.

'And now you can safely believe that nobody here speaks your language either so,' he said, as most of the mob began to shuffle away, their interest in me waning already. 'You can count yourself lucky, very lucky indeed, that none of them were bluffing to you about that.' I bent down and retrieved my hat from the floor.

'I take it an apology won't be forthcoming, then,' I said as I dusted it off. I received no reply and so then I went outside to look for Nick. He was nowhere to be seen, but then neither was the boy soldiers. I reasoned that there was no purpose in searching for him, as he would be able to look after himself and so stepped back into the shop again. 'How about an explanation though?' I said to the Irishman. 'Those blows will bruise and your Man of God over there don't seem too bothered.'

'You were spotted by a local,' he said as I rubbed my forehead to see if a bump had sprouted, 'coming up the road there. They didn't like the sound of you and your young friend, they suspected you of being police spies.'

'But why?' I asked, with real indignation. I could not imagine a deeper insult.

'Because you don't look right,' he said, surveying me from neckerchief to shoes. 'And because they expect spies on days like today. But not even the most suspicious among them would think that the authorities would employ an Englishman to report on us.'

I could see now that there was even more menacing characters lurking in the darker corners of this wine shop, all of them carrying firearms. A door at the back of the shop opened and revealed a staircase, down which some more women entered, followed by a dark-skinned man. However, I saw no one what matched the description of Hugo DeFarge.

'Why would a police spy be expected on a day like today?'

'Just the sort of question a police spy would ask,' the unsmiling Irishman replied. 'Now, do you want to buy a bottle of wine or not? I'm hoping you say yes as we could use the money.'

It felt strange to then follow him through this hostile bar, full of people who did not seem to be patrons but was just lurking there as if waiting on judgement day, all ready to beat up the first random stranger who walks into the place. I had been expecting DeFarge's wine shop to be a dangerous place full of criminals – a Parisian Three Cripples – but I saw now that this was not the situation. These people did not carry themselves in a furtive way like criminals do, but more like soldiers readying themselves for battle. It unsettled me, as the criminal mind was one that I understood well and had been prepared to meet here, but these revolutionary sorts was far less familiar to me.

'Is there a particular wine you were hoping to sample?' the Irishman asked me once he was behind the bar and had picked up a corkscrew. 'Do you have a favourite?'

'Oh, I'm happy to drink either,' I assured him as I opened my coin purse and hoped to make sense of the foreign money within. 'Red or white.'

'A sophisticated palate,' he remarked as he poured me a glass of the cheapest claret. I then ordered a plate of creamy cheeses and some bread to go with it. I told him that my young brother would be sure to reappear in time, although the Irishman did not seem much interested in me once he had taken the money.

'This your place, is it?' I asked him.

'I work here.'

'So whose place is it?'

'It belongs to the owner.'

'He about?'

'Why is that your concern?'

'It ain't. I'm just making conversation. How did an Irishman like you end up working in Paris, then?'

'I came to France on a boat.'

'And your name is?'

'My own concern.'

'Mine is Jack,' I said. 'How do you do?'

He had been avoiding meeting my eye until then, but the moment that I said my name he raised an eyebrow in this curious way as if he thought this an unlikely boast.

'Jack is it?' he peered at me. 'I thought you said you were just passing by?'

'I was.'

'What is your brother called, then?' He seemed troubled by my answers, as if they contained some sort of riddle that he was expected to solve. 'Jack too?'

'Who ever heard of two brothers called Jack?' I answered, becoming even more confused than he appeared to be. The

Irishman opened his mouth as if about to tell me something and then shut it again.

'Enjoy your wine,' he said at last and moved away from me.

Once alone I took myself over to one of the barrelled tables where I hoped to just sit there inconspicuous and get a proper feel of this dark hole I had come such a long way to rob. But first, I wasted no time in filling my glass and knocking back almost half of it in one strong gulp. The sensation was sweet bliss. A group of old soldiers sat at a nearby table all looked over at me in disgust at what I supposed was my unwillingness to swirl, sniff and savour the grape, but, considering how I had been thinking about little else other than liquor and puff ever since I had arrived in his country, they was lucky I was not just swigging it straight from the bottle. Once the contents of the first glass was done with, I started filling it up again with a view to taking this next drink a little slower.

So now that I was well ensconced within that shop, and with the warm reinvigorating medicine of the wine slipping down my throat, I set about surveying the glum interior to see whether I could glean anything useful about where the wedding certificate might be hidden. Behind the bar I had seen a well-guarded cash box into what the Irishman had put my coins, but there was no safe or desk where a valuable document might be kept. The door at the back what led to the staircase was unguarded for now, but it would be unlikely that I could vanish back there to explore the rooms beyond without drawing attention to myself. So instead I just tried to observe all I could about this front bar. Not only was there countless wine bottles poking out behind racks all along the rear wall of the bar, but they was also being employed on every table as candlesticks, and there was one on a windowsill what was keeping a faulty pane up. As this was a hot day, all the windows was open to let in the air but, like the front door, these too was screened with thin silk to discourage outside spies so that the shop was dimmer and more musty than it needed to be. Despite this, I could still get a good glim of the various characters what was all bustling about the place and saw that the wine shop was getting busier now. Those butchers what I had passed on the street outside had since entered, still wearing their aprons of dripping blood and clutching meat cleavers, yet they bought no wine. Then more tradespeople followed them in, then another clergyman, the washer-women, some families with young children, a lady in black widows' weeds, two sailors and plenty of strong coves wearing labourers' smocks. All of these people was armed in some way or other and they begun to mill around as if this was a sort of social gathering, rather than a dingy open shop. They must all be regular faces as nobody received the same rough treatment what I did as they stepped in.

Those two women what had stood with the men and brandished weapons into my face upon my arrival was now slinking their way towards my table with a new and far gentler attitude. They was both much more affectionate and appealing when unarmed and it was as if the whole unpleasant business of earlier was forgotten. The one in the red dress circled where I sat, stroked my back with her fingers and spoke in soft purring tones.

'*Salut monsieur*,' said the one wearing the white dress, who had earlier grazed my neck with the tip of her long sword. She touched her breast. 'Babette,' she told me.

'*Bonjour* Babette,' I smiled in return, impressed with myself at having mastered their language to a conversational standard already. 'Jack.'

'*Jack?*' repeated the red dress and she shrugged at her friend and muttered something I could not follow. Then she placed her hand upon her own chest. 'Adele.'

'Well, that's the introductions out of the way,' I continued in English, 'now perhaps you fair ladies would be so kind as to help me polish this bottle off. Pull yourselves up a chair.' I motioned for them to do just this and then clicked my fingers at the nameless Irishman behind the bar. '*Garçon,*' I called over, 'two more glasses, thanking you, and another bottle. After all, as I told you earlier, I'm partial to both the red and the white.'

As a child of the London rookeries, I have always enjoyed the company of an honest whore. Most of the women I knew, and had ever known, was what the reading classes referred to as 'fallen', including sweet Nancy who had been like a bigger sister to me before that bastard Sikes did her a permanent mischief. And so, in all truth, I had a lot more in common with these two than I did with either of the snobby Lamoreaux siblings, regardless of any language barrier. There was a natural affinity here and therefore I was more than happy to be convivial and buy the drinks for this fair pair, and in the absence of another paying customer, they was happy to let me.

The brute priest was back again and he stomped through the length of the shop with a furious face on, growling something unholy at me as he passed. Babette patted my hand in a *pay him no mind* gesture, continuing to try to convince me to take either her or Adele, or indeed both of them, upstairs to some room, through a series of skilful and well-practised hand gestures. But I was far more interested to see where the priest was going as he left through that back door to the staircase beyond and headed to the floor above, soon followed by bearded Armand. Now that I was listening out for it, I could hear all sorts of activity going on in the floor above this. There was a lot of stamping and raised voices coming through the ceiling and I pointed upwards and made a questioning gesture to the girls. They waved my concerns away and helped themselves to more of my cheese.

It was then that a great commotion could be heard coming up the lane from the open window to my left. Someone was approaching the wine shop, singing a jaunty marching song in a loud but unsteady voice and, for once, it was not *La Marseillaise*. Various other voices could be heard joining in with him, to the point where there was soon a full street chorus, although the lead singer himself appeared to struggling to stay in tune. The children what had been rushing about in the street was now cheering and laughing in delight and the man interrupted his singing to laugh too.

'Zhay Zhay!' the man roared and the children could be heard running towards him. 'Zhay Zhay!'

Every face in the wine shop, including the old cavalry men,

the two whores either side of me and the nameless Irishman, was all now turned towards the silk-screened door to see the man about to enter though it. There was a suspenseful pause and outside I could hear him say '*oof!*' as if some awkward kerfuffle had slowed him down.

Then we heard him counting. *Urn. Der. Twa.*

The silk curtain was ripped from its railings by a gigantic stonemason's hammer, the biggest I had ever seen, charging into the shop. Carrying this mighty tool was a smiling, muscular man, who had to crouch down as he passed through the doorway on account of the small child what was clinging to his shoulders in an ecstasy of giggles. Two more children trailed in after him and the whole room gasped and cleared a space as the hammer's head landed with a hefty thump in the centre of the room. Behind this man, two more huge hammers entered through the doorway, carried by two men apiece. Everyone laughed at what a muddle they all made of their own entrances in comparison to that of the first and I was surprised to see that among this small entourage of boys was my criminal assistant Nick, who winked at me as he cheered along with the others, as if they was all lifelong friends. I then noticed that somebody had locked the door behind them once the final man was in.

This entry man, who had on a brown waistcoat but was otherwise bare-chested and bronzed from the summer sun, straightened his back and exhaled as if he had been carrying that burden for miles. The entire shop, apart from my own uncomprehending self, burst into applause as he pulled a handkerchief from out of his pocket and mopped his sweaty but handsome face with it. He began to let the boy down from his back all gentle, the same boy what had collided with Nick just outside the shop.

On the evening before I had been shown a drawing of a cove who looked nothing like this here man, save for how they both bore sword scars down their left cheeks. It appeared that young Jerome had indeed allowed personal bias to get in the way of artistic realism.

'ARMAND!' roared Hugo DeFarge to the ceiling above. 'BRUNO! PIERRE!' he kept bellowing names with tremendous enthusiasm.

From behind the back door we heard what sounded like a herd of elephants come clattering down the staircase. In burst the bearded Armand, who was followed by the man dressed as a priest. They was both followed by about a dozen other burly men and just as many fierce women what I had not even seen before now. My red and white companions had deserted me by then as they pushed through the ever-growing crowd to see the excitement.

Armand embraced the chuckling DeFarge like they was long-lost brothers and the priest did likewise. DeFarge then appeared to challenge the priest, who he was calling Pierre, to lift the biggest hammer himself. Pierre obliged, but not without visible effort. Once he had it in the air, the priest could not resist swinging it and he just stopped himself from smashing one of the barrel tables in half. Uproarious laughter from all around, including from the priest himself, who seemed a much more jolly character now that the proprietor had arrived.

It was as though the whole place had been hit with a cannonball of charisma. DeFarge had lifted the spirits of the entire wine shop to such a pitch that it was hard to recall how sombre the place had been before his arrival. He then moved from person to person, greeting the men with manly embraces, calling them *mon ami*. The women – even the whores – he would kiss on the hand and call *ma cherie* – as though they was debutantes being presented to him at a ball.

An elderly man stepped forward. He had one sleeve of his faded cavalry jacket tied tight at the elbow and it was clear he had lost the limb in battle. A sword and sheath was buckled into his belt and as he greeted DeFarge, he seemed to shake a little. But he raised his good arm in salute and DeFarge seemed overcome with emotion and stood shaking his head at the nobility of it. Then, he pulled the little old boy into his chest for a manly embrace and kissed him on his bald head. It was, even for a disinterested observer such as myself, a most touching moment.

'*Messieurs! Mesdames!*' he began and clicked his fingers as if commanding something to be placed into his hand. Babette came forward with the same sword she had pointed at me and what was now sheathed. She presented him with the handle. '*Mesdemoiselles! Les enfants!*' he continued as he whipped the sword free and held it high enough to carve his name into the ceiling plaster. And then he roared a sentence what it seemed everyone in the room had been aching to hear.

'VOICI LA REVOLUTION!'

The eruption what followed, as all weapons was raised in the air and every man, woman and child roared back at him like warriors, could have torn the very roof off the place.

Chapter 11

The Club of a Thousand Jacks

I take a lesson in philosophy

The French, I had already observed, are a very expressive people. They go in for a lot more gesturing and physical performance than we English tend to, so things was easier to understand than I had expected. What followed then, and what according to the clock above the door went on for a good thirty minutes, was a rousing speech from this Hugo DeFarge what began with some archly satirical jibes at the cowards who was now quivering at home in their beds, turned into a sentimental tribute to these here brave revolutionaries what had joined with him today, then veered into a passionate and furious rant about the injustices heaped upon the poor by a complacent government, building to a battle-mongering call to arms which almost provoked a riot, before eventually rounding its way back to the sentimental stuff. Following political rhetoric is never that difficult, even when it is being spoken in a foreign language.

This crowd seemed to love him, some even looked like they was about to turn faint from the adoration. Throughout his whole performance – and it *was* a performance as much as it was anything – they shouted out what could only be popular slogans against the Second Republic. Among that chorus of sedition there was one voice what seemed to be even more passionate about it then anyone.

'*Mort au Petit-Bourgeois!*' screeched Nick and the young boys what he had been cavorting with outside all stamped their feet and cheered in approval. I could not tell if he was playing the part of a rabid revolutionary in order to fit in, or whether he had gone full native, but either way, he was accepted into the gang already. There was a pretty little red-haired girl of about his age, holding onto a strange tin and chanting along in just as vicious a way as the boys, while what seemed to be her parents stood either side of their sweet cherub and beamed down at her with tender pride.

Inspired by such happy displays of audience interaction, I decided that now was my time to stop playing the wallflower and to get involved with the party myself. After all, I had learnt a few revolutionary slogans in the short time that I had been in France.

'*Rappelez Rouen!*' I hollered from my position near the back corner of the bar and I thumped my fist upon the table to emphasise my strong feelings upon the matter. '*Rappelez Rouen* say I!'

At this, those closest to me all turned around and nodded in approval and my words was echoed around the room in tones of great gravity. Adele and Babette both clapped and somebody said *Bravo!*

Hugo DeFarge, however, paused in his oratory and craned his

neck over at me to see what unfamiliar voice had spoken. There was a sea of people between where he was standing high upon that barrel and where I sat around mine with a glass of claret still in my non-thumping hand. But it was clear that noticing someone he did not recognise in this little castle of his had an immediate and unsettling effect upon the man and, for the first time since his spectacular entrance, he appeared perturbed. He jumped off his barrel, handed the sword to someone else and began striding towards me, fists clenched. The sea between us parted as if for Moses.

He asked me a question as he drew up close and pointed a finger at me like it was another pistol. Then he repeated the question. The entire place went quiet and I flicked my eyes over our audience before answering. Each face had now taken their hero's lead and they all regarded me with deep suspicion once more. I could not see Nick now but, from somewhere at the far end of the room, I heard his helpful voice. 'He's asking you your name!'

'Jack,' I shrugged and then took another sip from the glass as if to say, 'what of it?'

There was a tense moment as DeFarge examined my face, what I was wearing, even the remaining cheese on my plate. Then, with a pugilist's swiftness, he circled the barrel and his arms was around me, pulling me close. I panicked and almost spilled my drink but was too relieved to care when I realised that he was treating me to one of his manly embraces, rather than a sharp left hook.

'*Bienvenue, Jacques!*' he laughed and ruffled my hair like I was one of the kinchins he had entered the wine shop with. The crowd burst into applause again and many of those closest to me patted me on the arm as if I had just won a competition. Then, DeFarge began jabbering on at me in French in an excitable fashion and it was clear that he expected my linguistic abilities to extend beyond just stating my name and repeating overheard slogans. I was much relieved when my assistant at last managed to shove his way through the crowd towards us so that he could act as my interpreter.

'Monsieur DeFarge,' Nick said on approach and he bowed towards him. He introduced himself as Nicolas but did not pronounce the Saxon-sounding s at the end of the name. He then continued speaking French but in that same grovelling manner that he had to me when he had broken into my crib. I could hear him repeating the word *monsieur* as often as he called me 'Sir,' and he seemed to be explaining who we was. DeFarge seemed to struggle to understand Nick's attempt at the language at first, but he was delighted to learn that we was English.

'*Jacques Anglay!*' he grinned and delivered me a matey punch to the breast. 'Englishman Jack! Welcome here.' He spoke English in a slow and concentrated manner and then he also bowed. 'It is pleasure to have you to fight with us.' He stepped backwards into the main area of the bar again, his disciples crowding around him in a circle. He lunged towards one and asked him his name, as he had me. The man laughed as if in on a joke and reached into his inside pocket. Out of that he produced a playing card what he held into the air and what looked to be the Jack of Clubs.

'Jack One!' DeFarge presented him to us, much to the room's merriment. 'Jack Two?'

Another man stepped forward and said *'voila!'* as he too pulled a card out of his pocket. This also displayed the Jack of Clubs. At this, another man whipped out the very same card from his pocket and declared himself to be the third Jack. Then, as if they had been waiting for this moment all along, the vast majority of the onlookers revealed that they all had about their person that very same card. Babette and Adele both lifted their skirts to reveal that theirs was kept inside their garters.

'A thousand Jacks!' Hugo DeFarge cheered and he swivelled on his boot-soles to face me, holding out his arms as if waiting for me to provide the capper to the whole comical scene. I could do nothing but smile back at him and hope that the moment would pass without comment.

'You're not a member of our club, are you Londoner?' said the Irishman behind the bar in a bored tone. 'Just some chancer with a coincidentally fortunate name. And when our man there realises that,' he adjusted his spectacles again, 'things'll turn awkward.'

Monsieur DeFarge seemed to have already realised it for himself and he lowered his arms, his face more disappointed than angry. At this, his people began hiding their playing cards again as if they regretted revealing them to us. I turned to Nick.

'I don't suppose there's any chance you've got a Jack of Clubs on you, eh?' I asked him. He bit his lip.

'I was sort of hoping you would,' he said.

The brute priest stepped forward as if readying to beat the last breath out of me at DeFarge's command. But his leader signalled for him to cool down and then addressed me himself.

'For why are you here, Englishman Jack?' His accent was thick and his wording uncertain. 'Are you *client . . .*' he waved his hand towards my wine and cheese, 'or spy?'

'My brother and I have travelled here to meet you,' I replied, knowing that the time for me to keep pretending that we was just passing custom was over. 'Hugo DeFarge.'

'Why?' he asked.

'You have a famous name,' I explained. 'You have a famous family.'

'In England my family is famous?'

'Among some, yes. Your grandparents was heroes of the revolution. They are admired in London, as are you.'

'You come here for the revolution?' he looked very surprised. 'From London?'

'Yeah,' I nodded. 'My brother and myself want to help you overthrow the government.'

DeFarge looked over at the Irishman, who was still behind the bar, and once my words had been translated, he turned back to me. 'Englishman and revolutions,' he said, dismissive. 'No such thing.'

'Wrong, cos there's a pair of English revolutionaries looking right at you,' I protested and Nick nodded in support. 'We've travelled all the way from London on account of how we heard you needed our help.'

'All them killings what went on in Rouen, Monsieur DeFarge,

sir,' Nick interjected 'was an *outrage.*' He had pronounced the last word in French, what impressed even me.

'And it ain't just us,' I smiled. 'There are hundreds of Londoners of our acquaintance what feel the same way. We are here to offer you their support 'n all.'

Nick began trying to translate that into French, but found himself interrupted by the sour-faced Irishman.

'This is all cockney shite,' the Irishman said. 'Londoners are not revolutionary people in my experience, you're all too in thrall to that fat potato of a queen. Even if you did have revolutionary blood coursing through your veins, there are injustices enough in your own country to be attending to. Why would you travel all the way down here to revolt?'

'I've got a French mother and a French father!' Nick responded before I had a chance to. 'Or I did until they died on me. Which means I care more about what's going on here than some bogtrotter would. More important, why are you here?'

'Because I'm fleeing the blight!' the Irishman replied with a flash of anger. For a short second, I wondered if he had just told me his name, Flean the Blight.

'Is that Irish slang for something?' I asked.

'I'm talking about the Great Famine, you ridiculous oaf. The one that has been devastating my land and starving my people to death, or ain't you ever heard of it? Because if you have not, and I can tell from your gawping English fizz that you haven't, then it's hard to imagine that you're so politically minded that you'd march to a whole other country to fight and die amongst foreigners.'

While he had been delivering this case for the prosecution, the rest of the wine shop had been watching us in uncomprehending silence, as if waiting for the verdict to be delivered. DeFarge himself had folded his arms as he tried to make sense of our conversation. It would be him who would decide the punishment if we was found guilty of lying.

'You're an imposter,' concluded the Irishman, 'it's as plain as your face. Your boy there is no more French than I am.' Nick began hurling French swearwords at him, but I touched his shoulder.

'Remember why we came here, *mon frère*,' I said to him in a calming voice, for DeFarge to hear. Then I reached into my pocket and produced something far more useful to me than a Jack of Clubs would ever be. I had brought along my very own Ace of Spades. An envelope with two pieces of paper inside.

'Monsieur DeFarge,' I said to him, 'I have been sent here to you on an errand. I said that you had admirers in London. It is true. There is a secret club of which I am myself a member. We call ourselves The Friends of DeFarge.'

From behind the bar I heard the Irishman snort his disbelief, but I kept my eyes fixed upon the shop owner as Nick did his best to translate my words. DeFarge smiled as I knew he would. Whenever anyone would stroll into the Seven Dials and declare that they have heard all about the legend of the Artful Dodger, I was always well flattered too.

'I have come to Paris to deliver this in your hour of need,' I said and held out the envelope. 'I think you will appreciate what it contains.'

DeFarge looked at my outstretched arm for a few moments and hesitated. But then he took it from me, opened it up, took out the first piece of paper, unfolded it and stared. There was a pause as I wondered how he was going to take seeing so unflattering an image but, to my great relief, he burst into laughter.

'*Zhay Zhay!*' he cried out then, turned to the little boy who had entered on his shoulders and beckoned him forward. '*Regardes!*' The boy, who had been clinging onto Adele's skirt all this while, came forward and was shown the drawing. '*Ton père, Zhay Zhay!*' smiled his father as he showed him the picture Jerome had drawn on the night before.

'It ain't a good likeness, I'll admit,' I said as this little JJ looked at me as if thinking that I was the one what had drawn it and shook his head in disapproval. 'But that there picture was given to me by someone in the secret club so that I could recognise you.'

'Who did this?' DeFarge Senior asked.

'It wouldn't be much of a secret club if I told you that now, would it?'

He shook his head in amused wonder and walked over to the counter, lifted the flap and went behind to where the Irishman was. Then he produced a pin from somewhere, came back out from behind the counter and pinned the picture up high on a wooden column near the stone fireplace.

'*C'est DeFarge!*' he announced to the room, smiling. Then, as his many minions all chuckled at the crudeness of the picture, he turned to me and wagged a finger like I was some mischief-maker whose satirical artwork he was prepared to enjoy with good humour.

'The only purpose of the picture is so that I would know who to give the true gift to,' I told him and pointed again at the envelope. 'Take a look.'

When Hugo DeFarge looked at the second paper that the envelope contained, he did not find it so droll. It was the one I had shown the Lamoreaux over dinner on the night before and I had been counting upon its impact ever since I was first told about this job. DeFarge blinked at it in disbelief and his face scrunched up as if the very confusion that it provoked was painful to him. He looked up at me and asked me what I meant by it.

'It is a British bank note,' I explained. 'The bank is Tellson's and the name on the account is a false one, but belongs in truth to the Friends of DeFarge. Between us we have been putting money into an account for many years. The note has been written out to you, and, as you can see from the figure written on the line there, it is a lot of money.' I turned to the Irishman. 'What is five hundred pounds in French currency?'

Once that figure had been translated, Armand and the brute priest ran up to DeFarge to see if the number was true. But the man himself kept glaring at me.

'Joke?' he asked in a way what suggested that for my own health it had better not be.

'No joke,' I assured him. 'Bank it and you'll see.'

In truth, when I had first thought of handing over such a note to Hugo DeFarge I had planned to do it on a Sunday. But what with this revolution seeming as though it was about to explode at any given moment, I thought it unlikely that any bank would be open today and so decided to risk it. The note itself had belonged to some unfortunate cove whose pocket I had picked months before and I considered it unlikely that he had anything approaching that figure in his account.

DeFarge conferred with his two principal cronies for a spell and I glanced down at Nicolas Rigaud. His face was all innocence, but I knew he understood how vigilant he would need to be if DeFarge was to accept the gift. I had gotten Celeste to write out the name and figures on the night before, as my own handwriting would never have convinced him of its veracity. When I had hatched this idea about the Friends of DeFarge I had only thought to exploit the memory of his grandparents, but the discovery that he ran such a large political club played into my hands even more. He was an ambitious man, this was evident, and ambitious men was not known to turn down funding.

At length, DeFarge looked back at me again and took a step closer. He sneered something that sounded ugly and then held the banknote up in the air as if ready to rip it into shreds. Then his sneer vanished and his laugh returned. He embraced me once more and called me something what Nick translated as 'brother until death.'

He thanked me for bringing him such a boon, folded the bank note up and placed it in his pocket. From now on, we had to keep this man under watch at all times. He would need to lock that note up somewhere secure. He would be bound to put it in a safe with other valuable papers and this would show us where the wedding certificate was. It was one of the oldest criminal tricks in the trade. If you want to know where a man keeps his valuables, give him another and see where he puts it.

By then, many of the thousand Jacks had grown tired of listening to myself and DeFarge talk for too long in a language they did not understand and a fair few, including Armand and the priest, had broken off into groups to discuss other matters. DeFarge was still preoccupied with me though and he picked up his son, whispered in his ear and introduced him as Jean-Jacques in a more formal fashion.

'His mother and I named him after Rousseau,' DeFarge said as he placed JJ down onto the floor. 'You know Rousseau?'

'As if he was an old friend,' I smiled back, although I had never heard the name before in my life.

Little Jean-Jacques and my Nick spoke to one another in a friendly way and I was glad to see that they had bonded well during their time away from the shop. A burgeoning friendship between them was something I might be able to use to my advantage later on.

'You wish to fight in a revolution, Englishmen?' DeFarge asked us.

'I can think of nothing I would enjoy more, Monsieur DeFarge,' I told him. 'Although my brother here must stay out of it for now. He is too young for danger.'

Nick shot me a look as though I had just betrayed him.

'Call me Hugo,' said our host, pronouncing it *Oogo*. 'And I do not let JJ here fight either,' he said, ruffling his son's black hair. 'Fighting is for men!' He slapped me on the shoulder again. 'Not children.'

'When do we start, Hugo?' I asked. 'I'm straining at the slip here.'

'We start when *Les Club des Clubs* tells us we can start,' he rolled his eyes heavenward as if talking about a bossy wife. 'Tomorrow, we hope.'

'Well, until that happy day my brother and myself are in need of lodgings. Any chance we can stay here for the night? That way, I can be up bright and early for the big battle tomorrow, if we should be so blessed with one.'

'*Bien sûr!*' he cheered and he placed his son back down onto the floor. 'After such generousness,' he tapped his pocket, 'I must not refuse.' Then he told JJ to take Nick upstairs and prepare a room for us. I was pleased about this development, as it would give Nick a chance to explore the house for any safes or locked rooms what might prove interesting. 'They play together well,' he said as we watched the two kinchins scramble up the staircase to the rooms above.

'It is good when boys make friends,' I agreed.

'It is good when *men* make friends,' he laughed and put an arm around me as he walked me over to join some of his other friends. 'We shall play well together too, I think, you and I.'

'Yeah,' I nodded. 'We'll be good and close.'

Chapter 12

Man is Born Free

But everywhere he is in chains

Soon after that they began revealing the secret hatches. Hugo, once comfortable that everyone who had gathered into his shop was either a friend of his, a card-carrying member of the Club of a Thousand Jacks, or a well-meaning foreigner like myself, began to order the many wooden tables and stools to be cleared from the middle of the floor and the rugs to be removed. The members did his bidding and uncovered three trapdoors what I suppose was for storing wine barrels, but, from the smell of metal and gunpowder as they was lifted upwards by hooks, they now contained crates full of artillery. There was two of these thick wooden boxes in each hatch, and the abler men of the club hauled them out. At DeFarge's instruction, they began taking them out the back of the shop and up the flight of stairs. The rest of us was then invited to march off after them up that tight passageway, and so, with one eye never far from DeFarge, I found myself following the scores of other revolutionary volunteers upwards through his crooked and many-storeyed home and into the long and spacious room above.

This was the room in which I had heard people stomping around in earlier. At the far end, there was a long table what had the largest tricolore flag I had seen draped across it as a makeshift tablecloth. The wooden crates was all placed upon this table and prised open. Inside was dozens of muskets, double-loaders and pistols. Such boxes can only have been looted from an arms factory, they was so well stocked. The brute priest began handing out weapons to everyone. I reached in and took out a handy pistol and it was not just for show. I did not much fancy being the only unarmed cove in the place.

There was not many children here in this room now, but the little red-haired girl was still among us and she went around with her small tin what contained many bullets. I took some from her to load my own gun with and said *merci beaucoup* as her ever-smiling parents looked on. Behind the table, a number of what I took to be DeFarge's closest disciples, including that horrible priest, jostled themselves into their seats at this long table as if about to commence a town meeting. The chair in the centre of the table was still unoccupied, but there was no doubt as to who was to sit there. The whole scene reminded me of a print I had once seen of *The Last Supper* and we all waited for DeFarge to plonk himself down in the Jesus chair. But he was still stood close to the entrance of the room, encouraging everyone as they entered.

Once the room was as packed with as many ready, willing and able revolutionaries as it would hold, and the huge window on the opposite wall what overlooked the street was opened to let in the air, DeFarge leaned out through the doorway and whistled. The Irishman appeared from below and I saw DeFarge peer around at the packed room, before removing the bank note from his pocket and slipping it to his employee as they whispered to one another. I tried getting closer to them so I could overhear what was being said, but considering it would have been in French anyway, such action was futile. After giving the Irishman what seemed to be a series of instructions, DeFarge reached down to his leather belt and unhooked a small bunch of keys what he handed over. Then the Irishman nodded, left the room and I saw him head up the next flight of stairs before DeFarge shut the door after him.

This was a most frustrating turn, as it was my job to follow that note, but I was now stuck in here with this hot rabble. If the Lamoreaux wedding certificate was indeed in this building, then there was a strong chance that it was where the Irishman was now headed. I knew that if I left to shadow him now, it would draw suspicion, so I had no choice but to remain with the club and continue my search later. DeFarge weaved his way through the crowd towards his seat behind the table. He remained standing, while in front of him someone had laid out a large street map of what I supposed must be Paris. It was the sort of map what a coachman might use and was covered in inky notations. DeFarge motioned for his congregation to huddle closer so they could see what he wished to indicate on it and, even though I could not understand much of what he was instructing us all in, I knew a battle strategy when I heard it being spelled out. DeFarge was pointing at various streets where he had already drawn bold marks. I understood only one word, which appeared to be the same both in French as in English – *barricade*.

The name General Cavaignac was spoken a lot, and without fail caused an outburst of violent cursing from the club whenever mentioned. By contrast, a mighty cheer would erupt whenever the name Blanqui was evoked But I did not much care who either of these people was, as I had no interest in fighting in no revolution anyhow. The social injustices what had beleaguered France of late did sound very terrible, but it was all far from being my problem. I had a shop to burgle. I was becoming anxious to do this sooner rather than later, so that I could get Nick and myself well clear of this shop, vicinity and even the city before the fighting began for real.

So I edged towards the door with a view to slipping out of it unseen and exploring the upper rooms alone, when a huge uproar was heard from outside the window what drew everyone's attention towards it. DeFarge rolled up the map again in a hurry, darted around the tricolore table and through the crush of people, to answer the many voices what was now calling to him from the street outside his shop. The crowd surged with him and there was great excitement at whatever was being shouted. I decided that there would be no better distraction than this. But, just before I could leave, Adele and Babette came up behind me and began trying to explain what the fuss was.

'Les Club des Clubs,' Adele beamed in excitement and so I had no choice but to smile back, as if I was as delighted about their appearance here as she was. I let them escort me closer to

the window, where DeFarge was questioning those who was shouting up at him.

From what I had already gathered, this club what Hugo DeFarge was the leader of was just one of a cluster of revolutionary gangs and they could not strike out against the government until a higher body, this Club of Clubs, had given all the smaller clubs the nod. I worried, as I watched DeFarge become even more impassioned by what he was hearing, if this here was that long awaited nod.

Stood next to DeFarge was that hairy ape Armand and he had in his hands a military rifle what faced the ceiling. He looked towards his master, as if awaiting an order and, once the men from the clubs had stopped speaking, DeFarge thanked them, clapped his hands over his head and cried out something to the whole district. Armand then pointed the rifle out of the window, into the air and fired two shots across the tops of the neighbouring houses. Roof-tiles was heard smashing, but in the next second, this sound was replaced with that of a crowd gone wild, the sheer roar of a people unleashed. They howled and stamped their feet together, this whole fallen community untied in a sudden frenzy. I even feared that the floor beneath us would give way and we would all go tumbling down into the bar beneath. Adele and Babette, in particular, seemed to be overcome with a furious ecstasy as they grinned at me and raised their weapons in the air. Outside, drumming commenced and there was a discordant, strangulated bugling from somewhere as several competing renditions of *La Marseillaise* sounded up. DeFarge then slammed the windows shut and cut through the stampers, as he began leading his ready army out of the doorway and back down the steps. I left through the door before him and, as he went through, I asked him if he knew where my young brother was.

'If this here is revolution at last, Hugo,' I said to him with a genuine urgency, 'I must speak to Nick first. You know, *mon frère*. Where did your son take him?'

Hugo paused and stared at me as if, for a moment, he was contemplating not answering. Then he pointed up the stairs to the floors above, as I knew he must. I thanked him and turned away to search, but before I had even reached the next landing on this tall house, I ran into Nick who had just appeared from behind one of the doors.

'This is it, Dodger,' he said, panting with excitement. 'Did you understand what those men out there was saying? I did, or most of it. It's time! They're going to fight the army! The proper French army!' He was bouncing on his toes as he told me this and, when he noticed the pistol I was holding, he regarded me with what can only be described as hero worship. 'Are you going to help them?'

'Of course not,' I whispered. His bouncing stopped and the buzz vanished. 'That ain't why we're here, is it?'

I cast my eyes about, both up the stairs and down, to ensure that we could speak unheard. 'The Irishman,' I spoke low, once I was certain we would not be overheard.

'His name's Brendan,' Nick replied. 'JJ told me.'

'He came up these stairs. See him?'

The boy nodded. 'JJ was showing me the rooms above. It's

a big house, bigger than it looks. Brendan walked right past us and went up to the garret.'

'Is he still up there?'

'*Nicolas?*' a high voice called out, pronouncing it the French way. It came from behind the door my assistant had just come out of, and could only be DeFarge's son. Nick turned and spoke in French but it sounded like JJ had not understood him.

'He's frightened,' Nick explained to me. 'Thinks his papa's going to get killed today.'

'He could well be right,' I said and stopped myself from making any further comment about how such a thing could be of benefit to us. The dark truth, that dead men are easier to steal from, had flashed through my mind but I chastised myself for even thinking it. Back when I was truly artful I had never wished death upon anyone I was stealing from, so I should not start now. 'Does he speak any English?'

'Not a word.'

'Then let's go in and comfort him. We can speak more free if we make it look like a nice brotherly chat.'

The room in which little Jean-Jacques DeFarge was hiding was small and messy, containing as it did one small bed, a chest with all the drawers open and a carpeted floor what was covered with toy soldiers what it seemed he had been showing to Nick. JJ was a sweet little boy, a miniature version of his father. He was stood on the bed, looking out of the window at the revolutionaries below who had gathered onto the street. A chant of *OOGO! OOGO! OOGO!* was getting louder by the syllable. As he saw us come in, I felt even worse about my hope for his father's demise just moments before, as his face was full of fear. Nick crossed over to him and spoke some French, his words sounded comforting. I noticed that JJ was still clutching hold of a small stuffed bear what I had even seen him with downstairs in the bar, a toy he was far too old for. It caught my attention, as it was not unlike the stuffed mouse what had belonged to my adopted son and the memory of baby Robin that it provoked caused an ache within me.

There was two small portraits in picture frames on the wall of this room and they was even more ugly than the rough sketch of Hugo DeFarge what was pinned up downstairs. The first was of a rough, square-headed man wearing a blue cap, who possessed all the good looks of a Toby Jug. He stared out at the viewer as if fixing to murder them. The second portrait was even more alarming, a woman this time, with wild, witchy hair and a merciless snarl upon her lips. Whoever this woman was, she looked like she would be a stranger to any soft compromise and I questioned the wisdom of placing such startling images up on a child's bedroom wall. No wonder the little lad looked so scared.

'Right, Nick,' I said, once I had sat myself on the end of the bed and placed the pistol down next to me. 'We ain't got much time. Come over here so I don't have to speak loud.' Nick moved away from JJ and came to sit close by me. 'The Irishman has a bunch of keys,' I said in a soft, low way so that JJ would just think I was bidding my brother a sad farewell. 'We need them. Once we get them we'll leave this place and come back whenever we think it's unguarded. Understand?'

Nick nodded. 'The document we want could well be in the garret but, if not, it'll be somewhere locked up and that bunch will find it for us.'

'If we do get the keys,' my assistant suggested, 'we could get them copied, then return them before anyone notices they was gone.'

'Yeah, but this ain't London and I don't know no locksmiths,' I said. 'Nice thinking, though. The good thing is that we can use this revolution business as a distraction. I'll hide myself–'

'*Zhay Zhay?*'

The door to the bedroom opened and in walked JJ's father. I realised then that the chanting of Hugo's name below was a question. His club wanted to know where he had gotten to. The answer was here, staring at me with a musket in his hand.

'*Papa!*' exclaimed the boy and he dropped the bear and ran into the arms of his father. DeFarge kissed him and spoke in a gentle, consoling way. Then he released the boy from his embrace and turned to me.

'You know Madame DeFarge?' he said. It took me some seconds before I could conclude what he might mean by it.

'Your famous grandmother,' I replied at last and pointed at the picture behind me. 'That's her, is it? Well, bust me. And this must be the grandfather what led the storm on the Bastille. They're an handsome pair.'

DeFarge blinked, as if unsure whether or not I had made the comment as a joke. I had the nasty feeling that he had been listening at the door and had understood that we had been discussing stealing from him. He opened his mouth as if about to say something, but we was joined then in that tiny bedroom by Brendan the Irishman who, before noticing that myself and Nick was in there, handed DeFarge his keys back. The shopkeeper thanked him and they spoke in French while DeFarge attached the keys to his leather belt once more.

'The Friends of DeFarge,' he said then as he looked from Nick's face to mine. 'Time for revolution, eh?'

The cries of his name from outside became even louder and I became very afraid of what this meant. Those keys was what I most needed to find and steal the Lamoreaux document, and they was attached to a man what was about to lead the charge. That meant only one dreadful thing.

'We fight together, *non*?' DeFarge grinned and offered me his hand so I could get up from the bed. 'Side by side. How did you say?' he clicked his fingers as he looked back at Nick. 'Brothers until death, yes?'

I smiled back, despite a sudden horror at where things was about to go, and then turned to my wide-eyed assistant. Nick looked up at me from his sitting position on the bed.

'Stay here and be safe,' I told him as both DeFarge and Brendan waited for me to exit the room with them. 'Keep away from the windows and do not leave this shop until I get back. Someone needs to look after little JJ here.'

'What about you?' he asked, with what seemed to be a genuine concern for my wellbeing that may have come close to matching my own.

'Me? I've got a government to overthrow.' I picked the pistol up again and checked that it was loaded right. 'Won't be long.'

Chapter 13

Stonebreakers

In which I hear the people sing and, mostly, they are out of tune

There are those who come to Paris for the sheer romance of it. Others come to admire the history, the architecture, or to just stroll through the serene, flower-filled parks. But how many can boast that, on their first whole day since arriving in this enchanting city, a full-blown and bloody revolution broke out.

I suppose I must be one of the lucky ones.

Adele and Babette was waiting for us in the saloon bar when we reached the bottom of the stairs and they was both delighted to see that I was armed and ready to go. They grabbed me by each arm and giggled all childlike as they tried to tug me towards the front door. But I resisted, on account of wanting to stay close to Hugo DeFarge, who had crossed over to those big hammers he had brought home earlier and seemed to be deciding which one he was going to select. There was several other club members lingering in the bar, including a young farthing-faced man of about seventeen who was sporting a dusty old musketeer's tabard what looked like it could have belonged to an ancestor, and he was stood frozen, filled with understandable fear. But along came the growling Armand to shove him with the butt of his rifle, until the lad was forced to follow the others out of the room. Then Armand turned his attention to bullying an elderly man out of a chair and handed him a big cosh what he seemed to think the old boy was going to need out there. Meanwhile, Pierre the brute priest was showing no sympathy for the grieving woman in her widow's weeds as he shouted marching orders into her black-veiled face. I saw the back of her shoulders shake in sudden sobbing. There was some middle-aged women here too who seemed shocked to discover that being members of the Thousand Jacks meant that, now that the whistle had been blown, they was expected to follow Hugo DeFarge to their probable deaths.

However, these reluctant revolutionaries found a champion in the form of Brendan, who was busying himself doing the very opposite work to Armand and the priest. He removed the cosh from out of the hand of the elderly man and let him sit down again, he assured the grieving widow that she did not have to go anywhere she did not want to and prevented anyone else who was either too old, too young or too scared for battle from joining in. This behaviour brought him into conflict with DeFarge's lieutenants, who barked and prodded the little Irishman, but found him unwavering. It was looking like these angry men might start using their weapons on each other before they got to face the army, but their altercation was interrupted by DeFarge. He had now lifted the largest of the three hammers so that it was resting against his shoulder and he shouted something over that seemed to take Brendan's part.

Armand and Pierre relinquished their positions and stepped away from the fight. Armand was then summoned to take the second hammer.

'English Jack!' DeFarge called over to me and nodded towards the last remaining one. 'Let us break stones together!'

Adele and Babette both laughed as I struggled to pick up its heavy weight, then rushed over to help me tuck the pistol into my belt so I could hold the hammer steady. Adele produced a ribboned cockade from somewhere and pinned it to my shirt, while Babette unbuttoned the top three buttons on my shirt.

'Ain't you coming with us?' I asked Brendan when it became apparent that, despite his weapon, he was not preparing himself for war. I was hoping that this shop would be unprotected during the battle, so I could come back here once I had stolen those keys and search it without disturbance.

'My job is to guard the premises and the lives of those who remain here,' he replied with an upturned chin. Then he indicated the hammer I was holding. 'Your job is to destroy the roads. Hurry now, your fellow stonebreakers won't wait.'

DeFarge then let out a mighty battle cry and charged out of the shop with his hammer held high. The crowds outside went wild for him.

'Don't worry about your brother,' Brendan said in a grave voice, just before I followed. 'I'll make it my business to protect him also.'

'Thanks,' I said, and meant it. Then I held my hammer aloft and yelled 'Up the workers!' before racing off after Hugo DeFarge and the bunch of keys what dangled from his belt.

Outside, in those narrow streets of Saint Antoine, gunshots was being fired into the air all around, sabres was rattled, war-whoops echoed from every house and I pretended to join in with this full assault on an as-yet unseen government force. And it fell upon me that I should be a lot more scared by all of this mayhem than I felt. Now that I was running through the city with all the other revolutionaries, I discovered, to my own surprise, that I was not afraid at all. In truth, there was part of me what was even enjoying the thrill of it. Myself and the other two hammer-bearers was all running close together, like a trio of mythical thunder gods, and as I looked down at my grip, I saw that my hands was steadier than they had been in a long while.

More men and women with cockades on their smocks was now pouring out from the houses, most of them armed with some makeshift weapon or other. We all had to run hard to keep up with our club leader, who kept on surging through the crowds. We had been bringing up the rear of this great procession, but now DeFarge was barking at those ahead of us to clear a path so that we could race through them and take our place at the front of the charge. Ahead of us, the sea of people parted and cheered as we pushed on through and many patted me on the back as I passed. It seemed that these hammers was to be a big part of the proceedings and I was very much looking forward to smashing some stones with mine. Adele and Babette was running either side of me and shouting things what I guessed was all 'Death to This!' 'Down with That!'

DeFarge was leading the Thousand Jacks away from the

Saint-Antoine vicinity and back towards the direction of that
great besieged building what I had passed with Celeste earlier
that morning – the one what I was now hearing called the
Hôtel de Ville. I was already good and sweaty what with the
weight of the hammer and the unforgiving summer heat and
this was bringing on a wicked thirst. The sweet Adele made
my burden much lighter though by producing a flask from
somewhere, taking a swig herself and then offering me one.
She herself poured the welcome liquid into my mouth as we
kept on moving and I gulped it down, expecting it to be water.
Adele giggled when I spat out red wine in surprise, spraying
it all over my shirt and even over Babette's pretty white dress.
Babette did not seem to mind though and we all joked together
as we proceeded on, my spirits getting higher just by the mere
taste of the grape. I asked Adele for some more and she obliged.
My gullet received another invigorating swig of the delicious
wine what she had no doubt pinched from the shop, as she put
the flask to my lips with much tenderness and allowed me to
sup. Both my red- and white-dressed companions seemed to
have taken a shine to me and I was being treated to all manner
of affections. They took turns kissing me on the cheeks and,
seeing that my own hands was full, they undid every button
on my shirt to cool me as we ran.

We hurtled onwards and turned onto the main thoroughfare what led back towards central Paris. It was here where
the first true shock of the revolution hit me. Because what
had, until now, appeared to my foreign eyes like the brewing
of an exciting local street riot, was now revealed to be a true

insurrection on a gigantic scale. In sharp contrast to how quiet the streets had been when I had passed through them earlier, it seemed that the entire city was now populated with countless angry, flag-waving revolutionaries. These impassioned and weaponised masses must have all crawled out of their holes to march upon their oppressors since hearing from the Club of Clubs. They now dominated the wide public road what led back to the Hôtel de Ville. Despite all the talk, I do not think I had hitherto appreciated how big this army of people was. It felt like here was the entirety of France.

They was all streaming in from other vicinities, chanting their defiance or crowing out *La Marseillaise* in full, fierce voices. A raggedy old woman with a cart full of rotten vegetables charged alongside us and she seemed in a great hurry to throw them at someone. Even the horses had a revolutionary air about them and it was clear that every vehicle in sight belonged to the uprising. Public omnibuses had been commandeered, draped in the tricolore flags and packed with rabid men and women of all ages banging pots and pans along with the many street drummers and trumpeters. The music was savage and discordant but I also thought it the most rousing sound I had ever heard and, had my hands not been full, I would have clapped along with enthusiasm.

And, for an odd and fleeting moment, I almost found myself pitying any opposing militia what might be compelled upon their honour to stand against this mighty mob. Because, without question, it seemed to me, the people here would massacre them. But I pushed such foolish thoughts aside, as I was too busy falling in love with the sheer lawlessness of what was occurring. It was all starting to seem like a wonderful street festival and I could not recall the last time I had enjoyed myself so much. The thought struck me that Nick would love all this and that I had been wrong to forbid him from coming. He should be here next to me, I thought, sharing in the fun of it. In truth, I was getting so wrapped up in the carnival spirit of the day that I had to remind myself that I was there for work and that I must not get distracted and lose track of DeFarge.

'Where's this army then?' I asked my companions as one unsettling thought niggled at me – that an uprising was not an uprising unless there was someone to overthrow. 'Why aren't they fighting us yet?'

I could not help but fret that the absence of any visible enemy so far was a little too convenient and I wondered if anyone else thought that this itself was very ominous. But Adele and Babette did not understand my question, of course, and they joined in with the singing and encouraged me to do the same. I still did not know a word of *La Marseillaise* but the tune was catchy and so I hummed along in my clumsy English way, much to the amusement of all around. Strangers from other districts cheered me as I did so, made friendly but incomprehensible comments and all around there was a general happy atmosphere.

Now the crush of people was becoming denser and it was harder to keep pace with DeFarge. He was still haring his way through the crowd ahead in a hot fury, his hammer aloft and shouting all manner of sentences, most of which had the word

Revolution! in common. But he was a tall man and he now wore an old blue cap what I recognised as being the same one his grandfather had been wearing in that picture I saw earlier, so keeping track of his movements was possible, even within this chaos. So far the rush of the revolution followed one consistent channel what led, at last, to the Hôtel de Ville.

Here was where the first of their famous barricades was being raised, in the streets all around. I had never seen anything like it before as sunburnt and sweating heroes toiled with the skill of engineers to create these magnificent street obstructions what would help us take possession of the city. First, they went at the paving stones in the street with huge hammers, not unlike the one I was holding, and before long it would have been impossible for the army to charge through towards us on horseback, so ruined was the path. Then the stones was piled upon each other to form the base of the barricades which was then covered by the smashed-up wood of overturned carts, coaches and barrows which strengthened and fortified them further. They even smashed public benches, iron railings and what looked to be public urinals, so that they could build up the barricades.

And so, with magnificent vandalism, the first real blow against the powers what be had been struck, even if the powers what be was still not about to witness it. Everyone within sight seemed to be either part of this revolution or in support of it, and those not fighting made a good show of offering their supplies of ammunition to those who was. If there was any *petit-bourgeois* out and about, then they was having the good sense to keep quiet about it.

'*Les Jacques Milles!*' bellowed DeFarge, as those of us from his club reached the first of the barricades. He turned to see who from his district was still following him and pointed at each of us. He then beckoned us to join him as he approached another man wearing a similar cap to his own who was orchestrating the raising of the street. I placed my hammer down as they spoke and looked over at the Hôtel de Ville. Those few guards what had been positioned outside was still there and from this distance you could see them trembling, as the enemy forces surrounding them had multiplied since we passed them earlier, like crows around carrion. Still, no violence had broken out yet but the mob surrounding the building was becoming savage. I cast my eyes across the dangerous crowd and was surprised to see someone I knew.

It was Maria, the belligerent servant-girl who worked for the Lamoreaux's aunt. She did not notice me, as she appeared too busy spitting at the soldiers guarding the building and waving a kitchen knife in the air, as if practicing a deadly cut. My first thought was that this must mean that poor Jerome and Celeste would have been compelled to make their own meals that morning, but then I began to worry about their safety. After all, Nick had overheard her making violent remarks about both the siblings and this was the day on which servants rose up against their masters. Could the Lamoreaux be in any danger, I wondered? Perhaps they was already dead? I hoped that this was not true as I had grown to like them, for all their haughtiness and, what was more important, if they was to die then who would pay me for stealing the document?

While I had been preoccupied with that, DeFarge had continued talking to the other capped man, who I would guess was a leader of a different revolutionary club, from the sense of rivalry between them. Now it seemed like there was some sort of confrontation between the leaders, and the other cap appeared to be telling DeFarge that we of the Saint-Antoine suburb was too late and that everything here was well under way. DeFarge cursed, indicated the hammers and asked a question. The other club leader shrugged, but from the highest part of the barricade, a tall man whose whole self was covered in stone-coloured dust shouted down some instructions. DeFarge nodded and turned back to his club.

'Boulevard Saint-Denis!' he commanded, which I took it was where we Jacks was most needed. Then he darted off down one of the narrow roads what led away from this district. Before I made to chase after him, I looked over towards the Hôtel de Ville once more and saw that Maria was staring right at me with all the affection of a murderess. She whispered to a nasty-looking cove beside her about me, but I did not linger long enough in that vicinity for her to cause me any trouble. Instead, I picked up my masonry hammer again and followed the rest of the club after DeFarge.

Despite having only been in that strange city for less than a day, I had made good note of various buildings, churches, signs and other city landmarks what would help me mark my path should I get lost. But, despite that, I was already thrown off by the maze of it all and soon could not have even told you if we was heading north-east or south-west. As DeFarge disappeared up yet another obscure alleyway, I considered that this must be how twisted and bewildering London can be to those less familiar with it. The running continued through more tight and winding alleyways and underneath wooden posts what buttressed the sagging houses either side. My smoker's chest was now all of a wheeze and I called out to DeFarge ahead of me.

'We getting there?' I queried, as we at last emerged from the warren of alleyways onto a wide main street. 'I mean, as much as I 'preciate the exercise!'

'We arrive!' replied DeFarge as we approached a mighty two-legged tower what was not unlike a smaller Arc de Triomphe, but right in the centre of a main city street. 'Porte Saint-Denis,' DeFarge grinned as if knowing I would be impressed not just by the monument, but also by how the multitude had claimed it as their own. The bridge of it was occupied by scores of revolutionaries, waving flags and brandishing rifles and covering its base with all sorts of interesting graffiti. There was hundreds, perhaps even thousands, of armed insurgents here arguing and shouting at one another. Their quarrelling seemed to be about what was the best way to construct one of those barricades in the middle of the street. They had already begun prising up the paving stones with far inferior tools to the ones we was carrying and so it was good that we had been sent there. DeFarge cried out to them as we approached, introduced us as *Les Jacques Milles* and encouraged us to raise our masonry hammers aloft. The revolutionaries here was much happier to see us than those at the Hôtel de Ville had been and another blue-capped leader laughed and embraced DeFarge with warm affection.

Again, it seemed like there was no soldiers or any other authority figures about to fight. The mob had the run of the whole city and everyone – including myself – was loving the experience. It was as if we had upended the natural order of things and turned society on its head. Every window was employed as a firing post, from where men and women was leaning out with rifles and even these ready warriors was grinning and making jokes with one another. One gunman was playing the fool and shouting out something for the whole street to hear, and everyone in earshot was in hysterics. I asked Adele to translate for me, as I've always hated missing out on a joke, but her attempts to communicate his satirical material was even more baffling. Another sniper began shooting down the street lamps at the far west end of the street and some applauded his expert marksmanship as the glass shattered on each one, while others appeared to be berating him for the waste of ammunition.

It felt like an honour to be a part of all this. I had the sensation of being a hero, like I was part of something important, something bigger than myself. If you had asked me why I was there at that moment I would have told you that I was fighting for revolution and I would have meant it. The business of Hugo DeFarge's keys was almost forgotten.

DeFarge then strolled straight over to where a group of workers toiled nose-down in the street, trying to prise up the stubborn stone, raised his hammer above his head and, without alerting them to his actions, struck it down onto the ground, shattering the stones beneath into bits and causing splinters to explode into the faces of the men around him. They all cried out in hot protest, but there was no doubt that the action had an effect. Other insurgents cheered and ran over to raise up the street as DeFarge ordered Armand and myself to follow suit and get to work smashing up that road.

I did as I was bidden. I went at the destructive work and helped the others drag up the stone to create our own huge barricade, and I did it because it pleased me. I was overcome by the camaraderie that now existed between myself and all these other cockade-wearing brothers and sisters, and I felt a genuine affinity for these French rebels. The heady thrill of vandalising a whole city to upset the rich and the powerful was too potent to resist and once I was finished here, I would go home to London and tell every slum-ear that we should do likewise in our own capital, if only for the sheer buzz of it. I was feeling alive again for the first time that year and I had forgotten all about the miseries of home. I no longer cared for opium, I no longer yearned for Lily. Instead, I realised with delight, once the road was ruined and a mighty barricade was formed out of paving stone, timber and overturned carriages, that the revolutionary life was just the thing to blow away all my cobwebs. My hands was steady, my heart was full and I looked towards Adele – who was busy loading more weapons with shot for the menfolk and refreshing them with the red wine from her flask – and Babette – who was helping to hoist up and unroll a thick roll of carpet across the barricade so it was easier to climb – and I considered as to which of them I would most like to marry once this revolution proved successful. We poor people was bound to be victorious and soon we would all be dining on pheasant and living in the vacated palaces of the rich. The Lamoreaux could stuff their precious wedding certificate.

Such thoughts helped me in my labours and soon we had the barricade raised across the whole width of the Boulevard Saint-Denis, reaching as high as the second-storey house windows. It was made out of paving stone, timber, furniture, even smashed doors and old grandfather clocks and, despite the exhaustion, I was well satisfied at having played my part in creating something so magnificent and unassailable. This must be the warm feeling that Sir Christopher Wren had enjoyed, I thought as I dropped my hammer and surveyed what we had created, after having built St Paul's.

It was when I was taking my first rest before climbing to the top of the barricade, as others was now doing, that a big hand landed on my shoulder. I turned to see Hugo DeFarge. He had been watching me throughout most of the building of the barricade, looking at my work in what I hoped was in admiration of my commitment to the cause. When he opened his mouth, however, he seemed to be unsure about what it was he wanted to convey.

'Madame DeFarge,' he uttered at last.

'What about her?'

'I . . . I . . . She . . .' He was struggling to express himself. I supposed that the emotion of what we was achieving that day must have meant a lot more to him than it ever could to me. I placed my own hand on his arm to let him know that I understood.

'She'd be very proud of you, my covey,' I told him. 'So would your grandfather be, if he could see you now.'

'I knew her hand,' he spoke at last, with a slight stammer. I was unsure as to what to make of that. It felt like something was getting lost in translation. Then he lifted his hand up, as if he was going to poke me on my exposed chest, but stopped himself. His face took on a haunted look. 'You are Catholic?' he asked me then.

'*Oogo!*' Adele called over to him and this snapped him out of this withdrawn state. She was about to clamber up the barricade with a flag-post what had a large tricolore at the end of it and it seemed that she wanted both of us to come with her. Hugo smiled over and turned back to me as if that odd moment between us had never happened.

'We fight as brothers on the barricade, Jack,' he said, after hugging me close. 'Death to the Republic!'

I repeated those sentiments and then I whipped out my pistol from my belt and followed him up a plank to the top of the mighty pile. There, I positioned myself between Adele and Babette and helped them to force their flag into the barricade so it could fly proud. Then I pointed my pistol in the air and shouted those three crowd-pleasing words that I had heard spoken so often since I had arrived in this country and that Nick had translated for me on our journey to Paris.

'Liberty!' I roared as my two lady friends flanked me on the top of the barricade, each of them embracing their English hero. All around, my new-found revolutionary brothers and sisters – even those high up on the Saint-Denis gate and the ones leaning out of the windows – thundered the word back at me. 'Equality!' I continued. The impassioned mob replied in force. Close by, Hugo DeFarge was loading a long military musket, not joining in with the popular chant. He was facing the other direction and staring west down the length of the road. 'And lest we forget,' I was still facing eastwards, addressing those countless insurgents what stood behind the barricades as if they was my troops '*Fraternity!*'

I had been expecting this word to be repeated back at me with the same enthusiasm as the first two, but instead, a very sudden, chilling silence descended over the whole street. It was as though the mood had gone dead at its mention.

'What?' I asked the blank faces what looked up at me from the street below. I looked at DeFarge, who was near the top of the timber planks and his smile was replaced with a scowl. 'Did I say it wrong?'

I turned to see what he was looking at. As I did so, I noticed that all the riflemen, what had until now been lolling out of their windows in so languid a manner, had tensed up and their weapons was pointed west at what had caused the sudden hush. There was a long line of stiff tall-hatted, blue-coated uniforms, all sat on horseback at the far end of the boulevard, their bayoneted rifles facing heavenwards and sharp blades all glittering in the sun. Our opponents, the National Guard, had at last graced us with their presence.

Of all the many revolutionaries what had gathered there under the Saint-Denis gate, it was of course Hugo DeFarge who first mustered up the courage to address the threat. He raised his hands to his mouth, and was brazen enough to introduce himself to the wall of cavalry what had appeared as if from nowhere.

The commanding officer of the guard, notable even from this distance by his taller hat, bigger horse and flashier uniform, trotted in front of his lined troops, all silence and threat, a drawn sword in his hand. He watched as DeFarge continued making angry statements at the top of his voice, seeming to make a study of us. I have seen cats regard twittering birds in the trees with the same quiet interest.

DeFarge received cheers from his people although – I could not help but observe – there was less enthusiasm in their voices now that the military had arrived. From his high place at the window, our satirical sniper made another of his jibes to the amusement of every French ear. To the left of me Adele whooped and raised her flask of wine in the air, as if toasting an already successful revolution. Armand was now brandishing a rifle and led the mob in an aggressive revolutionary chant. We all joined in as best as we could, and in the very act of singing we once again cast off the fear what these authorities had, for just a small moment, inspired in us. We was reminding ourselves that we was a people united, that we outnumbered them, that we was destined to win.

Brave Babette shrieked at them and made an insulting gesture with her arms what even I understood.

'You heard the lady!' I jeered at the guards myself. 'Piss off home, why don't you? This here is our city now!'

My prostitute companions hooted and they hoisted up their skirts to display their underwear to the troops, giggling like naughty kinchins as they did so and poking their tongues out. I recall feeling like I had never laughed so much before.

Then I heard a surprising noise. Somewhere over there amid that line of guardsmen a bottle of champagne had been opened. Adele's drinking flask exploded in her hands, and the remaining red wine was sprayed all over my left cheek. I flinched as another pop was heard, as I now understood that it was from no bottle. Another shot was whizzing towards me as we all began scrambling for cover. DeFarge jumped behind the barricade quick, followed by Armand, while Babette on my right dropped to her knees as the second musket-ball just missed me. To my left, Adele was dropping backwards down the barricade in a strange and unhurried way. I yelled to Babette that we should get down behind the barricade as Adele was doing, but she seemed to think that curling up into a little ball was a better idea. Adele's drinking flask had been dropped and was now tumbling its way down the front of the barricade, intact and with its lid screwed on tight. Where then, I wondered in slow confusion, had the red wine what was splashed all over me come from?

Another loud pop issued from the National Guard and this was followed by a torrent of gunfire from the front line of soldiers. The shock I was gripped with was itself surprising, because until then I had not imagined any sort of retaliation. I think there must have been a part of me what had expected the cavalry to just submit themselves, without opposing our revolutionary antics. My instinct for survival compelled me to jump backwards and retreat behind the barricade as everyone else was doing. 'We was only having a laugh!' I wanted to protest. 'There's no need for all this!'

I dropped my weapon, tripped and fell to the foot of the barricade and there was confronted with a horrifying sight. Adele was lying on her back with her whole body juddering. There was a wound in her neck and blood poured out of it, staining her white cotton dress. Eyes open, she stared upwards at the clouds, trying but failing to scream on account of the hole in her throat. I had never before seen such a severe wound up close and I was overcome by the obscenity of it. I held her close and did the screaming for her.

Babette collapsed down beside us, her hands still clutching at her belly where the second shot had struck her. She too was choking her last as blood seeped out onto the rubble beneath. I was caught tight between these wounded women and could hardly bear to move myself. I had a sudden sensation that I too must have been shot and not yet felt it but, after worming around on the ground and surveying my whole self, I realised that I had been luckier than these two women. A thunderous storm of bullets now flew above the barricade and all I could do was lie there in fear and watch Adele and Babette suffer, with no clue as to what I could do to help them.

That pair of beautiful women, who had befriended a stranger and shown me all that was best about the French character, in so short a time, was the first two casualties of this, the bloody June Days Uprising of 1848.

Chapter 14

Death to the Republic!

Wherein my true nature is tested and revealed

The next casualty of this vicious class war was that satirical sniper leaning out of his window. He had been firing off as many bullets as anti-republican jibes when there was no real infantry in view, but had now received a return shot straight through the head, before he even had a chance to squeeze his trigger. I looked up from my crouched position where I was still holding hands with poor, suffering Adele and saw the red-sprayed wall beside his window, as he dropped his rifle and his body collapsed onto the sill. Many of his fellow riflemen posted in other windows continued firing back at the cavalry, while others pulled the shutters closed in sudden cowardice. The dead man's rifle dropped to the ground next to me, but I did not hear its clatter because of the deafening sound of gunfire from every direction. The drumming had stopped, of course, and the only sound now was from the bullets ricocheting off the stone and ironwork all around and the cries of the already wounded. I couldn't even hear Babette's anguished weeping as she rolled herself up into a tighter ball on the ground beside me. I did not need to hear her though, as the agonised expression upon her face communicated enough. Her bleeding continued and her eyes pleaded for me to stop lying there and go and do something.

'I'll fetch a doctor!' I promised her, although she couldn't have heard me over the bullet-storm, even if she could have understood. 'Or a nurse! We'll get the shot out of your belly and fix you up Babette, I swear. Both you and Adele here'll be good in no time.' But I could already tell from the way Adele's grip was loosening in mine, how her body had ceased shaking, that it was too late for her. I turned to her just in time to see her die.

'*MORT À LA REPUBLIQUE!*' I heard Hugo DeFarge yell from somewhere and I turned about to search for where he was, certain that a man like him would know what could be done for Babette. But I saw that he was preoccupied, leaning over the top of the barricade with dozens of other revolutionaries and firing back at the infantry. I shouted up at him that we needed help down here, that the women – his friends – had been shot, but of course he couldn't hear me and, in truth, I do not know if he could have done anything. Up on that barricade, to the left of DeFarge, another rifleman took a hit to the head and tumbled down. DeFarge kept on firing regardless.

I heard Babette's pained and desperate voice calling to me then and crawled from Adele's corpse towards her. She was sobbing as I brought my face close to hers and then began choking. Her hand gripped mine and she tried to squeeze out her sentences. 'Don't get yourself all agitated, Babette,' I tried to shush her instead. 'Calm yourself and we'll try and–'

Another bullet interrupted me. This one whizzed by my left ear and struck her in her forehead. She was released in an instant from further misery. I was even more disturbed by this deadly shot as, not only had it grazed me, but it had come from such an irregular angle. I could not imagine that it had crossed from the guardsman on the other side of the barricade and this signified only one thing. She had been killed by a gunman on this side of the barricades.

This realisation brought on a whole new burst of panic and I turned to where the shooter must have stood. I saw a gruff bearded sniper leaning out of a different window. His still-smoking rifle was pointed at Babette and he nodded at me, acknowledging the mercy killing, before turning his attention back to shooting at the enemy.

I knelt there, on that street under the Saint-Denis gate, my shirt wet and reddened by the blood of the two women who, despite our short acquaintance, I had very much liked, and who had both died in my arms. It was then that I felt a dramatic and violent shift take place within me.

I have never been a coward. I will own to lacking a number of other heroic qualities, but bravery has never been a problem. And now that my shock and confusion was lifting, they was replaced by a hot fury, what made me want to avenge those women. I longed to strike back at the murderous army what had just killed my two companions, so I scrambled towards that rifle what had dropped from the hands of the dead sniper above and I collected it up, checked that it was still loaded and tried to hold it like a soldier might. Just then a new wave of armed revolutionaries appeared from behind me, as if summoned here by the sound of fighting and they all rushed to the top of the barricades too. I was about to join in with the stream of them when I saw that their climb to the top, where DeFarge and several other members was still positioned, was being hindered by several dead and wounded bodies what was tumbling down ahead of them.

As noted, I have never been a coward, but that did not mean I was about to turn stupid. There could be no doubt that to climb that barricade for a second time could result in the same end for me, so my finger loosened on the rifle's trigger as this sobering truth struck home. This was not my fight, I did not even really know what the National Workshops was, let alone why all these people was getting so het up about their closure. I backed up against the wall behind me so that there was less chance that I would be shot by stray bullets, and considered what the right thing to do was.

There was a strong temptation within me to flee this deadly scene. That was the most sensible course, if a cowardly one. I could return to the wine shop, get Nick and then leave Paris to its own troubles as we went home to our own city. But then there would be no triumph to boast of and I would be returning in defeat. And Hugo DeFarge would still have those keys about his person.

I wiped dirty sweat from my brow and watched him at the very height of the battle, fighting harder and with even greater courage than any other revolutionary. He was taking a lot of risks, sometimes raising his head high above the barricade and cursing at the army. It looked very possible that he could receive a shot at any given moment. I told myself, as my dark but simple plan formed, that it was not me who had convinced him to take on the French government. I could not be held accountable for his death, if it came, as all of this horror would be happening regardless of my presence here. So, if he should happen to do himself a fatal mischief and tumble to the foot of the barricade like Adele and Babette, then that was his own daft doing. I would take no pride in stealing keys from the body of a dead man, but I still wanted that Lamoreaux money. And if the course of history was about to conspire in my favour, then so be it.

'*Jacques Anglaze!*' DeFarge had turned away from the bullet-fire and was beckoning for me to climb up that mound of street rubble and fight by his side. 'Work, you devil! Work!'

'Death to the Republic!' I roared and began climbing up that bloodied barricade, showing as much bravery as any other warrior on it, even if my motive was a lot less noble. DeFarge had lowered himself from his shooting position so that he could wave me towards him in safety and he seemed most insistent that we fight side by side. He was grinning like a maniac as I jostled my way through the madness, to the part of the barricade where he and other Jacks was stationed. I wondered why he should be so keen for me to take my position in the vacant firing-post beside him. I also was shocked to see that just below the line of riflemen from Saint-Antoine, was that little red-haired girl with her tin of ammunition crawling about. She was offering bullets to whoever needed to reload, her ever-smiling parents now nowhere to be found. Seeing her risk her young life like that in the middle of a bloody street war made me grateful I had left Nick at home after all.

'Place yourself here,' DeFarge shouted over the deafening conflict as I reached the top. 'Fight beside me, if you are a rebel, as you say!' He spoke like he was granting me an honour, which was rum considering he had only known me since that morning. It was not until I had crawled upwards and poked the barrel of my gun over the top, that I recalled that this was just the spot where I had seen someone receive a mortal wound earlier. DeFarge then moved to a vulnerable space also. He was stood higher than any other shooter and was an easier target than most, but he did not seem in the slightest bit scared. I hesitated before getting high enough to see the enemy, but DeFarge left his position to grab me and then forced me upwards. It was a distressing moment and his handling was rough enough where I thought he was going to hurl me over the other side of the barricade. In doing this, DeFarge had raised his own self up to so perilous a level that his whole top half was exposed to enemy fire. Then he began shooting the last ammunition in his weapon in a fierce assault upon the guard what encouraged many others to do likewise. I remained crouched down just below the line of fire and shouted up at him not to be so foolish, even though his was just the sort of heroic behaviour what could play into my unheroic hands.

My head was close enough to the level of his waist that, should I wish to, I could reach out and touch the keys now. I made a note of how hard they would be to detach from the belt without him feeling me. Such an act would be almost impossible and, although I was well practised in such things, I felt that to even try now would reveal my thieving designs. Besides, DeFarge soon jumped back down behind the barricade, as he must have been clean out of shot by then. Then he whistled for the little ammunition girl to attend on him.

'You hold that gun like a woman,' he sneered at me when he saw how uncomfortable I was with the long army rifle I had taken up. I had never really held onto any firearm bigger than a common burglar's barker before, and it must have showed. 'Like this,' he said as he showed me what I should be doing and then gestured to me to start using the rifle on the enemy.

And so, for appearances' sake, I rose up and peered over the top very quick to see what the National Guard was up to, for the first time since they had started shooting. Through clouds of gun-smoke I could see that they had advanced much further down the street by now, the horses had been removed as they was finding it easier to attack us on foot. Many uniformed soldiers had managed to secure positions in doorways, alleyways and even occupied houses and they looked to have just as many snipers firing out from windows as we had at our end. I tried to take aim with my rifle to shoot at some of the moving targets, but they was scurrying fast as they tried to reoccupy the street and most of the infantry was employing their own military shields. On the other side of DeFarge was his lieutenant, Armand. He too had been risking his life by standing above the safety of the barricade and giving the National Guard ferocious hell with his two long muskets. It didn't look to me as though he was hitting anyone at all, just making an almighty racket and wasting bullets. I was confident that I could shoot with more precision than him.

So I squinted one eye, dared myself to rise a little higher on the barricade so I could take a cleaner shot and reviewed the situation.

The whole wide street was becoming lost in the fog of gun battle, the smell of cordite overpowered the air and it was getting harder to see where the troops was now positioned or how much closer they had advanced. However, the striking blue coats of the guard was easy to spot through the mist as they dashed from one position to the next. Halfway down the length of road I saw one soldier dart across to a make-shift blockade what was closer to us than most. He reached it unscathed, but I noticed then that there was two other soldiers already there, as now three of those big black hats was sticking over the top of it, all of them as tall and as offensive to me as those of the British constabulary. These hats had helpful red feather plumes sticking out of the top of them, and so they proved too tempting not to shoot at. My hands held steady as I aimed for the first hat, pulled back on the flintlock and squeezed the trigger. I shot it clean off and then, in rapid succession, I shot off the other two hats before I needed to reload. I was so impressed with my own marksmanship and by the grace with which I had handled my weapon, that when I scuttled downwards to avoid any retaliatory shots and to reload my rifle, I smiled at Hugo DeFarge and asked him if he saw it.

'I couldn't have done that a week ago,' I panted. 'My hands couldn't even hold a pen without shaking. That felt good, that did.' But DeFarge did not seem as impressed by my shooting as I was.

'Aim to kill,' he grunted at me as though I had missed the whole point of fighting in a war. 'Before you are killed.' Then he barked at the little red-haired girl to load my weapon next.

'You ought not to be up here,' I said to her as she took my weapon from me and opened the barrel. 'You're too young.' She spoke no English of course, and so ignored me as she attended to helping me work the bolt-action mechanism of my rifle. 'Where are your parents?' The battle raged on above our heads as she filled it with tiny bullets shaped like cones, which looked more deadly than the usual round ones I was used to seeing in London pistols. 'Go back to the wine shop where the other children are,' I persisted. 'You'll be safe there. Or safer than here, at the very least.' She clicked the rifle back into place and handed it to me. Then she crawled off to service other empty firearms further along the barricade.

I returned to my firing-post and tried to get as close to Hugo DeFarge as I could. He was firing at the guard too and I saw him kill at least two cavalrymen with ease. However, by now the bulk of the opposing force had swarmed much further down the street and was only a few houses ahead of us. Furthermore, many of our fighters had managed to occupy the houses just ahead of those, so the two warring factions was now close enough to engage in hand-to-hand combat. Our fighters appeared out of nearby windows and doors to shoot at the infantry and so we would have to take care not to hit any of them by accident.

However, my successful shooting of the three hats gave me confidence in my hands again and I edged towards DeFarge, hoping that now he would be too preoccupied to feel me untangle those keys I needed. But just as I was considering risking the dip, he whipped his head round to me as though he had predicted my approach.

'You are Catholic?' he demanded again and I have to admit, the question threw me. I could not work out why he was asking me about my religious upbringing at a time like this.

'No,' I replied, keeping my head down low. 'I ain't nothing of that sort. Should we not be fixing ourselves upon this here battle, eh, Hugo?'

'Then why,' he hissed and made a grab for my throat with his free hand, 'do you have this?' He seized hold of that valuable golden crucifix what I had been wearing about my neck ever since Jerome had given it to me in London. It had been on display ever since we had left his shop, my shirt had been unbuttoned to the navel. DeFarge yanked my head towards him so hard that the thin chain it was dangling from snapped. 'It is for Catholics!' he yelled.

I was stunned by this sudden assault upon my person and by the bizarre offence he had appeared to have taken at me sporting religious jewellery while unbaptised. I was all set to grab it back from him, when both of our attentions was directed back to the fighting by a tremendous noise provoked by something even more alarming appearing at the far end of the street.

Through the smoke we saw two mighty war machines being wheeled into view, pointing right at us. This must have been why the horses had been removed and there did not seem to be as many foot soldiers now. The path was being cleared for cannon-fire as doubtless this would be the best way for them to do our beloved barricade some proper damage.

DeFarge reacted to this new crisis by bellowing out some instructions what I would guess amounted to *kill before you are killed*. He even stood up from his kneeling position and held his rifled musket as if intending to shoot whoever was operating the nearest cannon. Whether he was capable of making such an ambitious shot, however, is something this history cannot record. For as soon as he was up on his two feet he was knocked off them again, struck by a wicked pellet from the other direction which was, even I will admit, impressive shooting in its own right.

Hugo DeFarge fell backwards and every revolutionary what was stood nearby – in particular those of the Club of a Thousand Jacks – cried out in dismay to see their hero hurt. He had spun around as he dropped, so the nature of his wound was not yet visible, but there was a trail of blood drips following him as he crashed down onto some broken paving halfway down the barricade. His supporters all rushed to his aid and there was an unspoken sense that if DeFarge was to die now then this would spell an instant defeat for the whole uprising, at least in this vicinity. I too left my firing-post in a show of wanting to help our leader back up again.

'Don't die on us, Hugo!' I pleaded as I clambered down

through the rubble mountain towards him. 'All of France needs you.' I could already see that he had fallen onto the keys and so it was going to be tough pinching them. 'Show us where you've been hit,' I said, in the hope that he would shift into a more accommodating position. 'I'm sure it ain't as bad as all that.' DeFarge rolled over, one hand clutching onto his other arm from where blood was leaking and he gritted his teeth. 'A manly wound,' I complimented him as I crawled closer to where the keys was. 'But it ain't fatal. Here, let me help.'

'You are no help!' he growled at me, before barking orders in French. Various attendants descended upon him then with bandages, medical implements and little bottles of iodine what they had brought along for just this sort of emergency. It made me burn to wonder where these ready nurses had been when Adele and Babette needed them. Even in the midst of a revolution it seemed like some people's lives was worth more than others.

As far as I could tell, DeFarge's wound was just a graze and there wasn't even any bullet to remove. No doubt it would hurt like hot hell, but if that was the worst that would happen to him today then he should count his blessings. He was having difficulty getting up without help, but I imagined this might be more to do with his fall than the shot. Armand was still up on the barricades and one of the few not to have let DeFarge's fall distract him from the pressing task of killing cavalrymen. He shouted for us all to return to our firing-posts, or so I gathered, and many did just that. However, I elected to remain by our fallen leader's side, crawling behind him so I could lift him up as he lay there, tending his wounds like I was Captain Hardy to his dying Nelson.

I helped to pour some water from a flask into his mouth but, after I had wiped his lips, he murmured something to himself in French, as his eyes fixed again on the crucifix what had hung around my neck. As his nurses did a hurried job of placing a bandage on him, I wondered if there might be a chance that I could get him to hand over those keys to me without me having to steal them.

'Maybe one of us should go home and check on our children, eh, Hugo?' I said in my best bedside manner. 'After all, they'll be worried, the poor little mites.' When he replied it was with a voice that was loaded with violent threat.

'I'll kill you first,' he snarled up at me. 'My son is not for you.'

'What are you saying?' I asked. 'I'm only worried for his safety.'

He glared at me and said nothing.

Most of the nurses what had patched him up was fleeing the barricade now, the job half-finished, and the sound of the fighting above was getting fiercer. If I made a lunge for his keys now he would fight me for them and would be wise to my scheme, but if I could move him away from this place it might be easier to take them unnoticed.

'Let's get out of here, Hugo,' I said in spite of his hostility. 'Before something horrendous happens.'

Just then, something horrendous happened. I knew that the first cannonball was about to strike seconds before it did as all the people from the upper windows, on the Saint-Denis gate and at the top of the barricade began screaming in terror at its flight. When it hit, the entire structure shook and everyone on it was hurled about by its quake. Many of those revolutionaries at the ridge of the barricade was thrown backwards by the mighty tremble as the ball struck the front and almost everyone else tumbled to some degree or other. The barricade was large and built on a solid base of stone paving and timber, but even that shattered where the second cannonball landed and that particular section collapsed under it, bringing many down with it. There was an overturned cart close to where myself and DeFarge was and it began a rapid sliding down the slope, as did a lot of the timber and the bodies of those already killed. I too went down with the wooden avalanche – it was impossible not to – and landed on my back at the foot of the barricade again just where I had fallen earlier, where the bodies of Adele and Babette still lay. I jumped out of the way just in time before a sharp sheet of metal, what been employed as a shield by someone above, came sliding down behind me and near guillotined my head clean off.

To say I was growing sick of this here revolution would be an understatement.

Others had been far less fortunate than myself. The dislocation of so much rubble and wood had caused even more fatalities and serious injuries than our enemy could have ever wished for. There was a number of crushed bodies lying close to me, some of whom was still twitching under stone boulders. But, as upsetting as that all was to see, I was still flint-hearted enough to pick myself up and look to my own survival. That is until I noticed the many empty tins and dropped cone-bullets at the foot of the barricade. I recalled who had been carrying those and I looked about to see where the little girl had got to. I saw her curly red hair and freckled arm sticking out from under the avalanche what had half-buried her. I dashed towards her to see if I could help, but her limbs was too still. She had been killed outright.

Even for a bastard thief such as myself, this was too awful. I collapsed down onto the ground and cursed out in anger. Before, when the two women had been killed, I had been furious with the army what had killed them. But this time my fury was directed at the revolutionaries themselves. Whatever it was that they had wanted to achieve from upending the Second Republic, it could not be worth all this death, least of all the death of a child. I was outraged by all of them for allowing her involvement and I told myself that I would never have done so irresponsible a thing.

But even as I thought this, I knew it was not true. Because there was a young boy back in DeFarge's wine shop who I had led with me to Paris and placed in a position of great danger while I pursued my fortune. I felt wretched as this truth set in, knowing that I was no better than this girl's parents, wherever they was, and I felt a terrible guilt at it.

Perhaps I remained there by that girl's side for a considerable time, or perhaps for no time at all. But I do remember that I was roused from my despair by the sound of Hugo DeFarge's voice shouting at his remaining troops through the smoke and burning rubble. He was making another of his many inspirational speeches and this one was having a miraculous effect on the bruised and fallen. Everywhere around, his thrown soldiers gathered themselves up, collected their weapons and charged back to the front of the fighting once more, as if they had experienced no adversity at all. It was as though his words had some sort of healing spell upon them, but I knew that even if I could have understood them, they would have done nothing for me.

However unlikely as this may sound, on that long and hitherto sunny afternoon of June 23rd, when the dead bodies was piling up on both sides and much of the street was in flames – deep grey clouds appeared and burst above Paris. This may strike some of my more discerning readers as something of a poetic fallacy, a storm above representing the storm below, but you can ask anyone who else was there during that uprising. A thunder clap came first, followed by a torrent of angry, beating rain what only added to the nightmare tone of the whole day. This storm spurred me to get up from my crouched position by the dead ammunition girl, wipe my eyes dry and begin staggering around near the bottom of that crumbling barricade. I had every intention of leaving the scene, as I had lost all interest in Hugo DeFarge and that rotten wedding certificate. I had other matters to attend to and, chief among them was getting Nick away from this revolution. But before I could, I heard DeFarge's voice call my name over the sound of battle and rainfall. I was surprised on hearing how close he still must be.

I turned and saw him there, drenched by the rain and lying

against an upright slab of pavement, blood running down the side of his cheek and his face contorted by pain. He looked to be crippled by the way he was propping himself up with his hands and not his legs.

'My son is not for you,' I heard him wheeze again.

I still had no idea what he was talking about and was ready to turn my back on him and leave, but then I saw that the bunch of keys was still hanging on his buckled belt. In his current weakened state it would be simple for me to just grab them from him, without no artfulness at all and there would be not much he could do about it. But robbing through force had never been my style and an undignified wrestle would demean us both.

'You,' he pointed at me, 'are in danger.'

A third cannonball struck the front of the barricade. This one did less damage, but splinters of stone flew into my range from close by and almost cut my cheek.

'What gives you that idea?' I asked him as I raised my hand to rub my hurt face.

'I killed a man,' he continued, as if this should be big news and he had not been killing people all day. 'He was *petit-bourgeois.*'

I stepped much closer to DeFarge then, as it was becoming hard to hear him over the hammering rain. I was curious to know if he was talking about who I guessed.

'What was this man's name?' I asked.

'Cupidon,' he told me. 'But he thought himself Lamoreaux.' Then he held up that colonial crucifix what he had stolen from around my neck, as if expecting me to account for it. 'This belonged to Cupidon.'

'I won that cross gambling,' I told him quick. 'I don't know who it belonged to first.'

'*Non*. You were given it by his children,' he said, leaning on his side, the wounded arm rested against the ground. 'I know this. They sent you to me. You and your boy.'

It was most disconcerting to learn that he had fallen upon the truth of my presence in Paris just by seeing that crucifix, but I tried no to let it rattle me.

'I was sent to you by the Friends of DeFarge,' I insisted. 'I don't know no Cupidon.'

'You were sent by my enemies,' he shook his head and then he rolled over to reveal something he had been concealing from me. A small pistol, pointed right at my chest. 'Lie and I kill.'

My bones almost jumped out of my skin in fright. I tried to stagger away, but the ground underneath was now treacherous from the rain and I could not move quick enough. Then he began laughing at me, an unkind laugh, but it reassured me that murder was not on his mind, at least not yet. The truth was that had he wanted to shoot me, he could have done so in an instant. Perhaps he would later, but for now he wanted to talk. He was holding the barker with both hands but one of his arms, I reminded myself, was wounded. With one well-timed pounce and snatch, that gun could be mine and then so would the keys.

'What do you want to know?' I asked, keeping a close eye on his shaky hands. All around us the bravest revolutionaries battled away in the storm, their faces black from the gunpowder and stone dust, but their souls burning bright. There was a lot fewer of them now though, hundreds rather than the thousands of earlier. The rest was either fled or dead.

'They have returned to Paris?' DeFarge asked. I nodded and wiped more rain away from my face. 'Both? Son and daughter?' I nodded again. DeFarge's own face was dripping wet too, but because his hands was occupied, he could not wipe it, so must have been becoming blinder by the second. I was growing confident that even one decent swipe at his weapon would overcome him. 'Does she hate me still?' he asked and it was hard to tell if it was the weather what was making him look so emotional. 'For killing her father? I know he does, but she?'

I shrugged. 'Killing someone's parent is not one of those things you forgive in a hurry, is it Hugo?'

'Grahh!' he replied, which, for all I knew, might have been something French or may have been just a noise he had made. 'It was either he or I!' he said then, straightening his aim. 'She knows this!'

The corner of the street we was sheltered in was becoming even more dangerous. Most of the paving stones was covered in these blue metallic spots from where the bullets had grazed them, and I glanced over and saw that some of those uniformed and red-plumed cavalry officers had made it to the front of the barricade on their horses. The more intrepid among them had dismounted and was clambering over the top with long swords; many was running our boys through with them. Armand had just put a bullet through an officer's forehead but even I, a cove with no military experience at all, could tell that we was on the cusp of defeat at the Saint-Denis gate. However well the revolution was getting on elsewhere in Paris, it was on its last legs around here.

'Now look here, Hugo,' I said in a firm voice. 'One of two things is about to happen to you and you ain't gonna like either of them. The guard are about to storm the barricade and they're going to win. You can either surrender or die.'

'*Pah!*' he spat.

'Go *Pah!* and *Grah!* all you like, *mon ami*, but it's the truth. Look at Armand if you don't believe!'

DeFarge turned his head towards the top of the barricade where I was pointing, just in time to see three separate soldiers descend upon the bearded ape of the Club of a Thousand Jacks. Two had already stuck swords into Armand's body as he continued fighting them. DeFarge cried out his friend's name as the third soldier shot Armand in the chest. It looked like a horrible way to die.

'That'll be us in a few minutes if we don't surrender,' I said. I had examined his legs closer now. There was blood seeping from out of his left boot. 'So why don't you put down that gun, eh?'

'*Never!*' DeFarge yelled in defiance and returned his attention to me. His gun was still aimed at my chest and I knew that there was no reason now why he would not shoot me, so I readied myself to dodge a bullet. But it seemed he had more questions first. 'You are here to steal my son?' he asked.

'No,' I blinked. 'What gave you that idea?'

'The brother ... Jerome ... he is ... not ...' DeFarge looked to be struggling to find the right English word for describing what Jerome was not, '... natural. He will ... never ...'

'Never what?'

'Have a son.'

'So what?' I asked, thrown by this random interest in Jerome's preferences in bed. Perhaps, I thought, it was some Catholic thing? 'That ain't nothing to do with it, Hugo,' I said, reasoning that now that the truth would serve me better than these strange ideas he was entertaining about our interest in his little JJ. 'What they're after is that wedding certificate you've been keeping from them. The one you want to sell to their old uncle what'd stop them from inheriting the big estate.'

DeFarge stared at me then as if he thought me an imbecile. He leaned an inch closer and inspected my face to see if I was serious. Then he started laughing.

'Oh, English Jack,' he shook rain from his hair as he sniggered. 'They have told you nothing about me at all!'

Then he fired his pistol.

Chapter 15

An Unlikely Assassin

Proving how the only tradesmen what ever prosper
in a revolutionary environment are the undertakers

The young cavalry officer what DeFarge had shot as he charged over the barricade towards us was not much older than a boy. But the bullet struck him right in the centre of the white cross on his blue uniform, a cross formed by two straps. He dropped like a puppet with its strings cut.

It had been a good shot – I will give DeFarge credit for that – and I had thought he had been aiming at me, so close was the bullet as it sped past my head on its way to its true target. My back had been to the soldier, so I had not seen him coming and nor had I realised that the National Guard had already swarmed over the barricade and was busy fighting the revolution off on this side. Doubtless that boy would have run me through with his sword had DeFarge not saved my life, but that did not mean things between us was about to get any more cordial.

'I will kill you still!' warned DeFarge as he pushed me off him. In the surprise of the shooting I had thrown myself forward and landed on his damaged legs, what had caused him to scream out in pain. He turned his gun back on me as another crack of thunder echoed across the skies. DeFarge surveyed the scene and saw how ruinous the storm had been for the uprising. The weather had become so punishing and difficult to fight in that most of the insurgents had fled. Meanwhile, the National Guard had remained fighting as they, of course, was all under orders to do so. The numbers had altered in a very short time.

However, the insurgents what had been on top of the Saint-Denis gate all this time had begun hurling large rocks from up there down onto the advancing guard and this kept most of them at bay for now. But it was only a matter of time now before more soldiers descended upon us and, while DeFarge's legs might not be up to the dash, mine very much was. I had no intention of lingering about here to get at best captured and at worst slaughtered. Nor did I wish for a poorly thrown rock to land on my own head. So I stepped backwards over the rubble-strewn slippery ground and prepared to depart the field of battle.

'You won't be killing no one else today, Hugo,' I said as I found myself having to step backwards all careful, over a bleeding corpse or two. 'Not with that little popper.' I didn't know much about rifles or muskets but I did know pistols, and whatever shot his had in it was now in the chest of that hapless sod a few feet away from me, groaning his last. DeFarge hesitated for one moment and then decided to find out for himself. He pointed the gun at my head, pulled the trigger and I was relieved to discover that my estimation had been right. The pistol hammer clicked down to no effect.

'Well, I must say we've had a magical day together, Hugo,' I said as he tossed the useless barker aside in contempt for both it and me. 'But I fear that the hour has at last come for us to part ways. Thanks for the local tour.'

Then, with a malicious delight, I showed him what I had been hiding in my fist ever since I had pretended to tumble into him after he'd shot the soldier.

'Thief!' he swore when he realised I had removed the keys to his kingdom from his belt buckle.

'The best in London,' I grinned back and tossed the bunch from one hand to the other. Even in that hellish setting I could not suppress my joy at feeling like the Artful Dodger again. I gave a little bow as he became enraged and started cursing at me in his rough French. I did not linger to ask for a translation for any of it, but instead I turned from him and began to leave.

'Tell her!' I heard him shout after me as I fled the broken scene. 'I knew her by her hand! Tell her that!'

But, although that once mysterious comment struck home with me and revealed its startling meaning, I did not let it keep me from running.

I ran from him with his broken legs and his furious soul, from the barricades and from the infantry. I ran from the dead bodies of Adele, Babette, Armand, and, worst of all, I ran from the corpse of the little ammunition girl. I kept on running away from the whole dreadful district, through the unfamiliar maze of the Parisian backstreets and alleys, turning corners what led I knew not where. That bizarre summer storm what had arrived so quick had now passed with just as much abruptness and the fighting too had stopped, at least for now. But the marks of both could still be seen everywhere, no matter how much distance I put between myself and the Saint-Denis gate. In my hurry to flee I splashed through deep muddy puddles and almost slipped into others who was running in the other direction from cruel clashes of their own. My path was often obstructed by people carrying wounded warriors away from harm and, in the centre of one narrow passageway, a long black lace shawl was being draped over the dead body of a man by two weeping women. To my shame, I vaulted over this sad sight, causing even more upset to his mourners but I was so desperate to keep moving. However, I should have seen that the trauma of the uprising had affected the whole of Paris and trying to outrun it was futile.

After about fifteen minutes of haring through the boarded-up and trembling city in a geographical confusion, I found myself at last somewhere along the bank of the River Seine. There had been plenty of fighting around here too or so it seemed. Near where I had emerged the pavement had also been ripped up to create a number of smaller, half-built barricades, the streets was littered with dropped weapons and bullet-holes had pockmarked the walls. Rainwater of a deep pink colour was running down these streets. Dead horses was stretched out across the width of the road and scared dogs raced half-mad from one place to another.

Although evidence of violence could be found everywhere, many of the human participants in the fighting had vanished as if they had been blown away by the storm. There was plenty of corpses, as well as some people scurrying about to cover their shot bodies with sheets or to remove them, but a notable cessation in the hostilities had occurred and the combatants on both sides had departed now that the sun was out again. Despite this, every now and again gunshots could be heard close by and, across the bridge called Pont-Neuf, infantry riders was careening back and forth over the river in a blazing hurry.

As soon as I stopped running I began to feel all the aches and pains what I had accumulated throughout the day and my cheeks smarted from the cuts. At any other time I might have looked most conspicuous in my rough, ripped clothes, all reddened with blood and with the beaten face of a pugilist. But most people I passed, as I walked eastwards along the riverside and past other abandoned barricades, looked just as bandaged, bloodied and as battle-worn as I was. I followed some stone steps down to the river embankment so I could stop and think without being harassed by soldiers. I was too tired to keep moving and I needed a place to slump down for a moment and think on what I needed to do next. Down here, the only people wearing army uniform was those bobbing about in the river.

Still gripped hard within my fist was those keys to all the important locks in Hugo DeFarge's wine shop. But, I had to admit, I was at a loss as to how I was now going to get back there. I had been trying to memorise all the important landmarks ever since I had arrived in Paris for just this very reason, but, like London, this city defied easy navigation. The river was on my right and ahead of me I saw the gargoyled glory of Notre Dame Cathedral, standing proud upon its island. We had passed it yesterday on our way to Les Halles and I knew that, from the big buttressed church there, I could find the Rue Montorgueil, which would lead me to the apartment where Jerome and Celeste would be. It made more sense for me to head to them, rather than get lost searching for the wine shop as one of the Lamoreaux could provide me with directions. And, furthermore, I had a few strong questions for those two about just what they really wanted from Hugo DeFarge.

I recalled how well Nick had been playing with Jean-Jacques back in the wine shop. They had reminded me then of when myself and Oliver Twist had first met. Nick the older, cocksure street kid befriending the younger, more innocent Jean-Jacques for criminal reasons of his own. I thought about JJ's worried expression as I entered his bedroom after the revolution had been declared. He had struck me as being very much like his father, but it had never occurred to me to question where his mother was. When DeFarge had entered the room and asked me if I knew Madame DeFarge, I had made the mistake of assuming he was on about his famous grandmother on the wall behind me. Now I knew better.

'Jerome! Celeste!' I shouted up at the window. 'It's Dodger, let me in!' It had taken me longer than expected to find their apartment, on account of the many barricades what had not been there this morning. Evening had fallen by the time I arrived and the wooden blinds above was drawn, but there was a light shining behind them, so I took it that somebody must be in. But, when I at last heard a voice answering my calls, it came not from above, but from the courtyard beyond the iron gate.

'*Monsieur* Dawkins?' It was Jerome calling from a shadowed corner and he sounded like he was afraid. 'Are you alone? Is my sister with you?'

'With me?' I asked as I saw his thin figure emerge into the dim light. 'No, why would she be? I'm alone. Come and unlock this gate, why don't you? I'm wearing a thin shirt and I need to put on something what is warmer and not as blood-drenched. It's getting good and cold out here.'

He begun scuttling towards me through the passage in his delicate way and he pulled some keys out of his coat pocket. But before he would unlock the gate he poked his unshaven face through the rusty bars and looked both ways down the street as if he hadn't believed me about being alone. Then he spoke in a distressed, self-pitying tone and I had the feeling that this former teetotaller had been at the drink. 'I have been the victim of an assassination attempt,' he whimpered.

'Jerome, unless you open this gate sharpish,' I rattled the bars with impatience, 'you'll be the victim of another.'

He jerked away from me and for a second I thought he was going to run back to his hiding place in the dark. Then he whispered.

'Do you have the wedding certificate?'

'Not yet,' I answered and showed him the set of keys. 'But I have the next best thing. If I take these back to the wine shop, it'll all open up to me like an oyster shell. But I need you to show me the way after I've changed clothes and washed. I can't crack a crib looking like this.'

Jerome unlocked the gate and, as I entered the passageway I noticed that the rightful heir to the Lamoreaux fortune had indeed been in a skirmish of his own. There was almost as many stains on the lower part of his shirt as there was on mine.

'That your blood?' I asked, once he had locked the gate again and checked that it was secure. When he turned back to me he shook his head and began to cry.

'Oh, what a punishing day for my sister and I to return to Paris!' he wept. 'This revolution has been so awful. Is it God's judgment, I ask, for our greed in pursuing a fortune? I think it very likely, *non*?'

'Not everything what happens in the world is on account of you, Jerome,' I told him, bored of his melodrama already.

'Oh, that angry storm. What a tempest! As if the skies above were somehow echoing our human storm below. As if He himself was commenting upon the tragedy of Man. As if the raging—'

'Yeah, yeah, Lord Byron, we ain't got time for all that,' I interrupted him before he got too carried away. 'Whose blood is that on your shirt?'

'Gaspard's,' he told me.

'I don't know who that is.'

'You do,' his voice was almost a squeak. 'The old servant.'

'Him with the wooden leg?'

'He tried to assassinate me.'

'No, he didn't.'

'You call me a liar!'

'I call you mistaken,' I said and then thought about it some more. 'Or perhaps I am calling you a liar. Listen, Jerome, I've known some murderers in my time, and that old boy who I met yesterday didn't have it in him. Now if you had told me that the servant girl had tried to kill you, I might have believed it. But Gaspard? No.'

'The lower-class always favours revolution!' Jerome trembled in fury at my scepticism. 'All of them, even the seemingly docile ones. This has been proved time and again throughout French history.' He looked though the iron bars to the empty street outside, as if fearful of everything. 'Times such as these make savages out of the meekest manservants.'

'So you're saying that this Gaspard turned savage on you on account of class revenge?'

'Perhaps for that or perhaps he was in the employ of my uncle Lucien,' he said, as if those two things had an equal chance of motivating an elderly man to become an assassin. 'He could have told my wicked relative about my return to France and they could have paid him for the job.'

'Tell me what happened,' I said, eyeing him hard.

'I thought myself alone in the apartment,' Jerome explained, neither of us moving from the shadows of that courtyard passageway. 'Celeste had not returned from taking you and your assistant to the shop and the servant girl was not around to make my breakfast.'

'I saw Maria earlier,' I interjected. 'Laying siege to the Hôtel de Ville. Not by herself of course.'

'You see!' he raised a finger as if his point had been made. 'Savages, all. Now, this devil who attacked me had secreted himself in my home, as I stared out of the shuttered front window through the slits in the blind. I was distracted by the mania below. Two barricades were being built at either end of the street and I knew that this would hinder my sister's return. The rabble was chanting 'Death to the *bourgeoisie*.' It was chilling. I was so terrified that I had armed myself, and it is a good thing that I did because otherwise he would have pounced on me from behind had I not heard the tapping of his wooden foot upon the floorboards.'

He reached into his other coat pocket and produced a sticky red knife.

'I turned and saw him there, scowling at me with sheer hate in his eyes. In his raised hand he had his own knife and it was poised to strike. But I was quicker and I stuck him with this.' Jerome stared at the weapon and his other hand went up to his face, as recounting all this became too much for him. 'He's up there now, the serpent.'

I was most taken aback by this story and for a few seconds I did not know how to respond to it. I now believed that he was telling the truth and I was beginning to wonder if the horrors of that day would never end.

'Is he dead for certain?' I asked at last. Jerome lowered the hand from my face and looked at me with pleading eyes.

'Will you go and see?'

★

A couple of short candles was flickering in that front apartment room when I entered. I imagined that Jerome had lit them earlier, on account of having drawn the shutters on the windows to protect him from sight. I took my first step inside the room and looked around for where the old servant might be.

'Gaspard?' I asked as I ventured further into the room, but I received no response. Jerome had told me that his attacker had fallen by the window and so I trod towards that part of the room. There, obscured at first by the position of a lounge settee, was a black shape upon the floor. I could see blood seeping out from under him. I repeated his name but, once I was certain that he was deceased, I stepped over to the shutters to let in some moonlight. This helped me get a better look at what had occurred.

The man on the floor had been dead for some hours, or so it appeared. There was a strong chance, I considered as I peered closer at him, that he had died as Jerome had struck him, considering his age and frailty. I remembered how decrepit he had seemed with his weak, wheezing voice and slow movements, so I was still bewildered by the idea that he should have attempted an assassination upon a young man like Jerome. I leaned down to look for his weapon. I saw the blade and then two other objects lying beside him. The sight of all three filled me with rage.

'Jerome,' I said, concealing this hot emotion as he stepped, all timid, into the room behind me. 'Do you recall requesting this old man to perform a task this morning? You told me you had asked him to do it before we all went to bed last night.' Jerome shook his head. I then darted over to him and grabbed him by the arm before he could escape the room again. He cried out in distress as I dragged him over to where his victim lay. 'That there is a razor blade,' I told him as I pointed at the three objects what Gaspard had been carrying. 'That is a flannel and that is a tub of shaving soap.' Jerome shook his head in denial. 'This man was coming to shave your beard, you fucking imbecile.'

Then I shoved him down onto the settee as he raised his hands to shield himself from the sight of the innocent man he had killed.

'No!' he protested and tried to back away as far as he could. 'If he was just coming to shave me, then why was he so secretive? Why did he not alert me to his presence?'

'Because he could hardly speak!' I shouted down at him. 'His throat was all worn out, which you might have remembered, Jerome, if you ever gave the people what serve you the slightest thought. In all probability, he may well have said something as he came up behind you, but you was too wrapped up in your own concerns to hear him.'

Jerome remained on the settee and was almost curling up into a ball as if to protect himself from my wrath, but I was already forcing myself to cool down.

'Bust me!' I shook my head as I watched this maddening specimen of the upper class feel sorry for himself. 'No wonder guillotines get invented.'

'Are you going to kill me?' he asked, once he had stopped weeping.

'Course not!' I replied, vexed that he would even think it.

'There's only one murderer in this room and it's you. I don't go around killing people, I've got too much mastery over myself.'

Jerome flinched as I sat myself down next to him on the settee and then, once he was assured I was not going to harm him, he uncurled himself and we both stared at the dead man in front of us.

'He needs moving,' I said after a very long pause. 'Before he starts attracting flies. As luck would have it, you've chosen the best day possible to stab a man to death. If we drag him outside onto the lawless street he'll just be one of the many dead bodies what are littering Paris tonight.'

'You expect me to carry him?' Jerome asked in horror as I got up again and crossed over to the window. It was dark enough out there where we would not be noticed disposing of a body, if we was quick about it.

'You can take his feet,' I said, turning back to him. 'Seeing as you've never carried a corpse before.'

'This will haunt me,' he declared once he had regained some composure, 'and for it I am bound to go to Hell, do you not think?'

'From what I've seen today,' I murmured, 'we might already be there.'

'I will go to church tonight. I must make a confession.'

'Nah, I've got a better idea,' I said as I walked back over to where Gaspard lay and glared at his killer. 'Once we've got rid of your faithful retainer here, you and me are going to have a nice little chat. All about what Madame DeFarge is up to.'

'Madame DeFarge?' he said, pretending not to understand me. I had seen that very same anxious expression upon the face of a little boy that morning and I was struck by how close the family resemblance was.

'Celeste,' I clarified. 'She's the wife of Hugo DeFarge and the mother of his son.'

Jerome opened his mouth as if about to deny such an unlikely claim. But he could not manage it.

'Take me to a church,' he sniffed instead. 'Before we go and search for my sister and nephew, I must pray to the Almighty for forgiveness.' He looked down at Gaspard again and his face collapsed in dismay at what he had done. 'And once I have prayed,' he told me, 'I swear I will confess to everything.'

Chapter 16

The Wretched

Revealing the true value of a mother's love

The outside of the church what Jerome led me into had suffered heavy vandalism during the day, its iron railings had been
removed to be used in a barricade. But inside was a haven of
safety, even now that night had fallen, and Jerome conversed
with a priest and some nuns on the door and tried to convince
them we was good Christians what would not cause any trouble
inside, even if we could not deny that we had been involved in
the fighting. We must have cut an unlikely pairing, he in his
affluent coat what identified him as *bourgeoisie* and me having
changed into cleaner clothes but still appearing more like a
revolutionary. Perhaps it was this what persuaded them to open
their doors to us, and to tend to my wounds. The appearance
of one vouched for the good behaviour of the other, although,
in these upside-down days, it was unclear which of us the priest
was more likely to approve of. Either way, we was granted
entrance and the doors was bolted after us. One of the nuns led
us through the aisle and found us somewhere quiet to sit, then
scuttled herself off. The church pews was half-full with people,

many of them also injured from the fighting and they was being nursed by men and women of the cloth and other volunteers. Poor families with young children was in here too, huddling together with pillows and blankets. Their mothers was trying to get them to sing sweet, comforting songs to distract them from what had been happening outside that day. A group of men was playing cards but they did not even speak to one another, nor did they much seem to care who won what hand.

'I see you have lost my father's crucifix,' Jerome remarked after he made the sign of the cross towards the altar, then sat down next to me. 'I was a fool to entrust it to you.'

'Hugo DeFarge snatched it from me,' I replied as I stretched my back what had been aching ever since I fell from the top of the barricade. My old whip-marks was burning again and what they needed was a good rub with tender, loving female hands. I could not help but wish we had gone to a whorehouse for our short recuperation rather than to this church.

'Ah,' Jerome nodded and he put his hands together as if in prayer. 'This is how DeFarge discovered that you worked for us.'

'Seeing it around my neck must have been a confirmation,' I whispered back. 'But he already suspected it from the bank note I gave him. Celeste wrote the figures on it and he recognised her handwriting. He even tried to tell me. "I knew her hand," he said. But I didn't understand what he was on about at the time.'

'This surprises me,' Jerome said. 'She did not write much.'

'There is a woman who I love,' I told him. 'She's called

Lily Lennox. And even if I never seen her again, I'd be able to identify traces of her for years to come. I'd know her from her scent, from her laugh, from an old item of clothing. You don't forget things like handwriting. If you'd told me about her connection to DeFarge, I'd have written the bank note myself. Why didn't you tell me?'

'People of my class do not divulge painful family secrets to tradesmen, especially criminal ones. You were engaged to steal something, you were told where it was. That was enough.'

Two nuns returned to attend to the cuts on my cheek. They had a bowl and a flannel with which they washed my face and then they dabbed some stinging liquid onto it. I tried hard not to flinch as they applied it, as I did not want to look soft in front of a pair of nuns. They spoke in French and Jerome translated that my cuts was not serious and would soon heal. And, as they had more severe injuries to attend to elsewhere in that church, they would leave us to contemplate our sins in private.

'I must pray now,' Jerome said and got up from his creaking pew, dropped to his knees and crossed his hands. 'For Gaspard,' he said. 'And for my soul.'

'Make it quick then,' I told him as he closed his eyes. 'I want to get back to Nick as soon as is possible.'

Earlier, after Jerome and myself had disposed of poor Gaspard's corpse and we had returned to the apartment to wash and change clothes, I had persisted in questioning him about what he and his sister wanted from the wine shop. Hugo DeFarge was under the impression that I had been sent there to kidnap his boy and, now that I knew that Celeste was JJ's mother, I saw why he might think that. I had been going over Hugo's strange words ever since I had run away from him and had, by then, formed an idea about why it mattered to Hugo that Jerome was bound to be childless. If the Lamoreaux estate could only be passed through the male line than JJ, Jerome's nephew, was to inherit it after his death. Hugo DeFarge had been hoarding the wedding certificate, not to blackmail or extort money from anyone, but because it was the key to his beloved son's future wealth.

Jerome had still not confirmed any of these assertions, but then neither had he denied them. He was, of course, preoccupied by the horrible mess he had just made of another human being and his whole body shook whenever he thought upon it. While he was praying I noticed something very queer about myself. Here I was in this church, after having experienced a day of being shot at and bled on, having witnessed more violent deaths within a few hours than I had ever seen before in my already harrowing life, and yet I was feeling alright. More than alright, I was fresh, alert and ready for the next challenge revolutionary Paris was to hurl at me. I was concerned about getting back to Nick of course but, despite worrying about his safety, I felt more clear-headed than I had in a very long time. Even the constant sound of distant gunfire could not dull my cheerful mood. Perhaps, I pondered as I watched Jerome's lips moving in prayer, this was because historically those of us with wicked hearts cope better during periods of evil than others. Or was it simpler than that? Was I feeling this sharp because I had not enjoyed a puff of opium in almost a week now?

A long queue was forming down the church aisle for this hot soup and bread rolls what the priest was dishing out near the altar. As I got up to join the end of it, I wondered when the last time that I had felt so lucid was. I decided that it must have been during my incarceration in the condemned cell of Newgate Prison. During that short period, when every minute what passed was one closer to my terrible appointment with the executioner, I had spent my ever-narrowing time concocting escape plans and holding myself with far more composure than my other doomed cellmates. It was only afterwards, when I was trying to enjoy my eventual acquittal and my comfortable life with Lily and Robin, that the nightmares started to come and I turned to the poppy tears for relief.

By the time I reached the front of the queue and was served my helping of soup from the pot, I had begun to wonder if I was the sort of person what needed a perilous life in which to thrive. The trick then to me never needing opium again, I concluded as I returned to Jerome to fill my belly, must be to spend the rest of my life in a state of perpetual danger.

If you are partial to soup what tastes like rainwater and bread what is as hard as stone then that little church near Les Halles would have been the ideal restaurant for you. But it was given free and it fed me for now, so I was not about to lodge a formal complaint. By the time I was licking my bowl clean Jerome had uttered Amen and lifted his head back up. I asked him if he was feeling better, to which he did not say much. Then the two of us moved over to a small, dark corner of the church, away from prying ears and the small congregation of miserable families what was singing mournful songs. I waited for Jerome to speak.

'Hugo DeFarge killed our father,' he began. 'We didn't lie to you about that. We did not lie to you about anything much. But we omitted to say that they were fighting a duel of swords and that my father lost. Guess who they were fighting over?'

'Your sister,' I replied.

'She was still studying at the Sorbonne when Hugo DeFarge seduced her,' he went on. 'And it was my father who first introduced them, would you believe? He liked to show off to his educated, *petit-bourgeois* children about what colourful characters he knew from the Parisian underworld. DeFarge was onesuch, a handsome young ruffian with infamous ancestors. My father had first met him in an opium den and he treated him like another son, much to my chagrin. Celeste adored him, though. Rich, spoilt girls like her will always be fools for his sort of low scoundrel.'

'You're telling me,' I nodded, thinking on all the rich, spoilt girls I had met in my time. 'He took her virginity then?'

'I don't know about that,' sniffed her brother. 'I said she was studying at the Sorbonne, not a nunnery. But her belly began to grow bigger, and once it became apparent that this was not due to gluttony, DeFarge was revealed as the culprit. Our father became apoplectic and challenged him to a duel. A brave thing to do, considering their difference in age and DeFarge's reputation as a swordsman. Brave, but mad.'

'So it wasn't murder, then,' I said.

'I beg your pardon?'

'If one cove challenges another cove to a duel and the first cove dies, that ain't murder. That's just sport with some risk involved.'

'My father *was* murdered!' Jerome shouted then, loud enough that we drew attention from every corner of the church. The priest glowered at us from his place at the altar. 'What else would you call killing a man in secret and then concealing the act for some years afterwards, eh?'

'I've heard of worse,' I said, thinking of Gaspard again. But Jerome seemed to have a short memory about that death and continued raging about the injustices done to his own loved ones.

'Nobody had been told about their night-time duel,' he said, 'other than their respective seconds and a handful of others. Nobody knew who my father had been fighting when his body was found and DeFarge – unconscionable villain that he is – married my sister the following week!'

A formidable looking nun came over to shush him then and he bowed to her, made the sign of the cross, and spoke soft once she had gone again.

'But I always knew that DeFarge was the killer!' Jerome leaned closer so that I could hear him. 'He had those cuts on his face, for one thing. I tried to convince Celeste but she was too in love with the man, she believed every lie that he told her. They moved into that wretched wine shop together and she gave birth to a boy. It was another two years until I received irrefutable written evidence as to the identity of the man who our father had fought with. When Celeste read it she recoiled from DeFarge, seeing him for who he really was, and she fled his home. She and I have been living in England ever since, working on our claim to the Lamoreaux fortune.'

'She abandoned her son?' I asked, thinking on little Robin again and how Lily had just given him away to other people. 'Cruel of her.'

'Celeste is a fine mother,' Jerome seemed offended on her behalf. 'She loves Jean-Jacques and she bitterly regrets leaving him now. But, at the time, it made more sense for him to remain with his father as her life was to become nomadic and most unsuitable for a child. However, she and I have a relative who is a lawyer and it was he who recently uncovered the existence of this wedding certificate that proves our legitimacy. How DeFarge managed to get hold of the document before we did is still a mystery to us but we know that he has it. It will make Jean-Jacques rich too, of course,' he concluded, 'once I am dead.'

'Think how special little JJ's going to feel,' I remarked with an air of heavy cynicism, 'when his long-lost mother reappears just at the point when it becomes clear he's worth a small fortune. It's just the sort of thing my mother would have done.'

'A slur against my sister's character,' Jerome replied. 'But it does not matter what you think. You are employed to rob a shop, not to pass judgment on our motives. And I think it is time for you to get back to work, no? I am worried for my sister, she never returned from delivering you to the wine shop early this morning and, in this vicious climate, she could be dead in a gutter. You must return to Saint-Antoine and look for her. I shall remain here where it is safe.'

'Sorry to disappoint you, my lion-hearted friend, but you're coming with me. I need you to show me the way back to the shop.'

Jerome looked horror-stricken at the suggestion that he leave this humble asylum, but I did not care much for his sensitivities in that moment. I was no longer interested in the affairs of these descendants of nobility and the same went for Hugo DeFarge's revolutionary cause. My one remaining responsibility was getting back to Nick to make sure that he was safe. I had been wrong to bring someone so young on a dangerous journey like this and, if anything bad had happened to him while I had been away, I would never forgive myself.

'I'll take you as far as the Hôtel de Ville,' Jerome at last conceded.

'You'll take me as far as I'll need you to,' I told him as I stood. 'Which will be much further than that.'

'You cannot talk to me like this,' Jerome protested as I loomed over him. 'You work for me, do not forget.'

I grabbed him by the coat collar and forced him to his feet. 'You seem to be mistaken, my covey,' I said as I pulled him towards the bolted door of this church, with a view to getting someone to unbolt it for us. 'I ain't your servant and I never was.'

Chapter 17

The Big Au Revoir

*Showing that there are two things what you should
never get caught up in — the revolutions of other countries
and the squabbles of other families*

It was the early hours of the morning as the two of us scudded
through the moonlit city and, although the fighting had ceased,
it was clear that the revolution was sleeping rather than over.
The streets was still foggy from gunpowder and gangs of armed
men, wearing the uniform of the people, labouring smocks and
tricolore cockades, roamed the streets. They would glare at us as
we passed, eyeing Jerome in particular with unguarded distrust.

'Take that rich coat off and dump it, you stupid horse,' I
hissed at him as we cut through the passage of a covered arcade.
'Before you get us both killed.'

Just the day before, I had passed through this fashionable
promenade and admired its checkered tiled floors, gas globe
lamps, fancy columns and high-class shops. But now the whole
arcade had been the victim of a looting frenzy. We crunched
the glass of smashed lamps and windows underfoot and the
keen shoplifter in me was disappointed to find that most of
the jewellers had already been stripped clean.

'This destruction is outrageous,' Jerome complained as he discarded anything from about his person what might identify him as *bourgeoisie,* including his coat and expensive pocket-watch. 'And these monsters will pay. General Cavaignac will prove victorious, you'll see. Brave and patriotic men will come from all over France to volunteer their services against this insurgency. More cavalry will come too and, soon enough, they will overwhelm the barbarian hoard and order will be restored.'

'Even in English you may want to watch that sort of talk, Jerome,' I advised him as we came to the end of an alleyway. We paused there to ensure that there was nobody about to cause us any trouble before we pressed on. 'And don't be so certain. French history tends to favour the revolutionaries, so if I was a gambling man – which I am – I'd bet on my class, not yours. The best thing that your government could do now, for all our sakes, is to surrender. It'll save everyone a lot of aggravation.'

Along the length of a wide commercial street known as the Rue de Rivoli there was several barricades what was taller and even more impressive than any I had seen yet. They was all manned by unfriendly men with guns and they decided who was permitted to pass over them and who was not. I had already suggested to Jerome that we continue to travel via the backstreets, but he was too terrified of shadows and knew those routes even less than I did. So instead we was compelled to negotiate our way past these stony obstructions. Jerome did a better job of convincing the barricade men that he was sympathetic to their cause than I would have imagined and there was a chance, I considered as we was waved over, that his dark skin colour helped to disguise the fact that he was of an enemy class. I wondered if this would make him feel grateful for his slave ancestry, but somehow I doubted it.

We soon came to the Hôtel de Ville, what was no longer under a state of siege. Battalions of the National Guard was encamped around that important government building and they too was showing hostility towards anyone who approached it without clear reason. They seemed to be tense enough where a change in the wind could have set them off shooting, so it was not I place I wished to linger around. In truth, it would be easy for me to find my way back to the wine shop alone now, but I was reluctant to tell Jerome that, as I was glad of his company. Neither of us was very likely to consider the other to be any kind of pal, but at least he could speak English.

'So I'm still prepared to steal that document you want, Jerome,' I told him as we turned the corner away from the Hôtel de Ville. We quickened our step now that we was not under so much military observation. 'If you're still prepared to pay me for it. But I ain't getting involved in no kidnapping plot. Lets be clear on that.'

'I never asked you to kidnap the boy!' he replied and seemed incredulous that I should have even suggested that he might. 'Such a thing was never part of my scheme. Celeste and I agreed. She would help me to secure the Lamoreaux fortune and I, in return, would make her son my heir. Our plan was a simple one. You steal back the wedding certificate. We use it to claim our fortune and then, once wealthy, Celeste would be able to regain custody of the son she abandoned. *Voila!* No need for kidnapping.'

'The little boy who I saw in that wine shop was a happy soul who loved his father very much,' I told him as we reached the edge of the suburb. 'Now you might not care much for Hugo DeFarge – and I can't say that I'm a great lover of him either, since he tried to shoot me in the head – but he struck me as being a good father to his son. Celeste, meanwhile, hasn't seen JJ since he was two. So maybe the boy won't want to come and live with you Lamoreaux. He might want to stay here with the people who care about him.'

'What? In this *pissoire!*' scoffed Jerome as he beheld the broken down vicinity of Saint-Antoine. 'I think not! With my sister and myself he will enjoy a life of great wealth and luxury. If you were offered the opportunity at his age to leave your London slum and live among a better class, would you have refused it?'

We passed by the spot where I had earlier seen the vagrant licking the spilt wine from the cobbles. Now there was dark scarlet stains of a different sort close by, but I ignored them and pondered Jerome's question. I had been very happy growing up in Fagin's den in Saffron Hill. If someone was to have come along and offered me a chance to leave there and live among the rich, would I have taken it? That it was taking me longer than an instant to think of the answer was in itself revealing.

'His father is most probably dead by now anyhow,' I said as we came to the corner of DeFarge's street. 'Or arrested. But there is an Irishman in there, guarding the place, so I shall have to be careful.' Before we went any further I stopped Jerome and took out the small bunch of keys from my pocket. 'You don't have to come with me,' I decided. 'You'd be a liability anyway.' He could not hide the tremendous relief on his face when I said that and, for a moment, it looked like he would turn on his heels and bolt before I had even finished the sentence. But then he hesitated.

'Perhaps I should remain and assist you,' he whispered after some deliberation. 'Who knows what you'll discover when you go in there? You might need my help.'

'Why would you want to help me?'

'I should not be a coward,' he winced. 'My father was never a coward, we cannot say that of him. He was a philanderer, true. A drunkard, a brawler, a bankrupt and an opium fiend. Let us speak plain, the man was a mighty fool. But he was never a coward and nor was his father, who faced the guillotine. If I am to be their legitimate successor then I should be braver than I am.'

I looked around the corner towards the wine shop. As before, all the windows was covered.

'I won't need you,' I assured him. 'I'm just going to knock on that door and see who is home. Then I'll ask to see my brother. Once inside, I'll slip him the keys and he can search the top rooms to find the certificate, while I distract the adults. Or, better yet,' I added as a good idea occurred, 'I'll just get someone to fetch it for us.'

'What if nobody is home?' Jerome asked. 'It looks like nobody is. What if those keys do not unlock the front door?'

'Then I'll just break in,' I said and studied the shop to see how I might do this. One of the first-floor windows had been smashed since the last time I was here and had been boarded up with what looked like thin wood. It was around the side of the building, a place not many other windows overlooked and it should be easy to climb up to if I used the low fence nearby. I pointed this window out to Jerome. 'That's an easy entrance,' I explained. 'A child could do it. But it would be helpful to me if you could act as a look-out should I need to enter through it. In truth, no matter how I get in, I could use somebody out here to warn me if trouble should come. Could you do that? A crow call or something of the kind?'

Jerome assured me that he was up to such a task, and he looked pleased to be making himself useful for the first time in his life. He wished me good luck and so I left him there, hiding in the shadows of Saint-Antoine while I returned to the wine shop, keen to find out how my young assistant had been occupying his time.

One sharp but loud knock upon that shop door was all it took for it to be flung open. I was most taken aback by this, as, considering the unsociable hour, I had been all set to have to make more of a racket before being allowed in. I twitched when I saw who had answered the door – Father Pierre, that brute priest who had welcomed me into this shop last time by punching me on the side of the head. His greeting this time was not much more gracious. He grunted upon seeing me standing there in the dark, looked beyond to check if anyone was with me, then grabbed me by the shirt and tugged me inside. I shoved him back as he did so, to convey that I was not going to be putting up with any more of his manhandling, but he was almost twice the size of me so did not seem bothered. Instead, he shut the door after me and said something in French for the benefit of other ears.

'Londoner Jack has returned, has he?' a flat, Irish voice said from somewhere in the dark of the main bar. 'I must confess, that of all the people I had prayed to see back safe from the fighting, you were not the highest on the list.'

The inside of DeFarge's wine shop seemed even glummer than it did upon my first visit. All the curtains was drawn and few candles was lit. It looked like a place of mourning. Most of the chairs was stacked up beside the tables, save for one. Around this I could see a solitary smoker and the orange tip of his lit cigar.

'Nice to see you 'n all, Brendan,' I replied as I stepped away from Father Pierre, as he went about lighting more candles, and towards the smoking Irishman. 'Still fighting the revolution from the comfort of your chair, I notice.'

'I take offence at that.'

'Take it how you like,' I shrugged and sat down in one of the chairs opposite him. 'Where's my brother?'

'Gone.'

'What?' I asked, in genuine alarm. 'Gone where?'

'He left here about an hour after you did. Kept going on about wanting to fight in the revolution. Wanted to follow after his big brother Jack.'

A tall candle flickered between us. Brendan had his head

turned away as he smoked and he seemed unconcerned by my obvious upset.

'You promised to look after him!' I pointed, in accusation. 'You should have kept him here. It ain't safe out there on those streets.'

'He didn't say goodbye or nothing,' Brendan said in a more defensive tone, after taking another puff. 'I'd have stopped him if I could.' He shifted his head towards the light then and his face looked even more anxious than Jerome's had been. 'We've had our own problems here without looking to your brother. Tell me, have you seen Hugo? Is he still alive?'

'The last time I saw him he was at the barricade by the Saint-Denis gate,' I told him. 'Alive, yeah. But his legs was all bust up. He was in a bad way.'

Brendan translated that for Father Pierre, who pressed his palms together and looked upwards in thanks. Then the brute priest asked something in French, what I gathered was supposed to be addressed to me. I recognised a name and the French word for dead.

'Armand is *mort*,' I confirmed. 'He died like a hero upon the barricades.'

Brendan did not seem too bothered about that news, but once it had been explained to Father Pierre, he cursed in grief and beat his fist against the wall.

'A child went with them,' Brendan asked. 'A little red-haired girl, you may have noticed her. Is she—'

I interrupted his question with a small, solemn nod. Brendan's free hand went up to his face.

'To hell with this revolution,' he said.

Then Pierre bombarded me with other names, but I recognised none of them. 'I tell you who did get killed though,' I said before they could ask after them. 'Adele and Babette. I'm very sorry.'

'Who?' asked Brendan.

'Adele and Babette,' I repeated. 'Them two prostitutes what was working here. They was both members of the Club of Jacks.' Brendan nodded at last. 'And you can take it from me,' I went on as he began translating to the priest, 'they was two of the bravest revolutionaries out there. They was among the first to climb the barricades and they suffered for their heroism. But they was still defiant in their deaths, you can trust me on that.'

But, as in my own city, while people will always be prepared to throw a festival of mourning for a bastard like Armand, nobody much cares about the whores. The priest shrugged at the news and I even heard him mutter *bien* under his breath. I wanted to kill him for that. It reminded me of how, in Bethnal Green, they all still sing songs about Bill Sikes, but nobody can even remember Nancy's surname.

'Not much of a Christian attitude,' I snapped at him.

'He's not a very Christian man, for all his posturing,' Brendan said, and I got the strong impression that he did not much care for Pierre either. 'He stole that priest's outfit from somewhere. Uses it to get up to all sorts. He's as religious as you are, I'd wager.' Then Brendan stubbed out the last of his cigar and leaned in closer to the flame. 'Here's a question for you, Londoner,' he spoke with urgency. 'And think on it hard. When you were here yesterday did you happen to see anyone who struck you as suspicious?'

'I ain't met a Frenchman yet what hasn't struck me as suspicious,' I replied.

'I'm speaking of a woman,' he said. 'Tallish, wearing widow's weeds. A very thick black veil covering her face. She was here, stood among the crowd listening to Hugo as he made his speech. She blended in well, as in these dangerous days, widows are commonplace.'

A sudden thought struck me. I had in truth seen a black lacy veiled dress twice yesterday. The first time was on my early journey through Paris when Celeste, Nick and myself had all stopped to look in that pawnbroker's window. Hanging from a rail, among many other rich clothes, was a mourning dress for sale. Then, only hours later, I had seen a woman wearing something very similar what concealed her face, in this here shop.

'Yeah, I saw a widow,' I said to Brendan once I had made the connection and realised what it might mean. 'Just after the revolution had been declared. She was among those what your imposter priest over there,' I pointed to Pierre, 'was trying to get to fight. You,' I pointed back to Brendan, 'defended her. You was saying she could stay here with the other women and children, under your protection.'

'Don't remind me,' he groaned. 'This is all my fault. Hugo will kill me if he ever returns.'

'What's happened?'

'Jean-Jacques is missing. We think this woman may have abducted him during all the fighting.'

'Hugo's son, you mean?' I asked. 'Little JJ?'

'He's been missing for hours and he isn't one to run away. This widow was seen playing with him before then. Whispering things into his ear and such. He seemed to like her. I got distracted when I had to go upstairs to board up a smashed window and when I returned down here,' Brendan raised his hands up to his temples in a gesture of shame, 'he was gone. And so was she.'

The distress on my face as he told me all of this must have been convincing, as it was not just for show. There could be no doubt now that the woman behind that thick black veil was Celeste and that she had abandoned all pretence at following Jerome's plan before reclaiming her child. It upset me to think that she might have endangered her own son just for financial gain.

'Pierre thinks he knows who she was,' Brendan continued and gave the man in the dog collar a hateful look. 'He didn't recognise her at the time, on account of the black veil but he now reckons it was Madame DeFarge. Hugo's estranged wife.'

'*Madame DeFarge,*' Pierre said in his deep gravelly voice and he picked up a short musket and pointed at nobody. He looked to be a little drunk.

'She the boy's mother?' I asked.

'Aye. And she's a wicked harlot from what I hear of her. Broke Hugo's heart and abandoned the family. She bedded half of Paris after that, and now she's stolen the boy who I was charged to protect, right out from under my nose.'

'Not very good at protecting kinchins are you, Brendan?' I

said in a proper temper. 'That's two you've failed to keep an eye on.'

When he spoke next it was in a quiet, mumbled voice, more to himself than to me. 'Hugo DeFarge saved my life once,' he said. 'Stopped me from hurling myself from off the Pont Neuf and into the freezing river when I was in one of my black moods. And I couldn't even repay him by keeping an eye on his only child. He should have just let me jump.'

Before I had entered the shop I had devised a scheme to find the wedding certificate, without even needing to search the rooms above. This scheme was simple and required so little effort on my part that I could not see how it might fail. But, now that I had heard about this child abduction and seen how much it had affected Brendan here, I was not so certain that it was a good idea. The atmosphere in this shop was too heavy now, these people too suspicious. On the other hand, I was at a loss as to how I could be expected to explore the rooms above under the same conditions. Both of these men had guns, so a conventional burglary, like the one I had described outside to Jerome, would be impossible. Nick was not here either, so there was nothing to stop me from just making some excuse, leaving and never coming back. But I had not come all this way, and gone through all I had that day, to give up now.

'There might be a way you can redeem yourself in Hugo's eyes,' I said to Brendan in a confidential tone. 'When I saw him last, at the bottom of a barricade, his legs was done in and all his other pals either dead or missing. He had nobody else to give orders to but me.'

'What orders?' Brendan looked sceptical.

'He wants me to fetch him some documents. That's why he gave me these.' I reached into my pocket and produced the set of keys to the upstairs rooms.

'And take them where? From the sound of things he could be either dead or in the Tuileries cells by now.'

'Perhaps, but perhaps not,' I said. 'He showed me a house near the Rue Saint-Denis where he could crawl or be carried to. He said the people who lived there would be sympathetic to our cause and that I should take the documents there if the revolution fell.'

'What are these documents?'

'The bank note of course!' I said. 'Hugo thinks he might need ready money if the republic win and he has to flee Paris. He'll want to bank it and start a new life. And there was something else but I can't remember what it was.'

'Think!' he demanded.

'Some legal document or some-such.' I tapped my chin with my middle finger. 'A wedding certificate? He said it was very old.'

Brendan reacted like he had never heard Hugo say anything about no wedding certificate before, but when he translated my words to Pierre, things became agitated. It seemed that the man dressed like a priest did know what I was talking about and they began conferring in a hurried way. When I heard Pierre mention the names Lamoreaux and Cupidon I knew I had hit my mark.

'Give me those keys,' he said and I let him snatch them from me. 'Pierre thinks he knows what Hugo means and that it could well be related to his wife's return.'

Then I followed him as he ran through the length of the bar to the back staircase, what led upwards through the house. Pierre grabbed his short but heavy musket gun and walked up the steps after me, grumbling something what could only be a threat. The climb was tight and steep but we soon reached the fifth and final floor. Here, an abrupt turn revealed a low door what led into a garret room and Brendan tried two keys on the bunch before at last finding the one what turned it.

The garret room was small and dim and only a small dormer window in the roof let in any light. It stank of old boots. There was a cherry-coloured desk in there, as well as matching shelves with dusty books and boxes on and two large chests on either side. Some lamps hung from the low rafters and Brendan handed me a match so we could get them lit.

'I suspect that Hugo only trusted you with all this on account of your close proximity at the time,' he said once the garret was better illuminated. 'So if we find this certificate he prizes, then you'll show me the house and, if he's there, I'll hand it to him myself.'

'Fair enough.' I was confident enough now in the return of my pickpocketing skills that I knew that Brendan's possession of the certificate would only ever be a temporary arrangement. 'I'm just happy to help.'

Pierre and Brendan grabbed hold of one of the chests and hauled it to the side. It revealed, hidden within the wall behind it, a steel iron safe. Brendan took one of the keys and unlocked it, as Pierre held a candle in a cleft stick close by. From inside Brendan pulled out the worthless bank note and handed it to me. Then he began searching through some other things what were contained within. I saw the sparkle of some diamonds reflected off the candlelight, a wine bottle and plenty of yellow, rolled-up legal documentation. Brendan pulled these out and placed them on the desk and Pierre began looking through the small bundle of papers for the certificate what would prove that the Lamoreaux's grandfather had married a slave. The rest of us huddled around in anticipation as he read the tiny text. But he cursed and threw them to the ground. Brendan locked up the valuables again and they both continued a frantic, disordered search through the many drawers in the chests and the desks. I tried to help, but considering all the paperwork was written in French, it was not likely I would find the desired certificate before either of them.

However, my attention was captured by something sat upon that cluttered desk what would not have appeared strange to their eyes, but what struck me as very peculiar. Here, in this hitherto locked room, was that same little toy bear what JJ had been holding onto when Nick and myself visited his room. I picked it up as Brendan and Pierre continued searching and I squeezed it as I thought about how it had managed to get through that door. There really was only one explanation and I smiled to myself as I placed the toy into my jacket pocket.

From somewhere lower down in the house came a violent crash of glass and a loud thump. Pierre started at the noise, grabbed the musket what he had laid down beside on the desk and crossed over to the doorway. There was some panicky chatter between the two men and then Pierre went downstairs to investigate. Brendan began to follow, but then stopped to point his own smaller gun at me.

'I'm not leaving you in here, Londoner,' he said and motioned for me to exit the room. As I left the garret room empty-handed and Brendan locked it after me, I could hear Pierre thundering down the many stairs to the first floor and then him shouting at someone. 'He says it's an intruder,' Brendan told me.

Then I heard a high, frightened voice from down there and a chill ran through me. Could it be my young assistant returning? And, if so, what would an armed and drunken man like Pierre do to a burglar?

'Wait!' I shouted as I began bound down the steps. 'Don't hurt him! He's with me!'

But of course Pierre could not have understood me anyway and, by the time I made it down to the third floor the shouting from both parties had reached an excitable pitch. The other voice was hysterical now and it sounded like they was both in that large room where the Club of a Thousand Jacks had met for our battle meeting. The intruder must have entered through the broken window. I was still a flight of stairs away, but I could hear the altercation getting worse. The familiar voice pleaded to Pierre for mercy.

Gunshots fired and they may have been the loudest ones I had heard in Paris yet. I had just reached the door of that room, but the blasts was so deafening that I had to stop and protect my ears. I no longer wanted to enter now, in fear that the firing had not finished. Brendan came clattering down the stairs after me and we looked at one another as if wondering which of us, if either, was to be the first to open the door and see what had happened. I decided that I needed to see and so went in.

That large room was now a tableau of just two people. The man dressed as a priest stood in its centre, still pointing his smoking gun. The intruder was lying on top the table, but about to slip off it, bringing the tricolore flag that the club had been using as a tablecloth down with him. I could tell who it was just from his expensive shoes.

'Jerome!' I cried when I saw his face and I dashed towards him to assess how bad the damage was. He was staring up at the ceiling and had taken three shots to the chest. It was a terrible sight, but at that moment I felt only relief that it was not, as I had first feared, the boy Nick who had placed himself in such peril.

For some bewildering reason Jerome had climbed through that vulnerable window just as I told him I was fixing to do earlier. His distressed eyes locked with mine as a red stain spread over his already bloodied shirt. He looked as though he was about to scold me for failing to protect his life, like a good servant should.

'What did you do that for, Jerome?' I whispered into his ear when I saw how serious those wounds was. 'You should leave burglary to the professionals!'

His lips was shaking in distress but he at last found a voice. 'Courage, Jack,' he rasped. 'I need to be as brave as a Lamoreaux shoul–' Then he slipped off the table altogether and the tricolore flag wrapped itself around him. I grabbed him and tried to pull him up again, but it was clear that one of those bullets had hit something vital. He died quick.

I cursed Jerome for his stupidity. He had earlier described his father as being 'brave but mad' and so it seemed that, in the end, he was a lot like him after all. Despite all the many good reasons Jerome had given me to dislike him during our short acquaintance, I instead found myself overcome with anger at another violent death of someone, I was then realizing, I had grown almost fond of. I turned back to face the ugly sod who had killed poor Jerome.

'This man was unarmed!' I shouted at Pierre, confident that he would now be out of shot. 'You're a murderer, you are!'

Pierre had lowered his gun by then, but was eyeing me hard. Brendan had entered and they had been muttering something to each other in French.

'Your intruder friend there was familiar to Pierre,' Brendan said. Then he walked over to the still open door and slammed it shut. 'He says that some years back he acted as a second in a duel for Hugo DeFarge. DeFarge had been challenged by his father-in-law.'

I began inching towards the open window what Jerome had just entered through, but Pierre barked at me to stop.

'The father-in-law himself was killed in the duel, so this isn't him. But Pierre says that your man there is his younger image. Hugo's father-in-law had two children. One was Hugo's wife, the woman we think kidnapped little JJ. And he also had a son.' Brendan turned to Father Pierre and asked, in French, what the son's name was again.

'Jerome,' the priest replied with a spit.

'Which means, Londoner,' the Irishman reached into his jacket pocket, pulled out his small pistol and pointed it right at me, 'that you are in a fair bit of trouble.'

Chapter 18

Bourgeois Bones

Featuring the fun French game of Cherchez La Femme

I could no longer even cry for help, as I was too short of air. What little air there was in my cramped subterranean box tasted of gunpowder, metal and wood shavings. I could feel tiny steel balls rolling around underneath my body, but there was not enough room in there to shift them so they was just adding to my intense discomfort. This coffin-like trap was not built for storing people, at least not living people, and so there was no natural air vent, just tiny holes where knots used to be. I had, to all intents and purposes, been buried alive.

The terror deepened as I scratched around the edge of the trap for some minutes looking for an inside lock what I might be able to turn, but gained nothing from that other than raw, splintered fingertips. I was unsure if screaming for help again would be a smart move as I did not want to use more air than necessary, but hopelessness was starting to set in. I tried to remind my panicking self that, if they meant to kill me, they would have done it by now. It was more probable, I tried to reason, as I placed my mouth close to the small holes in the wood, desperate for air, that they wanted to interrogate me and this was the first of many tortures.

I managed to raise one palm to my face, so I could feel the fresh bumps and bruises I had received at the hands of Pierre and they stung even more at the touch. To my credit though, I had left him with a few sharp ones of his own and I would wager that his hurt worse than mine. I had never engaged in fisticuffs with a man dressed like a priest before, but this Father Pierre had had it coming. I was so outraged by Jerome's murder that I did not even let the threat of Brendan's gun stop me from giving the holy imposter a good hiding. It was only when Brendan gave me a clout over the head with the pistol butt that I dropped to my knees and surrendered.

Pierre then shouted abuse at the Irishman and I guessed that he was telling him that, if he had been the one holding that gun, then I would have a bullet in my head already. But Brendan did not appear to be the cold-blooded executioner sort and, since Pierre had no authority over him, they instead had to endure my kicking, biting and colourful Anglo-Saxon language as I was forced down the stairs at gunpoint, into the main saloon bar. Pierre had pulled back the threadbare rug what covered one of the shops many secret hatches and pulled it up by its hook.

'I'd advise you to take short breaths,' Brendan said as he and his gun forced me down into it where the artillery had been kept. 'When we let you out we'll want to know where JJ is. Your life will depend upon us receiving a true and helpful answer.'

But, despite this promise of a reprieve, I had been left down there in the pitch darkness for what seemed like an hour, but on reflection, was perhaps closer to twenty minutes. That they would still want to question me about my involvement with the Lamoreaux family, or if I knew where little JJ was, was in my favour. What was not in my favour was that I did not know where little JJ was and so, on learning that, they might well kill me after all.

After a period of silence, footsteps was again heard crossing back and forth and I could tell from these that Brendan and Father Pierre had been joined by more people. I could hear a heated discussion going on above me and I was just about readying to launch another noisy assault upon the wood, when the lock turned and the trapdoor lifted. A spasm of coughing and blinking took grip of me as I breathed in better air and I saw four angry men looking down on me.

'The sun has risen already,' Brendan said as if he thought I would be interested. 'But then that's these long summer days for you, I suppose. Lets see if you can stay alive long enough to see the same one set.'

Then I was hauled out of that wooden hatch by the two ugly and armed newcomers, both of whom I recognised as being members of the Club of a Thousand Jacks. I was breathing hard as I was thrown onto a rickety wooden chair in the middle of the bar. Brendan took another opposite me. He removed his crooked spectacles, pinched the bridge of his nose and sighed as if this was all too much for him.

'You know, Napoleon Bonaparte once described the English

as a nation of shopkeepers,' he said as the three others all positioned themselves around me, guns by their sides. 'He flattered
you. Shoplifters would have been more accurate.' Then he
placed his awkward spectacles back on with some difficulty,
before continuing. 'I always knew you were no revolutionary.
I suspected you of being a thief and lo, it transpires that you
are one. A thief who's in league with the Cupidon woman
and her late brother, imbecile that he clearly was. Don't go
insulting us with a denial now, I've headache enough as it is.'

He had some nerve complaining to me about a headache
after the knock he had delivered to me, but I was still too
busy panting to point that out. I tried to say something in my
defence, but as forming words was still difficult for me, he kept
talking as if giving me time to get my voice back.

'You might be interested to know that the body of Jerome
Cupidon,' Brendan took care to stress the illegitimate slave
name, 'is wrapped up in that tricolore flag, which is now lying
in the gutter just outside in the street there.' He waved his pistol
towards the front door. 'On any other week, leaving a still
bleeding corpse to stink outside your shop would be considered
bad for business. But this is no ordinary week, is it? There's
anonymous bodies lying about all over the city and, same as
last night, a cart will trundle by before the dawn to remove
him along with all the others. He'll end up beneath the city in
the catacombs, I shouldn't wonder, with tens of thousands of
nameless others and they shall all turn into skeletons together.
Down there there'll be nothing to separate his bourgeois bones
from theirs and that, you thieving shit, is the final equality.'

To the left of him stood Father Pierre eyeing me hard and, at regular intervals, he would touch his musket gun which, I had no doubt, was by now reloaded. He rubbed the bruises I had given him whenever our eyes met and I knew that he would seize upon any excuse to shoot me dead. To the right of Brendan was a club member whose name I had not yet learnt, but who seemed less concerned with what was going on with me than he was involved with sticking his finger into his ear and inspecting the wax he produced from it. Behind me, the fourth man, who I had heard them call Etienne, sat on a chair in disinterested silence.

'Where is DeFarge's son?' Brendan asked once he had deemed that I had been given enough time to get my breath back.

'Water,' I said in a rough voice.

'Tell us where JJ is,' Brendan said, 'and you'll be given some.'

'Dunno where he is,' I answered after another cough. 'If I did, I would tell you.'

'Then what use are you to us?' he said and rose from his seat, as if about to give an order.

'Wait!' I stopped him. 'I didn't come to Paris to be part of no kidnapping plot and nor did my brother. We was hired by the Cupidons to steal that document I spoke of. I didn't even know JJ was Celeste's son until a few hours ago.'

'So what you said about Hugo hiding in a house in Saint-Denis,' he touched his spectacles again, 'that was a lie? We should kill you for that alone.'

But for all his tough talk there was a discernible shake in Brendan's behaviour. He wiped sweat from his brow with the sleeve of his gun arm and I got the impression that he was as shocked by recent events as I was. He was a man who had chosen to stay and protect a property rather than take to the barricades, and he had protected others from being bullied into fighting. He may have had no love for me, but I had known some killers in my time and this here cove was not born to it. Pierre and these other two was a worry to me, but I suspected that Brendan could be reasoned with.

'I am not a man you want to kill,' I insisted before he could prove me wrong. 'I am a man you want to put to work. If we can find out where she is, then I think I can talk some sense into Celeste. I'll help you get JJ back.'

'What sort of sense?'

'She don't want that little boy,' I asserted with as much authority as I could manage. 'She don't care for him one bit. She hated her brother, she put up with him because he was the heir. She just wants the Lamoreaux fortune and JJ's the key to it, especially now that Jerome is dead.'

'How would you know what she does and does not want?'

'Now, I don't claim to be her intimate friend or nothing,' I shrugged. 'But she's *bor jwa,* ain't she? So it stands to reason that she cares only for herself. I don't reckon she's got a maternal bone in her body.'

Brendan nodded as though this logic was inarguable, then translated it to the others. I felt the sting of disloyalty saying these dismissive things about Celeste's character, but although I had grown to like her during our short time together, I had seen little from her to disprove my claims. She had abandoned her son once before and so it followed she could abandon him again if he proved worthless to her.

'I'll tell her that I've searched this shop good and thorough,' I went on, 'and I never found no wedding certificate. I'll tell her that I have reached the conclusion that Hugo DeFarge never even had it. Then, once convinced that her son has no value to her, she'll return him unharmed. I guarantee it.'

'She won't believe that.'

'She will, because it's the truth,' I persisted. 'If Hugo had that wedding certificate, then it would have been in his office up there. We're chasing ghosts here and I can convince her of it.'

'Hugo does have it and his wife knows it full well,' Brendan told me after a short conference with the others. 'Pierre has even seen the thing. A lawyer friend of DeFarge's in Saint-Domingue unearthed a whole collection of old documents pertaining to the old regime and the wedding certificate was among them. DeFarge paid good coin for it before Jerome and his sister could outbid him, so she knows for certain that he has it.'

Before I could think of another reason for them not to kill me, we was interrupted by a hurried knocking upon the front window. Brendan went over to the door, slid back three bolts and in scurried one of those same messenger boys what had come to tell us that the revolution had been declared. It seemed like he worked for the Club of Clubs and he was circulating news about the fighting. Now that the door was open, I could hear the sound of cannon fire echoing again across the city. It seemed that the revolution could not even wait for both sides to enjoy a reasonable breakfast before firing up again.

The messenger babbled something about Hugo DeFarge and whatever it was it sent Pierre into an almighty rage. There was a line of six clean glasses standing on the bar and in his anger he swiped the lot of them onto the floor. This caused the others to jump and cry out at the destruction of it. From this extreme reaction, I took it that they had just been informed that their beloved leader had been killed. And, although it is never nice to hear about a person dying so young, I could not help but wonder how his untimely demise would affect my situation. Brendan's principal motivation in wanting JJ retrieved from Celeste seemed to be so that Hugo would not punish him for losing the boy in the first place, so perhaps I would be released now that it no longer mattered. This was unlikely, given the company he kept, though. The Club of a Thousand Jacks did not seem to be the 'say no more about it' types.

'Our little club has a spy in it,' Brendan said after he had thanked the boy, offered him a drink and bolted the door once he was inside. 'And whoever it is they have identified Hugo to the authorities and will make a political prisoner out of him. He was captured yesterday in Saint-Denis with his legs broken, so that part of your story was true.'

I looked at the other three club members from my seated position and wondered if the spy could be here with us now. Pierre's violent response to hearing of Hugo's capture now struck me as most theatrical. I saw Brendan regarding the smashed glass upon the floor in a distracted way and I wondered if he was thinking the same thing.

'They shoot political prisoners during revolutions,' he went on as he produced a jug of water from behind the bar and poured cups for all of us. 'Often in public.'

'Why are you telling me and not them?' I asked after he had walked over to hand me mine and I had wet my throat. 'Is it because you suspect one of them?'

Brendan looked tired and he removed his glasses so that he could rub his eyes. 'Sometimes it's just nice to give the French a rest,' he said, 'and speak an easier language. Don't read too much into it, I'll still kill you if you can't help me find Hugo's son. Even if his father is set to die I won't let that bitch take him. JJ deserves better.'

I wondered then what this here Irishman's real motives might be for wanting the boy back. Was he too fixing on exploiting JJ for his inheritance? Was there anyone in this city who cared about that boy for his own sake? The answer to that question, I concluded, was probably yes. But Hugo DeFarge had a date with a firing-squad, so his parenting days was almost over.

While we had all been enjoying this brief respite from my interrogation, the man called Etienne had been talking to the messenger boy from the Club of Clubs. It sounded like he was telling him to circulate the word about JJ's abduction while he was on his rounds. But then, after some questioning, the young boy began nodding his head with a sudden vigour. Brendan and the others all responded in surprise and those sat on stools stood to their feet at the import of this news. The boy turned and pointed somewhere in the direction of the street outside. He was pointing, it appeared to me, to the very place where

Brendan had said Jerome's body had been dumped, further down the street. Whatever it was he was saying had a startling effect upon everybody, as if they had all just been told that outside the body of Jerome had got back to his feet and was now staggering back towards the wine shop.

Pierre, Etienne and the earwax man all brandished their weapons and rushed over to the front door what Brendan was already unbolting.

'What's occurring?' I asked him and made a big questioning gesture as the door was being opened.

'Madame DeFarge,' said Pierre, in a grim voice. Then he and the other two Frenchmen rushed out of the door yelling Gallic obscenities. I followed too, hoping to make my escape during the chaos, but Brendan slammed the door in my face before I could exit.

'You're still a prisoner!' he said and pointed his gun at me again.

'But if Celeste is out there, I can help!'

'Get back on your chair!' he commanded.

Once I was sat down again, both Brendan and the messenger boy moved over to different windows so they could see what was happening outside. I continued pestering Brendan with questions but received only taciturn responses. It was clear that the boy had spotted someone outside who answered to Celeste's description, but it did not sound as though they had found her. At length the earwax man was readmitted into the shop with something in his hand what, for once, it did not look like he had burrowed out from his own head.

It looked at first like a black lacy flag, and it was only when he got closer to me that I saw that it was a widow's veil.

'He found that lying across Jerome's face,' Brendan told me in a huff. 'And the boy says he saw a beautiful dark-skinned woman weeping over it. So that disproves your notion that the Cupidon sister cares nothing for the Cupidon brother, doesn't it!' Then, in French, he ordered Earwax to go through the bar to the back door and outside into the courtyard beyond to see if she was hiding behind the back fences. I could not help but notice that Brendan had become even more disturbed by the return of Madame DeFarge to this wine shop than he was before.

'It wasn't you what murdered her brother, Brendan,' I reminded him. 'You ain't killed anyone yet and I'm prepared to tell her so, if need be.'

'Why should I care if she thinks me a killer?' Brendan asked. 'I think she's a whore!'

However, by the way in which he had been making the sign of the cross whenever he thought I wasn't looking, I was starting to suspect that Brendan cared very much about not wanting to be thought a murderer. I did not doubt that he might have it in his political heart to shoot a man in combat for the sake of a revolution, but a cold-blooded kill was not something I thought he would ever be proud of. I decided to put this theory to the test.

'Keep still,' he ordered as I got up from my chair and crossed over to the saloon bar. 'I'll shoot unless you sit down again.'

'Is it too early, I wonder,' I said as I walked over to the part of the long bar where Pierre had been sitting and picked up a corkscrew, 'to open a bottle of wine? I mean, if that clock up there is correct it ain't even nine o'clock, but then I ain't been to bed yet. Would you want to share a glass with me?'

'Stop moving about!' he said as I avoided the smashed glass on the floor and searched for some unbroken ones. He had the door open now, still searching for signs of Celeste and his attention was divided between the street outside and me. I reached down behind the other side of the bar and fished up a pair of upside down glasses by their stems. I had my back to the room, but could see where everyone was through the smeared and scratchy mirror what covered the length of the bar wall. Although bright daylight was streaming in through the open window and door, DeFarge's wine shop still had all the convivial atmosphere of a medieval dungeon. It was the sort of place where even a summer's day could not rid it of its dark gloom. There was plenty of shadowed nooks, arched snugs, wooden partitions and discreet crannies what made it a perfect drinking den for those occupied with sedition and villainy.

'Boy at the window,' I called over to the boy at the window, whose head was almost half out of it as he watched the others. 'Fancy a drop?' The boy did not respond until I whistled and then, when he turned to see me grinning back at him through the mirror, wiggling a now uncorked bottle, he shook his head. 'Please yourself,' I said as I poured my own, 'what about you, Irishman?'

Brendan was now so distracted by the search for the black widow that he did not even deign to answer me. This was most encouraging. I was forming a plot what would involve creeping up to him from behind, clocking him with this bottle, disarming him and taking that pistol for myself. Not a sophisticated plot, I grant you, but these was not sophisticated times.

However, just as my tongue felt the first taste of claret, I saw something so unexpected that it caused me to spit some up. And I wondered, for a short moment, if my hallucinations had come back again.

'Not a good year?' Brendan asked from his position at the door.

'This here is corked,' I said by way of explanation, hoping to conceal the sheer sensation of shock what I had just experienced from looking in the long mirror behind the bar.

'Ask for your money back, then,' sniffed Brendan and he returned his attention to the street. I turned back to the mirror, where I had seen the alarming vision, but all I saw now was my own bashed face staring back at me, a fright in and of itself, but it was not what had caused me to start like that. Because, just seconds before, I had seen another face staring back at me.

It was Celeste. Her face had been paler than usual and there was an expression of utter malice upon it, but it was her alright. She was somewhere in this room with us.

I swivelled around on my stool to see if I was dreaming her. From the reflection behind the bar she looked to have been stood in a far dark corner. I was even more troubled to see that there was no longer anybody there. 'Stop fidgeting, Londoner,' said Brendan, his eyes still fixed upon the street. 'Or you'll be put back in your hole.'

I kept on searching the room for Celeste in as subtle a way as I could, without drawing attention to myself, but I saw no further trace. I turned back to the mirror where I had just seen her and she was gone from there also. So I examined the scene again and noticed something I had missed on my first inspection. In the corner of the wall where I had expected her to be was another mirror, discreet and dull, but there all along. Celeste's image must have been reflected in that, which meant that she had in fact been standing at the exact opposite side of the bar where the door to the staircase was. In a slow, relaxed motion I turned my head to see if she was still there, but now there was just an empty corner where some coats was hanging.

I remembered that Celeste had once lived here as DeFarge's wife and that therefore it was plausible that she would know of any hidden entrances or passages that this shop might have. And a crafty old place like this was bound to have plenty of them.

Father Pierre then bounded back through the door and into the shop, swearing about something at the top of his voice, with Etienne following after. 'Any joy?' I asked as I took another sip of wine. But Pierre just shoved me aside as if I was just some irksome cur that he was growing tired of and pushed on through to the door what led out to the courtyard where the earwax man had earlier gone. He must have been out there for less than two minutes before he began bellowing out in horror.

We all of us raced out into the courtyard to see what was wrong and, because I was the nearest to the door, I was the first to see the horrible sight what awaited us out there. Lying face down in the middle of the cobblestoned yard was earwax man, with blood pooling out from under his head like a red halo. His throat had been slit and then the murder weapon, a small but sharp blade, had been discarded nearby. There was no sign of his killer.

Brendan, Etienne and the young messenger boy bundled into the yard behind me, and all expressed their revulsion upon seeing the murdered man. Brendan ushered the child back inside and away from the scene of the crime, but Etienne was more concerned with grabbing the knife and rushing at me with it. But he soon found that my hands was quicker than his and I grabbed his wrists before he could do me any mischief. We wrestled like that and again I think I could have bested him if it was not for Brendan and his gun, who stopped one of us from killing the other.

Pierre was still shouting curses against the unseen killer and he pointed toward me as if warning her that I would be next. I heard him mention Jean-Jacques, but if he was hoping she would trade her priceless son for me, then he had made a gross misinterpretation of my relationship with her.

'None of this is my doing!' I protested as I was forced at gunpoint back into the bar where Brendan had opened the hatch again. 'I haven't killed a soul and neither have you,' I told him as he insisted that I either get in there again or receive a bullet. 'Don't start now!'

The hatch door was shut over me and I heard its lock turn. Having already survived a session down there I should have known that, despite my fear, I was not going to suffocate if I measured my breathing out in a calm way. But being trapped in a very cramped space with no power to free yourself is not a state of affairs known to promote cool thinking, and so mortal dread took over once more. I was banging against the trap and shouting for help again within seconds.

'Hark this, Brendan!' I called through the small holes. 'I know where the wedding certificate is! It's in my pocket. Let me out and you can have it!' I pressed my ear against the wood above to hear if my lie had been heard, but it had all gone quiet above. A very strange sort of quiet, considering all the drama what must be occurring up there.

Then, a very sudden roaring was heard, an inhuman but somehow familiar sound. Voices began crying out in alarm at it and, I realised in an instant, that my terrible situation had just become far worse.

Someone – Pierre I think – went shrieking from one side of the room to the other. His heavy footsteps as he passed over my hatch even managed to shake the wood. There was plenty of stamping about then, in what must have been a fevered panic and the shouting increased. Brendan seemed to be giving people orders and, by then, I realised that no matter how loud I was to cry, nobody would hear me above that almighty din. So I turned on my side and shoved hard into the trap with my shoulder. I knew they would be able to see the trap throbbing as I pounded upon it and I hoped that somebody might be merciful and release me. But they all sounded far too pre-occupied and Father Pierre was busy snarling that word *putain* in fierce repetition.

Then, a gunshot silenced him. This was followed by the

heaviest thump yet as his burly body must have collapsed to the floor not far from where I was. And that was when the real terror began, both up there and down here.

Another gunshot and another loud thump. Some return fire from a different pistol. Then, the sound of glass shattering. The heat was becoming impossible to tolerate too and I thought I could smell smoke. It was only then that I realised, with a whole new horrifying jolt, that the room above me must be on fire.

'HELP!' I cried, loud and as desperate. 'Don't leave me down here! I'll burn! Let me out!'

The chaos above me was not abating though and I knew then that expecting any of those people up there to come to my aid was becoming less likely by the second. So I renewed my battery against the door, reasoning that if anyone was going to save me from a live cremation, it would have to be me.

Fear though makes us stronger, so now that the smoke was beginning to blow through the holes in this hatch I found that my redoubled efforts was producing a result. There was a definite crack appearing in the wood and I was starting to think that I should be able to punch my arm through and then force myself up. So I put everything into my next heave, but nothing budged. I cried out in despair as I dropped back onto the base of the hatch exhausted, with the bleak thought that I was really going to die.

That was when, above me, the lock turned and the trap-door lifted. I felt an overpowering wave of heat enter the hatch and had to blink hard to see who my saviour was, as a spasm of coughing took grip of me. The room above me was a deep orange now from the flames and smoke obscured the standing figure looking down at me. All I could see from my low position was a dark blue dress and a silver pistol what she then tossed aside.

'You look like a goose cooking in an oven, Dodger,' Celeste said and she crouched down to grab for my hands. 'And you have about your person just the thing I came back for. So get up, and let us flee this wretched shop before it roasts us both.'

Chapter 19

Paris Burns

Something stolen is at last returned

It felt like the whole city was on fire as we ran from the scene. The uprising's second morning of fighting had been even more destructive to the city than the first and so the blazing shop we was leaving behind us in Saint-Antoine was just one of its many problems. The gunshots what had been fired in there also was as nothing compared to the storm of bullets what could be heard everywhere for miles around. The murdered bodies what remained after the rest of us had escaped the flames just added themselves to the tally of the dead.

I had needed Celeste's help not just to escape from out of that hatch but also to support me away from the burning building, as my coughing was heavy and my body so bruised. We had staggered through the fiery shop, past the shot corpse of Father Pierre, towards the front door and there could be no doubt that she was guilty of both murder and arson. Black smoke followed after us, as we at last made it out of that furnace and through the open door. We did not stop running until we was well clear and on the other side of the street.

DeFarge's wine shop was on a tight corner between two lanes, so it had no neighbouring buildings what the fire could spread to. There was, however, some tall tenements what backed onto the shop, and so extinguishing the blaze before it became a full inferno was a priority. Not far from the shop was a water pump and it was there that I saw Brendan and the messenger boy both filling tin buckets and crying out for people to help them fight the flames.

'Should we help?' I called to Celeste before we fled the vicinity. 'We should help!' I knew how devastating such a disaster would be if it had happened in one of the London rookeries I called home. Such an emergency required as many fire-fighters as possible. She stopped running and looked back to the destruction she had created with an impassive expression. Other locals was, by then, running to the shop with buckets and blankets and it looked like there might be a chance that the fire could be contained before it spread.

'I have a child to return to,' she said and took my hand, yanking me further down the street and away from her violent crimes. 'As have you. Nicolas is safe with me, Dodger. Come with me to him.'

In truth, the fire looked like it could be extinguished without my intervention, so I kept following her as she turned a sharp corner into an unprotected yard. Here a beautiful black saddled horse had been hidden, tied to a tree. This horse belonged to her, so it seemed, and she stroked its nose most soft before mounting her. I did likewise and held on tight to her waist as she rode us out of that warren of streets, away from the building she had set alight and from the body of her murdered brother, which was still lying beside the road, wrapped up tight in the French flag. She did not look back.

Celeste proved to be a skilful rider and she raced the horse through tight alleys and around severe corners, until we came to a thoroughfare along which other buildings was on fire and soldiers was fighting insurgents. Many of the hysterical populace screamed at us to stop and help them, but we thundered through to the next beleaguered vicinity. The horse was a splendid specimen but there was only so much fighting and destruction what she was expected to pass before she became agitated, and I began to feel that Celeste was struggling to control her. Soon, we reached a long, wide boulevard, up which Celeste tried to travel but there was several barricades built along it what made easy passage impossible. So we returned to the back streets where we continued heading northwards, up through crooked byways and endless courtyards.

'Where are we going?' I shouted into Celeste's ear as we galloped further away from the centre of the war-torn city. We was heading up a steep incline by then so the horse had slowed but the rumble of violence could still be heard behind us. 'And where did you get this here horse?'

Even from my position behind, as Celeste told me to be quiet, I could hear the crack in her voice. I still had my arms around her waist and I could feel the soft judder what comes when people weep.

'Find somewhere safe and stop,' I told her as we reached the top of a long street what was built on a hill and where things seemed to be, at last, more peaceful than they was below. 'You ain't in any state to keep riding.'

She did not reply but, after some more minutes of traversing this more peaceful suburban section of Paris, I at last felt her body sag in defeat. She brought us to a discreet and flowery park where we could dismount and I collapsed onto the grass in exhaustion, my battered self aching all over. As I did this, Celeste led the horse over to a nearby water trough and I watched her as she treated the beast with much more gentleness and care than I expected from a woman what in the past twenty-four hours had kidnapped a small boy from his home, murdered some men and set fire to a building and, perhaps, a whole vicinity.

I turned from that strange puzzle of a woman and looked around to inspect where we was. This green and hilly mound what we had stopped at seemed to be in a more genteel part of town and I supposed that on an ordinary day it would have been abuzz with the wealthier citizens. However, it seemed that the rich and idle had all had the good sense to flee the city as soon as the poor and hungry rose up and one glance back towards where we had travelled from proved that their decision had been a wise one. From up here we had a perfect overview of all the different districts below and, if I was a painter and wished to capture the entire panorama of this devastating revolution in glorious detached detail, then I could not have asked for a more suitable spot. From up here, I could see far, to Notre Dame's island and beyond. Gun smoke rose from all corners of the metropolis like unnatural clouds, loud cannon-fire was heard booming from the main thoroughfares and I could see every house what was on fire, and there was a fair few of them. I tried to identify from up here the wine shop of Saint-Antoine among the countless garreted rooftops, but my geographical knowledge of the city was still too poor. I hoped that Brendan and the other locals had managed to put it out before it spread. But one thing was for certain as I gazed over the once beautiful city of Paris – the revolution had made a right unholy mess of the place.

The weather was pleasant, though. I raised my face up to the midday sun so that these high summer rays might do my injured face some good and breathed in this finer air. Behind me I heard the horse whinny once she had drunk enough. I saw that Celeste was tying her to some post and heard her saying things in French to the mare what sounded very comforting. Soon, I saw her long and slender shadow lengthen on the grass ahead of me, as she approached from behind. Without making a sound she sat next to me in that now ruined dress and for some moments we both watched the fighting what raged below us. It was as if we was two generals, surveying our battlefield – although I very much doubted that we was supporting the same side.

'Sorry about your brother,' I said after a few more minutes of silence. 'He didn't deserve that end.' She acknowledged my condolences with a small nod and a sniff.

'They just wrapped him up in a flag and threw him out for the dustmen to take away,' she murmured in a tone of disbelief. 'My sweet Jerome.'

'He was too gentle for this cruel world,' I agreed, deeming that now might not be the most sensitive time to mention that he had stabbed an old man to death.

'Indeed,' she said. 'Of the two of us, at least, he was the good one.'

Somewhere down there in the city, there was the biggest explosion yet. I thought I saw the roof of a house collapse.

'Celeste,' I asked after a respectful moment of silence had passed. 'Is it true that Nick is safe?' She nodded and the relief of it was so great that it almost made me forget my bruises for a minute. During that brief moment when I had thought that the imperilled intruder that Pierre was confronting was Nick, I had been gripped with a guilt the like of which I had never before known. If that young rookery boy had ended up dead outside the wine shop, I would never have forgiven myself for bringing him.

'He is with my son in a horse farm just outside of Paris. Our lawyer,' she stopped and corrected herself, '*my* lawyer lives there. He and his family are treating the boys kindly. He also lent me that horse.'

'So JJ is your son, then,' I said to no immediate reply. 'And yesterday you snuck into his home and stole him away without telling anyone. That weren't very nice, was it?'

'Should I have left him down there in the middle of all that?' she cried with indignation, as the noise of the fighting below us grew even fiercer. 'As a war rages around his innocent ears. What mother would not want to pluck their child away to safety?' She had a point, but I was not going to let her off that easy.

'I heard you abandoned him when he was young,' I said, as we remained sitting side by side, staring down at the urban chaos. 'Why the sudden interest?'

'You think I only want him back because of the inheritance, is that it? Because my son is next in line after Jerome? You think me a villainess?'

'The thought had occurred.'

'Well, I don't care what you think of my motives, you impudent shit! You have a very short memory, to speak so ungratefully. I could have left you to burn, don't forget.'

'You rescued me from that hatch because you thought I had your grandparents' wedding certificate in my pocket,' I spoke without anger. 'You might have even heard me say so through the floorboards. Well, I don't have it, I'm sorry to tell you. It was just something I said so they wouldn't leave me down there.'

'No, I rescued you because I did not want you to die!' She was crying angry tears as she spoke. 'You are very welcome – do not mention it!'

'You said I had something about my person—'

'I was referring to this!' She reached for my jacket pocket and snatched at the item I had forgotten was in there. It was the small toy bear I had seen JJ playing with and had found again the garret room. 'I was hidden within that wine shop, watching you before you saw me. I noticed this bear sticking out of your pocket.'

'You risked returning to that shop for a toy bear?' I asked, incredulous.

'My son is inconsolable without it. He has not stopped crying since I removed him from Saint-Antoine and I hoped it would comfort him. It was a toy I gave him when he was just a baby. He doesn't even remember me, but I thought if I presented him with it again he might stop hating me!'

'The mother and son reunion is not going so well then?'

'He doesn't even believe I am his mother,' she sighed. 'Him with his dark skin and Caribbean eyes, how can he not be my son? But he cries for his father constantly.'

'Well, what sort of reaction did you expect from a child after you snatch him away from his happy home, wearing black widow's weeds? You must have looked like a witch from a fairytale.'

'It wasn't like that,' she explained. 'He liked me at first when I had approached him in the shop. We played games and I sang him songs while everyone else in there was distracted by what was happening elsewhere in the city. Then your Nicolas reappeared from somewhere and saw me without my veil on. I was able to communicate with him in whispered English what the situation was. He believed me when I said that JJ was my son. He saw it confirmed in both our faces.'

'There is a slight resemblance, I'll give you that. But if you ask me, he takes after Hugo.'

'If it were not for your assistant I never would have been able to lead my son out of there. Jean-Jacques adores Nicolas. But as soon as we were clear of the shop and I revealed to him who I truly was, he rejected me utterly. And I am heartbroken by it.'

Her face was all sorrow. A tear had travelled down the length of her cheek, but she kept staring towards the city as it tore itself apart.

'I've known much more wicked mothers than you in my time, Celeste,' I said as she flopped herself against me and kept crying. 'You're alright in my eyes.' I put my arms around her and kissed her head. Then I thanked her for pulling me out of that bonfire.

After a short period she stopped crying and told me that she had something for me. She reached into the seam in her dress and pulled out a small brown paper package what was tied up with string. I wondered if this package contained some sort of food as it seemed soft as she touched it.

'I did not wish to leave this at my lawyer's house,' she said after wiping her eyes. 'He or his wife might have found it and got the wrong impression of me.' She untied the string and handed it to me. 'I am returning what I stole from you.'

I already knew what the package contained before I had even finished unwrapping the paper. I could smell its heavenly contents before I even saw the brown substance. I felt the old familiar sensation, what I had hoped I was done with, shiver through me again. I took a strong sniff and inhaled its beautiful fragrance.

'You said you threw this into the sea,' I said, once my nose had established that this opium was mine.

'It was always my intention to return it you,' she said. 'But not until after your task was complete.'

It was with a strange mixture of emotions that I found myself reunited with my old drug. I had just begun to feel free of its influence, although considering that I had spent most of the past couple of days trying not to get shot, it had been easy to forget the stuff. But seeing it again here reminded me of the hook it still had in me and I felt it tug at me once more.

'But my task ain't complete, is it?' I said, and wrapped it up again. I was glad to find my hands was still steady, despite their contact with the poppy. 'We haven't found that wedding certificate yet.'

'The bargain you struck was with Jerome, not me,' she said as she got to her feet, her composure regained. 'I don't care about the Lamoreaux estate. Never did. That was his obsession, mine was with regaining my son. There is a strong chance that the old wedding certificate has burnt inside that shop by now and, if so, good riddance to it. It has caused us nothing but trouble ever since it was rediscovered.'

'So is that it then?' I got up also to confront her. 'After all I've been through! Tearing around after Hugo DeFarge during a dangerous revolution, getting beaten up, almost burning to death and you mean to say that I ain't going to get one sou for my troubles?'

'You have been given plenty of valuable jewels as a deposit,' Celeste said, as she walked towards a nearby apple tree. 'Considering your lack of success, I think you have been more than well rewarded.'

'What about little JJ?' I went on, as she picked a crunchy red one and then walked it over to the horse. 'It's his inheritance now. Don't you care about him reclaiming his estate?'

'Of course, but I will love him in poverty also,' she said as the horse was fed. 'Even if he continues to despise me.'

And, for all my outrage at learning that my efforts here had amounted to naught, I was pleased to hear her say that.

'I am now going back to my lawyer's house where I will return this Milady here and see my son,' she mounted the horse. 'Perhaps he will have softened towards me by now, but I doubt it. I take it you wish to be reunited with your assistant also. My lawyer's family will be certain to offer you both bed and board until you are ready to return to your own city.' Behind us the fighting still raged. 'London will seem like a quiet country village after your time spent here, I think.'

So I climbed up onto Milady with her, and the horse began to trot on, further away from the centre of Paris. Behind us the sound of cannons became fainter as the trot became a gallop, but that did not mean that the savage revolution was coming to any kind of close yet.

Chapter 20

Heroic Beasts

Showing how I came to witness a daring duel
between two well-matched opponents

The letters etched into the stonework of the outer gate declared this house to be the Maison de Regnaudot. Celeste and myself had been riding for under an hour and had managed to pass through a city tollgate, travelling deeper into the green and peaceful countryside. As we approached the house, a young black girl had been waiting for us and she began yelling for Celeste in a joyous way. She then ran up to the main house to alert the owners to our arrival. By the time the two of us had dismounted, the girl's father, a tall, middle-aged man dressed in light attire, had appeared through the front door to greet us, accompanied by his younger, lighter-skinned wife. This couple exchanged wary looks as Celeste introduced me, but when she told them I was the older brother of Nicolas, they both smiled and nodded. I returned them a courtly bow and I was told that this was Maximilian and Françoise Regnaudot. We all shook hands in a very cordial manner. Max, I was then informed, was the Cupidons' lawyer and was related to them via the Saint Dominguan branch of the family tree. It seemed that neither he nor Françoise spoke much English, so, once our nodding and smiling was exhausted, Celeste asked them where her son was.

Max indicated that her son was to be found in the fields behind the house and he walked us all back there as his daughter took Milady the horse back to the stables. But, before these Regnaudots could lead us through a wooden, floral-decorated archway what would take us around the side of the building, he asked where Jerome was. Celeste stopped us all, breathed out and in French told them that her brother had been killed. The couple both seemed to be stricken by the news and I could tell that their relationship with the Cupidon siblings was built upon more than just a professional arrangement. Françoise asked a question and Celeste answered with the word revolution. They all bowed their heads in sorrow before continuing on.

We could hear childish giggling from the fields beyond and Celeste stopped again, this time explaining that she wanted to change into a dress what did not smell of fire and gunpowder before greeting her son. Françoise escorted her into the main house, while Max and I continued on to the paddock beyond.

There was a small group of children playing on ponies back there in the late morning sun, and, even from a distance, I recognised both my boy Nick and JJ DeFarge sitting on the same animal. There was also some other boys of Nick's age, what may have worked there, who was on bigger horses and showing my assistant how he should ride. Nick was holding the reins with confidence and JJ was sat just in front of him, with Nick's arms acting as his protection from falling off. As far as I knew, Nick had never ridden a pony in his life, but he looked most adept at it already. I could hear from JJ's laughter as Nick said something that he was comfortable here among these people. It all struck me as a very carefree scene.

'My eyes, it's the Artful Dodger!' Nick beamed as he saw me approach. 'Alive, despite the odds!' He showed he was able to turn the pony and ride it towards the paddock fence. 'I am glad of two things, Mr Dodger, sir,' he grinned as he drew near to where myself and Max was leaning. 'First, to see that you survived the barricades. And second, that nobody ever asked me to wager money on it, as I for certain would have bet the other way. How are you, my old mentor?'

'I'm very well, thank you, Nick,' I smiled back as I scratched the pony's nose. 'Good to see you're hard at work, smashing the hated *petit-bourgeois* from within.' Nick chuckled and tapped his nose in a gesture of conspiracy. '*Bonjour* JJ,' I said to the little boy. 'Remember me? I'm a friend of your father's!'

Nick translated that to Jean-Jacques as best he could, but the boy seemed to be very distrustful of me, which, in all honesty, showed that he was a decent judge of character. My battered face and blood-specked clothes was unlikely to endear me to any child. Then, the avuncular Max said something to the boys what suggested that their time on the pony had drawn to an end. He reached over the wooden fence to help JJ out of the saddle and encouraged Nick to dismount. He told the boys to say goodbye to the pony.

'*Au revoir*, Dartagnan,' they waved, as one of the older boys led the pony away to the stables. '*Au revoir!*' Nick turned to me.

'You ever heard of the Three Musketeers, Dodge?' he asked.
'No,' I replied. 'Why? Have they heard of me?'

'They're characters in a famous French book,' he said as he climbed through the fence posts and embraced me. 'Max here was telling us about them last night. I didn't understand the half of it, but he's named most of his nags after them. That there is Athos!' He pointed at a great big brown brute what one of the older boys was riding. Then he pointed to another, sleeker grey horse. 'And he's Aramis! There was one called Porthos, 'n all, but he died.'

'*Les Trois Mousquetaires,*' Max grinned to hear those names being spoken and we began strolling around his grounds as he held the younger boy's hand. Then he said something what I did not understand and Nick had to concentrate hard on before translating it.

'One for all and all for one!' he said at last as we neared some woodland what touched the edge of the paddock. 'That's their motto! Or perhaps it's the other way around . . .' Nick continued chattering in his excitable way and he seemed glad to be demonstrating a working knowledge of French historical adventure fiction. He started telling me the parts of the story what had been explained to him and made up the parts he hadn't understood.

'Sounds like a bloody good book,' I told him as we began to make our way back to the farmhouse.

'Yeah, I'm going to read it!' he said. 'It'll help me learn the language better.'

We was strolling past some kindling what someone had

piled up and Nick broke away from us and darted towards it. He grabbed the longest stick, whipped the air with a heroic flourish and pointed his makeshift sword heavenward. Then he repeated the musketeer motto in French. Max laughed, but corrected him on his pronunciation. JJ broke away from Max's hand then and grabbed his own wooden sword. A duel between the two boys commenced.

'*Bravo Jean-Jacques!*' cheered Max as we two adults watched the swordfight. For so young a boy, JJ whacked at Nick's stick with the same kind of ferocity that I had seen his redoubtable father display atop the barricades. That said, Nick could have defeated him whenever he wanted.

'He's half your size, Nick,' I said. 'Kick him in the belly or something.'

But Nick fought with more valour than that and even let JJ think he had won, as he let him strike his chest with his stick. Nick doubled over and pretended to die and JJ lifted his stick in the air and declared himself victorious. Both myself and Max cheered at this, but Nick then pounced back up and grabbed him unawares. JJ squealed with laughter and soon all four of us, both men and boys, was having a hearty old chuckle together.

But then the spell was broken and JJ's happy smile vanished. Because that was when he heard his mother's voice calling him from the farmhouse.

We looked over and saw Celeste approaching us in a pretty summers dress, smiling wide and trying to look as maternal and as inoffensive as possible. In her hand she had the bear what she had snatched earlier from out of my pocket. Her son took one look at her and started shaking his head in obvious distress.

'*Non, non, non,*' he protested and ran towards Max for protection. Then he began crying something what was in dramatic contrast to the high spirits Nick had just worked him up into. I needed no translator to know that he was telling her that he hated her and that she was not his mother.

Celeste stopped in her path, looking as though she had just been punched in the gut by his response.

'Nicolas,' she then said in a heartbroken voice. 'Would you please hand my son his bear back?' Nick crossed over to her to take it from her hand. 'I shall leave you all alone until lunchtime. I am sorry for disturbing your game.'

Then she walked back into the house and I followed after, wishing to console her in some way, but knowing that it was going to be hard work.

Later, after Celeste had finished crying over the twin sorrows of her brother's death and her son's rejection, she began to tell me more about her personal history with JJ's father. We had been left alone in one of the Regnaudot's guest bedrooms, just the two of us, and she had confirmed some of what I already knew. She had met Hugo through their father, theirs had been a mutual seduction and he had gotten her pregnant with JJ. She even hinted that she had known all along that her husband had killed her father in that duel, but that she was so in love with him that she chose not to see it. Why then, I asked, did she flee the wine shop when Jerome revealed hard evidence as to Hugo's role in her father's death?

'Oh, I don't know, it was all such a horrible time,' she said, her hands on her temples. She had been complaining of a headache ever since we had left Paris. 'Jerome was so angry and persuasive. He had always hated my marriage to Hugo. He had been jealous of my husband's close relationship with our father and so proving that he was the killer was a terrible vindication of his hatred.'

I looked around the nice chamber as we sat side by side on the bed. These Regnaudots seemed like good people, but my ever-professional eye could not help but notice that they had lots of pretty things about their home what might be worth the thieve. However, they had been nothing but gracious hosts ever since I had arrived and had offered me both food and a bed to nap in, so slipping their valuables into my pocket would have dishonoured even me.

'But there were deeper reasons,' continued the miserable Celeste. 'I was finding motherhood a challenge. I was finding wifehood a challenge. I hated the poverty of Saint-Antoine. I hated the politics of my husband and his repulsive friends. I was too young and too *bourgeois* to live like that. So I left them.'

After she had said all of that, I thought of how I had left my own mother's home when young and how she had never seemed to care very much. And then I thought on how, years later, Lily Lennox had left me in a similar fashion.

'Did you not love him anymore?' I asked.

'Hugo or JJ?'

'Either.'

'Earlier today I set fire to a shop to avenge my baby brother,' she said. 'For Jean-Jacques, I would burn down all Paris.'

'You may have to hurry,' I said. 'Paris is doing a decent enough job of burning itself down.'

'As for Hugo,' she said with her head resting on my shoulder, 'I find that, in spite of myself, I loved him very much. He was a better parent to our son than I ever was, or could be, and I know in my heart it was not his fault that my father died. Someone would have killed him sooner or later, he was that sort of man. Yes, I think now that Hugo was the great love of my life. How sad it is that we never appreciate such things until people are dead.'

'He isn't dead,' I told her.

'Of course he is,' she insisted and lifted her head to check if I was joking. 'He died in the revolution. Otherwise, he would have been in the wine shop this morning. I had expected to see him there. I wanted to see him, if I am to be honest, so I could tell him that JJ was safe.'

'Well, he might be dead,' I informed her. 'If not, he'll be dead soon. That Irishman who works for him told me that they captured Hugo alive at the foot of a barricade. They'll shoot him, along with some other political prisoners any day now.'

Celeste seemed to be stunned by this news and she began muttering to herself about it. Then she straightened herself up and spoke in a steelier voice.

'What a holy fool the man is!' she said. 'He has a son to raise and he gets himself involved with this ridiculous uprising. You know, he deserves to be killed. Our son will be far safer with me.' Then she stood up again and walked over to the window what overlooked the paddock where JJ still was. 'I didn't start this revolution, did I? Nor did I in any way conspire for my son's father to get himself captured. These things would have happened without my intervention, so why am I cast as a witch all of a sudden? It is a good thing I arrived when I did, or he'd be orphaned!'

'You know what, Celeste?' I interrupted, still sat at the edge of the bed, her back now to me. 'You're starting to remind me of my mother.'

'Oh really?' Celeste replied in a snide tone. 'Was she educated at the Sorbonne as well?'

'If she was, she never thought to mention it,' I said. 'Kat Dawkins was a dreadful mother in most ways. She used to frighten the breath out of me with her volatile and dangerous behaviour. I ended up leaving her and going to live with a kindly old man named Mr Fagin, who provided all the parenting I would ever need. Sometimes she would just turn up in my life though, like you have done to your son, and I would spend the whole time wishing she would just leave me alone, as I was happier without her.'

'Why are you telling me this?' she asked from the window. 'To be cruel?'

'Nah, I just thought you'd be interested,' I continued. 'Because last year I ran into my mother again in very surprising circumstances. I won't burden you with the whole story, but she ended up saving my life. And ever since then, well, I ain't felt so raw towards her.'

'So your advice is that I should wait until my son is an adult and then save his life in some way,' Celeste turned away from the window and stared at me with her still wet eyes. 'Because, until then, he will never accept me. Thank you for trying to comfort me, Jack Dawkins, but I think I would like to be alone now. You must be very tired, so please sleep. We shall wake you for dinner.'

She left me alone in that comfortable bedchamber then and, considering that I had not slept in over a day now, I should have been crashing into a slumber with ease. But I sat there on my own for some minutes and felt nothing other than alert in both mind and body. I knew enough about opium withdrawal to know that sleeplessness was one of its many symptoms, so I reached into my jacket pocket and pulled out that brown package and considered what to do with it. It would be so pleasing, I thought as I peeled back the paper surrounding it, to take some now and allow myself to drift off into a well-earned reverie.

'I wouldn't do that if I was you, Mr Dawkins, sir,' said a voice from the doorway. 'You'll want to be lucid for what I'm about to say, I should reckon.'

'No Nickname Nick,' I smiled as I folded the package up and placed it back into my pocket. 'My trusty assistant.' He shut the door behind him and came closer, that same toothpick in his mouth that he had had when he visited my home. 'There's something I've been meaning to ask you as well,' I said. He leaned against the bedpost and raised his eyebrows. 'What was JJ's toy bear doing in that garret?'

'He must have dropped it in there,' Nick shrugged. 'When he was showing me around, after you'd gone.'

'But the door was locked.'

'So was the door to your crib when I cracked it that time,' he pulled the toothpick out of his mouth and showed it to me. It was made of metal. 'JJ thought it a giggle.'

'Nice implement,' I complimented him. 'Can it open a safe?'

'It didn't need to,' he grinned and, from inside his sleeve, he pulled out a yellow rolled-up document what looked delicate enough to have belonged to another age. 'Do you want to tell her, or shall I?'

The sun was at its deepest crimson and was setting over the fields. There was then only three of us, sat around a table on the wooden veranda at the back of the house, as well as a bright orange cat what was letting me stroke him. Since arriving at the Maison de Regnaudot that day I had enjoyed a refreshing sleep and a bath and had borrowed some of Maximilian's clothes, which fit, but was stiff enough to make me look ten years older then I was. Earlier, over dinner, Max had tried to tell me more of his love of the novelist Alexandre Dumas and, despite the language barrier, he had managed to communicate that every animal he owned was named after a character from his book. This feline in my lap, for example, was named after the villainous Cardinal Richelieu and the title suited him as, like all cats, he had a very devious look fixed upon his face.

But now, the Cupidon family lawyer had placed on some *pince-nez* spectacles and was reading very different material. Celeste had shown him the document what Nick had found inside a desk drawer in Hugo DeFarge's wine shop soon after we had shown it to her. Across the top of this document was written CERTIFICAT DE MARIAGE in big letters and further down, where it mentioned the betrothed, was the names Jean-Phillippe Lamoreaux and Cessette Cupidon, both with accompanying signatures. After staring at it for some time, he raised his head and spoke to Nick in French.

'He says it proves things beyond doubt,' Nick turned to me, as I sipped at the apple juice I had been served and looked over the now empty paddock. 'Celeste and Jerome was never bastards. So JJ up there can inherit the entire Lamoreaux estate if he wants it.'

There was an open window above where the three of us was sitting and out of which we could hear the inconsolable JJ sobbing, as one who is in captivity would do. The boy knew he was destined to be rich anyway. He had boasted to Nick during their short time together in his father's home and had even told my assistant where the document was kept. But he was reacting to the news that his hated mother had arranged its theft with very little grace, as he had wanted to share the wealth with his father instead. We could hear Celeste in his bedroom, trying to sing him lullabies and convincing him of her love, but he continued raging against her.

Soon his mother's voice was replaced by Françoise Regnaudot's, who did a better job of soothing the angry little boy to sleep. When Celeste at last joined us on the veranda, we had lit several lamps and the air was heavy with mayflies. She looked overcome with exhaustion and I wondered when the last time she had slept was. Nick poured her some of the juice from the jug into a glass and she sat between her lawyer and myself as they conversed for a few minutes in French. Her voice sounded strained. At length, Max stood up with the document in his hand and retired into his study to peruse it at length. He wished us all a *bon nuit* and then Celeste was left to discuss business with her two thieves.

'Apple juice?' she said when she saw my glass. 'Did Maximilian not offer you any wine?'

'Yeah, but I ain't always in the mood to be drunk,' I told her, and was surprised by the truth of it. 'Now that we've got the pleasantries out of the way, the time has come for my assistant and myself to raise the delicate matter of our fee.'

'You were promised an awful lot of money to recover that paper for us, weren't you boys,' she said.

'Indeed we was.'

'But by my brother. Not by me.'

I glared at her. The distant booms of the Paris cannons could just about be heard even then.

'Don't toy with us, Celeste,' I told her as I placed my glass down on the table and leaned in closer. 'Because if there is one lesson you French should have learnt by now, it is to never upset the workers. I went through a lot of aggravation to get that document '

'And from what I gather, much of it was needless,' she smirked. 'While you were risking your life up on the barricades, trying to steal keys from my reckless husband, your assistant here was the one who succeeded in his task.'

Nick lifted his own glass up to his lips and smiled, as if he had been waiting for someone to point that out.

'Be that as it may,' I conceded. 'He never would have been left alone in that wine shop to explore its rooms unhindered without my inveigling. And you never would have hired him without me on account of his age. So you still owe us what we was promised.'

'Oh, do not fear,' she raised her palms in a defensive way and smiled. 'I have every intention of honouring the bargain you boys made with Jerome. As soon as Paris becomes safe again, Max will present the document to the Lamoreaux lawyers and, once all the tedious legal matters have been taken care of, you will be paid the figure you were both promised. However,' it was her turn to lean further in. She lowered her voice to a whisper even though nobody else on the premises spoke English, 'I have been doing a lot of thinking since our conversation earlier, Jack.'

It was dark now and the day was nearing its end. I had the strangest feeling that I was not going to like the turn this conversation was about to take.

'I wish to make a new bargain,' she told me. 'But with you alone. Not with Nicolas.'

'Why not with me?' he asked.

'Because what I am about to ask is far too perilous for one of your age.'

'In which case it's far too perilous for me 'n all,' I told her. 'What is it?'

'I want, if it is still possible, for you to help me rescue my husband from the firing squad.'

Nick and I looked at one another. I cannot recall which of us started laughing first, but we did not stop until Françoise leaned out of the open window above and told us to keep it down.

'I'm a thief, Celeste,' I shrugged. 'Not one of the Three Musketeers. You've got the wrong man.'

'I'll double your fee if you agree to help,' persisted Celeste.

'Double of everything is worth nothing if you're dead.'

'You think it cannot be done?' she asked. I considered this, as the orange cat jumped from my lap to Nick's.

'Most things can be done,' I admitted. 'Its only a lack of daring what makes people think otherwise. But the risk is far too great and I'm happy with my earnings as it is.'

I leaned back and swirled the last of my apple juice around as if it was a glass of brandy.

'I cannot do this without you, Jack,' she pleaded. 'I wouldn't know where to start. But I truly feel that the only way I can earn forgiveness for abandoning my son all those years ago is if I can save his father's life. And there isn't time for me to go to anyone else about it.'

I found myself troubled then by the way in which Nick was looking at me. It was with a worrying air of misplaced faith and I hoped he was not thinking that I ought to agree to so lunatic a suggestion. On his lap, meanwhile, Cardinal

Richelieu was regarding me as if he thought I was an imbecile either way.

'Triple my fee,' I said at last, once I had drained the last of the juice. 'And perhaps I'll give it some thought.'

Chapter 21

A Far, Far Better Thing

*Wherein I sample some of the famous French cuisine
and even dare to attempt an improvement upon it*

By the time I returned to the backstreets of Paris, the June
Days Uprising had been raging for three days. The same city
what had struck me as so majestic when I had first arrived, had
since been reduced to a right old rubbly, pitted and smoking
mess. The revolution had not yet been defeated but there was a
marked change in the street warriors I passed as I negotiated my
way through the urban battleground. Gone was the celebratory
spirit what had carried us all onwards when the fighting had
been first declared, gone was that sense of a fun day out for the
poor. The insurgents was still out in force, but they was halved
in numbers and all looked as if they would welcome defeat, if
only for the chance to rest. A great many of the houses what
I had passed when entering the Saint-Antoine vicinity a few
days before had now had most of their plaster shot off by stray
bullets, exposing the timber, the pipes and even many of the
rooms behind. It was like walking past a giant set of open dolls'
houses, so visible was all the decoration within. Meanwhile,
straw was scattered over much of the streets to cover the blood

and uncleared bodies, while many of the front doors had been kicked in. Evidence of looting and vandalism was everywhere as criminals of all stripes, most of them doubtless without a single revolutionary thought in their head, had taken advantage of the chaos around them.

It was early evening by then, and almost a whole day had passed since Celeste had tried to convince me to act against my natural inclinations and save the life of a man who she now claimed she had never stopped loving, despite everything. And yet it was still not dark. I could feel the shadows around the room lengthening though and heard the sounds of fighting in the distance get fainter. Night was creeping up slow again and this would bring about another ceasefire, until morning. I peered out of the first-floor window of the wine shop to see who, if anyone, would be returning from the barricades after a hard day of battling the militia.

Before long, I saw a man turn the corner at the end of the lane and, even from this distance I knew he was the one I'd been waiting for. He had a musket slung over his shoulder, a cartridge belt strapped around his tunic and he walked with his shoulders slumped. Every so often he would adjust his pair of spectacles as if they was threatening to fall off and he spoke to nobody that he passed. He cut a very lonely figure. I moved back from the window, dropped the cigar what I had been concealing from view onto the floor and snuffed it out with my foot. I wasn't concerned about starting a fire anyway, the room was already gutted and charred from the arson of yesterday. I had spent the past hour exploring every room of the now vacated wine shop and, even though the fire had been extinguished before the main building was destroyed, there was a strong smell of ash even as high up as the garret.

The downstairs bar though, where the fire had been lit, no longer resembled anything other than a burnt out shell. The saloon bar itself was now like a lump of black charcoal, the panelled walls was blackened and weak, the barrel tables now burnt to a crisp. All the bottles what had not melted had been removed and stored down in the cellars. The thick iron posts what acted as columns had all had their paintwork burnt off. There was no good reason for anyone to enter this bar now, other than to pass through it to the rooms above and there was not much reason to go up there either. However, my exploration of the various upstairs rooms and their possessions had revealed to me that one person was still living here.

The Irishman entered through the dark main bar, as I had expected he would. I watched him from deep within one of the hidden nooks, as he removed the cartridge belt from his shoulder and lowered the musket. It was not until he had rested the weapon against the wall and taken several steps away from it that I at last cleared my throat to alert him of my presence. He almost died on the spot from fright.

'Mother Mary!' he exclaimed when he saw me emerge from the shadows with Celeste's silver pistol in my hand. 'I didn't spend the day getting shot at by the cavalry to return home and get felled by a burglar. Lord, let me go with more dignity than this!'

'Cool yourself, Brendan,' I said and pointed the pistol away from him. 'This barker is just for security. I came here to talk, not to pop a ball into you. And my guess is that there ain't no more ammunition in your musket anyway, so lets not even pretend this is going to turn into a shooting party.'

'Then what are you doing here?' he demanded. 'Why must you Englishmen continue to torment me? Is it about that wretched wedding certificate? I tell you, I don't know where it is and I don't much care! I've got my own problems.'

'Ain't we all,' I said and placed the pistol down onto what remained of the bar, stepping away from it in a generous gesture of trust. He was stood as rigid as the iron post beside him. 'My problem is that I'm an opium fiend, Madame DeFarge's problem is that her son hates her and your problem seems to be that you live in an ashtray by night and fight for a country that ain't even yourn by day. Answer me this, what do you care if the French government shuts down the National Workshops? You ain't from here, you can just move on to somewhere else if you don't like it.'

'I'm a rebel and I'll die a rebel,' he answered. 'I'd oppose the ruling classes in their infamy, no matter where I was.' He held his chin high and proud although again this could have been on account of the slippery spectacles. 'And I fight because I'm one of the few surviving members of the Club of a Thousand Jacks. Most of the others are dead or captured by now and I daresay that one of those fates will befall me if I keep heading out with my gun every morning. But, damn, I have little else to live for. My job here, when the revolution began, was to guard the women and children and defend Hugo DeFarge's shop. I failed on both counts.'

'What have you heard of DeFarge?' I interrupted, as I was growing bored of his self-pity already. 'They shot him yet?'

'Not yet, but they will. More importantly, what have you seen of his son?' he fired back. 'You're still in league with that bourgeois bitch that took him, aren't you? Is he safe?'

'He's living with some very nice people on a horse farm just north of Paris,' I answered. 'About an hour's ride away. He's better off there than he would be in the middle of all this mayhem, so don't go beating yourself up about letting him go. He has everything he needs. Trouble is, he misses his Papa. I'm here to see what can be done about that.'

'What does that mean?' Brendan asked, with a cold expression. 'His Papa is soon to be killed and his mother only wants him for his fortune. Don't come around here and start pretending you're any friend to the boy, you're his kidnapper's accomplice and nothing more.'

'*Au contraire,* as the French say. I'm his fairy godfather,' I replied as I stepped even closer to him. By now, we was close enough to punch the other if we cared to and it was possible that either one of us might try at any moment. 'Because I'm going to grant him his dearest wish. By which, I mean that I'm going to rescue Papa DeFarge from the mouth of death.'

Brendan's spectacles was almost slipping off his face. I noticed now that only one of the eyeholes still had glass in it, the other had been smashed away in battle. He raised a finger and pressed the ridge of the glasses back up his nose. Only then did he begin to smile at me.

'You're an amusing one, London Jack, I'll give you that,'

he patted me on the arm. 'But I'm exhausted, so, if you don't mind, fuck off and bother someone else with your nonsense. I'm going to what remains of my bed so I can be up bright and early for the slaughter tomorrow.'

'Where is DeFarge being kept?' I persisted. 'Under the Tuileries palace, yeah? That's what we've learnt so far. In situations like this, the government puts all their prisoners down in these cells below the palace on the waterside terrace. That's where they locked the captives up during a similar uprising in February, that where they're likely to be putting them now. Are we right?'

'Who is we?' Brendan asked in irritation.

'The heroic trio what are going to rescue him,' I answered. 'The Three Musketeers I like to think of us as.'

'You're insane and you belong in an asylum,' he said and turned to walk away. 'All three of you. Goodnight, *Dodger*.'

'You told me yesterday that they was planning on shooting the leaders of revolutionary clubs as an example to others. That means that they're doing it somewhere visible to the public. That therefore means they ain't done it yet, or you'd have heard about it and that, in turn, means he can still be rescued. Stands to reason.'

Brendan turned back to me and snapped. 'D'you think that he's some sort of romantic highwayman from the last century? D'you think that you can simply turn up to his hanging, fire off a few shots and dash off with him in the back of a carriage? He's a political prisoner with a famous name. The Republic will be guarding him and the other leaders tight. They'll expect a rescue attempt to be made and they'll have a whole battalion to cut down anyone who tries.'

'A whole battalion?' I scoffed. 'For a handful of troublemakers? When there are tens of thousands of revolting Parisians, marauding about the place, laying siege to all the important buildings, trying to kill the men in charge of the cavalry? If Hugo has more than six people guarding him, I'll be amazed. Most serving soldiers will be otherwise occupied.'

'But those six will be armed and waiting for you.'

'Nah, they'll be waiting for revolutionaries,' I countered. 'They'll be waiting for club members, for an angry mob. It'll be people like the late Armand or Father Pierre who they'll expect. They'll not be waiting for the likes of me.'

'You flatter yourself.'

'I'm a thief,' I explained. 'And back in London I'm considered a top-class one. I'm going to slip in behind them and run off with DeFarge like he's Marie Antoinette's final jewel-box. They won't even know he's missing until they go to fetch him for the firing squad. Not only that,' I held up a finger to stop him from pouring more scorn upon my reputation, 'they will not be expecting someone like Celeste.'

I could tell from his expression that he had not been expecting her involvement. 'Madame DeFarge?' he said. 'She's one of your three musketeers?'

'The rescue was her idea.'

'But she hates her husband, she made his life a misery when they were married and betrayed him at every turn. She's not even on the side of the revolution, so why would she do it?'

'She has her own reasons for wanting Hugo alive what neither she nor I need to explain to you. The point is, as you was correct to note earlier, she's a bourgeois bitch what has no sympathies with the revolution. That is why she's been able to find out information about where they're keeping him and what sort of security he's under, which is more than any spy among your ranks ever could.'

I moved over to the bar window so I could see if anyone else was approaching from behind him. A full white moon was hanging above Paris by then and many desperate figures was seen darting about this way and that. Nobody was approaching this shop, however.

'Celeste spent this morning visiting some old friends of hers what are high up in the Second Republic. They all know her to be a staunch conservative, so suspected no underhand motive what might harm them.'

'How high up?'

'The highest, so she says. You ever heard of a cove called Napoleon Bonaparte?'

'Yes, and he's been dead for over twenty years.'

'Well, Celeste reckons she's been on intimate terms with his nephew and heir.'

'Louis-Napoleon?' Brendan was more incredulous than impressed. 'Of the National Assembly? When you say intimate terms, do you mean . . .?'

'She knew him in the days after she left Hugo, yeah. Put it

this way, she never met his wife. She's also been friendly with a lot of other important men. Politicians, generals, famous novelists and – what did she call them? – Orleanists.'

'She has lain with a hundred devils then.'

'Judge the woman all you like, Brendan, but these connections make her an exceptional spy for our purposes. She's learnt a lot of helpful stuff regarding how the battle is going from their end. And the government think that they're winning this war. More cavalry and other reinforcements are on the way to Paris to double the numbers but, until they get here, things are delicate. The troops are being driven like donkeys, are underfed, deprived of sleep and are ready to drop. Civilians are volunteering to help them, but from what Celeste has learnt, they are proving more of a hindrance than anything. Such untrained volunteers are guarding the prisoners down in the Tuileries so, if we can get to DeFarge before the real reserves show up, we'll have an advantage.'

'There's that mysterious we again,' observed the Irishman. He was still stood steadfast near that iron post and I was now perched on the windowsill facing him. 'The English thief. The French whore. Who's your third? Not that little boy again?'

'The Irish rebel,' I smiled.

'Be off with you,' he replied. 'And I don't just mean out of this building, I mean out of France. Go back to London, you're making a nuisance of yourself here.'

'I'm going to need another accomplice if I'm to do this right,' I told him. 'You and me speak the same language and you're the only person I know what cares about the man. I can hardly expect someone of Nick's age to risk himself, can I?'

'You can't expect me to, either!' he shouted in a sudden and surprising burst of anger. 'The woman killed two of my friends and burnt down this place, which was both my home and my livelihood. Not to mention the matter of the stolen child. Hugo always said that I shouldn't trust his wife – before I had even met her – and, from our short acquaintance, I can see what he meant. I almost died in that blaze myself!'

'There's hurt feelings on both sides, Brendan,' I fired back as I paced around the room. I circled him slow as he held his position by the post. 'You helped to wrap up her murdered brother in a flag and you dumped him in the gutter. So it ain't going to be that easy for her to cooperate with you, neither. But she's willing to do it. And why? Because she wants to rescue a man she once loved and thinks that she still might. A man, I might add, what you told me saved your own rotten life when you was readying yourself to end it. Don't you think you're under some obligation to return the favour now you've the chance?'

I had stopped circling him by then. He removed his spectacles and rubbed the one glass lens with his thumb before replacing them on his nose. He seemed to be regarding me anew. I was determined to say nothing to break the silence, I wanted him to speak next.

'Where is she now?' he asked at last, in a softer voice. 'Is she coming here?'

'She was here earlier,' I told him. 'About two hours ago while everyone else was on the barricades. She's borrowed a horse and carriage from one of her old gentleman admirers and I helped her load Jerome's body onto it. So you ain't the only one what's had a horrible afternoon.' Brendan seemed unimpressed with that. 'I'm leaving here now to meet her in an apartment near Les Halles what belongs to her aunt. We're going to plan Hugo DeFarge's rescue together. I've already got some good ideas as to how it can be affected. Come with me. Be our third man.'

Brendan looked over to his musket what was leaning on the wall and then to his cartridge belt hanging from its hook. He walked over to them.

'So tomorrow I can choose between being cannon-fodder for the barricades, or getting killed trying to rescue my only remaining friend.' He slung the belt over his shoulder again. 'I suppose it's not much of a choice either way. Very well then, Londoner, lets go to her. As much as anything, it's an excuse to get away from this blasted shop.'

A cove named Victor had proven to be the most helpful of Celeste's old acquaintances. It turned out that Bonaparte's nephew was not even in Paris and many politicians was either under siege in the Hôtel de Ville or some other important building while others had fled the city. This Victor though had remained in his home, as he wished to write about the unfolding drama and, when Celeste had managed to pay him a visit, he had proved himself to be a veritable gossip. He had always enjoyed telling her things, Celeste told me, as I was busy preparing a stew in that apartment on the following morning.

'They killed the Archbishop of Paris yesterday,' she complained, making a big show of addressing me and not Brendan. 'He stood before one of the barricades, quite courageously, so Victor says, and he tried to reason with the revolutionaries. Revolutionaries! A heroic name for a bunch of barbarians and marauders. They shot the brave man down like a dog.'

'Meanwhile,' Brendan said after sipping from the coffee I had made him, 'the talk in Saint Antoine is of cold-blooded murder.' He too was addressing me, as not a single word had passed between himself and Celeste since I had brought him here, late the night before. 'Committed by the Mobile Guard against any rebels who surrender.' They had grunted at each other when they needed to and both seemed to accept the presence of the other, but the chances of these two political opposites becoming friends anytime soon was not high. 'Mass executions on a grand scale, is what it is. So you can understand why it would be hard for the barbarians – as she calls them – to sympathise with a corrupt old churchman when he suggests that they should lay down their weapons.'

Celeste was not to be outdone.

'Victor claims that the insurgents have prisoners of their own,' she said, still to me. 'Soldiers of the guard who have fallen into savage hands. And that rather than release these soldiers, they cut off their heads with a hacking knife. Then they desecrate their corpses and burn them. So is it a surprise that the guard would show such butchers scant mercy when they throw up their own hands and expect civilised treatment?'

She blew on her coffee as if she had just been discussing the weather. If the two of them was having a competition to see which could make the other angry first, then Brendan was about to lose both his temper and the game.

'I would have thought that the struggles of the poor and downtrodden,' he snapped as he slammed his coffee cup down onto the table, 'would mean something to a woman of slave ancestry. Or do you never notice the colour of your own skin? Answer me this, was it your husband's idea to name your son after Rousseau? Because you're evidently oblivious to his teachings.'

This seemed to get her back up and she looked ready to throw her coffee into his bespectacled face. I decided that the time had come to interrupt this fascinating debate, by banging my ladle against the stew pot and drawing their attention back to me.

'Alright gang, that's enough politics for one morning,' I said, as I threw the many scrags of meat into the massive pot. 'Let us agree that horrible things are being done to both sides and that, regardless of who we might want to win, we'll all be glad when the violence is over. In the meantime, Hugo DeFarge ain't going to rescue himself, so we've a busy day ahead of us. Pass me that onion what's rolled onto the floor before the ants get to it.'

It had not been easy to acquire so many ingredients for the flavoursome stew what I was cooking up, but somehow we had enough. I had earlier raided the windows of a smashed local butchers and helped myself to what little was left, collected some veg from underneath an overturned cart and added these findings to the stock what was already here in the apartment's larder. The floorboards of this residence was stained red from where poor old Gaspard had fallen and the small rug covered less than half of it. Because of this, and also on account of the heat, there was many insects about, but as long as they stayed out of the stew, I was unconcerned.

'This is going to be delicious, if I do say so myself,' I smiled as I chopped into a carrot. 'I'm just sorry that I won't be tasting it.'

'So your man Victor tells you that many of the soldiers aren't getting fed enough,' Brendan asked Celeste, straining hard for a more civil tone, 'how is that possible?'

'He says that there are few people left working in the army kitchens, as most have been ordered to fight the threat,' she explained again. 'And food is not easy to acquire when the people who normally supply it are among those shooting at you. Victor says that many households are doing their best to provide their own charitable contributions for the soldiery, though. It is not uncommon for the wives of republican heroes to arrive at the barracks with food for them.' She picked up the fallen onion and placed it on the kitchen table next to me. 'This is the service we are going to provide for those who are guarding my husband.'

'So,' Brendan nodded his head in dark understanding, 'poison is your game, is it?'

'Course we ain't poisoning 'em, Brendan!' I cried out in offence at the very suggestion, as I tossed half a dozen dumplings into the pot. 'What sort of diabolical chef d'you think I am? This is going to be the most enjoyable stew they've ever had.'

'And I would sooner poison a hundred revolutionaries before I would endanger the life of one patriotic soldier,' Celeste added, staring at him with her arms crossed.

'You won't need to, Madame DeFarge,' he said as he tapped his now loaded musket what was propped up beside him at the table. 'As I'm happy to put lead balls into the lot of them.'

'Tell him about what you've learned about the prison arrangements at the palace, Celeste,' I said as I began chopping up the onion. 'And about where they've been executing people up to now.'

'If what Victor tells me is true,' she said, ' it is likely they will want to shoot Hugo in the orangery.'

'That's part of the palace gardens what is made up of these little orange trees,' I informed him as I wiped the water from my eyes. 'And not slang for his bollocks.'

'Apparently, they do this,' Celeste explained further, 'because the orangery is not far from the underground dungeons where hundreds of prisoners are caged. The thought is that if those prisoners below can hear the firing squad killing men before them, then they will be more likely to collaborate and give evidence against others, to spare themselves. This detail struck my friend Victor as especially chilling.'

'Victor seems very informed for someone not actually in the military himself,' Brendan remarked as I dropped the chopped onion into the stew and continued stirring it with my ladle. 'How does he know so much?'

'He likes to be kept abreast,' she replied. 'And he knows a lot of important people who tell him many interesting things.

He is a famous novelist, so people are often keen to impress him with the details of their profession.'

'A famous novelist called Victor?' Brendan asked and he sat up to attention. 'Its not who I think it is, is it? What's he written?'

'Oh, I don't know,' she said and raised her fingers up to her temple, as if conversing with Brendan was just one of the many things that she was finding a trial about today. 'Something about a hunchback and a gypsy girl. What does it matter? More to the purpose,' she turned her full gaze on him for the first time, 'is it true what he tells us? That you revolutionaries have been capturing and killing guardsmen?'

Brendan seemed annoyed by her bringing the ugly business up again, but this time he had misunderstood her intention.

'It's hard to behave with honour during times such as these, so yes,' he admitted, 'they probably are executing those who they capture. But are they hacking their heads off as your Victor claims? That sounds like his novelistic fancy to me!'

'Dodger wants to know if you can get some of their uniforms from them?' she said, much to his surprise. 'Two of them, one for him and one for you. Its one of the reasons I let him involve you in this.' Brendan turned to me and looked as if he was about to ask me to elaborate on this ghoulish point, but I was distracted by how tasty the stew was smelling.

'*Voila!*' I announced and kissed my fingers in triumph. All the innocent elements had been placed into the pot and it was on the stove, cooking well. 'This'll be ready in no time. Once it is simmering it'll be time for me to add the final ingredient. Celeste!' I clicked my other fingers to summon her over. She reached into a little bag and produced what I was not trusted to take care of myself.

'I for one am glad that you won't be sampling this yourself, Jack,' she said as she handed me the package of yellowy brown, tar-like substance. 'I find nothing attractive about an opium fiend.'

I looked down at my precious stash of the Poppy Drop and, for one weak but potent moment, I considered calling the whole plan off so I could consume it myself. Opium is not pleasant to look at, but I knew what sweet pleasures it gave me when burning in a pot and being inhaled through a pipe. But this moment passed and before it could return I began breaking it up with my fingers to be added to the stew. The opium stuck to my hands like glue as I did so, but Celeste stood ready with a cloth to wipe my fingers clean so I would not be tempted to eat any.

'So you see, Brendan,' I said to him as he walked over to the stove to see what culinary delights we had in store for the already tired prison guards, 'neither poisoning nor shooting will be the game.'

'Instead,' Celeste said as she sniffed my stew in approval, 'we're going to be treating those brave boys to a well-earned rest.'

Chapter 22

Dressed for all Seasons

We make a delivery

Whenever my life is in mortal danger, my hands are as steady as steel. It is only afterwards, during periods of reflection and inactivity, that the shakes had been known to take hold and it is then that I find I must dull my senses with opium. But ever since arriving in Paris, I had maintained a complete mastery over myself and there was no doubt that this was due to the high jeopardy of the uprising. Nothing blows away mental lethargy quite like relentless shootings, beatings, suffocations and burnings what cannot help but accompany a revolutionary atmosphere. As a result, I had managed to push all thoughts of the drug away for sometimes more than two or three hours. But, even as I prepared myself for the task of risking my life to save that of a man who, during our last encounter, had tried to shoot me dead, I found that I couldn't stop thinking about Lily Lennox.

There was a long dressing mirror in that apartment what belonged to Celeste's aunt and, as I surveyed my reflection and adjusted the ill-fitting blue National Guard uniform, I wished that Lily was here to see me dressed as a soldier. It would have been nice to have shared a smile with her over it.

I was alone in the apartment as my two accomplices was busy loading up a cart in the courtyard outside, and so I was allowing myself a melancholy moment before launching myself back into the hazards of Paris. There was a bullet-hole in my jacket down by the lower waist and red stains covered the bottom half of my outfit. I touched this hole with my finger and knew that there was not a thin hope I would ever see my love again. What I was planning on doing that day ran a very real risk that I would be killed, like thousands of Parisians had been already. And besides, even if I was to survive and return to London a renewed and richer man, she had made it plain that she wanted nothing more to do with me, so it was about time I took the hint and left her alone. I wished that I could tell her though, before I went to a far, far better rest than I had ever before known, that she was right about me. I would never have made a good father and so it was right of her to have taken our adopted child away to a more stable home. Robin was bound to grow up better off far away from my bad influence. I had learnt more of what it means to be a parent during my time away and I was no longer sure that I was up to the job. But, most of all, I wished I could tell her that I was sorry to have made her miserable, that I still loved her and would never stop.

'That uniform is even more conspicuous than mine,' said Brendan, as he entered the room and saw me fiddling with the jacket what was too loose around my waist. 'Look at all the blood on it.'

'It's ideal for the purpose,' I replied, returning my full attention to the matter at hand. 'And these boots fit better than the
first pair we found.'

I cannot pretend that stripping the clothes from off the backs
of dead men whose bodies had fallen in territories occupied
by the insurgency was a fulfilling task and both Brendan and
myself expressed discomfort in more ways than one. The red
feather plume on top of my black hat was bent and ready to
fall off, but all of this added to the illusion that I was a soldier
what had been in the wars. So I held my hat underneath my
arm, took a deep breath, saluted myself and then we left the
apartment to join Celeste in the yard below. She was readying
the two mares we had borrowed from Max's stables – Milady
and DeWinter – and everything we needed, including the
drugged pot of stew what was big enough to feed about ten,
the thick coil of rope with a hangman's knot at the end and
three loaded muskets, had been loaded up onto the wooden
cart and an old blanket placed over them. Celeste had already
tightened a bloodied bandage around Brendan's head, so he
looked like he had sustained a nasty head injury and he was
using this to fix his spectacles on straight as we descended the
winding iron staircase into the yard.

'Hurry, Dodger,' she said as she sat at the reins of the cart.
Brendan was putting a thick and baggy labourer's smock over
the top of his military uniform. 'Hugo could be executed
whenever the fancy takes them!'

Brendan threw me a similar loose revolutionary garment
and, for now, we hid our hats under the blankets. Our plan

hinged upon us being able to pass through the city unhindered by either side, so this ability to change identities fast was essential. Then Brendan hopped up onto the back of the cart, clutched his bandaged head as if he was in horrible agony and I ran through the dark passage to unlock the doors what led out onto the bright street. Celeste cracked her reins to get the horses moving and our rescue party was on its way.

It was Monday, June 26th, and this uprising was well into its fourth day. And, although more willing revolutionaries had been rushing into Paris from other parts of France ever since it began, the death toll was increasing at an even higher rate, so it seemed unlikely that reserves would keep coming for much longer. The mood of the people, as we travelled through the backstreets, taking care to avoid the barricaded thoroughfares, was even lower than before. When this revolution had begun you could sense the fire within every soul prepared to die for it, but now that too many had, much of that burning passion was dying out too, or so it seemed to my foreign eye. You did not hear *La Marseillaise* being sung much now.

'If we were ever going to win this revolution,' Brendan muttered in a miserable voice, as he too noted the dejection of the people, 'we would have done so by now.'

I was sat in the back of the cart with him as we trundled across the blasted terrain of the city, both of us covering our uniforms with those smocks so as to avoid getting killed by any snipers still occupying the high windows. These districts was populated with many armed and unhappy insurgents, still marching towards a battle what by now they must all be able to see that they was bound to lose. There was a bunch of riflemen walking with their heads down towards the sound of a supportive drum, but whereas before the beat had been rousing and quick, now it just sounded like the slow rhythm of a funeral dirge.

'Look, Celeste,' I patted her on the shoulder and pointed ahead as we turned onto one street. 'It's the old boy from the hostelry, recall him? The one who told us to remember Rouen!' But if Celeste did recall the ageing firebrand, what had woken us all up that morning with his loud and fiery rhetoric, then she did not show it. She just kept her eyes fixed ahead as she drove past a smoking wreckage what was once a building, her horses picking up speed. But as we passed the weary countryman I stood up and raised my musket in the air to salute him as we passed. *'Rappelez Rouen!'* I shouted, hoping to stir his subversive heart. He did not acknowledge me. He just kept on marching forward in a slumped and defeated way, as if he could not remember anywhere anymore.

Celeste had dressed in an attractive way that morning, without making it seem too obvious that she had done this in order to charm those who she needed to. Every so often we would have to draw up the horses at various blockades, where truculent men with weapons questioned her about where we was headed and why. When it seemed that they was detaining her longer than most, Brendan and myself would have to lay behind in the cart, groaning and clutching the bloody parts of our costumes so that they could see we needed medical attention and must be waved through fast. But Celeste took the opportunity offered by the delay to ask some subtle questions about what we could expect at the Tuileries.

The Tuileries palace was a former royal residence situated on the right bank of the Seine. The Second Republic was then employing it as some sort of military garrison and it had spent the last few days under a sustained attack. On this desperate day, when the revolution was on its knees and making its last stabs at victory, such buildings had become the focus of the struggle. Celeste was told by the men at the blockades that the revolutionaries thought that if they could take the palace, this would be such a triumph that it could topple things their way again. There was already thousands there, she was told, laying siege to the place.

'Do you not consider that a problem?' asked Brendan, our leading pessimist, once our vehicle had been waved through.

'I consider it good news,' I replied as we emerged somewhere along the left bank. We saw the beleaguered palace on the other side of the river and heard the raging musket-fire what surrounded it. 'What better distraction for a crack than an entire revolution happening outside? It'll mean fewer guards down in the cells too, I reckon. Now stop fretting and help me learn these French phrases. How do you say 'I am wounded!' again?'

'*On m'a blessé!*' he answered, taking care with the accent.

We remained, for now, on the other side of the river to the palace and, as Celeste continued driving westwards, I was able to get another good look at the long exterior wall what ran along the gardens all the way to Place de la Concorde. That was where the Egyptian obelisk what Jerome had spat at on our arrival was standing and the gates to the palace garden was also there. Cracking into a palace was always going to be a difficult proposition, but breaking into palace gardens was less problematic. From this side of the river it was apparent that there was a siege under way near the garden gates too. But Celeste's friend Victor had revealed to her that there was a hidden entrance close by, where the wives of the men inside had been delivering food to sustain the republican volunteers who was guarding the prisoners. The hungry guards would no doubt be keeping an eye out for such women. Before our cart crossed the bridge to approach these gates, Brendan removed his smock to reveal his blue guard uniform and put on his plumed helmet. He then climbed onto the front next to Celeste, to take the reins from her as I passed her the pot of stew. I kept my smock on for now, as before I left the two of them to worry about getting to the garden gate without incident, I alighted the carriage on the left bank. My job was to steal a boat.

It would need to be sturdy and reliable, but also, the plainer and less noticeable it could be, the better. The embankment on this part of the river was crowded with small vessels, many of them abandoned, but a lot of these looked untrustworthy, so I ignored them and kept searching for something more robust. Further along the bank I saw a lone fat man wearing a beret, sitting on a stool with a paintbrush what was touching the canvas of an easel. In front of him was a wooden dinghy and two long sculls what would serve my needs very well. I wondered, as I approached him, whose side he might be on.

Should I leave my smock on and appeal to his revolutionary sympathies, or reveal my uniform in the hope that he sided with the government. Either way, it did not matter, as by the time I had got close enough I saw that he was dead. He was slumped on his stool with his paintbrush pressed up against the canvas. It appeared that he had been killed by a passing shot from behind him at some earlier point in the day, and he had died mid-stroke. I shook my head at the tragedy of it as I untied the rope from its moorings, jumped in and began rowing over to the other side of the Seine as fast as I could.

The river was busy with ships ferrying people away from the danger of the city, but I had crossed the Thames enough times in small boats to be confident that I could make it to where I was supposed to meet the others. Halfway across, I looked over my shoulder to see what was occurring on the Tuileries side. Compared to the eerie quiet of the left bank I was rowing away from, the right side of the river was a sweeping panorama of mob rule, violent action, rising smoke of gunfire and pulsing, panicking crowds. Once I was closer to the other side I rode upstream, as there was too much activity along the bank to moor up anywhere safe. At last I saw Brendan in his soldier's uniform, waving to me and yelling in French from a discreet part of the bank. For appearance's sake he was pretending to arrest me, so that other soldiers wouldn't want to bother me in my smock, so I made a gesture of surrender as I let him pull me into the bank.

'Celeste is in the palace kitchen,' he whispered, once I had thrown him the rope to tie up on the tight mooring between some others. 'The men who took her in are unsophisticated. I bet I've had more military training than they have. They had their sweaty paws all over her posterior as they led her through their small door. It almost made me wish we were poisoning them, God help me.'

We walked up the bank to where the horses was tied to a tree and waited for her to return, while keeping an eye on the boat. He kept a gun trained on me the whole time so it would not look strange to see a soldier and a revolutionary in each other's company.

'*Là-bas!*' I checked with him. 'It means "over there," right?'

'Yes, but you must stop pronouncing the final letters.'

We spent the rest of our short time there with him going over other helpful phrases again and I felt I was becoming quite the linguist by the time Celeste reappeared. She was walking down the embankment towards us, her movements very slow and unsteady. She was using a wooden rail to help her move along and her face showed an expression of strong concentration. It looked to me like she had been punched in the stomach, and just as I was about to call out to ask if she was alright, she stumbled to the ground. We ran up to help her, but as we drew close we saw that she was giggling.

'I congratulate you on your culinary excellence, Jack,' she said as I helped her up, 'your stew tastes *formidable!*'

'You had some?' I asked as we helped her back to where we had left the cart and horses. 'Could you taste the opium?'

'*Oui,*' she sniggered as she began stroking Milady's nose in a slow and sensual way. 'And I begin to see why it is so popular!'

'Did the guards have any?'

'All ten of them!' Celeste said, and held up eight fingers. 'Eight of them!' Then she raised her arms up to the sky and began rocking her hips as if readying to dance. 'They made me have some with them after I shared it all out. They are such imbeciles.'

'Clearly your potion is strong, Dodger,' Brendan observed. 'But that's her first taste of the stuff. The men may have stronger constitutions.'

'Then I had best get to work,' I said as I helped Celeste into the back of the cart. She looked like she would be grateful for a lie down. 'She's done her bit for now.'

I collected my military musket from the back of the cart and, using a small fishing hook, let it dangle from my trouser belt. Then I threw the knotted rope over my shoulder and headed back to the stolen boat with Brendan as we left Celeste with the horses.

All of the Tuileries gardens was surrounded by a high wall. I had already scouted these walls and had seen mobs of men try to climb up from the roadside to gain access to the gardens, only to be shot down by guards positioned in windows on the opposite street. But mobs only become mobs because none of them think for themselves and I knew that a riverside approach would be the thief's best way in. Brendan rowed the boat to the part of the riverside wall what I had selected as the best place to make my ascent. It was chosen as it was just close enough to the guards what was patrolling a nearby bridge, but far enough away from them that they would be unable to shoot me as I climbed. Then Brendan and I ran up through the short sloping patch of trees what led to the foot of the wall.

'Is all this worth the money, Jack?' asked Brendan then, using my first name for the first time in our acquaintance. I had just swung the rope upwards and hooked the noose part over the top of a wall post. I was tugging on it so it would tighten. 'I mean, I owe DeFarge my life but you don't. And you're the one taking the biggest risk.'

'I'm the Artful Dodger, Brendan,' I said and glanced over to towards the Pont Royal where I was surprised to see the guards had not yet noticed us. 'Taking risks for money is what I'm all about. Now stop fretting and give me a leg up, can't you?'

'Best of luck then,' he nodded in his sombre way and knelt down to give me a strong heave up the palace wall.

Chapter 23

Trespasser

Exploring a once royal residence

It was a high wall, but in my extensive career as a burglar I had climbed many higher. I scrambled upwards using the rope and my every movement was assured and swift. Soon my hands grabbed hold of the top of the wall and, with great exertion, I hauled my body onto it.

Once safe at the top I was able to breathe a little easier and I looked down over the Tuileries gardens what I had heard so much about. They was every bit as glorious and as symmetrical as Celeste had said they would be. There was fountains, statues, neat curved hedges and tree-lined avenues and, best of all, plenty of tall, strong trees what would be easy for me reach and climb down. So I scurried like a squirrel along the wall until I reached a good and bushy spot and then I turned my head back to the riverside. Brendan was already rowing back towards Celeste, and the National Guard what was stationed on the Pont Royal had still not spotted me. They was all occupying themselves with blocking anyone from approaching the palace, so my fast climb had gone unmarked. It was time to rectify that, so I placed some fingers into my mouth and whistled loud.

'Bollocks to Napoleon!' I hollered and that got their attention. They all began calling out to each other about the revolutionary on the wall. I unhooked my musket and waved it high in the air. 'Remember Waterloo! Down with the Republic! Your cheese stinks 'n all!'

Then, before they could test if their rifles could shoot this far, I blew them a kiss, grabbed one of the trees and began my descent into the Tuileries gardens. Gravity did most of the work as I climbed down using branches, falling most of the last part into a hedge in a concealed part of the gardens. I had selected this spot as there was a long lane of neat, high hedgerows what helped me to vanish from sight. I was much closer to the palace, where the prisoners was, than I was to the garden gates and I knew that the soldiers on the bridge would be informing the palace about the British intruder who was dressed like an insurgent and brandishing a gun. I removed the smock, hid it deep in a hedge and I lay down onto the gravel in my blood-splattered soldier's uniform, waiting to see how many guards would come to apprehend me.

From my position I had a good view of the huge round fountain what occupied much of the space between myself and the palace. It took longer for my would-be captors to appear than I had given them credit for. But I soon heard some disordered shouting approach, and at last around six or seven rifle-bearing uniforms hoved into view. They seemed to all be quarrelling with one another and few of them was running in a straight line. One of them did not even appear to be running at all, just moving in a slow plod as if he was readying to collapse. It looked like my stew had done its job.

I began calling out again, only this time in my practised French.

'*Intru!*' I shouted, taking care with the pronunciation of this word for intruder. '*Intru!*'

Then I pointed my weapon in the other direction, through a grove of chestnut trees and towards the far gate, and began firing random shots what hit only tree bark. I looked back at the approaching guards and saw them cower at the sound of sudden gunfire. A number of them even looked as if they was ready to turn and head back to the safety of the palace. So I screamed out '*Merde!*' in an agonized voice and hid my now empty musket under some earth, beneath a hedge. I then staggered to my feet and appeared to them from behind a thick tree, clutching the wounded part of my blood-soaked uniform, crashing over some lower hedges and shouting the other phrases I had been taught.

'*On m'a blessé!*' I said as I reached the opposite side of the big fountain. '*Merde! Merde! Merde!*' I dropped to my knees and nodded my head behind towards the cluster of trees. '*Là-bas! Intru! Intru!*'

Then I collapsed face down as most of the guards rounded the fountain, raced past me and headed off to catch the imaginary culprit. Some of them had even started firing, as if they could see something. Two of the slower ones reached me then as I writhed on the floor, swearing every French curse word I had learnt in the past few days – which was a lot. As I had hoped, they treated me as though I was one of them and tried to get me to roll over so that they could see my wound better. Instead, I began yelling '*Aidez-moi!*' and '*Medic!*' until they was forced to grab me under each shoulder and help me back to where they had come from. I kept my hands pressed tight over the uniform's bullet-hole and continued with my performance as I was led up the stone steps towards the palace.

Whether or not these volunteer soldiers would have believed my ruse without having been made so foggy-minded from the stew, is a question that shall never be answered, but when I was shoved inside the small tradesmen's entrance what led down below the palace and into a rotten little kitchen, I saw that the huge pot Celeste had delivered had almost been licked clean. There was three more soldiers in that kitchen and, when I was brought in still screaming and cursing, two of them jumped up from wooden chairs as if I had woken them. The guards carrying me shouted orders at them, they grabbed a couple of rifles from an upright rack and bustled their way outside to help in the search. I collapsed into one of the vacated chairs and leaned over, still clutching the bullet-hole in my side and refusing to let the remaining soldiers inspect it. The wound what had killed the uniform's previous owner had done enough bloody damage to the garment to suggest that I was done for and so the guards left me there to suffer alone. They ran over to a door, opened it and began calling down for more help. Two more musket-wielding guards emerged from the dark staircase then in answer to the call and, as they entered the kitchen, I could hear terrible screaming sounds coming from below and I wondered at what tortures the prisoners here must be undergoing. I could tell from their more assured movements that these two prison guards had not been at the stew, but still they exited into the garden along with the woozier pair what had brought me in here.

There was one elderly guard left with me in that kitchen and he was enjoying a deep snooze in a corner chair, so I had a feeling he would not prove to be much of an obstacle. I straightened myself up, crossed over to the wooden rifle rack and selected one of the three long weapons what rested upon it and held it as if it was loaded. I then moved over to the door, from which that horrendous screaming could be heard and I peered into the dark. A narrow and winding staircase led downwards and there was a riot of voices calling up in desperation. One voice though could be heard louder than all the others and this one was commanding and threatening. I had only stepped down two or three steps when the sudden cracks of gunshots rang out, the sounds ricocheting off every wall, almost deafening me.

After that, the cries became even more outraged and hysterical and every step I took down there just increased my dread as to what terrors I would find below. I got to the final step, with my gun pointed ahead, and saw what was happening down in that torch-lit dungeon. There was four arched cells to the right of me and far too many men barred up behind them. To see so many men cramped up in so small and confined a space, so tight that it was hard to imagine how they could breathe, let alone move, was to see a great barbarism being committed.

There was then only one remaining guard left there overlooking that cruelty and it was clear that he was becoming overwhelmed by the many arms what was straining for him through the bars and the violent taunts directed his way. A flask of water had been dropped upon the ground and it seemed like there had been some sort of tussle, as they had tried to grab him. He seemed to be most agitated by having been left here to guard this savage human zoo and so, even though he was still protected from the rabid mob by the bars, he had taken to firing into the cells to keep them at bay. Now at least one man had been killed in there and this had created even more havoc. The prisoners' bodies was now pulsing hard and some was getting bashed against the iron bars. The murderous guard loaded his musket and looked ready to commit another atrocity. It was a horror to behold such brutishness.

I stepped into the lamplight of that underground passage and the guard glanced towards me and gave me an order. But then he looked at me a second time in a manner what suggested that he had enough wit to see that I was far from being a real soldier. He called out in alarm and moved his firing arm in my direction, but, before he could do this, I crossed over to him, took hold of my rifle by its barrel and then swung the weapon into him hard. He collapsed under the strike, dropping his weapon. My audience of over a hundred imprisoned revolutionaries let up a rabid cheer.

I kicked the fallen man's weapon away from him, then shouted '*Vive la Revolution!*' so that even the slower-witted prisoners could tell that the uniform was a lie. Over on the far wall a big bunch of keys was hanging, so I darted over there as the crowd all roared in approval.

'Hugo DeFarge!' I cried out as I turned to face all four cells. 'Its London Jack, come to rescue you! Where are you?'

The prisoners stamped, spat, and raged as if they thought I was teasing them. Down at the bottom of one cell, amid all the kicking legs, one long arm was stretching out, its fingertips pulling the guard's weapon towards him. I always had every intention of freeing the lot of them and so I crossed over to the first cell and began to unlock it, still calling for Hugo DeFarge as I did so. But before I could turn the key, the sturdy guard was back up again and he charged into me. He was a stronger man than I had given him credit for and he pulled me away from the cell and slammed me against the brick wall behind.

However, the first cell burst open as we struggled and around thirty sweating, starved, thirsty men charged out to attack their persecutor with a shocking violence. Some even patted me on the shoulders, embraced me as their saviour, said *bravo!* before hurtling up the steps in a bid for freedom.

'Hugo DeFarge!' I shouted again as I crossed over through the rush of people to the prison doors, to retrieve the keys. 'Which cell you in?'

But there was too much noise to even hear a response so I unlocked the second cell and freed those poor beggars. A gunshot was fired behind me as I unlocked the third cell, causing me to start in fright. Then a cheer went up. The released prisoners had killed the guard.

It was only when I got to the fourth and final cell, what contained less than half the amount of prisoners as the other three, that I received a reply to my question. Twelve men pointed to a figure lying on a blanket at the back of the cell as I unlocked the gate. This cell had more space and light than the others and there was more evidence that the prisoners had been fed. This, I supposed, was where they kept the important prisoners, the ones what was to be shot in full view of the public and so needed to be kept alive for that.

I could not yet see the man I was being directed to as he was lying on an old mattress, facing towards the barred window as if enjoying the last of the summer sun before his execution. I crossed over through this straw-strewn, piss-smelling cell towards him, but he addressed me first.

'The Friend of DeFarge,' I heard him mutter, as my head formed a shadow over him. He smiled at me as though our meeting was a very pleasant surprise. 'How do you like the palace?'

'So far I ain't seen much of it, to be honest, Hugo,' I said as I crouched down beside him, 'but I would imagine that this isn't the nicest room in the building.' The only ones what remained in that cell by then was myself, him and some mice. One of his legs was covered in bandages after his fall from the barricades and so was his other foot. 'Are you going to be able to move or not?'

DeFarge raised his hands to his face so he could see me

better and winced in pain as he did so. He was wearing an unbuttoned white shirt what was wet through with sweat. That colonial cross what he had swiped from me was dangling around his neck on a new string. He tried to say something, but began coughing as I looked around the cell for anything what might help. I was glad to see a wooden crutch leaning against the wall what the guards must have brought him down here with.

'Pierre,' he murmured.

'Pierre ain't with me,' I said as I fetched it over. 'I'm in league with Brendan on this. And another.'

'Pierre,' he repeated the name of his friend with more of a growl this time, ignoring my efforts to try to heave him up. 'Pierre was my Judas!' Then he spat at the nearest wall. 'They crossed his palm with silver.'

'Did they now?' I asked and recalled my own suspicions about how the man in the priest's outfit might have been the police spy they was all worried about, the one who had identified DeFarge as a club leader. 'Well, you'll be glad to hear that Father Pierre was killed.'

'*Bon,*' DeFarge nodded. 'By you?'

'No, by someone else,' I said, as I tried to pull him into an upright position. 'Up you get!'

'*Zhay Zhay!*' he cried, then once I had him hobbling with great difficulty out of that cell. 'Is my son . . .' he searched for the word, '. . . safe?'

'Very safe,' I nodded as I took his weight and we hobbled at a slow pace towards the cell door.

'Who has him?' he asked, as we managed to shuffle past the brutalised dead body of the prison guard.

'Some good people, just outside of Paris.'

This confused him and, as we came to the foot of that tight stone staircase, he paused and his fist grabbed my shirt. 'Tell me,' he breathed into my face. 'Tell me what you do not tell me.'

'They are friends of your wife's,' I explained. 'It was her idea to rescue you.'

'Celeste?' he exclaimed. 'That *putain!*'

'Yeah, that's her,' I said, as I reviewed how difficult it would be to climb those stairs. He was a heavy man and there was not going to be much space in that passage for the two of us. 'She's outside, waiting for us in a cart just now so, y'know, lets get a wriggle on.'

But instead, Hugo DeFarge pushed me away like he thought me a viper.

'You go to her!' he seethed. 'I would die first!'

'Don't be like that, Hugo!' I said as he pulled away from me some more. 'She wants to save your life.'

'She wants to ridicule me!' he said with a snarl. 'She is my Judas!'

'You seem to have a lot of Judases,' I pointed out and, even from down here, I could hear the chaos what was going on above us up those stairs. 'Now hark this,' I said. 'You're being an ungrateful shit. We've all gone to a lot of trouble to free you, me most of all. And you killed Celeste's father, don't forget. So she's forgiven you your trespasses.'

'He wished to kill me!' DeFarge protested.

'Also, one of your friends killed her brother Jerome two nights ago, so she's having a hard week.'

'Jerome is . . . *mort*?'

'And you'll be too, if you don't hurry. But, if you'd sooner stay down here and be a martyr, then sod you.' I kicked his crutch away and he toppled to his knees. Then I began climbing the steps alone. 'I hope they shoot you right in the orangery.'

'Wait!' he called before I reached the top. I turned back to him and saw a chastened figure, wounded in more ways than one, struggling to get back to his feet again. 'Take me to her,' he groaned. I returned to help him up. 'Take me to Madame DeFarge.'

Chapter 24

Blood on the Oranges

Showing that high adventure is all well and
good until someone gets shot

Le Jardin des Tuileries, as the French know it, is famous throughout the world for being a tranquil haven for fashionable visitors to walk arm-in-arm, up and down the lanes of well-manicured hedges, admiring the shrubbery, fountain-work and wondrous architecture of the landscape. I should have liked to visit the gardens on such a peaceful day. The day I crossed through them, however, they was a bloody and ridiculous battlefield.

The hundreds of prisoners what I had set loose from the dungeons below was running riot through the gardens, causing all sorts of trouble for the armed guards. One escapee was trying to flee the garden by climbing up the same tree as I came down. The guards laughed, shot him and he landed in the same bush what I did. Another was not even trying to escape, but was climbing up the plinth of a statue of a naked Roman lady as if trying to kiss her. He too got shot. Elsewhere, a soldier and prisoner was wrestling over the possession of an infantry rifle and they had somehow managed to get themselves ankle-deep in the big fountain. In that instance, it was the soldier who got shot. Also in the fountain was two freed men trying to drown one in uniform, but DeFarge and myself did not linger long enough to see the outcome of that particular struggle.

'Keep close to the walls,' I told him as we hobbled along the shadier outskirts of the garden, hoping not to be noticed amid the riot. My entire rescue plan, from first move to last, hinged upon the hope that the military of Paris would have too many other problems to notice that I was stealing DeFarge away. 'If we draw any unwanted attention,' I said as I helped him along, 'protest loud that I'm arresting you and we'll feign a conflict as if I'm trying to drag you back.' His full weight was leaning into me, he had one arm around my neck and the other working the crutch. I was straining to push him along at any real speed as my other arm carried the rifle.

'Give me the gun,' he panted. 'I shoot to kill. You shoot only hats.'

'If you had the gun, they would try and shoot you,' I said and kept on surging forwards. 'But I'm just another soldier. Now move quicker.'

'I cannot,' he complained.

Just then a nearby plant pot shattered as a stray bullet hit it. Had the pot not been there, the shot would have gone right into DeFarge's head. He began moving quicker.

Soon, we had managed to hobble beyond the fountains and the statues and into a grove of trees. I noticed that the large gates over by the Place de la Concorde had opened, which at first I thought was good news. I had hoped that this meant that escape would now be a simple matter of walking through them, but I then realised that they had been opened to let in more armed guards. And, unlike those guarding the prisoners, these men was unlikely to be volunteers and had not been at the opium pot.

They ran towards us in two ranks of five with their muskets at the ready. So I propped Hugo up against a tree and pretended to be arresting him. The reinforcements therefore ignored us and started firing at the more threatening prisoners, who had begun charging at the gate. The Concorde ranks all knelt down in unison and began firing at the bolder prisoners until their numbers was much thinned.

'We must die here!' moaned DeFarge when he saw the strength of the forces we would need to get through before our liberty could be assured. He indicated my gun again. 'We die shooting!'

'Just stay behind this here tree and stop being so melodramatic,' I told him, annoyed with his persistent defeatism. 'Let them charge and pass us by. Then we'll make our lucky escape.'

'Non!' he cried and made a lunge at the rifle. 'Shoot to kill!'.

We wrestled then and, although I should have bested him, his crutch gave way and he pulled the rifle down with him as he fell to the ground. I then heard one of the guards running towards us from the direction of the orangery and so dived backwards behind a tree to safety. If Hugo DeFarge insisted on dying in combat, then that was his business, but he could leave me out of it.

'For valour!' he then yelled, and aimed the rifle at the

guardsman who I could hear getting closer even from behind this tree. DeFarge fired, I could hear the bullet find its mark, a man cried out and his body skidded onto the nearby gravel. I was still shielding myself behind the trunk but I could see DeFarge lying on the floor and a pained look across his face. 'Brendan!'

I looked around the side of the tree trunk and saw that it was indeed my Irish accomplice who had just been shot on approach. DeFarge began gibbering his apologies as Brendan wailed and writhed about in the orangery, clutching his wounded arm.

'That's the last time I try and do you a good turn, DeFarge!' he swore. 'Could you not see I was coming to help!'

'It has to be said, Hugo,' I remarked, still from behind the relative safety of the tree, 'I have never known anyone be such a hindrance to their own rescue party as you.'

It sounded like the battle behind us was nearing its close and that soon all the prisoners I had released would be dead. That said, the gates to the palace garden was now wide open, unguarded and close enough that I could see that Egyptian obelisk just beyond. One dash and I could be free, but I had these two dead weights to worry about.

'If you pair of stumbling clowns could get back onto your feet sharpish,' I told them as I readied us to make a collective bolt for it, 'then we could all be home before dinner.'

I then scrambled over to DeFarge – he was, after all, the one I was being paid to return alive – and tried to help him up again. But he expressed such agony now whenever I tried to move him that I began to think it impossible. Meanwhile, over in the orangery, Brendan was getting to his feet while holding his injured arm and swearing through his teeth. He looked like he was enduring a lot, but I wondered how useful he would be in helping me shift DeFarge now. I knew that at any moment, some of these guardsmen would turn their attention around to us and they would soon see that Brendan and myself was imposters. I was beginning to despair at our situation.

Just then, through the tall and ornate open gates of the Tuileries gardens, came a cart travelling at a tremendous speed. It was pulled by Milady and DeWinter, those two beautiful horses – and Celeste was at the reins, looking a lot more lucid than she had the last time I saw her.

DeFarge had been lying face down as the woman who had abandoned him years earlier reared her horses up as close as she could and called over to him in their native language. Whatever it was she said, it sounded like an order and the only word I understood was the name of the child they shared. He glared up at her, spat out some dirt and said something back. It did not sound affectionate.

Brendan had staggered over to us by then and I got a better look at his injury. It looked like the bullet had torn through the sleeve, hit his arm but not entered it. He was plugging the blood in with his fist, but bleeding was sure to follow and he gritted his teeth. Despite this, he helped me haul DeFarge up and onto the cart and it looked like we might all get out of here after all.

But there was one armed infantryman walking towards us, away from the battle in the chestnut-tree grove. His head was cocked as if he might be suspicious of Brendan and myself and he shouted something aggressive at us. I was busy helping to heave DeFarge up onto the cart as Celeste hissed at us to hurry. Brendan replied to the approaching soldier with what sounded like an explanation for what we was doing, but this guard kept coming. He seemed to be of a higher rank than most and had a stiff brush of a moustache, which twitched upon hearing an unfamiliar accent.

Brendan stepped towards the officer to try to convince him that we was just following orders He held his injured arm with one hand and his weapon in the other. I jumped onto the cart once DeFarge was loaded and now we was just waiting for Brendan to clean things up. But the officer was running towards us by then, shouting out for other soldiers to apprehend us. He raised his musket as he did so. DeFarge shouted something to Brendan. A final order to kill from the leader of the Thousand Jacks.

A shot rang out. Someone had fired first, but it was impossible to see who as the horses panicked at so near a blast, charging away from the orangery and through the gates in fright. DeFarge and myself toppled forward as they did so and he cried out Brendan's name as we retreated. But we had turned out of the gate by then and so the outcome of the confrontation went unseen.

DeFarge cursed Celeste as she cracked the whip for the horses to move even faster and it sounded like he was accusing her of abandonment. But she ignored his command to go back for his imperilled friend and instead circled the obelisk and fled the Place de la Concorde, the very place where decades before, her ancestors had been guillotined. Her husband was made incandescent by her defiance but she had done what she and I had agreed to do and she was obligated to do no more. She kept her eyes fixed frontwards until we was safe from capture.

We had been successful in rescuing one man from his execution. But we had doubtless left another to face the very same fate.

Chapter 25

Recalled to Life

A historic conflict between two sides reaches its conclusion

The horses tried to pull us through Paris as fast as they could, but the journey was jagged and beset by interruption. The principal reason that the prison cells had been manned by volunteers was because every true soldier was out on the streets, battling the insurgency. There seemed to be twice the amount compared to how many there was a day ago. Many men and women could be seen throwing down their weapons and surrendering to them, each road where a barricade had been built seemed to have been reoccupied by the government and the streets was already under repair. The cavalry occupied almost every corner we passed and the only dead bodies we saw lying about now was not dressed in uniform. This was the fourth day of revolution and it was obvious to all that there would not be a fifth. I was sat in the back of the cart looking at all this evidence of revolutionary defeat and when I glanced over at DeFarge I saw that he was crying.

'Why am I free?' his voice croaked when he saw me looking at him. His face already looked agonised from the pain in his legs but the surrounding scenes was causing him even more torment. 'Had I been executed, then I would have died never knowing of this.'

I shared his dismay. This was not my country and I had not come here to help in any struggle, but I hated to see my own brave class being brought to its knees once more by those who rule.

Celeste was fighting hard to forge a path northwards through the beaten districts, but there was so many blockades and skirmishes to avoid that it was impossible for her to keep heading in a straight line. To pass by some obstructive soldiers she had been compelled to yell '*Bravo à la Republique!*' so they was in no doubt of her support. DeFarge looked as though he had just been stabbed in the heart as he heard his former love cheer for his victorious enemy.

'You'll be seeing your son again soon, Hugo,' I said as I removed my soldier's jacket and kept my head low in the cart. 'Fix on that.'

'I do not want to see him like this!' he cried then and clenched his fists. 'I am ashamed! I am a failure with broken legs. Saved by a woman I detest and, worse, by an Englishman! I want JJ to remember me as a proud Frenchman. I promised him revolution!'

From her position up on the driver's post, Celeste turned her head and said something to him in French, the tone of which sounded like 'tough'. Then she returned her attention to the road, riding the horses through tight passageways and round difficult corners.

At length we reached a higher district what seemed untouched by all the fighting and the military so Celeste slowed the horses down to a trot. She rode them into a small but empty cemetery and reared them up in an unstoned patch of grass so they could rest. Then she turned her whole self around to address the man she had offered me so much money to help rescue.

'*Salut mon cheri,*' she smiled with a sarcastic sweetness and blew her estranged husband a kiss. DeFarge grumbled something back at her as I jumped off the back of the cart, knelt down and kissed the earth beneath me. I, at least, was glad to be alive. I removed those military boots what, by now, was causing me great discomfort and the long socks underneath. Then I stood barefoot, let my toes feel the grass beneath them, faced the sun and grinned at my own brilliance. I had just saved a man from a firing squad.

Celeste should have been proud of herself also, considering that it was her idea to rescue Hugo in the first place, but she seemed far less elated as she too climbed down from the cart and crossed over to stroke Milady's nose. Now that she and her husband had begun exchanging terse and unfriendly words, her face was gloomier then ever. I could not, of course, understand anything of what passed between husband and wife as I sat on my little mound of grass and watched their awkward reunion, but often you do not need speech to understand what passes between people. Hugo was groaning on at her in much the same manner as he had to me and she looked to be exhausted by him. Soon both of them was crying, but his sobs was loud and passionate whereas hers was quiet and more concealed. Now, although I was also finding the stubborn and ungrateful martyrdom of Hugo DeFarge to be most wearying, I could not help but feel some affinity with the man. Here was someone who had been loved by a woman and was then abandoned by her. I too knew the pain of that and so could understand how hard meeting his wife again under such circumstances must have been.

'*Non!*' Celeste cried out then after some sort of accusation had been made, causing both the horses and myself to flinch at the violence of it. She began hissing at him in retaliation and he seemed shocked and chastened by her words. Then her face dropped into her hands and she wept. When Hugo spoke next it was in an apologetic voice.

'Englishman,' he said to me, lifting up the string what hung around his neck. 'Give my wife this, please. It belonged to her father.' He extended his hand to me and offered me that gold crucifix what he had snatched from around my own neck on top of the barricades. I was disinclined to do his bidding and almost considered reminding him that I was not, in truth, one of his followers. But Celeste looked so stricken by the sight of the cross what had once belonged to her late brother, that I decided that I would do it for her. As I fetched it and handed it to her, he spoke with a greater softness than he had before. He mentioned Jerome in a way what sounded like condolences and then, as Celeste took the cross and looked at it with great emotion on her face, I heard him say *merci beaucoup* for the first time since we had rescued him. Celeste shut her eyes, squeezing out two long tears and kissed the crucifix. Then she pocketed it and wiped her eyes and chin.

'Monsieur Dawkins,' she said to me in a more composed manner. 'I find my husband is as impossible to reason with as he ever was, so perhaps you could be so kind as to tell him what I want in exchange for having rescued him.'

I turned to Hugo and saw him squinting at us both with suspicion. 'Divorce?' he asked.

'She wouldn't have gone to all this trouble just to ask for that, Hugo.' I laughed at the very idea. 'She would have let the firing squad divorce you for her.'

'Tell him,' Celeste said and stepped much closer to Hugo, 'that all I want is for my husband to speak well of me to our son.'

'Tell her,' he grunted, 'it will be of no matter. The boy hates her.'

The tollgates around the city had been blocked with people trying to flee Paris now that the revolt had been beaten. So it was many hours later when our cart returned to the Regnaudot farmhouse, and again their little daughter was waiting to greet us, we came up the lane. This time, however, instead of running to her parents as we approached, I heard her call for Nick and JJ. My assistant stuck his head out of one of the top windows and howled in celebration when he saw our successful return. By the time we had reared up outside the front of the house, JJ DeFarge had bounded out of the front door, scrambled to the cart where his father was and was crying with joy. Max had followed him through the door and he lifted the boy up so he could kiss and embrace his favourite parent. He ignored Celeste.

I disembarked and looked at the touching scene between father and son as Hugo took his delighted child and squeezed him close, covering his head in kisses. It made me yearn to be a father all the more. But, just as I was about to entertain melancholy thoughts about what had been denied to me, No Nickname Nick came hurtling out of the door and into the porch.

'Jack!' he cheered, running down the steps to embrace me just as hard. 'I told JJ you'd do it! I said to him, "if there's anyone who can steal your old man back then it's the Artful Dodger!" And you went and proved me right!' Then he shouted over to his younger friend something what had a ring of 'I told you so!' about it.

'Nice to hear you've such confidence in me, Nick,' I said, remembering that this was one of the boys what had witnessed my disgrace at the zoo. 'But it weren't all me. Celeste played her part to perfection.'

But, as I turned to congratulate Madame DeFarge on her successful delivery of my opium pot, as well as her tremendous driving, I saw that she had already dismounted and was handing the reins to Max's daughter. She cut a forlorn figure as she stepped away from the cart and made to climb the steps up to the porch, as if ready to collapse upon a bed inside. But before she could leave us, her husband called out her name. She turned and he encouraged her to come over and then whispered into JJ's ear. It was clear he was agreeing to Celeste's request and then he encouraged the boy to give his mother a kiss. JJ did this in a reluctant fashion, but soon all three of them was talking in a tender way. By the time Hugo was being lifted out of the cart and helped inside, Celeste had her son in her arms and, for once, he was not fighting to get away from her.

From the open window above the veranda, Nick and myself could hear Celeste putting JJ to bed with a soothing lullaby. That was about three days later and it had taken a lot of work on her part, but now they was as comfortable together as any mother or son could be. I looked out into the quiet night and tried to hear if there was any more gunshots from the city, but none had been heard in days. The revolution was over and the state held power once more.

Hugo DeFarge was gone. The truth was that if the government ever caught up with him again, he would be executed as one of the leaders behind the failed uprising – this time with greater efficiency. So on the day after his escape, he wrote a letter on Regnaudot stationery and sent it to an address in Paris of the only person who, he said, he could trust and who might still be alive. Days later, a woman arrived in an old brougham carriage to take him away. She had with her fresh bandages and other medical supplies for his legs and had made immediate arrangements for them to leave France. None of us was introduced to this woman in a formal way, but she and DeFarge seemed very familiar with one another. Jean-Jacques cried when he was told that he could not travel with his father to Spain, or Italy, or wherever it was he said he was going. Everyone else was delighted to see the back of him, especially Max and his family. His bloody legs had made a proper mess of their best linen and his constant moaning about the revolutionary defeat had been spoiling the otherwise ebullient mood of the house. But before we all waved him off, he had told JJ that he must live with his mother now, and that he should treat her well once he inherits the Lamoreaux estate. And, although the boy wailed about not wanting to part from his father, it seemed like Celeste had won the lad over already and so it was happy endings all round.

'Nick the Fingers,' I suggested as I puffed on one of our host's cigars and blew smoke rings towards the direction of the empty paddock.

'There already is a Nick the Fingers,' my assistant told me as I handed him the cigar. 'From Deptford.'

'Alright then,' I said, 'The Crafty Fox.'

'Don't like it,' he replied as he blew a bigger smoke ring, much to my envy. 'Sounds like a tavern.'

'Lucifer Nick.'

'Why am I a Lucifer?'

'On account of your red hair,' I explained. 'Or better yet,' I took the cigar back from him again, 'The Elusive Pincher!'

'That one sounds more lecherous than thieving,' he observed, which to be fair was true.

'I'll tell you something,' I said after I had taken another puff, 'Fagin made coining nicknames seem a lot easier than it is.'

Earlier that day Max Regnaudot had returned to Paris for the first time since the fighting had ceased and he was not back yet. He had taken with him that vital document what he was going to present to those now in possession of the Lamoreaux estate. How they was all going to react to the news that they had to clear out to make way for young master DeFarge, was not a thing I was letting trouble me as I waited to be told that my large payment was ready for collection. I was happy enough there though, sat on his veranda with my feet up on his garden table, enjoying plenty of food and drink from his larder. His wife was starting to act like she might be keen for me to move on though.

'I keep telling you, Dodge,' Nick sighed. 'I don't want a nickname anyway. I'm happy being Nick.'

'Please yourself,' I decided. 'And it won't matter anyway. Because as soon as we get back to London I'm telling all the Diallers about what an exceptional thief you are. Your reputation in the rookeries will soar like a hot air balloon when they see how rich we both are and hear as to how we acquired it.'

'Yeah, well, that's another thing,' he said as he reached for the glass of that brandy what we had found in a locked cabinet. 'I ain't going back to London. I'm staying here.'

'Here in France?'

'Here on this farm,' he explained. 'Max has offered me a job working with the horses and I'm going to take it.'

'But what about your promising career as a London crim?' I cried out in bewilderment. 'When we first met you told me you was buzzing about coming on this job for the opportunity of it. I thought you wanted to advance yourself and be a top sawyer one day.'

'Nah, I was just buzzing about coming back to my true country,' he shrugged. 'Where I was always from.' He took the cigar from me again and had another drag. 'But I don't imagine you'd understand that.'

We had heard a carriage draw up outside the front of the house while we had been talking and I knew that Max the lawyer had returned. We had listened as he entered his house and had gone straight upstairs to talk to Celeste. Nick passed me back the cigar and I thought about what he had just told me.

'Did I ever tell you why I wanted to come on this excursion?' I asked him.

'For the money,' he said.

'Yeah, but it wasn't just that. It was for the adventure of it,' I replied. 'When I first met you in that zoo, I was a shadow of the old Artful. I was a slave both to the poppy and to my own festering laziness. But the danger of Paris has cleared me of all that, just as I hoped it would. Now I feel like my old self again and, well, that is a greater reward than I ever could have wished for.'

'I am glad to hear it, Jack,' said a voice from behind me. I turned and saw Celeste stepping out of the back door with the wedding certificate in her hand. Max was standing behind her with the expression of a pallbearer. 'Because we have learnt some disappointing news.'

Chapter 26

A Complete Revolution

Concluding my French narrative to a rapt London audience

'So, after all that, you didn't get nothing for your troubles?' complained young Joe Muckraw. 'That is the shittest story I've ever been told.'

It was not just the Slippery Soap what cried out in protest to hear that the Lamoreaux fortune was a bust, but also about thirty other orphans from the Seven Dials vicinity, who was sat clustered around me. They had all been very much enjoying my tale earlier, as no story pleases rookery ears better than that of poor children of their own age inheriting unexpected wealth. But now that the truth of it had been revealed, they was all turning nasty. I was standing on a flat roof of some derelict building what the homeless kinchins around here had taken possession of and I was in the company of two of my closet Diallers, Tom Skinner and Georgie Bluchers. They had been sharing out these crates of fizzing soda what my gang had stolen from a warehouse, as well as some jars of stolen sweets. The purpose of my visit here was to demonstrate to these grubby ingrates that I was back to being our local top sawyer, and also because it was the sort of thing what Fagin might have done.

'Remember earlier,' I said as I raised my finger to silence the mutiny, 'when I told you about old Lucien Lamoreaux? Which of you can tell me who he was?'

'He was the old uncle,' the Boy Chimp piped up, 'what had inherited the fortune instead of Jerome's Pa.'

'Correct,' I said and threw him another toffee. 'Eat that before it melts. Well, it turns out that old Lucien had been dead since February.'

'Dead all along!' laughed Sticky Jill.

'And it transpires that Lucien was a gambler, a spender, a debtor and a drunk. He had squandered all the fortune away over the years, so when Celeste's lawyer approached his heirs to tell them that JJ was set to inherit the estate now, they all fell about laughing and told him he was welcome to it. The mansion had already been sold to pay off his debts.'

It was the last days of summer, but the sun was still all of a blaze and so we all wore protective hats. To the west we overlooked Soho and to the east Covent Garden. I was most happy to be back in a city with a geography I knew well.

'But there was still treasures to be had,' I consoled them. 'Two big boxes of portable property what had not been sold off yet and so was delivered to JJ and his mother. These included some brass candlesticks, silverware, fancy hairbrushes and some clothing what had very much gone out of style. But I managed to stuff my travelling trunk with as much of it as I could and that, as well as the jewels I had received earlier as a deposit, was my lot.'

'What did the boy get?'

'Jean-Jacques received the other box what was mainly full of items of sentimental value.'

'*Sentimental value?*' One of the girls spat the words in disgust. Every child there knew a consolation prize when they heard it. 'Poor little sod!'

'Chief among these,' I continued, 'was a small but old painting of his grandmother Cessette, what had been painted by her secret husband in the previous century. Celeste told JJ that they must hang that picture upon the wall of their new home so that they would always remember their Caribbean heritage. Someone had written on the back of this picture a line from the philosopher Rousseau, who JJ was named after. It translates as 'To assert that the son of a slave is born a slave is to assert that he ain't born a man.' Now ain't that a lovely note for us to end upon?'

'No it ain't,' answered Venetian Vince, as the confectionery was passed to him. 'Cos I say Dodger has more humbug than this jar. I don't believe half of it and the other half he zagger-ates.'

'I believe him!' cried a new voice from right at the back. She was a dirty-haired girl standing on the ledge of the roof, with all of North London behind her. 'I believe every word of it. And you know what part of the story I liked the most?' Every head turned towards her as she raised her fists in the air. '*Revolution!*' she declared. A great many others on that rooftop cheered at that. 'We should have one of them upris-ings here,' she announced and waved her arm over the city behind her. 'I'd be first upon the barricades if we did. Who'd be second?'

A chorus of solidarity arose from many, but not everyone was so quick to follow the firebrand girl into a class conflict.

'Wasn't you listening to the story, you daft chit?' sneered Soap. 'The revolution lost, dint it? They all got shot up, dint they? Is that what you want to happen to you? The lesson of Dodger's story was to not bother with no revolution as it's only for fools and Frenchmen. Look after your own selves, that was the lesson of the thing. Right, Dodge?'

By now, both Tom and Georgie had indicated to me that they was bored of entertaining kinchins and wanted to get back to adult affairs, so it was time for me to leave. I smiled at my youthful audience and bowed before making my exit.

'I'm like a historian, me,' I told those urchins before I left them all with the bounty of sweets and drinks I knew they would remember me for. 'I just relate events as they happen and you are free to draw your own lessons. Now, if you'll excuse me, I have other escapades to involve myself in. Enjoy the treats!'

When I emerged onto Monmouth Street below, I could still hear all those kinchins quarrelling up on the roof about the relative merits of rising up against the higher classes. The loudest voice though was still that firebrand girl and she was now leading her supporters in a rousing rendition of the tune I had taught them all earlier. I could still hear them humming *La Marseillaise* all the way out of the Dials.

★

'Afternoon Ruthie,' I greeted the landlord's daughter as myself, Georgie Bluchers, Tom Skinner and Herbie Sharp all pushed through the double doors of the Three Cripples tavern and strolled up to the curving bar. 'Porter ales for all, and you can start me up a new bill, considering I've paid off the old one.'

'This goes on the second bill,' Ruthie said as she pulled the first pint. 'Which is almost getting as high as the first. You planning on paying this one off too, are you?'

'One day soon, Ruthie, one day soon. Tell me, how you getting on with that new barman I set you up with?'

'Useless,' she complained as she handed me the glass and started work on the second. 'His right arm can't pull the taps and his spectacles keep falling off. Not to mention all the ruddy politics we have to listen to, God spare us.'

'For the pittance I'm paid,' Brendan defended himself from the other end of the bar, where he was serving Greta and company, 'they're lucky I even turn up. How are you, Dodger? Grand?'

Just after we had abandoned him in the Tuileries gardens, Brendan Kennedy, it turned out, managed to shoot that approaching officer in the orangery. Then he fled through the gates on foot, still clutching his wounded arm and leaving a trail of blood in his wake. He described the pain as being awful, but that the Catholic guilt he was subjected to at taking a life had been worse. I had been right earlier when I had judged him as not being the kind what takes easy to killing.

Before leaving France I had revisited the burnt-out old wine shop in Saint-Antoine and found him there, his wounded arm all bandaged up and crouched in the corner of a dark room staring at a loaded weapon in his hand. So it was fortunate for him that I arrived when I did, as I was able to talk him out of doing anything stupid and convince him to travel back with me to London. 'We all get low,' I had assured him. 'But that don't mean we have to stay that way. And now that Nick ain't with me, well, I'd be grateful for the travelling companion. How about it?'

Once these pints had been served, I was set to shift off to a smoky corner of this tavern with my criminal colleagues, so that we could discuss the shadowy dealings of the day. It was good to be head of the gang again after all those months lost in opium dens. These old pals of mine had welcomed me back as though I had never been gone, even Tom, who had assumed leadership of the Diallers during my absence. And, although I had not returned from France as rich a man as had been expected, it was obvious to all that I was a cove renewed. I had even completed some other well-paid cracks since my return from France, most of which had been arranged through Barney at this here tavern, and I had reasserted myself as the top earner of the rookeries.

However, today I was in no mood to involve myself with any new business, as I was only interested in spending some time in the company of my fellows. So when Brendan accosted me before I moved away from the bar to tell me that there was someone I should meet, I was happy to let another thief take the job.

'This woman was asking for you in particular,' he told me,

away from the others. 'She says that she's in trouble and that you're the only thief in London what can help her.'

I had just taken my first swig of the ale as he said that and I let it slip down my throat before responding. 'What did she look like?' I asked.

'Beautiful,' Brendan said and he adjusted his specs. 'Very much so.'

'The last beautiful woman what asked for my help was Celeste DeFarge and remember the bother that all caused,' I said.

'This woman is brown-haired and wearing a green dress,' Brendan elaborated. I lowered the pewter pot from my lips at that description. 'And she's sat in the taproom now. She's been waiting for you for some time.'

I slammed my pot down onto a table and surprised Brendan with my sudden urgency. 'How do I look?' I asked. The Irishman shrugged as if he had no opinion on the matter. So I crossed over to that large scratched mirror they have in there and tried to survey my reflection. The scars and bashes what I had sustained during my time in Paris had healed a fair bit, but was still visible. I adjusted my collar and fingered about with my hair until I was satisfied that I was presentable. My gang of Diallers had vanished behind a wooden partition by then, but Brendan was still stood there and he attempted one of his rare smiles.

'Best not keep a lady waiting, eh, Dodger?' he said and I stepped through the busy bar, ignoring various old acquaintances on my way, and went through the door what led to the corridor where the taproom could be found.

Once away from the noise of the bar, I breathed out hard and placed my hand upon the doorknob. Then I entered and saw her sitting by herself around that same table where I had met Celeste and Jerome over a month before. She was nursing some sort of hot drink and looked up as I entered. She was as lovely as ever.

'I hear you're looking for a thief,' I said as I stepped closer.

'And not just any,' Lily replied as she shifted in her seat so I could get a better look at her. 'But one thief in particular. Cos, as you can see, I've gone and gotten myself into a fair bit of bother.'

I looked down and saw the full belly she was displaying through that loose green dress. Then I looked up at her face again and saw that she was anxious about how I might respond.

'Never fear, my dear Miss Lennox,' I said as I walked back to the taproom door and shut it so that the two of us could have some privacy. 'Because – as I told another lady who was sat in that very seat some weeks ago – you have come to the right man.'

Acknowledgements

With this third book in the Dodger series the debt that I owe to Charles Dickens has grown even greater. Not only was he the author of *Oliver Twist*, a novel that has plainly inspired me more than any other, but also of *A Tale of Two Cities*. It was a tremendous pleasure to be able to combine the two stories and introduce the Artful Dodger to the ancestors of Monsieur and Madame DeFarge. I hope that their original author would approve of this meeting and of a tale which takes the reader from the Three Cripples in Saffron Hill, to that notorious wine shop in Saint Antoine, and then back again.

I would also like to acknowledge two other people who have very much informed my vision of who the Artful Dodger is over the years. George Cruikshank, the original illustrator of *Oliver Twist*, showed us a Jack Dawkins who was vibrant, comical, smirking, arrogant and flamboyantly over-dressed and he could easily be viewed as the character's co-creator. Also, I don't think there is anyone of my generation who doesn't see and hear Jack Wild, the young star of the 1968 musical film *Oliver!*, whenever they think of the Dodger. It was of course his grown up voice that I imagined as I wrote the narration.

I am also indebted to various works of non-fiction. The most important and helpful of these were: *Recollections – The French Revolution of 1848* by Alexis de Tocqueville, *1848 – Year of Revolution* by Mike Rapport, *Dickens on France* a collection of Dickens' travel writing edited by John Edmondson, *Emperors of Dreams – Drugs in the Nineteenth Century* by Mike Jay.

A sincere thank you to Stefanie Bierwerth and everyone else at Quercus for the wonderful work they have done in bringing this book together. And of course to everyone involved with Heron books.

Most of all, I would like to single out my editor Jon Watt. It has been a great honour to be able to write this trilogy over the past few years and it all sprang from his faith in me as an author. His encouragement, advice and support throughout that process were always invaluable and my warmest thanks are reserved for him.